DON'T LOOK BACK

By Juanita Tischendorf

Also by Juanita Tischendorf

Who Says I'm Small

Til Death Do Us Part?

The Madman, The Marathoner

An Unfair Advantage (A Murder In Oklahoma)

The Selfie (Adolescent/Teen Girl Self Development)

DON'T LOOK BACK

Juanita Tischendorf

J. Tischendorf Services

2015

Don't Look Back

First Printing: 2015

ISBN 978-1-928613-68-8

Paperback Edition

J. Tischendorf Services
Rochester, New York 14617

Published In The United States of America

http://jtischen.wix.com

Dedication

For my husband, Mark whose love will keep me young forever.

Thank you. Without your support and patience, I would have never achieved my dream.

Acknowledgements

I would like to thank my, my creative writing course and my family without whose help this book would never have been completed.

Thank you for your patience and guidance and belief in me.

Foreword

More than 2 million marriages are celebrated each year in America. Some last forever. Some don't. A simple divorce is the solution for the vast majority of couples when wedded bliss loses its fragrance. Yet not all women can come to terms with ending a marriage.

Angelo Maglioni, II, sits in his plush office reviewing the case of Samuel Stillman. When Angelo sees the name of the prosecuting attorney, his interest peaks. At that moment, Samuel Stillman becomes the pawn in a case that will have a surprising ending for all that eventually become entangled in the episodes that unfold.

Healthy, strong and headed for success with her business, Computers systems Unlimited, Skye should be brimming with hope and decisively planning for her future. Instead, her childhood fears haunt her, taking the shape of nightmares and daydreams as she struggles with her personal and business obligations. She is yet to realized that the most threatening episode in her life is about to unfold and the magnitude of her nightmares will shrivel in comparison.

Not until it all culminates in a confrontation at the Sanders residence does Skye finally realize what has been taking place around her. By then it is too late. In this powerful domestic thriller a chilling story unwinds in which terror and devotion plague a middle-class housewife, mother, and business owner. The question is whether she can remain alive and sand through it all.

Introduction

Marriage and divorce are both common experiences today. It has become acceptable for children to be raised in a single parent environment. How common this has become is that about 40 to 50 percent of married couples in the United States divorce.

There is not one theme that can cause a divorce to happen. There are many.

If love is the tie that binds couples together, money is often the pliers that pull them apart. Money antagonizes couples. It sometimes invites divorce. And though finances have always raised tensions for couples, it may be harder than ever these days to avoid conflict. That's because today's range of family complications are many. There are moms leaving and re-entering the workforce, late life marriages that bring debt and adult children to mesh together, along with shrinking pensions and baffling health care choices — all pulling us into making more financial decisions and the pressure can lead to divorce.

If you think that sexual infidelity is the leading cause of divorce, you've wrong. The top reasons married couples split, is the lack of communication because humans need to communicate.

So with divorce being common and actually quite easy to obtain with a little bit of pain. Why would someone go through the trouble of concerning murder to end the relationship.

Today there are so many people who dwell on the worst case scenario and get so engrossed in it, they cannot see the light at the end of the tunnel. The course they take is worse, it will ruin their life forever. .

Juanita Tischendorf **Don't Look Back**

CHAPTER 1

IT WAS A cold and snowy January so typical of Upstate New York in midwinter. It had been snowing for several days in succession with no visible sign of the sun poking it's welcome face through the muddy, gray skies. It was the scene that filled her vision as Skye stared pensively out the window, recalling a cold January day so long ago.

***

The phone rang. Skye picked it up.

"Hello?"

"Hello, Skye, is that you?"

She recognized the voice immediately and in the same instant she felt a hint of dread. "Yes, Adam, it's me."

"I hate this. I've been sitting here for hours wondering if I should even make this call. God, I feel like I'm five years old and tattling on my brother."

"What is it?

Again silence on the other end while Adam tried desperately to figure a way to not have to tell her, but knew it was too late.

"Skye?"

"Yes, Adam?'

Skye placed her hand on her forehead and began kneading it as though trying to force herself to concentrate. "Come on, tell me Adam. Is it about Hank?"

"Yes, it's about Hank" Adam said. "How much do you want to hear?" His tone was like that of someone who has been forced into a corner and had no way out.

Skye replied without hesitation, "All of it. Everything. I want to know as much as you can tell me."

"Are you calm?

"Yes, Adam. Come on and tell me." Skye toyed with the handle of her mug of coffee as she tried to keep her irritation under control. "Whatever my husband does no longer holds any surprises," she said cynically. "So give it to me straight."

Adam did just that. Skye listened with no remorse or hurt evident in her expression. Adam, on the other hand was feeling very uncomfortable wishing he hadn't been put in this predicament. When he finished telling her, he stopped talking immediately, glad that it was all over and done with.

"Don't fret Adam. You know me well enough and you know enough about the state of my marriage to not feel guilty."

"Well, at least we won't play a stale scene," he said trying for a little humor then blatantly added, "but I can't believe you're going to play the complaisant wife. If you were older, perhaps I could imagine you tolerating the bastard, but Skye, for heaven's sake, don't take this laying down. It's been going on too long!"

"I think Hank can vouch for my non-complaisant reactions, Adam, and I am not one to take anything lying down. It's just that... Well, there is Scott to consider."

"I won't even comment on that issue as you already know how I feel about your determination to keep the home in one piece until he's grown. Skye..."

She didn't allow him to continue as she interrupted.

"Adam, thanks. Now, don't worry about me. I'm fine."

She heard something invading the silence of the house.

"Listen, Adam, I think I hear Hank. You take care and I'll call you later."

Not waiting for his reply, Skye hung up.

The atmosphere suddenly seemed airless, as though something tumescent was about to burst, pushing against her. For a second, she wanted to cry out. She despised feeling as though she labored along while he did no more than grasp the joy out of life. And it was even more unbearable knowing it took practiced skill to outwit his caginess. Hank Sanders had a sixth sense that worked with alarming clarity.

When Hank entered the kitchen her back was to him. Quickly she twirled around to face him. "So, you slept with her, didn't you?"

Hank stood before her, his face masked with confusion. He was a tall man and quite handsome. His curly hair was worn in a big Afro that crowned his brown face. From his thick black eyebrows that arched above the startled expression in his brown eyes to his slightly parted full lips it was apparent at that second, Hank was unprepared for the confrontation.

Skye continued to study his profile, saw the firm jaw slacken and witnessed the tightening expression about his mouth. The phone call and his reaction made no answer necessary.

Hank didn't respond right away, his mind going a mile a minute as he searched for a way out. He thought back to the criminology course he had taken. What was it that the professor had said? A frown appeared on his face filling his smooth forehead with wrinkles. The wrinkles incinerated as it came to him. The professor's theory of defense was simply to deny. Deny and keep on denying and never admit one fact of evidence that would indicate guilt. And why? Because the proof of guilt was on the accuser.

Now he was himself again, feeling superior as he said, "What are you babbling about now?"

"Forget it. There is nothing you can tell me anyway that I want to hear. Nothing."

In confusion, Hank stared watching her composure grow before his eyes. This was not her normal reaction. He could deal with ranting and raving, but not this apathetic behavior. It made him feel as though she really didn't care and that scared him.

"Skye, tell me what's going on," he said innocently, his arm coming forward and his hand reaching out to touch her.

"Don't touch me, and don't deny the truth. I just finishing talking to someone on the phone who saw you. I have to admit I thought you were smarter, Hank, but I guess I was wrong. You were caught in the act this time. You were seen coming out of the motel room with some woman and driving away with her."

The words spilled from her mouth. "True, no one saw what you were doing in there, but I tend to think it wasn't innocent and that's what matters. As far as I'm concerned you slept with her, and maybe others. I don't know or care."

"You're wrong, dead wrong Skye. For once in your life just listen to me."

"I've done all the listening I intend to do."

"At least hear me out. Give me a chance to explain."

"What's there to explain, Hank? That you went to bed with another woman or that it wasn't the first time? In either case, I don't want to hear about it."

She started to walk away, but Hank grabbed her arm, his composure broken and desperation setting in.

"Listen to me. I admit I gave the girl a ride, all right? I admit the girl was in my car. But that's all there is to it." Whatever else anyone told you is a lie! He drew a great sighing breath and shook his head forlornly. Then he looked up and attempted once more to dissuade Skye. "I expect you to be bitter and I deserve that, but at least hear me out."

Skye's emotions were strung out to the limit, her heart cracked against the walls of her chest while the sight of him made her ill. She wanted this over with, now.

"I swear I am innocent. I'll swear it on the Bible."

She flung the words at him, "The Bible! When were you last in church?" "What would you say if I admitted that I'm afraid to talk to you about it?"

She said nothing. Nothing was required. Right now all she wanted was to be finished with the matter. "Let's stop this," she said, trembling. I've heard quite enough." She turned as if to leave the room.

Hank covered the distance between them and grabbed hold of her elbow, but she easily shrugged loose.

"Skye, wait!"

"Leave me alone," she flung over her shoulder, "Just leave me alone!" Irritated by her refusal to stop, he moved quickly and grabbed her arm again, forcing her to a standstill. "No, you're not going anywhere. You'll hear me out first."

"I said leave me alone, Hank."

"No."

"I mean it, Hank."

He swallowed hard, pressing his head back, glancing first into her green eyes, then aside, afraid of the determination he saw clearly at this close range. He had to try to make her understand.

"You're always listening to what people say and that's why..."

Skye pivoted roughly, managing to free her arm. She hurried down the hallway and went into the bathroom, shutting the door behind her. She tried not to hear the tapping on the door or Hank's voice as he desperately tried to persuade her to come out. There was no way she would subject herself to be being treated like a complete idiot.

She continued to stare at her reflection and what she saw was a face that was attractive rather than beautiful, a face that reflected pride and courage and sensitivity. But right now she didn't feel either courageous or sensitive. She was scared. Exactly why, she didn't know.

Finally she heard Hank's footsteps moving away. Then the tension broke. All the outrage at the injustice, the humiliation of defeat flowed out in torrential tears. She didn't fight it; she just allowed herself to cry until finally empty, she splashed water on her face and reached for a towel to pat it dry. She peered into the mirror, fully expecting to see the evidence of her crying written on her face. Instead she saw sober eyes staring back at her without a trace of tears.

It had been over for some time. Her relationship with Hank had gone through all the stages possible a long time ago. It was the embarrassing humiliation that hurt her now and that usually passed once she let him know she wasn't dumb. She'd be fine and she knew it.

As she opened the bathroom door she repeated to herself, "It's only a matter of time. Only a matter of time."

***

Skye had felt the warmth of each summer day, looked out at the bright yellow and reds of autumn foliage, suffered through the cold whiteness of winter and rejoiced in the colors of spring flowers and greenery and it helped her past the time. As for Hank, well she didn't know what Hank was up to any more or how he felt. Nor did she care. Outside of a bruised ego, she was intact. She had fallen out of love with Hank a long time ago, if indeed she ever loved him. So why did she continue to stay she wondered.

"Poor Adam," she said out loud. He was her watchdog, the one who always seemed to be in the wrong place at the wrong time, or was it the right place at the right time?

Skye took a deep breath that was almost a shudder, turned, and walked stiffly over to the table. Her hand brushed against a glass and knocked it over, and it rolled across the linoleum floor to her foot. She stared at it, completely still, then lifted her foot and brought it down, hard, so that the glass shattered into fragments on the floor.

Her mind was racing backward again into a blur of years, and she was seeing in one swift glimpse after the other where she had already been until suddenly her head was filled with a scene that had taken place just yesterday.

***

Hank stood in the center of the room wearing a pair of denim jeans, a light blue pullover shirt, and a pair of heeled dress boots that added unneeded inches to his six foot three frame. There was a smile on his face as he prepared to go out and shoot some pool with his friends. His check was in the stack of mail left that morning and after stopping at the bank to cash it, he could be on his way. Just as he was about to open the door, Skye entered the family room.

"Did the mailman come?"

"Yeah," he said as he picked up the rest of the mail and held it out toward her. "Here it is."

"Did you get your check?"

Hank's face changed. As if a hand had passed over it, his eyes no longer shone with anticipation, the smile crinkles at the corners of his mouth disappeared. Except for his eyes, which reflected the intensity of his anger, Hank Sanders managed a calm stance.

"That's none of your business," he stated bluntly, thinking it served her right since she was never happy with anything he did any more.

"It is my business," she said. "And what's more, you should be offering the money to help pay for all this!" Her hands swept out in a gesture that took in their whole environment. In all honesty she was jealous because his lack of responsibility forced hers to greater depths. Because of him she lived in constant fear of not making ends meet.

She grew impatient. "Well, what can you give me toward the bills?"

"Nothing," he said adamantly.

It was he who should be on the defensive, he who should be apologetic, but the tables were always turned. And she murmured, almost coaxing now, "Why nothing, Hank, I can use some help?"

"You know damn well, why nothing. I don't have enough to even make it through the week and you want me to give it all to the bill collectors!"

Hank could feel his anger spinning out of bounds. He had to release it. He picked up the lamp, raised it high, and brought it down hard, splintering the base and ripping the lamp shade from top to bottom as it smashed against the arm of the sofa.

This was unexpected. Skye stared in amazement but did not back down. "You disgust me!" she cried. "Just look how much you care about the things you force me to pay for."

The urge to strike her grew from the pit of his stomach until he felt he could hold back no longer. He felt the room slowly tilt around him and he knew he had to get out of there. He glared at her, his equilibrium shot to hell, then turned and stomped out of the house before she could say any more.

But he needn't fear. Skye was exhausted and ashamed for allowing herself to lose control. She thought she was beyond such agonized rage, far beyond it. As she stood there alone now, she knew the only reason she had allowed herself to lose control was because of the anxiety she felt when bills became due and she wondered where the money would come from. But now as she cooled down she knew she'd find a way, she always had. .

With Hank gone, Skye spent the rest of the day and on into the evening working madly. She sifted through the jobs that had piled up in her office, pulling out the smaller ones that she could complete quickly. Skye worked steadily, stopping only to call each client once a job was ready for pickup, then turning to the next. By the time she called it a day, she had earned the money she needed to pay the bills. Feeling much better now that she had managed to overcome yet another obstacle put in place by her illustrious husband, she allowed herself to relax. She picked up a folder from her desk and carried it into the family room where she sat editing the contents until she exhausted herself.

CHAPTER 2

The next day began with disaster. The alarm failed to go off and she had awakened in panic. Her finger punctured her last pair of pantyhose and she couldn't find the shoes she planned to wear so ended up changing her clothes. She was an hour late in getting her workday underway as she hurried into the kitchen to start a pot of coffee, forcing herself to pay attention as she placed, one, two, three scoops of coffee into the filter and then filled the reservoir with water. She then turned on her heels and headed toward her office at the front of the house.

"Darn," she yelled, remembering last night she had left her notes for the Jamison project on the end table in the family room. She twirled again as she hurried across the kitchen toward the family room, only to find Hank standing at the front door, his hand on the door knob. "Darn," she said again, only this time under her breath as Hank turned, startled by the unexpected visitor.

"Well, aren't you going to say something? Yell at me if you want to."

"I don't feel like yelling. I've had a terrible morning."

Hank found himself thinking she had a charming way of widening her eyes to express her emotions. Today her hair was pulled back into a ponytail which made her look like a little girl and he felt a sudden need to be near her, or at least try to please her. "Can I get you anything while I'm out?" he asked amiably.

All she wanted was to be left alone, his presence was an annoyance. Skye, only thinking about that, replied, "Sure. Can you give me something toward the mortgage?"

As soon as the words were out she regretted them. The last thing she needed was a confrontation with Hank, but she couldn't help it.

"Come on, let's not start that again. I'm broke and you know it."

"Okay, okay, forget I said it." Aggravation was written all over her face as she waited for him to leave, but he didn't budge.

"Look, didn't you say you were just leaving?" she said impatiently.

Seeing her irritation made Hank want to linger.

"If you're going, go!" she said in frustration.

"You know," Hank said taking a few steps into the room, "I'm beginning to think you want me to go."

Skye allowed her eyes to move to the papers on the table, then slowly back to Hank. "Oh will you please..." she groaned.

"What? What is it you want? I'm beginning to feel like you're throwing me out!"

"You want to know? Well, what I want is for you to pay the bills! Now what do you think about that?"

He stared at her with one eyebrow raised. She was stepping on his pride and she knew it. Where he came from the man was the breadwinner, the provider and the woman ran the house. He knew the tables had turned but she didn't have to keep reminding him. He had to defend himself. "What I think about that is all you want from me is money. Well I don't have any!"

He looked at Skye for so long that she had to shut her eyes. His face was full of rage until gratefully, he finally turned on his heels and left. She watched the door close behind him and heard the sound of the garage door going up, the gunning of a motor and then nothing.

Skye hesitantly continued to stand where she was. She gritted her teeth as she wished, just once in her life she'd like to know what went on inside Hank's head. She knew what would upset him and she wasn't proud of using it to get the results she wanted, not in the least, but what else could she do. Slowly she shook her head then walked over to the table to retrieve the papers.

Glancing at the papers in her hand she regretted her words even more as she started back across the room and up the two stairs into the kitchen. She stopped to lay the papers on the table before going to the cabinet to get a mug, and fill it with coffee. As she took her first sip of coffee, her eyes gazed out the window over the sink to look into the backyard. No wonder she was tired, she thought. With everything falling on her shoulders, she deserved to be tired.

Skye shrugged her shoulders now and carrying her cup walked over to the table and picked up the Jamison project. "I have a job to do," she said aloud. Balancing the coffee in one hand and carrying the folder in the other, she went into her office and used her elbow to flip on the light. She moved around the desk and turned on the computer then went to the window to open the blinds. She was already calculating the time it would take to complete the job before she sat down with the folder opened in front of her. By the time the computer sat waiting for her command, her mind was already cleared of all thoughts except the job at hand.

Her fingers moved effortlessly over the keyboard, pausing only now and then as she collected her thoughts or contemplated a change. She was interrupted by a client calling to find out when he could pick up his job. Skye glanced at her calendar and scheduled him for two o'clock. Two more calls came in. Both were for jobs to be dropped off. She penciled in the times and returned to the Jamison project.

At precisely two o'clock the doorbell rang. Skye pulled out the Andrew's folder and laid it on the center of her desk before going to open the door. He was her two o'clock appointment. She walked Phillip Andrew's to a chair and once he was seated in her office she turned over the job to him, sitting patiently while he reviewed the contents.

"This is great. You did an excellent job. I appreciate it."

"Well thank you, but your instructions and information was what made the job come out so well."

She watched as Phillip smiled and accepted the check he offered in payment. Looking at it she began shaking her head.

This is much more than we agreed on Mr. Andrew's.

"I know, but that was settled before I knew how much time and effort you were going to put into the project. This is far more than I asked for and I'm very pleased with your work."

"Well, thank you," she said smiling sweetly. "But really, you allowing me to be your base for computer services is enough. I enjoy my work and having a challenge makes it just the more interesting. I'd rather you consider me for any future jobs you have."

"Now that you mention it, I do have another job for you." Skye listened carefully as he went over the details for another project he would like her to do. She assured him she could foresee no problems and he could stop by with the project on the following day. After seeing him to the door, she again returned to the Jamison job.

The next interruption came at three thirty and before the client, Emily Rose, left, her next appointment arrived. Sandra Randolph was a new client, which required Skye to spend at least an hour of her time. Patiently she asked the right questions to determine what Sandra expected, listened carefully to everything she said, and took notes. She looked over the job and gave Sandra a date to return to pick it up. When the meeting was concluded, she walked Sandra to the door and only after the door closed did she move swiftly back to her desk and return to what she had been doing. There were no further interruptions and Skye was able to finish the Jamison project.

Slowly she got up from the chair and went into the kitchen. Every muscle, every nerve, was stretched yet there was no sleep in her. Skye's ears picked up every sound, the swish of a passing car, the far high drone of a plane passing overhead, and the switching of channels on the TV in the rec room downstairs. Hank was home. She hadn't heard him come in but that wasn't unusual.

Skye walked over to the top of the stairs and hesitated. She wasn't tired and she knew what would happen if she tried to force herself to sleep, but what else could she do, she wondered. Nothing. Sadly she climbed the stairs and prepared for bed.

CHAPTER 3

It was mid-March. The days, weeks and months that had seemed to pass by so slowly now were to the endpoint of winter. The entire world seemed to hum and bustle beyond the walls that enclosed her, yet the night seemed empty.

Skye had been jolted awake by yet another nightmare. When the nightmares first started she had been more frightened by trying to understand them, than by the scenes that pervaded her unconscious mind. Now she found herself accepting them as a mere tool to keep from thinking about reality. Admittedly she was having a hard time coming to terms with her life, yet the dreams were always so weird and so illogical.

At first only brief snatches of the dream came back to her as she laid staring at the ceiling. She could recollect her breath coming in gasps and an almost drowsy terror stole through her veins as frightening visions possessed her mind. She stood in a hotel lobby, the floor covered with a plush brownish carpet. Looking down she sees a spider of abnormal size burrowing through the carpet. She jumped back in fright forcing her gaze to fall on another area of the lobby where rats the size of puppies were eating away at a corpse lying in clear view of the hotel guests. Only, she realizes, she is the only one able to see this horror.

A sound comes from behind her and she identifies it as the clatter of dry leaves crackling under the weight of something. Frightened, she looks down to see the carpet has been replaced by a bed of foliage and the clamor she heard was of something approaching from behind her.

Skye freezes, too frightened to turn around though aware that whatever is stalking her is moving closer and closer. The rustling sound seems inches away yet she is unable to move. Suddenly she feels a cold claw close around her ankle and in the throngs of sleep, a scream catches in her throat, forcing her to gasp for air. She struggles and struggles to allow the scream through her lips until her effort forces her awake.

Skye took a deep breath, then another, her body still frozen in panic, her mind still captured in the confines of the dream. Slowly her heart stopped racing and she was finally able to move. Her first action was to reach across the bed to flip on the light. "Bad things only happen in the dark," she said, "Never in the light."

When her arm returned to her side, it brushed over the book lying open on the end table and she realized then what had caused the nightmare. Reading The Shining before retiring was not the smartest thing to do, especially for someone who is admittedly scared of the dark.

It seemed unusually quiet then she remembered it was Saturday. Her neighbors would be sleeping in a little longer, luxuriating in the chance to finally finish their dreams. She wondered if their dreams were troubled or pleasant, or maybe they were whitewashed by delusions of not having to scrape snow from their driveways and automobiles before they could be on their way to work.

Even though she had been working out of her house for the last four years she remembered having to travel the icy streets with other stressed-out motorists who irritably plowed along on salted expressways that cut the life of an automobile in half. She knew what it was like, yet there were times now when she missed the bustle of getting up in the morning and going to another place and leaving all semblance of her personal life behind. Rare as it was, a different mise-en-scene did seem appetizing at times.

She was feeling melancholy as she made her way to the kitchen. Silence greeted her as she took a seat in one of the captain chairs, scooting it up close to the edge of the trestle table. She sat there surveying her surroundings as if seeing it all for the first time. The room was cheerful and seemed to lift her spirits as she sank deeper into the cushion of the chair.

Skye allowed a deep sigh to pass through her lips as she tried again to consider her alternatives. What could be worse than not knowing what needed to be done or even where to start? Deep inside she knew that it wasn't going to get easier, or any better until she came to terms with her life.

The last time she had been this confused was when she had started up the business. It had been frightening to strike out on her own but at least she had had Abe, who helped her make the right decisions. The business was going well and she could easily afford to set up outside of the home, but why challenge success? Secretly Skye believed her clients sought her out for two reasons. Her office was in her home. It made them feel comfortable and they believed that the money they paid her was for services and not overhead.

That day dragged on forever before finally it was officially over

CHAPTER 4

The first knowledge of a new day came when her bedroom was invaded by glints of sunlight that forced her to squeeze her eyes closed. She was not tired, but just not ready to face facts. With her eyes tightly closed there was no Hank to contend with, no clients filling precious hours with their demands. Laying here there was only the truth that there was a new day. But she forced herself to come to her senses.

She moved her head an inch closer to the outside of the pillow, then her whole body followed slowly as if pushed inch by inch. The sun caught her full in the face and she was forced to open her eyes. That's when she made a decision. She would not compromise her time. She would concentrate on her problems.

She slipped her arms into her pink shortie robe and drew it close around her body, absently drawing the ties as she padded down the carpeted hallway to the kitchen.

She sat down at the table wondering how to weed through all the demands she placed on herself. Where to start and how to focus on what it was she wanted. It felt like the way that someone with anorexia feels as they stand before a full length mirror, buck naked and the reflection is that of a fleshy body out of control. What do they do when their view is distorted? Probably they tell themselves they'll just stick their fingers down their throat just one more time, or take another laxative, but that wouldn't solve her problems.

Skye frown as she thought, whenever she tried to deal with reality, she just took a trip into fantasy world instead. "Sick," she said, "very sick."

Getting serious, Skye admitted that technically she had stretched herself and her mind to the limit. She sat for some time going over everything, trying to discover what it was that held her back from happiness. Instinctively her body stiffened and she sat up straighter in the chair with her eyes staring off into the distance. She knew!

"I'm scared," she said slightly puzzled. Then firmly, "You bet your ass you're scared!"

Hank came to mind. He had served in Vietnam and was trained for combat, trained to remove himself from personal feelings except the drive for survival. It might sound harsh to say it, but in all honesty she had witnessed the effects of his four years in the service. He could be hard and brutal, his mind so bent out of shape he could not think along rational lines as he never took the time to separate the soldier from the man, the situations experienced in war, from the relationship with a family. And there was the key. The word relationship was foreign to him. He knew better how to win and conquer.

"What a pointless waste of two peoples' lives," she said. Twenty-one years of enduring one hardship or another, something uncomfortable or difficult, or frightening or threatening always brewing in the background. It might have been better if they had loved each other, but then again it might not.

Skye pushed her chair back and went over to the kitchen sink. Absently she reached up in the cabinet for a coffee filter and placed it in the basket she held in her hand. She slid the basket in place and filled the pot with water which she poured into the reservoir of the coffee maker. As she placed the coffee pot back on the burner and flipped the switch to the "on" position she envisioned his face. He was a man with no need to turn out like he had.

She didn't wait for the coffeepot to finish before filling her mug. As she poured her first cup, she thought, she used coffee much in the same way that Hank used booze. And there was another issue to contend with. Hank was a heavy drinker. When they had first met he would have one or two beers in front of her. Once they were married he stocked the cabinet with liquor, adding it to his morning cup of coffee. He drank enough to inebriate a herd of elephants but rarely did he appear drunk. If she had to pick his two greatest vices it would be drinking and spending money to excess.

She was tired of the roller coaster ride with Hank and she needed to love and be loved in return. It all boiled down to the fact she needed peace, and peace could not be found in her marriage. If she wanted stability and happiness she had to strike out on her own. Hank was not going to change.

She was forty-two years old, supposedly in the prime of her life. Skye thought about that and another brilliant saying came to mind, "You're as old as you feel!" Bullshit. You're as old as you are, was nearer the truth.

CHAPTER 5

She had covered a lot of ground that morning and was just about to go get dressed when Hank seemed to materialize out of nowhere. It wasn't easy for a man of his size to sneak up without warning, she thought, but in her present frame of mind a herd of elephants could have passed unnoticed. Noticing the magazine on the table Skye picked it up, pretending to be interested while he moved about the kitchen fixing himself something to eat.

***

This morning he had awakened feeling the need of a warm body, hand or foot beside him. He should be used to it now, but he wasn't. The only blessing in living together, yet apart, was not having to be concerned with someone else's feelings or let them know of your coming and going.

Skye hadn't dared to look up during the whole time for fear he'd be looking her way. She flipped through the pages of Ebony until the strain became overbearing.

"Hank, I need to talk to you!"

Taken totally by surprise he was unprepared and found himself saying, "What is it now, Skye?" Someone need money? No, let me guess," he said sarcastically, "you want me to face my responsibilities. Am I right?"

Careful not to turn it into an argument, she said, "In a way that's part of it, but not all of it."

"Well do tell," Hank said not trying to conceal his contempt.

"Hank, I have had it. I can't keep trying any more. All we do is fight and never get one thing settled."

"So, what's your point?"

"It's becoming too hard to face living like this. I'm tired of arguing and having to ask you to do things you should want to do on your own. I can't take it anymore."

A look of self-righteous rage distorted Hank's features as he stared at her.

"Do you hear what I'm saying, Hank?" she said with her voice raising an octave or two.

"Yeah, I hear you. How can I help but hear you with you screaming like that."

She could tell by his attitude he might have heard but was not comprehending her meaning. His attitude was like a poison flowing through her veins, but it was too late to back down now. How she wished she could bluntly lay her cards on the table but something told her it was not the time yet. Instead she said pointedly, "I'm serious. I've taken all I can take."

Hank's face remained enraged and Skye felt herself melting until she found herself adding, "Either we figure out something right now or it's over!"

Before she had finished she knew she should have kept quiet but the words were out. To appear in control she stretched herself up in the chair as if stiffening to match wits with him, the master.

Her change in posture did not go unnoticed and Hank took it as a challenge. He knew just how to take the wind out of her sails, too. Just who did she think she was demanding him to make a decision at her whim. All he could think now was how much he hated it when she tried to stand toe to toe with him. Every time she tried it took away from her femininity, leaving him to deal with her like any other person who foolishly forced him into a corner. He could show her just how forceful he was, but there was no need for drastic measures, yet. He waited a few seconds before forming his retort.

"Right this minute at your command and convenience, huh? That's so like you." He paused to let his words sink in before continuing. "Well, I don't have the time right now and I won't have the time later, either."

She was livid. Oh, what she'd like to do to him at this moment. She wanted to fly out of her chair, put her hands around his neck and squeeze the life out of him but there were two reasons she didn't. Hank knew she was no match for his strength or his ability to verbally chastise her. He could toss her aside like a wet washcloth if he pleased or come back with something with ease to silence her. Instead all she could do was stare at him in defiance until he turned and walked away. Before totally out of view, Hank turned around and gave her one last look of utter disgust that turned her stomach inside out.

Skye moved into the bathroom to shower and dress. While she was applying her makeup a knowing expression covered her face. "That's it," she said to her image. "That's it, of course!"

***

The rest of the day raced by as Skye busied herself until late at night. She typed up several address listings, finalized a presentation package that was due the next day for one of her long-time clients. When the phone rang she picked it up while she continued to look over the presentation.

"Hello, Skye Sanders, can I help you?"

"I hope so, Ms Sanders. This is Mr. Davidson and I got your name from one of your clients."

"How can I help you?"

"I wanted to know if you install software?"

Skye leaned back in her chair thinking silently to herself. If she wanted to get enough money to take control of her life she couldn't turn down any jobs. She knew how to install software, but depending on how many packages were involved, it meant being out of the office for a length of time. She decided to play it by ear.

"Yes, I can do that. What do you have in mind."

"Well, I have a computer, a PC, and I need the software I purchased put on it. I don't know what's exactly involved, but the salesman I purchased the equipment from said that it would take some time and cost quite a bit. I thought I'd at least check around before I let them install it."

"Well, tell me what you have and I'll give you an estimate of time and cost."

As Skye listened, she jotted down numbers on her desk pad.

"Well, I figure it will roughly take four hours to set up your system. Now, I have a suggestion for you. If you can bring the computer here and leave it, I'll set you up for two hundred dollars. How does that sound?"

The line was silent for a while and then Mr. Davidson said, "That sounds great. When can I drop it off? I haven't even unpacked it yet so any time is fine with me."

"Any time? Well, can you drop it off this afternoon?"

"I'll be there in the hour."

"Good. I'll see you then."

Skye hung up the phone, smiling as she turned to the presentation again. That was easy money. She could set the system up and continue working at her other jobs while the programs were being installed. Not a bad deal. Not at all.

Satisfied with the presentation she checked the calendar and picked up the next folder. There were letters and reports to be completed and she worked steadily until she had everything in order.

Occasionally when Skye worked late with Adam Snyder, they would go out to dinner. Adam was probably twenty years older than she, yet Skye considered him among her closest friends. When he had stopped by with this job she had been so busy she told him she couldn't get to it right away and had sent him on his way, knowing he liked to sit with her and chat. Now, she was feeling remorseful for not giving of her time. Adam had done so much for her and asked so little in return.

She had first met Adam Snyder when they had needed a family lawyer. Skye had found him in the phone book and over the years they had become good friends.

He was an extremely likeable man with curly salt and pepper hair that he wore short and close to his head. His thick black eyebrows provided a backdrop for his intense light brown eyes that seemed to be always smiling.

Over the years Skye had called Adam when Hank had gotten his speeding ticket and his license was going to be suspended. Several times throughout the transpiring years she had called him just for legal advice on matters that had surfaced. When she had set up the business, he had offered his assistance. Later, she had hesitantly solicited his help in finding out what Hank was up to and he had willingly helped her, as a friend.

Her reward for diligent work was fatigue and she gladly put the papers neatly in the folder, shut down the computer and turned out the lights. She turned in that evening feeling positive she was in for a good night's sleep.

***

Long before he approached her, Skye knew of Hank's reputation. Hank was physically attractive and charming, and his intelligence seemed to add an extra dimension to him that was unexpected. He had an easy sureness about him that woman found challenging and because he showed interest in her, co-workers were all pushing her toward him saying that she needed to socialize more with the opposite sex, something she did only when pushed into a corner. It was quite obvious the man was infatuated with her, but she held him at bay.

Skye knew his type and was prepared to defy him, to tell him to do whatever he pleased with his life, but leave her out of it. But somehow when the opportunity presented itself to tell him just that, she backed down. He was very polite and undemanding when he talked with her and she found she liked hearing his quiet voice. When he asked her out to dinner she surprised herself. Skye said, "All right."

It had come as a shock when she heard Hank ask, "Will you marry me?"

It was wrong, she remembered thinking. They hadn't known each other long enough, but who set the standards for the length of a courtship she argued with herself?

"Do you mean it?"

"Yes, silly, I mean it. Will you marry me?"

"Yes," she said, "I'll marry you."

There hadn't been a day that Skye could remember when she didn't chastise herself for making that hasty decision. But she had. Maybe that was the force behind the drive she had to excel in the world of business and the all encompassing love she had for her child. For the next nineteen years she had paid royally for her mistake.

As she continued to lay in bed she smiled up at the ceiling. She had made a success of her business and that was something to be proud of accomplishing so it wasn't all a lost cause. Skye turned over and looked at the clock. It was after three in the morning yet she still could not get to sleep. She picked up the book on the end table and began to read. When she reached the end of the chapter she paused to rest. She pushed her body back against the pillow and closed her eyes, no longer able to concentrate and gratefully allowed her body to be consumed with its need for sleep.

Skye heard a voice scream out, "Stop it! Stop it!" and was astonished to realize the screams were coming from her. Her heart pumped like thunder in her chest and she had to take deep breaths. She inhaled slowly and then exhaled, over and over again. A tight mask of fear embodied her.

Slowly she came around. Her eyes blinked several times, movement of the covers meant her body was stirring and finally she was fully awake. She chanced a fearful look around her and let out a sigh of relief. She was lying in the bedroom, her bedroom, and she was totally alone. But it was dark!

Her breath came in uneven gasps, a sign that she'd be hyperventilating if she did not calm down soon and she focused her attention on composing herself while her eyes skated around the room. Her breath began to slow to a normal pace as she realized no one was in the room, no threat to her. But the lamp! Where was the lamp? She didn't have a clue as the last traces of the nightmare slowly ebbed from her mind.

Skye got out of the bed, and wearily walked down the hallway to the bathroom. Her eyes inspected the area before each deliberate step until she was able to reach beyond the door frame and flipped on the light. While the tub filled, she pinned up her hair and washed her face and with one last frightful look to make sure the door was locked, she sank into the tub.

The water, warm and soothing soon relaxed her and the events of the evening faded as she felt into a deep sleep. She didn't hear the footsteps in the hallway or the turning of the doorknob.

***

Hank, hearing sounds coming from upstairs had awaken and gone to check. He could have sworn he heard something crash to the floor as he ascended the stairs, peeking first into the family room and then turning his eyes toward the kitchen. All was quiet, nothing seemed out of the ordinary as he moved silently through the kitchen and down the hallway.

He stopped at the bathroom door, turned the handle and found it was locked. A worried expression crept across his face as he turned toward the master bedroom. He walked silently to the open doorway and stood listening. There was no sound, not even the sound of Skye's breathing. Cautiously he moved into the room. Skye was not in the bed. He moved to his right to check out the other bedroom, moved further down the hallway and turned left to check out the laundry room before looking at the locked bathroom door. Though he could not hear a sound, the light showing under the base of the door and the fact that Skye was not in the bedroom now added up. Slowly he retraced his steps back downstairs.

***

Meanwhile, the water began to chill. Trying to turn over in her sleep, the shock of the water lapping against her naked body, woke Skye abruptly. Her eyes flew open and at first she was disoriented until remembering she was lying in the tub. The water was tepid, but felt icy cold as she gingerly stepped out to dry herself. After she had her robe wrapped around her body, she let the water out of the tub and turned on the water in the sink. She splashed water on her face until all traces of the facial and Vaseline were removed before reaching for a washcloth to pat her face dry. She had no idea how long she had lain in the tub. "What time is it?" she wondered as she drifted toward the door and unlocked it. She moved determinedly down the hallway toward the bedroom, her earlier terror forgotten. She climbed into the bed and instantly fell asleep.

***

Hank had slept fitfully after having his sleep disturbed. He was tired as he lay staring up at the ceiling thinking. He had come home late and had been shocked to hear Skye still working in her office. He half hoped she'd hear him and come out, but she didn't and after a time he had dragged himself downstairs to what he now called "his room." Though all his belongings were here, it still didn't seem like his room. Why he allowed Skye to force him out of the master bedroom was still a puzzle to him as he sat up on the bed. He stretched, searched through the dresser, and got out some clean underclothes and went to take a shower in the downstairs bathroom. He continued to think about the rearrangement of his house to benefit Skye. First it had been the elimination of the living room into her private office and then she had forced him out of the master bedroom. How had she done it? It still amazed him. Why had he let her take over his living room, his bedroom? As he stood drying himself he continued his train of thought. On his return to the bedroom, he dressed, still thinking about it until he was in the kitchen making a quick cup of instant coffee in the microwave which he seasoned with a shot of whiskey to clear the cobwebs. "Hair of the dog," he said as he stood drinking the coffee and already feeling it's warming affect. When the cup was emptied he sat it on the drain board before going to get his coat and heading out the front door.

CHAPTER 6

Several weeks and then months had passed and the weather was warming up, making it hard to want to stay in and work, but she did. With a short break for lunch, Skye met the mailman and chatted for a while before taking the mail to the office.

For the next few minutes Skye sorted through the pile separating the bills, the magazines, the junk mail into separate piles. She thumbed through the magazines and flyers until she was left with a small stack of envelopes. These she sorted into a pile for the office mail and another for the household mail. Skye opened and finished with the office pile first and then turned to the next pile. This was not exactly her idea of the way to spend the day, but it needed to be done. A sigh escaped her lips as she faced the fact that this may well be the highlight of her day.

She opened everything. She stacked the household bills on the desk and flipped through the junk mail. After discarding the last of it she picked up the bills, let out another sigh and started opening them.

The first one on the pile was the gas and electric bill. With some hesitation she lowered her eyes to the bottom line and was only slightly surprised by the amount due. She laid it aside and picked up the next one which turned out to be a late notice on Hank's van payment. This didn't surprise her as she placed it on top of the other bills that needed to be paid. She'd take care of it for him. The next was the American Express charge account statement, which she started to lay on the pile unopened, knowing there would be no balance, but having nothing better to do, she looked inside. Her eyebrows arched as her expression changed to disbelief. She stared fixedly at the amount written below.

"This is impossible! There has to be a mistake!" But even as she said it, Skye knew it was no mistake. Hank was at it again.

"Why does he keep doing this to me? He knows he can't afford to pay this bill." She pauses for a moment, then shook her head adamantly. No, she assured himself, he had no way of knowing how much her income had increased over the past few months since he was never home.

Skye fumed, she ranted and raved. Nothing would please her more than to hit something, hit it hard right now. But it was Hank she wanted to hit and thinking about it did no good. He was not home.

Skye left the office, making her way to the bedroom, only vaguely aware of what she planned to do. In the bedroom, she snatched open a dresser drawer and grabbed a pair of exercise tights. Then trying to balance, quickly worked one leg, then the other into place, before tugging them up over her hips. She reached back into the drawer and removed a body suit which she stepped into and began tugging it up over her tights.

She practically ran to the closet and got down on all fours, madly searching for her sneakers. She found them, put them on and like a raging bull, she raced downstairs. Into the DVD went her workout disk and she stood ready to follow instructions as they flowed from the speakers.

"Stand with your legs, hip distance apart, stomach pulled in, shoulders back, this bone, the pelvic bone tilted up toward your navel..."

Her body worked feverishly while her eyes focused on the bodies on the screen. Blissfully, her mind barricaded all but the commands from the screen as she stretched, bent, swung her body around, her mind concentrating on each movement and the feel of her muscles as the tension was replaced by fluidity of motion. It was something Skye could count on, and right now she needed someone to depend on and not confront her with any nasty surprises. An hour later, her body glistening with sweat and feeling physically rejuvenated, she went to take a shower.

Under the spray of water, it all came tumbling back to haunt her again. "Just where does he get off thinking he can charge to his heart's content?" The words energized her resolution to let him have it with both barrels.

When she stepped out of the shower she dried her body before escaping to the bedroom. There she haphazardly threw on some clothes cursing the day she had met Hank. That's when she heard a noise that had her running back into the bathroom to look out the window.

At the far end of the road, less than a house distance down the street, Hank's blue van appeared. Skye felt the force of her anger blossoming even more as it spread through her, manifesting itself in a throbbing pain at the back of her eyes. She winced as she focused on the van turning into the driveway.

Her time had come, and the knowledge had her moving at breakneck speed. One minute she was at the window, the next she was standing before the entrance to the garage.

CHAPTER 7

In the garage, Hank sat for a moment contemplating. What was Skye up to now? He stretched luxuriously in the confines of his van even though he was limited in space to extend his body. His neck was tense and he lowered his arms so that his hands rubbed the area just below his hair line. After the day he had, he needed some sanity and he was actually relishing the idea of seeing Skye. He thought about the conversation he had with the man at the Circle Bar. A pleased smile spread on his face as he thought about what he had done, and wondered if maybe he should take it a step further. That brought him around to thinking about how much pleasure it would give him to see the look on Skye's face when she found he wasn't just sitting back taking whatever she dished out. But his pleasure was short lived. He felt a tinge of regret. What he wanted was Skye. As if to put things in their proper perspective he said aloud, "Why should I care what the hell Skye is doing?"

It was so confusing. On one hand he sought to outwit her, yet he wanted to be with her. In frustration he shook his head then proceeded to climb out of the van, slamming the door hard. He walked nonchalantly across the garage floor and felt more in control as he approached the door to the family room.

Inside, Skye stood like a sentry waiting for Hank to enter, mumbling to herself.

"He thinks he deserves nothing but the biggest and the best of everything. That stupid van of his, this house.. Well, let's just see how he likes the other side of that coin."

While she grumbled, it dawned on her she had forgotten the evidence. Listening for a moment and not hearing a sound, she quickly flew up the two steps, slide across the kitchen floor, banging her hip against the table before finally maneuvering her body into the office. She swept up the American Express bill from the top of the desk.

Skye was out of breath with her hip aching but she was not about to let that stop her from hastening back to her post, determined to be the first thing Hank saw when he flung the door open. Her foot caught in the nap of the tri level carpet in the family room, almost throwing her off balance, but instinctively she reached out, placing her hand on the wall as she covered the short distance to the door without mishap. She planted her body in front of that door thinking she'd either be standing or face down--it was no never mind to her.

***

Hank now stood at the garage door entrance checking through the keys on the ring until he found the right one. He stared at it, as though not sure it would fit the lock. His mind drifted, caught up in a TV version of the sweet little wife awaiting her husband's return home. A sarcastic smile planted itself on his face while the vision quickly changed to that of what he could expect to be waiting on the other side of the door--nothing and no one. Yet he couldn't help wondering in his present state of mind, what would it be like to open the door and have Skye run into his arms. Grumbling he said, "Fat chance of that."

Despite his inability to keep his mind precisely on what he was about, Hank managed to finally insert the key in the lock and turned it clockwise, then leaning forward, pushed it wide open. For a moment he was stunned into silence as his gaze fell upon Skye. Then slowly, recognizing the look of anger blazing in her eyes he entertained the idea of turning tail and running before the onslaught began. Only that was not his way.

Skye stood stiffly erect with her left hand on her hip, and before Hank could close the door behind him she said, while waving the bill about the air, "How could you do this?"

At first he was at a loss, having no idea what was on her mind as he moved his head back to avoid being clipped by the edge of the paper waving near his face.

"Back off Skye. What, are you crazy."

"Ha! Yeah, I'm crazy alright. Look at this. Just look at the balance on this bill!"

He pretended innocence for two reasons. First, if it was what he thought it was, it meant he would have to think about the fact of what he had done, and he did not want to think about that right now. Secondly, he had acted smartly, taking a cash advance against his card. There was no way Skye could have an inkling of what he had used the money for. He looked at the hate on her face, and unwillingly took possession of the paper.

He glanced at it. It was the American Express bill. Then showing no concern said, "So?"

"So! Look at it Hank, or don't you have to? Huh? Do you already know what it says? Come on, tell me."

They were in the family room, the room he enjoyed most. As if he hadn't heard her, Hank took off his coat and sat down in his favorite chair, the one with the beautiful wooden arms. He fantasized thinking he could feel the strength of the tree under his hand as he touched it. He stretched out his legs. Oh, it felt good. He even closed his eyes, bathing in a pure moment of thoughtlessness--his mind relaxed. He had had a lot to drink and enjoyed the numbing sensation that stole over his body. "Will you answer me, you stupid, selfish pain in the ass!" Skye screamed loudly, annoyed by his lack of concern.

And there went his tranquility. Hank sat straight up.

"Shut up, Skye! If you know what's good for you, you will shut your fat mouth right now."

He paused for a moment, registered the extent of her anger that fed his anger and yelled, "I don't care how mad you get, you're not going to force me into doing anything, so you might as well calm down."

"Calm down? Is that what you said? How can I calm down when you're acting like an asshole? You don't have the money to pay this bill and, furthermore, I'm not going to pay it for you. Do you hear me? I am not even going to try and pay it this time!"

Skye's voice cracked and her throat was raw by the time she spoke the last sentence. She was screaming at the top of her lungs and acting like a maniac. But it didn't matter; nothing mattered now. As much as she despised arguing, she was unable to hold herself back. This was the last straw and Hank's attitude threatened her sanity.

The expression on her face blazed in his soul and fed the fire glowing within Hank now. He was amazed at the audacity of this five-foot, four inch person trying to get the better of him. She had guts, he had to give that to her. Standing up to him, who was twice her size and weight. Somewhere deep inside he felt a need to ease the pain he had caused her and he tried to shake the feeling. He knew he was guilty and he felt sorry, for just an instant. Sorry because he knew he had played his cards already and she was the victim all the way around. But it only lasted for a minute.

"Well, what are you going to do about it, Hank? Got a magic wand to make it disappear? Just what were you thinking when you withdrew all this cash against a charge card that has to be paid all at once?" There was barely fire in her words that were spoken softly so as not to irritate her throat. Her stance wavered and he knew her energy was sapped, yet he ignored it.

"Just don't you worry about it. Don't pay the damn bill if you don't want to because I don't care what you do with the bill. Stick it up your ass for all I care. Only now you had best get out of my face!" He started to walk away.

"Please, Hank, this is serious." Skye said meekly, all the fire gone from her voice. "It's out of hand. I can't live like this anymore."

A thick cloak of silence descended on the room and Skye felt the tears as they flowed freely. Hastily she tried to wipe them away with the back of her hand, but not before Hank had taken notice. He could be callous and was never one to let a person walk all over him, but even though he resented her attack he knew he had the upper hand. Her fate rested on him and he figured he could afford to let her have the chance for retaliation.

"Stop worrying about it, Skye. I just ran into several bad breaks, but I'll take care of it." Hank started to let her know that he knew what she meant. He knew she wanted to end the marriage, but he kept quiet.

Skye could feel her body weaving as she stood in front of the chair, misreading his expression. Right at that moment she felt an urge to grab hold of the wood base lamp on the end table next to his favorite chair and swing it as hard as she could until not only that self righteous look, but his whole face disappeared. The realization that she wanted to hurt him stopped Skye in her tracks. Violence was not her forte and the fact that she thought like a savage scared her. Silently she said to herself, I've got to get away from him.

"Okay Hank, okay, I can see I am wasting my time trying to make you understand that I'm serious. Just forget I even mentioned it." She turned and started up the stairs, feeling a heaviness of body and spirit.

By the time Skye reached her office she knew she would pay the bill and any others he decided to make for her. She took a deep breath and allowed it to slowly escape as she paced in her office. "Damned if I do, damned if I don't," sadly she said stopping in front of the office window and looking out. She had managed to set aside quite a bit of money and still keep up with the bills and now, this bill, this one bill would wipe her nest egg clean.

Everything seemed so normal, so unchanged around her, she thought, yet her world was falling apart. Or was it? Suddenly her expression changed from sadness to determination. As clear as the sound of the noon time siren that pealed and without checking you knew it signaled twelve o'clock, she did have an alternative. Divorce was her way out and she would make it so. Only not now. She must be calm, cool and collected when she confronted him.

She looked up at the trees that had overnight grown new leaves and felt rejuvenated. She would ask for a divorce when they both were rational and everything would go well because... She paused, then finished by thinking, because it just must.

Skye settled back in her office chair and rested her head against its back. A worried look came to her face as she realized something for the first time. She was a passenger! She frowned, causing lines to appear on her forehead. She had never thought of herself in this way, but realized it was true. Why did it take her old boss to convince her she could make it in business? Why did she still continue to want Hank to take control of things? Why was she always asking her friends or family for their advice on things they knew nothing about? Why? She knew why. She didn't want the responsibility of being the driver because it was so much easier to place herself in the other seat.

Skye could feel herself relaxing. She could do it. This new awareness restored her confidence and she knew she would get a divorce before it was too late for either of them to have a second chance at happiness.

CHAPTER 8

Angelo Maglioni, III, sat in his plush office looking over some papers on his desk when the intercom buzzed. His features were distinctly of Italian ancestry, his black hair having hints of gray at the temples that added distinction to his appearance. He was successful, his year round tan and excellent physique supporting the claim, while his soft brown eyes spoke of kindness and honesty.

"Yes," he said.

"Mr. Maglioni? Some papers were just delivered by a messenger. Would you like me to bring them in?"

"Ah, yes, Lisa. I've been waiting on them."

In a few minutes he heard a light tab on his door. "Come in Lisa."

Lisa opened the door and walked over to hand the envelope to her boss. She stood in front of his desk, waiting patiently until he looked at her. "Can I get you anything else?" she said inquiringly.

"No, thanks Lisa, that will be all." He smiled at her, then watched as she moved across the carpet to the door. She was a proficient secretary, quite capable of handling more than the routine jobs. Lisa was pretty, dressed quite attractively, and had a pleasant personality. All his clients commented on her refreshing welcome and her honest show of respect, which more than made up for her minor inabilities. He waited now until the door closed behind her. Once he was alone he reached across his desk to pick up his letter opener which he slid gently across the sealed top of the envelope, a look of disinterest on his handsome face. He removed the pages and laid them down and with a sigh, wondered why he had even bothered, but they were here now so he might as well look it over.

Angelo's head was down as he read through the pages until suddenly his heart leaped as though a gun had sounded. Now, just calm down, he said to himself. Just stop it. That business is all past. It ended years ago. It's finished, remember? Finished.

But it wasn't. He looked sharply at the name that stared up from him on the page. Mr. William T. Taylor. That name caused tumultuous anger. He no longer was disinterested.

William T. Taylor was his archenemy and this was the first opportunity that had come his way to pay him back for the injustice he had caused him. It didn't matter that Taylor's influence was not threatening to him now. This was a question of self-respect. It was a personal vendetta that had to be settled and one that had begun seventeen years ago.

Had it really been seventeen years? It must have been somewhere in that time span because it had happened early on in his career when he was first staring up his law practice. A terrible fury took over his being as he reminisced. If Taylor had been in the room and he had a knife, Angelo would have plunged it into Taylor's heart. But that phase of his life was over, he tried to tell himself.

Angelo turned his chair around and looked out the window where a fine snow was falling. The skies were pale, with smudges of low gray clouds. Bare trees stood out in crisp distinction and he sighed, closed his eyes, and told his heart to beat right. But it beat all the more erratically as he envisioned what was now in his grasp. For so long he had waited and hoped for this opportunity. He had his man assigned to Taylor for so long he was beginning to wonder if he was wasting his money. Once Taylor became District Attorney, the man had asked for more money to continue his surveillance. He understood what it would mean for him as well as himself if the man got caught so he agreed to pay him more. Spying on Government and State officials did not lend itself to light sentences and tampering with the mail could put a person behind bars for a very long time. Angelo leaned back in his chair.

***

He had been ambitious back then when he made his decision to become the best damn lawyer this city had ever known. He worked hard through high school and later in law school to get the best grades he could muster. Because of his family's money, he was able to concentrate all his efforts on his schooling and he took full advantage of it. He passed the bar exam with flying colors and went about starting his legal practice. After getting several successful wins under his belt, he was on his way up and was soon influential enough to pick and choose his clients. Back then he had the world in the palm of his hand and never doubted he could make it all happen just as he dreamed it would be.

His determination all stemmed from his upbringing. He came from a highly respected family in the mafia, if you could call it that, and had grown up watching his father always keeping an eye out behind him. His father lived in fear of his life, or was always on guard for a possible takeover, which was where all his attention went. He used to hate him for his lack of feeling, his lack of time for him and his mother. But later he realized he had no alternative. His father couldn't afford to care for, or about anyone or anything except the business. There was many a time he wondered why he was born, or why his parents had married.

His father's business influenced his childhood. There were times when Angelo, who was too young to understand, was told not to play with certain kids or was not allowed to join after school events or go to the hangouts with his peers. Being too young to understand he saw it as a punishment that caused him to miss out on a lot of enjoyment during what should have been the best years of his life. As a result, early in his young life he resolved he would not be like his father.

He didn't know when he actually came to the conclusion, but once he understood his father's business he vowed then that no matter what it took he'd turn the Maglioni name into one that was legally respectable. He vowed also that when he married and had a family he would give them all the attention and love that he had been denied. He added one more vow later on after witnessing a scene between his father and mother.

Angelo was looking straight ahead. His face held sadness as he remembered that day.

He had come home early from school and was seated in the livingroom when he heard his mother and father in a heated argument. Silently he crept into the sun room and hid behind a chair. His mother was crying and his father stood in front of her with his arms hanging at his side, in a straddled stance.

"Angelo, you can't, she's my best friend," his mother said.

"I don't give a damn who she is."

"But..."

Her sentence went unfinished. He could see his father's eyes burn right through his mother. He watched as his father as he advanced toward his mother, his arm drawn back and breathing heavy until he was in reach. He saw the hand as it made contact with her face.

His mother, up against the wall of the sun room had no means of getting out of his way, but she twisted her body helplessly. He saw his father's open palm as it again came up and struck swiftly, hitting one cheek, then he backhanded her in a repeating process. The ring he wore must have cut her face as he could see blood on her cheek. Not relenting his father hit her again with such force her head slammed against the wall and he heard her helplessly crying out. "Stop, Angelo, please stop." In response he heard his father say, "You remember that and remember it well. You stay out of my business and out of my way or I will have you replaced. You understand that?"

Sobbing, his mother crouched in the corner of the room now as Angelo stared directly into the pain in her eyes when she looked up and shook her head. At that precise moment he hated his father and wanted to kill him.

He never forgot what he saw or forgot his father's words on that day. He knew his mother was always trying to please his father and she never raised her voice. How could he strike her, he kept asking himself. No matter what she said or what she did, there could be no sane reason for it. He vowed as he squatted, whimpering softly behind the chair, that he would take care of her. He also adamantly affirmed he would never hit a woman.

***

As the years transpired his attitude softened toward his father. He reached an age of understanding and once he did he felt sorry for him. He grew to realize that the kind of life Angelo Maglioni II led, forced him to become a man who was incapable of loving another human being. It was as though he was only half a man. And with this understanding, Angelo couldn't help wondering if his father had always been that way. He didn't know.

He did know that he wouldn't, and couldn't like that kind of life. The day he approached his father with his decision to go to law school, he knew it was only by virtue of the profession that his father agreed and paid his way. It wasn't until after he had graduated did he dare tell his father he had no desire to play a role in his business.

At first his father was beside himself with anger.

"What have I ever done to you to make you so ungrateful. I built this empire to turn over to you to make your life easier and you show me no gratitude or respect!"

Angelo, if he had been half-witted, might have challenged the validity of his father's words. He might have told him the truth. His treatment of his mother, his style of living in fear of his life was not something to brag about. But he had a level head on his shoulders.

"Father, I understand why you feel that way, but you must try and understand that I am like you and want to make my way on my own. It has nothing to do with any lack of respect."

They might have argued the point for years if Angelo hadn't used his brain and gotten his father's right hand man, Bruno, on his side. Bruno had been with the family longer than he could remember and was the only man his father truly trusted. And rightfully so. Bruno would have died for his father if it came to that. But Bruno also cared immensely for the young Angelo; and after using this handle to the maximum, he knew Bruno would go to bat for him. He never knew what transpired, but though his father wasn't happy, he finally gave his consent, even offering his support to help him until he got on his feet. What that meant was that whatever money he needed, his father would front.

He never expected it, nor did his father ever tell him that he was proud of him. But why shouldn't he be!. Angelo knew he was brilliant. His grades, the marks he obtained on the bar exam all proved that. The only one to express any pride was his endearing mother and that seemed to suffice.

Even though he was confident, it wasn't only to soothe his father that he accepted financial support. He was too used to having money to consider being without it. So, unlike the usual starving lawyer starting up a practice, he had not only unlimited finances at his disposal, but the resources to help him solve even the most difficult of cases. Angelo never turned his back on using his father's men to get information that could win a case.

***

Now Angelo sat up straight and stared ahead. He had been able to stand on his own two feet and make it big in the law profession. He had accumulated a respectable body of clients and the largest and prestigious law firm in this city. He didn't question the fact that he had started out with an advantage, but that didn't lessen the fact of what he had managed to achieve on his own. He was a great lawyer and had legitimate clients now. He had worked long and hard and was leading a clean life.

That brought him to the issue of William T. Taylor. Taylor was a fiercely ambitious man, fighting his way up the ladder with neither money nor connections to boost him. His only stronghold was a convincing veneer of being a civil servant to the people, but underneath he was what Angelo termed a gutter fighter who would go to any means to discount the credibility of his opponent. Add to that the fact that he was vindictive of anyone who hadn't struggled to reach success and you had the full picture. Taylor was a man who neither forgot nor forgave a colleague who had a hand up.

Angelo swung his chair back around to face his desk. He again looked down at the papers on his desk, imagining that just like himself, Taylor wouldn't have been in that courtroom for this case either. He was the District Attorney now and had a large staff of senior assistants who were capable of handling cases for him. Why he had taken it upon himself to defend the victim was still unknown, but Angelo determined there had to be a payoff involved somewhere along the line, or something that went outside the boundaries of honesty. But did that matter? Angelo again thought about that long ago courtroom event.

***

It was Michael Zorreli, one of his father's men who was on trial that day and as a favor to him Angelo took the case. That was the first time Angelo chanced to meet Taylor; the case was Taylor's first and he was just as determined to win. Taylor had called on the best private investigator he new, Daniel Malone, to gather every piece of information he could come up with on Michael Zorreli and Daniel had come through for him. He was confident he would win the case.

"Mr. Zorreli, do you care to tell the jury of your connection with your lawyer?"

"Objection, your honor. My knowing Mr. Zorreli has nothing to do with this case."

"Objection sustained."

"I'll rephrase the question. Mr. Zorreli, do you work for a man named Angelo Maglioni?"

"Yes I do, but not this Angelo Maglioni."

"A simple yes will suffice."

Zorreli fell for it. His jaw was clenched and his face was filled with anger as he responded to the questions. Somewhere along the line Zorreli managed to clarify that he worked for Angelo's father, but the damage was done.

Throughout the interrogation, Taylor took every opportunity to make the jurors aware of the connection between the man on trial and his attorney. Angelo, determined to not get into a bout of defending his family name, backed down. He lost that case. Michael Zorreli was sent to jail and Angelo's reputation was badly soiled.

For a long time he tried to correct the damage on his own, but without success. No respectable clients came to his door. It was his father who came to his rescue. For the first time he listened to the man and believed in what he said. His father told him that he'd get all the clients he wanted regardless of his name, if he could prove his ability to win their cases. And on that premise he defended the stream of clients his father sent to his firm. Each client was hand-picked and only the ones that could not be traced back to connections with the mafia were sent to his doorstep. It was a long, painstaking process, but eventually the business prevailed.

He didn't recognize his success until he sat at the head of the biggest and most sought after law firm in the city and maybe the country. Only the most brilliant and promising lawyers were asked to join his firm, and they came to him. His firm was being sought after by the rich, and the famous, the people who had the money to pay for the best damn lawyer around and Angelo's firm charged the highest fee for their services.

Now with this new case before him, one that he normally would have turned aside, he remembered with vivid clarity. He had been on his way to the top when he met Mr. William T. Taylor in that courtroom so long ago. It was this man who had almost forced him out of the legal profession. A man who didn't respect the guidelines of the profession nor feel any guilt for what he might have done. He had been unjustly accused as being part of the mafia and out of respect for his family name only, he had to back down. Oh how he wanted to defend himself against the wrongful allegations, but he could not, and it left him with a feeling of vengeance. Just as he swore to not lead a life of crime, he vowed to seek justice for those fraudulent accusations.

For all these reasons he made the decision to defend the man Samuel Stillman. The man whose case was now before him. He picked up the phone and dialed a number. When he reached his party he said, "This is Maglioni. Go ahead and set it up."

Seeing the name of William T. Taylor brought back all the old memories, and Angelo decided he would get satisfaction one way or the other. This was something he had to do for himself. He had to pay the man back for all he had taken away from him. He had the power and the means to stop Taylor in his tracks.

It had been a long time coming, a very long time, he thought, but the time was now near. "Taylor, you had best watch out because two can play your game," he said as his fist came down on the desk.

CHAPTER 9

Sitting in a not so plush office in the District Attorney's office, Taylor was doing some thinking of his own. A caricature of a man who has succumbed hard times and finally got a leg up, William Taylor sported a pot belly from too many beers. His hair now thin and graying made him appear older than he was by calendar years. But time hadn't washed away the contempt in his piercing washed out blue eyes or the snarling curvature pasted on his thin lips. He had already gotten word that Sam Stillman was going to be defended by Angelo Maglioni. Before the ink had a chance to dry, he had the paperwork delivered that established proof that Maglioni was indeed going to take the case of Sam Stillman.

It didn't come as any surprise to him. Taylor had always believed that Angelo would try to even the score some day. That's why he was always cautious, thinking that he could bet on Maglioni keeping tails on him. Only not like that time so long ago when he had to do his own leg work to come up with the information to put Angelo Maglioni III in his place, he now had men at his disposal. He had made a lot of connections over the years that would now pay off and add some excitement to the drudgery of his job as District Attorney.

He wasn't totally dissatisfied with the position, but he had thought that with the power of sitting in this seat came respect. But it hadn't turned out that way. The people who worked for him did what he asked because of who he was and not because they respected him or for that matter, felt he was capable. And he needed that respect, he needed to know they knew he was smart.

Taylor looked down at the papers that laid on his scarred desk top and focused on the name of Angelo Maglioni. Even after the smear he had put on his reputation, the man had made it back to the top. He could have been a good lawyer with a large practice too, but he didn't have the money to see it through. To his credit he had realized that and gone for the job of District Attorney, only it wasn't enough. He wanted what Angelo had and he wouldn't be happy until he made the man feel what it was like to have to make it on his own.

He had almost succeeded that time some fifteen or so years ago.

***

William Taylor was a poor kid from a broken home, raised by foster families and put on the streets right after graduating from high school. He worked the night shift at fast food places to finance his way through junior college. He graduated, barely, and had a time of it trying to get into law school. His grades and lack of finances made him settle for the cheapest one he could find, which of course was not one of the most prestigious institutes. It was then that he really hit the books, managing to make his studies beneficial, if not outstanding. He hadn't graduated with honors, but at least he graduated. Again he met with disappointment as he hit the pavement going from one law firm to the next and being turned down. He passed the bar exams by the skin of his teeth while living hand to mouth not knowing where or when he'd make his next dollar. The day he hung his sign on the door was the first feeling of accomplishment he had, but that was all it reaped.

Many a day he sat in his one room office looking at the chipped paint and ripped drapes wondering when his time would come. Finally he got smart. If work didn't come to him, he'd go out and get it. He started hanging around police stations, passing out his card to anyone who would take it. He managed to keep busy enough to pay his bills and that was all. He worked within the realm of the law until he realized it wasn't getting him a name. That's when William decided that his only objective was to win the case. So, using every possible means, following every conceivable trail, he did just that until finally he received some recognition for his ability. Luckily he wasn't one of those law school students with the noble idea that a lawyer was just a person trained and licensed to prepare and manage a court action as an agent for his client, nor did he consider himself a defender of individual rights, protecting the oppressed. His experiences taught him that any crook with enough money to pay his fee was worthy of being represented in court and proven innocent. That meant he would investigate the facts and the evidence as presented to him by his client, and in a court of law introduce evidence, interrogate witnesses and argue questions of law and fact that would help him win the case. As far as loyalty went, he must be loyal to his client and himself. Loyalty did not extend to the community or his associates in practice until he had made a name for himself. That meant that in order to win he must turn over every stone in the process. No one and nothing was too sacred for his scrutiny.

At first the work dribbled in until finally he had more than he could handle. It wasn't big or impressive cases, but enough to put food on the table and eventually allowed him to move to more plush furnishings. And that was when his ship came in.

He had been young back then, and for William, trying his very first case of notoriety, was not about to stop at anything. He had suffered enough to realize he'd never make it big until he was picked up by some prestigious law firm or successfully tried a widely publicized case that would put his name in print and pay him a lot of dough. That's where he set his stakes.

He became a news hound, reading about every important person, their connections and what they were up to. He read about murders, kidnaps, wife-beating cases without discrimination until he became a walking book of knowledge. He kept up on any newsworthy items that could benefit him either now or in the future.

He distinctly remembered that day as he pored over the newspaper, running across the announcement that the District Attorney was retiring. It wasn't immediately important to him as he read the article of the man who had served the city for some time and was now stepping down. It came to him slowly. He could become the prosecuting officer of the judicial district, but in order to get there, he had to make a name for himself.

With that purpose in mind he had to act fast. From that second on he worked toward his goal. The day the phone rang and he was asked if he would be the prosecuting attorney in an upcoming case, he accepted even before learning the details. When he began the tedious job of preparing his transcript he knew this was his ticket up. He would be prosecuting Michael Zorreli!

It was as much a surprise to him as to anybody. Here he was still a young, unknown attorney, given the opportunity to prosecute a case against the mafia! Sure he knew he hadn't been the first lawyer approached, or one chosen for his track record. This was a case that not just any lawyer would touch. By eliminating those who had already made a name for themselves, those with family, and those with connections in high places, it left only those who were hungry or who had nothing to lose. That was Taylor to a tee.

From the moment he took the case, William spent every hour trying to gather the information he would need to win. That was when he had first met Daniel Malone who proved to be invaluable to him in getting the details together. As far as he was concerned, there wasn't a private investigator better than his friend Daniel.

When he met with defeat in trying to dig up information that would prove beyond a shadow of a doubt that Zorreli should be put behind bars, he felt the first tinge of failure. That made him put his thinking cap on. There had to be some trail of evidence that had been overlooked by the mafia, something he could sink his teeth into.

He went back and reviewed the details for the trial and found what he was looking for. The defending attorney was a young lawyer named Angelo Maglioni. The name, Maglioni, immediately set off a bell in his head. He knew that name! From that point he focused all his efforts on the attorney. That's where Daniel came in.

At a lost, he had to admit he needed help. He buzzed his secretary, asked her to pull out the business cards for private investigators and bring them in immediately. He'd remember once he saw the name. He had met with most of them at some point, but one stood out in his mind as a possibility. When his secretary came and handed him the business cards, it was the third one down. Daniel Malone.

"Dial this one for me, please."

"Sure Mr. Taylor."

In a few minutes the intercom buzzed and he picked up the line. "Mr Malone's on line two?"

After completing the formalities, Taylor invited Mr. Malone to come to his office. They met and Taylor hired him for the job. He gave him copies of everything he had uncovered to date and explained how he wanted him to proceed. He was not surprised when he learned that Maglioni was the son of the head of one of the largest of the four eastern mafia families.

Angelo was his age, already with a thriving legal practice. He came from money and was making more money in a successful law practice. He was married to a woman named Kay, and had two children; something Taylor hadn't the time or opportunity to achieve. Angelo had graduated with honors from Harvard University, ranking in the top ten of his class and immediately set up a private practice which grew by leaps and bounds. Yet, as Taylor went over the dossier of Zorreli and did some further investigation into Maglioni he found that most of the cases Maglioni had tried had been of public interest, but with no connection to the mafia. That didn't stop him as he made his case. He had no proof to sustain his judgment, but he'd go for the jugular vein and convince the jurors that the young Maglioni was representing the mafia family.

He knew that a good attorney would have concentrated only on the accused and seek the proof he needed from that standpoint. A good attorney would not even consider aiming his sights toward his associate in practice. Yet it was not beyond Taylor and he considered himself a good attorney, slightly desperate, but good. Besides, from all he had read, Angelo's connection was a logical assumption. A rich and successful lawyer and only son of a mafia mogul, who wouldn't draw the same conclusion? He made up his mind. Instead of going into the courtroom to prove that Michael Zorreli was guilty of washing mafia money, he went in to prove that Angelo Maglioni III had a stake in the outcome of the case.

The day after the trial the papers were ablaze with details of the trial that ran for three weeks. He had played it shrewd and his name was in print as the man who had succeeded in putting away Michael Zorreli. With that prestige, he got enough notoriety to be recognized and even sought after. It also got him the position of District Attorney.

***

Taylor sat forward in his chair now. As for the young Maglioni, he had managed to get his point across so that it wasn't easy for him to rebuild his practice. Yet he wasn't too surprised, as he followed the man over the years, to learn he had not only managed to rebuild his reputation, but he now headed one of the biggest law firms in the city. Yes, he had stopped him, but money talks and it managed to blot out the bug he had placed in the public ear.

Taylor had an odd little smile flickering over his lips as he sat up in his chair There was something else he had managed to do. He had read several months after the case that the Maglioni marriage had ended in divorce. That was something the man would never get back in place.

Now as William reveled in glory, he was full of confidence. He had succeeded once and he could succeed again, he thought. His mind was already working on the case now before him that appeared to be a sure thing. But he was going to play it smart and gather every thread of evidence and information he could find. When he walked into that court room and faced his adversary he would be thoroughly prepared.

He reached across his desk and picked up a pencil, chewing on the eraser thoughtfully as he wondered what was it he wanted this time. He had the position he had wanted and in a sense he had Maglioni to thank for that, because without that win under his belt his name would never have been plastered all over the newspapers. As District Attorney he was earning a respectable salary and had a staff that could handle a case like this. But he knew why--it was because he wanted Maglioni himself. After winning that case, Taylor never had a night's sleep or walked without checking behind his back. He lived in fear until he was able to hide behind the title of District Attorney. What he wanted was for someone to pay for the anguish he had gone through, the money he never had, the family he couldn't afford to start.

Taylor looked again at the papers on his desk and his hatred was visible on his face. He didn't know how he would get even and he didn't know the facts of the case, but he was confident he would win in the end. Maglioni had managed to claw his way back up, but he wouldn't escape again. Besides, he thought, he still had nothing to lose and everything to gain by trying. He also had the protection to survive the outcome.

CHAPTER 10

The next morning Skye woke feeling exceptionally refreshed. She had slept peacefully through the night with not one nightmare. As she moved about getting her morning routines out of the way she hummed a happy tune. By eight that morning she was seated at her desk and ready for work. She had just started her first job when the phone rang.

She managed to get out her usual greeting before the woman on the other end identified herself as the personal secretary of Mr. Angelo Maglioni. She didn't know any Mr. Maglioni. Quickly she searched her mind and registering nothing get out a pad and pencil to take notes. This was obviously a new client.

"If you are available, Mr. Maglioni would like to meet with you this morning at ten o'clock."

She didn't hesitate or take the time to check her calendar as she recollected the name. Everyone knew his name! "Yes, I can be there, but do you know what this concerns?"

"No, I was just asked to call you, and to ask that you be prompt."

"I'll be there."

Skye was used to dealing with small company owners, but when it came to the owners of large, prestigious law firms, she had only dealt with their secretaries and so far hadn't gotten one foot in the door. She had finally given up. Now that she had a nice listing of clients and new ones being added everyday she no longer did much advertising. Maglioni headed the largest law firm in Rochester. It was the most prestigious firm in the area. If Mr. Maglioni wanted to meet with her personally, it must be something really big or else he would have utilize his own staff for the job. Dollar signs filled her head as her mind wondered what it could possibly be. A firm that size asking for outside assistance must be contemplating a sizeable project.

She didn't have much time to dwell on the matter as it was almost nine thirty. Quickly Skye closed down the office and turned on the answering service. In the bedroom she pulled out her black wool skirt, a tan wool jacket and her tan silk blouse with black trim at the neck and cuffs. For accessories she put on a simple pair of gold braided earrings and her tan and black spectator shoes. She stopped in the bathroom to refresh her make up and pull her hair back, clasping it at the nape of her neck. Satisfied with her reflection, she grabbed her purse and her briefcase, put on her black wool cape and was on her way.

As Skye drove downtown she fantasized on the prospect of meeting Mr. Maglioni himself, and again she was assured it had to be something major in store for her. She smiled, wondering which one of her customers had given him her name. It would have to be one of her more prestigious clients, but which one? She had a meeting with Angelo Maglioni. Who would have thought....

Skye arrived early and had a few minutes to kill. She walked around outside the office building on State Street. At precisely ten o'clock she was giving her name to the receptionist. An hour passed before she was finally ushered into the office of Mr. Maglioni.

He sat behind an antique cherry desk that shone like glass with shelves of thick leather law books as a back ground. Everything in the room spoke of wealth and prestige including the man himself.

Maglioni stood erect behind the desk in a tailored navy blue suit, a shirt so white it shone and a one of a kind silk tie of blues and peach tones that set off his tanned face. His black hair had hints of gray at the temples, his features were distinctly of Italian ancestry and she was able to surmise that from what she saw, he kept himself in tip top shape.

He did not offer her a chair as he spoke with a huge smile and a hand thrust forward. "Miss Sanders?"

"Mrs. Sanders," she corrected as she shook his hand.

"Nice to meet you, Mrs. Sanders. I'm Angelo Maglioni. "I've heard about your work." He paused for a moment. "I have something I would like to have you do for me."

Angelo had given this matter a lot of thought. If something should go wrong, he didn't want his firm to be tied to any scandal or suffer any repercussions so he determined the best action to take was to handle this matter outside the firm. The lady who stood before him seemed qualified for the job. He had found her business card, company flyer and a resume in the file that his secretary kept of advertising sent into the firm. He liked the idea that she worked out of her home and so had contacted Frank Jaffe, a PI he used often, and had him check her out. The report back was good. Her clients were respectable people who solicited her services on a regular basis which meant they must like her work. The background check revealed nothing unusual and now that he had met her, she seemed ideal for the job.

Without taking the time to be seated, he picked up a thick folder on his desk. "This is a transcript that I want you to look over. It is a matter of complete confidentiality that requires a short turnaround time." He hesitated a moment. "I think you will have no problem handling this assignment."

"I'm pleased to here that." She watched Mr. Maglioni who still stood holding the folder. Skye took this as a signal and walked up to the front of the desk to take it from his hands. It was thick, and required her to use both her hands to keep from spilling the contents. Carefully she lowered it to the corner of his desk and leaned down, folded back the top of the folder and scrutinized the contents.

The folder contained a pile of loose notes; some typed, some handwritten.

"Oh, please, take a seat Mrs. Sanders. I'm sorry, where are my manners?"

Skye smiled while secretly thinking to herself he hadn't forgotten his manners. He was testing her to see if she had enough culture to wait until she was offered a chair.

"Thank you, Mr. Maglioni," she said as she mindfully lowered herself into the chair nearest the desk. Skye was careful to smooth her skirt and sit on the edge of the seat with her ankles crossed.

She could tell by his expression he was impressed. He came from behind his desk and stood beside her chair, looking over her shoulder while she again turned her attention to the pile of papers. Everything seemed pretty explanatory.

"There's a sample of how it should be organized in the back."

Skye quickly flipped to the back of the folder and picked up the sample. She studied it, having a good idea of the contents she would be placing in the format.

"I don't think I'll have any trouble with this. Everything seems straight forward."

"That's just fine. If you need to make minor changes, go ahead if you think it works best with the transcript. Just two things to keep in mind. First do not change any of the meaning, and second, this is confidential work." He paused and then looking directly in her eyes said. "But of course, I don't need to tell you that."

"You've been very thorough, Mr. Maglioni, and I would be disappointed if you hadn't."

She swore he almost chuckled, almost before he caught himself. He beamed instead, then asked, "Do you think you can finish the job in a week?"

Skye leafed quickly back through the pages, paying careful attention to the handwritten sheets to make sure she could read the writing. After a few minutes she looked at Mr. Maglioni and said, "I'll have to shift my work plans somewhat. This will take some time to complete... Yes, I don't see why not. I can have this back to you in a week."

"Good. Well all that's left is the financial arrangements. I'll pay you twelve hundred dollars when you deliver the job."

Skye was sure she had misunderstood him as she mentally calculated the folder to contain at least thirty sheets of paper, but most did not represent a full page of typing. "Did you say twelve hundred dollars?"

"That's what I said." He added, "That's if you can have this ready by the end of next week, of course."

"But..." She started to say that this was much more than she charged for a job of this nature, but wasn't able to finish.

"Mrs. Sanders, I'm setting the fee at the value I place on the work, the short notice and time I can spare and the extreme need for confidentiality. Do you understand?"

Skye tried not to think about what she could do with twelve hundred dollars. Tried not to show her excitement as she replied as calmly as she could muster. "Of course. I will have the job ready for delivery by next week."

"Well, Mrs. Sanders, it was a pleasure meeting you."

Skye took his extended hand, replying, "The same here, Mr. Maglioni."

Once in the confines of her car she let out a whoop. She had thought the Jameson project was big, but it shrunk in light of this one. She still didn't know how he learned about her business but it didn't matter.

***

The balance of the week she worked frantically on the jobs she needed to get out, anxious to start on the Maglioni project, but reminding herself each of her clients were important. It wasn't until Monday of the following week she found some time to embark on the project. She opened the folder and pulled out the instructions for the design layout. Pensively she studied the format then leaned back in her chair staring off into space.

Sunlight streamed through the office window, making patterns on her upturned face, yet she took no notice. In the background the radio played the familiar tune of the group, Simply Red, and every now and then a word or two of the song, "If You Don't Know Me By Now," penetrated her thoughts, but her mind quickly strained them out. She was so thoroughly engrossed that when the home phone line rang, she practically jumped out of the chair.

At first, not wanting to be disturbed she tried not to answer it, but by the fourth ring she changed her mind. Quickly Skye got up and banging her knee against the side of the desk she limped hurriedly into the kitchen. Breathlessly she picked up the receiver.

"Hello?"

"Hi, Skye, it's me!"

"Oh hi, sis," she said. It wasn't often that her sister, Mary, called during the day. Mary also ran a business out of her home that took up most of her time. She was a seamstress, specializing in wedding gowns, and had an overabundance of work that she scheduled throughout each year. If she was calling during their business hours, it had to be important. Skye quickly cleared her mind to give her sister her full attention.

"I know you're busy so I won't keep you long. I wanted to remind you that tomorrow is Anna's birthday. I know how you forget the dates."

Anna was the daughter of her younger sister Barb. Barb and her husband had one son, Brandon, until last year when they adopted three beautiful little girls, ages six, seven and eight. She remembered her sister then telling her to mark the birthdays on her calendar, but she had forgotten and now Skye had to admit she hadn't remembered. How Mary managed was beyond her. Mary had dates scheduled for fittings, delivery, and weddings that she had to keep straight and she managed it all competently and still stayed on top of all the personal family events. Skye, on the other hand, had no problem with her business schedules, but not wanting to mark personal matters on her business calendar, she often forgot birthdays and family get-togethers.

"What would I do without you, Mary. It amazes me how you do it. I bet you didn't even have to check the calendar."

"Well... I wish I could agree, but I did. Fortunately I figured you hadn't followed my advice and put the dates on your calendar. I'm right, aren't I?"

"You know me too well. I did do something right though."

"What's that?"

"I bought a supply of cards and have them in my desk."

She heard Mary laughing on the other end of the line and suddenly wanted to talk with her.

"Mary, are you in a hurry," she said hoping she wasn't.

"No, what is it Skye? You sound like something is bothering you."

"No, not really, I just wanted to tell you that I've made a decision that will affect the family, sort of." She wasn't sure how to tell her.

"What is it, Skye?"

"Well, I've decided to leave Hank." She paused then forced herself to say the word. "I'm going to tell him I want a divorce."

There was silence on the line.

"Mary, did you hear me?"

Though Skye wasn't aware, Mary was smiling, happy that her sister had finally come to her senses.

"Yes, I heard you and all I can say is it's about time. I don't know why you've put up with him so long and I can tell you right now that the rest of the family will be happy for you, too."

Skye felt tension she hadn't realized was there begin to ease from her body. Her family was very important to her and knowing that they were behind her made it all that much easier to face.

"Thanks Mary, It means so much to me to know that I have the family support. I wanted to tell you before I talked with Mom."

"Well, we're pretty close you know so you never fooled us. We could tell you guys weren't happy and I might as well confess that it wasn't easy trying to pretend we liked him. He made it very hard because he always acted like we had to go overboard to make him feel welcomed while he did nothing."

They talked for a while longer and then said their goodbyes. Skye hung up the phone and started toward the office, but changed her mind. She picked up the phone and dialed her mother, telling her the same news and getting the same reaction. Her final call was to her sister Barb who was just as supportive and when she had finally finished with the phone she felt relief. Now the decision was out in the open and it seemed to spur her on to take the steps necessary to conclude her marriage. Pleased, Skye went back to work.

***

Two new clients came to her that day which was not unusual.

The first was a well-dressed woman who appeared to be in her late forties. She introduced herself as Paulette Locke, a real estate agent. She wore a well-tailored bright red suit with a paisley print scarf at the neck. Her hair was red, her eyes blue. Paulette had a broad forehead, arched brows and high cheekbones, all accentuated with just the right amount of makeup and a genuine smile that had Skye liking her instantly. As she review the contents of the folder she handed over, Skye studied Paulette. From her experience she had learned that what a client suggested they wanted, and what their actual needs turned out to be could differ, so she listened carefully as she planted an image of the woman in her mind. She had also learned that producing the work was only part of the job, the other was making it match the client's personal expectations. By setting aside an hour or more to visit with any new customers, Skye assured her work would meet with their approval.

"Well, Mrs. Sanders, what do you think? Can you handle the job?"

Paulette Locke had mentioned she needed the work completed by the end of the following week. That would be tough, but not impossible. As Skye looked over her schedule, Paulette watched.

"I know this is an imposition, but I've already settled on having you do the work. If I can be so bold--I have anticipated it will take several hours to look over the information, then another hour to familiarize yourself with the requirements--that leaves probably two or three hours to put it all together." Smilingly she added, "How close did I come?"

"Almost identical to my anticipation." "Yes.. " Skye started to say she'd do the job but was interrupted.

"I'm going to tell you right up front that I will make a commission in the range of ten thousand--give or take a little. I am paying you twenty percent to meet my very demanding deadline. Please, say you will do the work," she said in a teasing, but sincere voice.

"I was going to say yes before you made it so appetizing. This is way over what I would have charged you, Ms. Locke."

Paulette smiled sweetly at Skye. "I like honesty and I like you, but because this is a very important project and I'm getting paid well to do it, I am willing to offer you two thousand dollars. I also know I can count on you to keep the contents confidential and I'm willing to pay for that privacy. So if we have an agreement, I'll just leave this with you now and expect to hear from you by Thursday of next week."

Still in shock, but knowing she could use the money, Skye agreed. While seeing Paulette Locke to the door, Skye couldn't shake the feeling that something was not quite right.

She was still looking over the Locke job when another customer came to her door. Quickly scooting out from behind her desk she went and opened the door to see a pair of beautiful light brown eyes shining and smiling at her.

"Hello, my name is Mitch Cayman. Can I come in?"

Skye hadn't realized she had been staring. It was not only those vivacious eyes that drew her, but the hand he extended with its long, patrician bones caught her attention. He was an extraordinarily handsome man. She estimated him to be over six feet. His hair was dark brown with auburn highlights that looked to be natural. He had a strong jaw and a dimple in his left cheek that make him look much younger than she estimated his age. He had to be somewhere in his late thirties or early forties, was her determination. From his light brown complexion and his features, Skye could tell he was the offspring of a mix marriage. One parent, for sure, was black. Whatever the other parent, the results were indeed striking. Right now this handsome, well dressed man and waiting on her doorstep to enter.

"Sure, I'm sorry, please do come in," she said quite flustered.

Skye stepped aside and watched as Mr. Cayman walked steadily up the stairs into her office. She followed, holding tightly to the handrail. She had a hard time concentrating as he talked about the job he wanted her to do. He laid a neatly tied pocket envelope on her desk as he explained he was a lawyer and had just finished a major project that needed to be documented.

As he talked Skye listened intently. There was an aura about him. He spoke with absolute confidence. His diction was perfect, his clothes were perfect and she felt that he demanded perfection of everyone around him. Again she heard the word "confidentiality" stressed and a substantial sum of money.

"What is going on?" she thought to herself.

"Well, Mrs. Sanders..."

"Yes, just give me a minute," she said shakily. Skye finally pulled her eyes away and managed to open the package. Carefully she looked over the contents and seeing nothing out of the ordinary, lifted her head and said, "I can see no problem..."

Catching the hesitancy in her voice, Mr. Cayman asked, "Is there something bothering you?"

"Oh no, nothing, it's just that you're offering so much and..." She caught herself before she mentioned the name of Paulette, somehow sensing she mustn't disclose that detail.

"Well then, if it's settled, I have to run. I have an important meeting in an hour and I need to be prepared."

Mr. Cayman stood and Skye followed his lead.

"So, I can expect the job by Thursday of next week and we agree on the sum of twenty three hundred?"

Skye took a deep breath, smiled and said, "Yes, it's settled."

She walked to the door with Mr. Cayman, shook his hand then watched, mesmerized as he climbed into his car. Finally she closed the door and managed to navigate the steps up to her office.

She stood in the middle of the room unable to understand what had just happened. Two jobs totaling over four thousand dollars. She still couldn't believe it. It was with great effort she managed to calm herself and get back to work.

***

The following day was no less eventful when she met Mr. George Palma, a private detective. Mr. Palma was of average height, average weight, average looks. There was a challenge in the quizzical expression in his hazel eyes, and an endearing boyishness in the sandy hair that was wind tousled that day. As she listened to him talk she felt a comforting steadiness in the authoritative way he presented the job he wished her to perform and again she felt that feeling of anxiety. He too offered her a large sum of money, thirty three hundred to be exact. The fact that he needed the job the following Thursday didn't phase her at all. Everyone wanted the job done by that day.

This time Skye was more in control as she looked over the papers briefly and agreed to the deadline and the amount. She had played the scene twice now and knew that there was no need to express he surprise or even convince the client of her ability to do the work. Someone must have given a raving review of her capability and her company. Hopefully she 'd soon find out just who had sent these new clients to her door. Even as she wondered, she felt she already knew...

CHAPTER 11

In the morning, Skye's first sane thought was, it's Saturday. She rolled over on her side and stared toward the window where light streamed through the slats in the blinds. It was going to be a brilliant morning, she thought and outside of wanting a cup of coffee, she was content. She quickly scuttled from beneath the covers, swung her legs out and let them dangle over the side of the bed, then quickly sat up. She had worked late last night and accomplished a lot. Thus the high spirits of today.

She was in rare form as she moved about the bedroom gathering articles of clothing while humming a Whitney Houston hit. She brushed her teeth, ran warm water and washed her face before applying a light coat of makeup. By the time she finished dressing she had organized her day. With everything caught up, she had earned a break away from the house. In the bedroom, she put on a pair of jeans and a neat cotton shirt already making a decision to take this day for herself. She would go shopping, something she hadn't done in quite a while. She started a pot of coffee then went off to gather up her purse and coat. She drank two cups before going to the garage and climbing into her car. Soon she was on her way to Marketplace Mall.

Skye walked without purpose, stopping now and then to look closer at items that caught her eye. She ducked in and out of dressing rooms as she tried on articles of clothing, not really searching for anything in particular. She wandered from store to store, inspecting racks of clothing until something caught her eye. She saw a green silk dress crammed tightly among a colorful array in front of her. She pushed against the clothes until she was able to pull the hanger out and immediately fell in love with the dress. It was the color of an emerald. She held it up in front of her as she walked over to one of the full length mirrors. It was stunning. Quickly Skye looked around for the dressing room and disappeared inside. The dress seemed to float down over her body as she raised her arms over her head. When she stepped out into the corridor to walk toward the mirror, she watched as it floated in and away from her body. It looked good. Without checking the price, she removed the dress and placed it back on the hanger, her mind made up. She flinched only slightly as the sales lady told her the cost of her purchase which she paid in cash. When she passed by the fragrance counter she thought, "What the heck," then treated herself to a bottle of Fendi spray.

Shopping seemed to be exactly what she need as she continued to meander through the mall, gazing into shops and stopping when something caught her eye. It was a new experience for her to indulge herself in this way and she found she liked it. Her mind was free and unencumbered. She passed by a public phone and on a whim paused to dial Janet's number. As she stood waiting for someone to pick up the phone she reflected.

People said they looked alike yet Skye couldn't believe herself to be even half as attractive as Janet. She smiled to herself, knowing she liked the comparison. Janet was extremely attractive, had married a responsible loving man, and had a lovely home and family. Her life was filled with love and comfort that she could depend on lasting for years and years, while she... How many times had she wished that she had a husband who loved and cared for her like Daniel cared for Janet. He was always surprising her with little presents or flowers when he returned from one of his business trips, always looking admiringly at her whenever she came into his view. Skye envied her and wanted what Janet had for herself.

You're not to covet your neighbor, she thought, but she did. While she was on the verge of trying to start over, Janet was still growing in her relationship. A sadness came over her, but it was soon interrupted when she heard Janet's voice on the line.

"Hello," Janet whispered into the phone. Skye was all attentive now.

"Hi Janet, it's me, Skye. I'm over at the mall and was wondering if you had time to join me for lunch?"

Janet was surprised, not expecting Skye to call, but it made her happy to hear her friend's voice. Well aware of Skye's habit of working around the clock, she found it more than a bit curious. What ever had gotten Skye out of her office?

"You want to have lunch?" she said, not hiding the surprise in her voice as she raised her head to smile at her husband.

"Don't act so surprised. I know what you're thinking Janet." Skye said happily. "A simple, Yes will do."

"I'd love to, but just a minute, hang on." Her eyes still looking at her husband, Janet placed a hand over the receiver and whispered, "It's Skye. She's at the mall and wants me to join her for lunch."

Her husband who was standing by the sink, smiled at her whispering back, "Well, go ahead darling. I can manage on my own."

Janet looked lovingly at him and nodded her head as she removed her hand from the mouthpiece.

"Skye?"

"Yes, I'm here."

Janet paused, remembering. "Wait a second." Again her hand pressed against the mouthpiece. "Daniel, are you sure? Jamie has to go to practice this afternoon and you're parents are coming over for dinner."

"It's all right baby. Go ahead and have some fun. I'll take Jamie to practice and there's plenty of time to worry about dinner. You go and have a day to yourself."

"Okay, if you insist," she responded, then into the phone said, "It looks like you've got a date, Skye. I'll be there in thirty minutes. Where should I meet you?"

Skye who had heard most of the exchange on the other end of the line, smiled. Daniel Malone was a wonderful man who worked hard everyday, but never lost sight of the fact his wife worked hard too, raising two kids and running the household. She knew his answer would be yes before he even said it. Janet probably knew that too. If only..., she thought, but then didn't finish.

"Meet me at the Eatery," Skye said, already anticipating the fun ahead of her.

"Okay, see ya in about a half hour." The line was disconnected.

Skye hung up the phone and wandered in the direction of the Eatery. She had a little time to kill as she stopped in a shop that had interesting pieces of paraphernalia that would occupy her until Janet arrived. There was a stone carved chess set on one of the shelves. Skye ran her hand over the surface, picked it up and inspected several of the chessman. She found herself thinking of Hank. He loved chess sets and had accumulated a few of them, though he rarely played.

Why not, she thought to herself. It couldn't hurt to purchase it and give it to Hank as a peace offering. As she carried it up to the counter she began to like the idea a lot. This would please Hank. It might even please him enough to make him listen to her. Even if she had to play him a game so she could get his attention, she was willing to give it a try. Skye made the purchase then quickly headed toward the Eatery.

Janet was already seated at a table, looking around at the faces, trying to find her. Skye walked over and plopped down in the chair across from Janet, smiling and feeling pleased with herself.

"I never thought I'd see the day!" Janet said in amazement. "You, taking the time to shop and looking so relaxed, too! What gives?"

"Do you have to act so shocked." Skye said trying to appear hurt by the remark. "I just figured I needed to get out and have some fun for a change."

"Well, you have to admit this is not like you, Skye," Janet said.

"I know. It's just that I've been so boggled down with work lately. This is the first time I could claim a minute for myself and I took it."

"Makes sense to me," Janet said happily. "Does this mean you're not on a time schedule today?"

"That's exactly what it means. I plan on just taking it easy for the rest of the day."

They talked idly as they stood in line to purchase their food. As they carried their trays to a table, they continued their conversation.

Prompted by Janet's inquiry, Skye cautiously told her about her recent windfall.

"I've got a few new clients who seem to be somehow connected."

"You sound troubled by that, Skye. I should think it would make you happy."

"It does. It's just that when I work on the jobs it gives me an eerie feeling that I can't explain. I'm probably being paranoid, but the fact of them paying me so much money and setting their own price makes me feel like something is not right. Do you know what I mean?"

Janet just stared at her for a moment, thinking. She knew that Skye worked on jobs that required confidentiality so didn't ask for further explanation. Heck, Daniel came home at times wanting to talk about his business, but only able to say just so much and she understood. She'd sympathize with him and respond in kind and he'd feel much better. So she did the same with Skye, though honestly she didn't have an inkling what was bugging her.

"Skye, I don't know what to tell you. If it makes you feel apprehensive, maybe you should consider letting the jobs go."

Skye peered into Janet's face. "I just don't know. I'm just confused."

She was used to hearing that too. That kind of response meant there was something else at the root of the problem. Cautiously, Janet countered, "Maybe it's not the jobs that are confusing you, Skye?" Suddenly she remembered that night when Skye had blurted out, who cares about orgasms anyway, and she felt she was right. She had looked so miserable that evening and Janet's heart had gone out to her knowingly. Abruptly she thought, that's what they should be talking about now.

"Maybe you're right. I've been under a lot of pressure lately...." Skye sighed.

Janet sat back. She wanted to change the subject, but feeling the time wasn't right.

"Listen, Skye, you deserve to earn some good money, you need it and you are only doing your job. There is no law against earning good money and if the individuals are doing something illegal, you're not, so I would just forget it."

"You're right, Janet. I know you're right. Why should I let it bother me when I know that I am doing nothing wrong." She paused. "It's just that it made me feel so uneasy, and I can't for the life of me figure out why except that it just doesn't seem to add up." Again she hesitated. "I mean, why would someone pay more than I charge for a job?"

"Yeah, I agree. But then again we're talking about people who you say seem to have money. I don't know about you, but I've always wondered what makes people with money tick!"

Skye laughed and her laughter made it all seem right. She picked up her fork and started eating her crabmeat salad. Suddenly she felt hungrier than she had in days. Janet, following her lead, picked up her fork and quickly devoured her salad, then stuck her fork into Skye's plate, popping pieces of cheese into her mouth until both their plates were empty.

They sat drinking their coffee when Janet sensed the mood was right.

"Skye, I need to ask you something, but if it's none of my business, just say so, okay?"

"Sure, Janet, what is it."

"Well, remember when we all got together over at your house? I had the feeling that something was bothering you and you needed to talk it out. Am I right?"

Skye, not wanting to go into it, but figuring she must, shook her head. "Yes, I was miles away that night but I don't think I was ready to really talk about it then."

"What about now?"

Skye took a long sip of her coffee with her eyes on Janet's face. She did want to talk about it now. Carefully she organized it in her mind before she began.

"I've been thinking about leaving Hank. I wasn't sure I could do it, but I am now. I am going to ask Hank for a divorce." There, it was out.

Janet looked at her sympathetically for a long while. She knew things weren't right between Hank and Skye, knew it for a long time and had wondered if Skye would get around to doing something about it. She worried about her friend a lot lately, especially because she seemed to be trying to bury her sorrow in work and had recently taken to keeping her problems to herself. Now she had an opportunity to help and she took it.

"Skye, I think you are doing the right thing. You are a wonderful person and more so because you have put up with Hank's antics longer than I ever could. You deserve better and I'm glad you finally realize it."

Skye smiled through her tears. She felt relieved to know Janet understood and was on her side. She reached across the table and grabbed her hand. Janet smiled at her and lightly squeezed her hand before their hands parted and they finished the last of their coffee.

"One more thing, Skye. If you need help, any help at all, please let me know. Promise."

"I promise."

"Well, what about doing some shopping," Skye said gaily. It felt like a load had been lifted from her shoulders and she felt wonderful.

"Let's do it."

They pushed back their chairs and after emptying their trays in the garbage, they were on their way. They walked down the pathway, popping in and out of stores, now and again stopping to admire or try on clothes. Janet loved to shop and got as much joy out of it as Skye. When Skye saw Janet fingering a lovely silk scarf, she cajoled her into letting her purchase it for her.

"No, I couldn't," Janet said.

"Come on Janet. I want to buy it for you. Think of it as a thank you gift for letting me unload my problems.

"No, I... Oh well, what the heck. Okay, it's your money."

That purchase made, Skye saw a rack of hair accessories in one of the small boutiques that were scattered throughout the mall and stopped to admire them while Janet went over to look at the makeup. Finally she made a few choices and went to pay for them, asking the sales lady to put the items in two separate bags. When Janet joined her she handed her one of the packages.

"Here, these are for Jamie."

"Skye!" Janet said trying to sound reprimanding. "Stop it right now."

"Okay," she laughed, "but make sure you give them to Jamie and tell her their from her Aunt Skye."

They continued through the mall until tiring, Janet turned around.

"I don't know about you, but my feet have had enough."

"Party pooper."

"I'm sorry, but I can only handle so much fun. Besides, I've got to be getting home. I'm having my in-laws over for dinner tonight and I haven't an inkling of what to fix them. Got any ideas?"

Skye thought for a moment. "Whenever I have that problem I usually end up making a stir fry. Everyone seems to enjoy a good stir fry. Why not fix them a chicken or shrimp one and have rice on the side?"

"That's brilliant! I like that idea. Okay, that's what I'll fix and you have to come to dinner too. What do you say?"

She started to say, no, but then thought about what was waiting for her at home. The day had been so enjoyable she didn't want it to end. There was no reason she couldn't, and she wanted to.

"Okay, you've got one more dinner guest. What time."

"Oh, I don't know... Why don't you just follow me home. We can make the dinner together and talk some more?"

"Why not! But I think I'm all talked out."

"You better not be because I need you to help me come up with a good excuse."

"Excuse for what?"

"Well, my in-laws' big thing lately is wanting to take the kids to Florida with them. It's not that I don't trust them, it's just that the thought of being without the kids for the whole summer bothers me. Besides, Jamie doesn't want to go and she wants me to tell them for her."

"Oh, I see. You think if I'm there they won't insist?"

"They will, but at least I'll have your support."

"What about Daniel?"

"Oh, he is only thinking about us being alone and not how much he'll miss the kids. He says it will be like a second honeymoon and I keep reminding him we already had a second and a third honeymoon."

Skye found herself laughing and then finally said she'd give her support, adding that it was for Jamie she was doing it. Instead of going home, she followed Janet.

Once they arrived, Janet fixed them both a large glass of ice tea with lemon and sitting at the kitchen table they started going through cookbooks looking for a recipe that would be exciting to fix for dinner.

"Janet, this looks promising. How about a spinach lasagna?"

Janet took the cookbook from Skye and looked over the ingredients. "Sounds fine. I have all the ingredients. Let's do it?"

Laughing and talking they started the preparations with Skye taking care of putting the ingredients together, while Janet ran around getting all the supplies.

"We can fix a salad... I know, why not some garlic bread. I can run over to Wegmans and pick it up."

"Sounds great," Skye replied, "but let's make the bread. We have time."

Janet stared at her dumbfounded. "I hope you know how to make it because I don't"

"No problem." She told Janet what she'd need and Janet quickly laid out the ingredients.

They worked steadily and within an hour everything was prepared. The bread dough was set aside to rise and Janet and Skye sat down at the table, happily exhausted. They talked for an hour and then Skye let Janet knead the dough and shape it into a long loaf. She placed it on a cookie sheet, covered it and set it on the stove to rise again. By the time Dan came into the kitchen they were set.

"Look's like you two have been busy."

"Hi honey," Skye has prepared a real treat for tonight.

"Correction," Skye said, "we've prepared this together."

"How's business, Skye?"

Dan sat down at the table with them and picked up his wife's glass of tea.

"It's really going good. Thanks for asking."

"Skye, tell Dan about your new clients."

Skye hesitated at first and then decided to tell him what she had mentioned earlier to Janet.

"It's really nothing, but I told Janet that these new clients seem somehow connected. I'm not sure, but I think they were sent to me by Mr. Maglioni."

"What makes you think that?"

"They are new clients and they came to me right after I had a meeting with Mr. Maglioni. He had called to request a meeting with me and gave me a sizable job to complete. When I looked over the papers I noticed that the same people seem to be mentioned in all the jobs. It's some kind of legal case that I really can't get into, but it looks pretty serious."

"You've done work like that before. Haven't you?"

"Yes. Only... I don't know. It's probably me. I've been very busy and it's catching up with me."

"Tell him about the money, Skye," Janet chided.

"What about the money," Dan asked.

"Well, they are paying me a lot of money. More than I ask for in doing this type of work. Not only that. They are all paying me in cash which I'm not use to. That may be all it is, too." Skye paused, realizing she shouldn't really be discussing the matter. " But, enough about business. I want to forget about business now. Let's talk about something else."

Dan wanted to ask more, but could sense that Skye was done talking about the clients. Yet he wondered about this. She was right to be concerned, yet he didn't dare press her for more details.

Janet's in-laws kept praising Janet for her choice for dinner and after glancing over at Skye who was shaking her head, Janet graciously accepted their compliments. At one point during the meal while Skye was listening to Daniel who was telling a funny story about the neighbor's husband, the phone rang.

"Excuse me Skye. I'll get it Janet."

"Thank's honey."

Daniel picked his napkin off his lap, wiped his mouth and pushed back his chair. "I'll take it in the den." He smiled at Janet and then disappeared down the hall.

When he arrived in the den, Daniel moved behind his office desk and picked up the phone.

"Hello, this is Daniel Malone".

"Hello, Daniel, this is Taylor."

Slowly Daniel pulled out his desk chair and sat down. Whenever Bill Taylor called Daniel knew to expect being tied up for some time. He had known Taylor for a long time and liked him because the man had always done good by him. It was Taylor who had got his business going good and Daniel never forgot it. When Taylor was appointed to the position of District Attorney, he had called Daniel and asked if he could still count on him for PI work. Daniel had been surprised by the request, knowing that Taylor would have all the manpower he needed, and yes, he had been flattered by the request. Taylor continued to request his services for cases that didn't require Daniel to overtax his time and he continued to be at Taylor's service, never regretting his decision.

Daniel reached across the desk and grabbed a pencil and a piece of paper.

"What can I do for you this evening," Daniel said.

When he finished his conversation with Taylor, Daniel sat back pondering the matter. Taylor had a job for him which wasn't in itself unusual, but he had an intuitive feeling that what Bill was working on was somehow connected to the conversation he had earlier with Skye. He wasn't sure why he felt this way. He continued to concentrate on the phone conversation, going over it carefully in his mind. Taylor had briefed him on the case, mentioning the name of Maglioni as the defending attorney. Daniel knew the name and immediately his quick mind connected it to that long ago case.

Now Daniel worked through the details that Taylor had shared. Taylor had said he wanted him to find out what the defending attorney was up to and was quite sure that Maglioni would be working the case outside the firm. Daniel was to find out all he could and report back to Taylor. Daniel frowned, knowing he was on the right track and even if he wasn't, he had to start somewhere. Skye's mention of the new clients may only be a coincidence, but he had a feeling it was much more than that.

A worried expression on his face, Daniel made a decision of where to start, knowing he would have to handle the matter with kid gloves. The last thing he wanted was for Skye to become suspicious of him. After all she was his wife's best friend. After a few more moments he decided he was going to have to get help.

He wrote down some more notes and then carefully took the pad he had been writing on and locked it in his drawer.

By the time Daniel returned to the dining room, his wife was already in the process of winding up the evening.

"Forgive me for taking so long. It was business."

"It's okay, Honey," Janet said, "I already explained that to our guests."

Daniel smiled lovingly at his wife and then turned to his parents and Skye.

"I apologize for breaking up the evening. Thanks for understanding."

He moved toward the front door with his arm around Janet's waist as they saw his parents and Skye to the door. Gently he kissed Janet's cheek before moving away from her side to hug his parents.

"Did you enjoy yourself?" He asked.

"Oh yes, Daniel, we had a lovely time." This came from his mother, who added. " Janet was, as usual, a gracious hostess." Daniel's father shook his head to show he agreed with his wife.

His parents turned to Skye. "It was wonderful seeing you again, Skye. You're such an interesting person and a great friend to our Janet."

"Thank you," Skye said. "I really enjoyed the evening."

A few more hugs and kisses and Daniel readied himself to walk them to their car.

"Skye, thank you for coming. I hope we see more of you." He paused, then added, "If this matter with the new clients really bothers you, maybe I can help."

"Thank you Daniel. It's always good to see you and I appreciate your offer, but I think I'm being paranoid." She smiled pleasantly and then turned to Janet.

"Janet, thanks again for asking me to come. It was a nice relaxing evening. Anytime you need support, just call." The last was said with a wink. They hugged and Skye made her way to her car.

That was how Skye spent her Saturday. It was late when she finally pulled into the garage, not noticing the car that pulled around the corner, turned off it's lights, and sat with the occupant watching her.

***

With four new clients and her regular work load, Skye was too busy to think. She had to spend the morning running errands as she needed postage and had a large mailing to take to the post office. Later that day she spent a couple hours typing the Maglioni project, due that Friday. When she started printing out what she had so far, the printer thimble broke. "Darn"! she said, "Just what I need." She didn't have a minute to waste, but she needed the printer. Quickly she put on her coat and boots and soon was on her way to the computer store to purchase another. Out of habit she glanced at her office calendar. "Darn!" she said again noting she had a luncheon meeting to make. She hurried across the room to her files and pulled out the folder for Marcia Kaplin, tossed it into her briefcase and then ran into the bedroom to change into more appropriate shoes. She stopped in the bathroom and ran a comb through her hair and a half hour later she went flying out the door. She was in too big a hurry to notice the car parked on the corner of their lot.

There was an unanticipated line at the computer store counter that put Skye even further behind schedule. When she finally paid for her purchase she hurried into the parking lot, opened the car door and dropped into the driver's seat. She was mindless of the hem of her coat hanging out the door until practically running up to the front door of the restaurant she glanced down to see the smudges.

"Damn!" she said as she headed toward the rest room. When she emerged she seemed much calmer and followed the waiter to the table where Marcia Kaplin was already seated. She was ten minutes late for the appointment.

"I'm so sorry Marcia," she said as she seated herself across the table.

"Calm down Skye, it's okay." Skye tried to do just that but she was not one to be late, hated to be late, especially for an appointment scheduled ahead of time. But she told herself there was nothing she could do about it now.

They talked while they ate and once the meeting was concluded, Skye forced herself to wait patiently until Marcia got up to leave the table. She then offered her hand, accepted the job that was turned over to her and walked at an even pace beside Marcia Kaplin until they parted in the parking lot with Skye again apologizing for her lateness.

"Will you forget it. I understand and besides we're talking only ten minutes here. It's not a major disaster to be late once in your life."

Skye dropped the matter then and thanked Marcia for understanding. Soon she was at her car and unlocked the door, slid behind the wheel and turned on the ignition.

Once she was in her car she told herself she had best be glad that Marcia was a long standing client and friend, because if it had been a new client she would have just ended the relationship. Being a small business in the home, it seemed that clients were firm about appointments and gave her the same consideration, knowing she ran a one woman office.

Instead of heading home, Skye went to the Kinko copy center where she had left a job earlier last week for duplicating and then was finally on her way home. Once she pulled into the garage, she wasted no time as she threw her coat on a chair and quickly went in to the office to change the print thimble, start up the system and began sending a document to the printer. When the printing was done she looked it over, liking the way it looked and finally allowed herself to take a breather before working a couple more hours, finishing off a few of the smaller items on her desk calendar. By the time exhaustion set in, Skye was happy with her progress.

***

The following day was Thursday and Skye was again laboring on the Maglioni job. She worked steadily and reread it twice before she allowed herself to feel comfortable with the results. The job had to be perfect, but unfortunately the brief encounter with Angelo Maglioni supplied little detail about the man himself and what he expected beyond the sample he had given her. Finally satisfied that it met the criteria and unable to find any mistakes, she organized the papers and placed them back in the folder.

She turned to the new job given to her by Marcia Kaplin and after a thorough review, blocked out the anticipated time for completion on her desk calendar. While she had it in front of her, she looked over the dates. Satisfied that she was on schedule, she finally set the calendar aside, spending the balance of the day and well into the night working on the projects demanding her attention.

She was so engrossed in her work that she didn't notice when Hank came to her office door and peeked in. He stood there for a moment watching her, so immersed in her work. These last few days, these last few months, had been different. Before then it had been a battle, God knew, but wasn't pain a part of life too? Miraculously now, a silent hush had come over them and as he stared at her now he felt something. It was as though Skye was no longer showing her disappointment with life, it was like she had discovered a remarkable peace.

What was she thinking or doing that had her looking so self-assured? She hadn't spoken to him since that day they had that big fight and he knew she wasn't happy with the outcome. What could it be? After a while he moved away, going downstairs to watch television.

CHAPTER 12

At four o'clock on Friday morning, Skye awakened feeling tired and heavy-eyed. She had slept badly, her mind pervaded with doubts that she could not explain. She tried to go back to sleep, but found she was too nervous. She rolled over on her side and moved her legs over the edge of the bed until her feet touched the floor. With effort she stood, grabbed her robe and padded down the hallway and into the kitchen to fix a pot of coffee.

For the first time she found it easier to concentrate on Hank. The last few days had passed quickly with so many surprises she hadn't had time to contemplate her personal life. When had she decided to ask him for a divorce?

Skye poured herself a cup of coffee and went to sit at the table feeling totally out of it. It was the wee hours of the morning, she was tired, yet she could not sleep. There was just so much she could fit into a day, she told herself. And lately her days had been very demanding of her time and attention. Yet, she admitted to herself, she'd have to find time to speak with Hank sooner or later--best if it were sooner.

She sipped her coffee as she tried to sort out how she would go about sitting him down and telling him straight out she was going to apply for a divorce. She tried to imagine his reaction, but couldn't. Tried to determine what to say, but no words came to her. All she knew was that she expected nothing from him. She didn't want any alimony, anything that would tie her to him, and she couldn't help thinking there was nothing she needed anyway. Somehow everything had fallen into place on its own. She didn't understand it and was quite shaken by the events of the past few days, but she had to admit she was grateful. Who would have figured she'd come into so much money in such a short period of time.

She started to get up and make a note on her calendar then decided against it. She could schedule all she wanted to, but the one thing she had no control over was Hank's appearance. He'd have to be home and that she couldn't command by a schedule.

Pensively she sat at the table for what must have been several hours. At six-thirty came the first flicker of sunrise and she no longer felt sleepy. As she bathed and dressed she was relieved as she had made a decision to approach Hank at her first opportunity. By eight she was in her office and working steadily. When nine o'clock came, she sat back to review her work, then went to get dressed for her meeting with Mr. Maglioni.

In the bedroom she looked through her closet. Skye felt like wearing black, but chose a green Chanel copy she had bought on sale at Loehmann's as it looked rich and cost more than she usually spent on clothes. Everything must be perfect--no run in her stockings, rubber tips intact on her high heels, make up applied tastefully but enough to camouflage the results of a sleepless night, and every hair in place.

Skye was expected in Maglioni's office at ten thirty. At ten o'clock she pulled her car into the parking lot. As she entered the lobby she was faced with a crowd of people standing in front of the elevators and had to wait her turn. When the third elevator arrived in the lobby, she finally was able to enter and once inside she looked at her watch. It was ten twenty. When the elevators finally stopped at Mr. Maglioni's floor, she patiently waited to get off and hurried down the hall to his office. Another glance at her watch as she stood before his secretary's desk indicated it was ten twenty-five. This time she was immediately ushered into Mr. Maglioni's office.

Angelo Maglioni was seated behind his massive desk dressed in a European-cut dark blue suit, crisp white shirt and a powder blue patterned tie. Skye was glad she had worn the Chanel copy.

Maglioni looked at her for a long moment, then slowly got to his feet, towering over her as he extended his hand. His handshake was firm and the smile on his face appeared sincere, yet even in all her finery, she felt apprehensive and unsure of herself. She was glad when he finally offered her a chair and quickly got down to business.

"May I see the transcript?"

Skye reached down beside her and placing the briefcase on her lap, undid the clasps and pulled out the folder. She handed it across the desk, placing it in his hand, then closed the briefcase before setting it down beside her chair.

Mr. Maglioni seemed engrossed. Skye sat nervously watching for a hint of his approval or disapproval of her work, but she couldn't see his face.

"I know what a disruption in your business this job must have caused," Angelo remarked. "I have to tell you, this is perfection!"

Skye controlled the urge to smile in triumph. "I always try to do my best to satisfy my customers, Mr. Maglioni."

"Well, you have succeeded and this work is more than I expected. I have another job for you, if you're interested."

Skye didn't hesitate in her response. "Yes, I'd like that."

"I'm very happy you feel that way." A stern expression appeared on his face as he continued. "Each job will require the same confidentiality and I will expect you to hand them over to me personally. I prefer we don't discuss the contents of the jobs, but any questions on the work itself I will answer. Is all of that clear?"

His voice accentuated each statement making her feel as though a giant fist was closing around her heart, as if she was being manipulated. There was nothing condescending in his manner, but she felt like a little girl being taught how to act and what she should say. The feeling was real though, and she had to swallow before she could reply.

"It's all perfectly clear and I will respect your wishes."

His tone became friendly again as he remarked, "Fine, Miss-er-Mrs. Sanders. My secretary has an envelope to turn over to you with your payment and the next assignment. All the instructions have been placed inside, but if you have any questions, just call."

As she shook his hand and allowed him to guide her to the door she was nervous. She had set out to impress him with her work and had succeeded, yet it gave her no happiness. For the first time she admitted she had been shocked by the transcript she had just turned over to him and she wasn't anxious to work through another. Yet, she thought, this was her ticket out, but admittedly she was confused by her feelings. Skye stopped at his secretary's desk and collected the envelope that contained payment for the job, and the folder with the next assignment. With effort she managed to find her manners and smiling said, "Thank you. I'm sorry, I don't know your name."

"It's Lisa, Mrs. Sanders. Lisa Caldwell."

"Well, thank you Lisa. I'm sure we will be seeing each other again. You take care now."

"You too, Mrs. Sanders."

Skye continued to hide her nervousness behind her smile as she walked over to the coat rack. Setting her briefcase down and laying the envelope on the chair she quickly put on her coat, picked up her belongings, and walked out of the office. It wasn't until she was seated inside her car that she finally relaxed and noticed the envelope that was still in her hand. Her hands pressed against the sides of the envelope. There was an uneven thickness, as if pages had been folded down. Inquisitively she opened it, sticking her hand inside and felt a smaller envelope inside. She felt its thickness as she carefully withdrew it. She turned it over and ran a nail along the top edge of the seal so she could peer inside. It was very thick.

"My God," she gasped, pushing her body against the back of the car seat. Inside was a stack of bills that would choke a horse. The man had paid her in cash! Cautiously, Skye glanced around the parking lot and not seeing anything suspicious, removed the bills from the envelope. She counted them, glancing up now and then to make sure no one was watching. There were twelve one hundred dollar bills! She counted it again, unable to believe she was holding this amount of money in her hands.

Out of her area of vision was a car with one lone occupant. The man sat silently in the automobile looking over in Skye's direction. He couldn't tell what she was doing from his vantage point, but he continued to stare in her direction. Besides, whatever she was doing wasn't what he was being paid for anyway. So he waited.

Skye, getting over the initial shock of being paid in cash, now leaned back taking in deep breaths while she put the money back in the envelope. Skye was careful to keep it down on her lap. She reached across the front seat to the floor of the passenger side until her hand grasped the handle of her briefcase. She tugged until it rested on the seat beside her, then quickly flipped the latches and placed the envelope inside. Again she looked around and seeing nothing suspicious, turned to the larger envelope that still laid on her lap.

Inside the papers were arranged neatly. Again, some were handwritten while others were typed. In the back was a stapled pack of instructions. Skye removed them from the folder, taking the time to quiet her pounding heart as she looked them over. The instructions were thorough and only slightly different from the ones she received with the first assignment. She noted that the deadline for completion was set for three weeks from the day. She got her appointment book, flipped to the day prior to the turnover and made a note, then laid it aside. She then placed the papers back in the folder and was about to close it when something fell to the floor. Reaching down, Skye picked up an envelope--just as thick as the one she had just opened.

Her hands were trembling as she tried to insert her nail under the flap and slit the envelope across the top. She didn't look immediately at it's contents, but instead stared straight out the windshield, her heart pounding in her chest. When she allowed her eyes to return to her lap, she spread the top. Again she looked straight ahead.

It was filled with money! Skye frantically looked from side to side, then back down to her lap. She pulled out the bills and started counting. There were twelve crisp one hundred dollar bills inside.

"I don't believe it!" She pushed her body back, hard against the seat. "It must be some kind of mistake!" But she knew it wasn't. Mr. Maglioni was not the type to make mistakes. His secretary seemed efficient enough to not make one either, especially not one of this magnitude. She was being paid in advance!

Quickly Skye flipped open her briefcase again and threw in the second envelope. She reached into her purse and located her briefcase key and with shaking fingers finally managed to get it into the lock. She twisted it until she heard the lock catch.

The man seated in his car now wondered what was taking her so long. He glanced at his watch and noted they had been sitting in the parking lot for almost a half hour. What was she up to? Parked two car lanes across from her, he had to raise up off the seat to get a good look at her car. What he saw was the woman sitting immobile behind the steering wheel. His first thought was that she was waiting for someone. Well, he said silently, if she could wait, so could he. He was being paid by the hour whether he produced or not so it was no matter to him.

***

Skye was lost in thought, unable to make herself start the car. She wondered what was going on, should she go back in and confront Mr. Maglioni or just drive away and not ask questions. She had never been in this position before and wasn't sure of the proper course of action to take. Somehow the whole matter didn't seem quite right.

As she sat there she recalled her initial shock when she began typing the transcript. The transcript dealt with a man named Samuel Stillman. It seemed Samuel was being tried for the murder of his wife. From what she could gather, Samuel had come home unexpectedly to find his wife in bed with the neighbor's son who was said to be eighteen. Samuel, who was a known felon, had several guns on the premises and took a .357 magnum and shot his wife in the head. The boy, who apparently had tried to run from Sam, got it in the back. They both died instantly.

It gave her an eerie feeling all over again. From the wording of the transcript she surmised that Mr. Maglioni was going to defend this man who appeared from her point of view to be guilty. She knew that both sides had to have a lawyer and even the guilty party had a right to be defended, but Mr. Maglioni did not look like the type of lawyer who would or needed to get involved with a man who would do such a thing. Mr. Maglioni also seemed to not be a lawyer who lost many cases. From the looks of his law firm and his reputation in the city, Mr. Maglioni definitely didn't need the money. So why defend a guilty man? It puzzled her but the more she tried to understand Skye was convinced it was legal and she really shouldn't concern herself with it. Still she had to lay the papers aside and remind herself.

Why was he paying her in cash and why in advance? She wanted to know the answer, but after a time she realized she had made up her mind. As she turned the key in the ignition she knew she was not going to say anything to jeopardize the business. Besides, she told herself, she was not doing anything wrong. Carefully she glanced behind her and to the side of her as she backed out of the parking lot. With effort she smiled at the parking attendant while she waited for him to hand her the change. Finally she was on her way home, not seeing the man start up his car and trail behind her.

As Skye drove she reflected on the money and what it meant to her. She thought of Hank. What would he do if he found out about the money? She had to resolve the matter immediately. She had to ask him for the divorce even if it meant staying up all night seated by the door, she'd do it. By the time Skye pulled her car into the driveway and drove into the garage, she seemed to have forgotten what was in her briefcase. Instead she was determined to talk to Hank. How had she allowed so much time to slip by?

But the work that waited for her was enough to keep all matters aside. The first was a resume that was scheduled for pick up later that day. Next she began typing some address labels that were needed by Mrs. Peters.

Skye typed away thinking about the woman. Mrs. Peters ran a successful interior decorating company for the past ten years, and had been one of Skye's first clients. How she managed to be successful was beyond comprehension. The woman was always behind schedule and hadn't met a deadline as far as Skye was aware. Yet her client base kept coming back for more and new clients were always being added to her mailing list. She knew the woman quite well and could say she didn't get repeat business because of her temperament--she was blunt, opinionated and quite overbearing. So she had to believe what she had heard, Ms. Peter's reputation was built on her flair for creating the drabbest room into a show place.

When the last name and address was entered, Skye prepared her billing and placed everything in the folder marked "Peters."

A glance at her calendar verified she was right up to date again, so she took the time to sort through the mail.

One envelope caught her eye. A large manila envelope laid face down. She picked it up and turned it over. The front carried the return address of a computer publishing company that she remembered sending a writing sample. Her fingers trembled as she turned the envelope over and tried to undo the clasp. When she tried to lift the flap she found that it had been glued in place. Her hands now shook as she reached for the letter opener which she attempted to place carefully at the corner and push gently until the tip disappeared under the sealed edge. Cautiously, trying to steady her hand, Skye moved the letter opener across the top. Then she paused.

For a long moment she studied the envelope before she allowed herself to reach in and remove the first sheet of paper. It was a letter and she trained her eyes on the text absorbing the words. Skye gave a startled gasp. Her face was illuminated as she whispered, "Dear God." She continued to read, her hand flying up to her mouth, pressing against her lips. In three short paragraphs the letter told her that they were impressed with the sample of her writing she had sent and were offering her a contract to prepare a book for their company.

She felt tingly and alive and energized just thinking about it. To have such a feeling was rare and she stood basking in the glory before finally reaching into the envelope to remove the balance of the contents.

There was a letter size folder with a glossy cover that had the embossed emblem of the computer company. She waited a few seconds to allow her hand to press across the cover before she laid it open on her desk. Inside were pockets. One side held a stapled pack of papers that covered the contents and format for the book. The other side held the contract.

Carefully, Skye lifted out the contract and began reading each word. Having seen many contracts, she realized it contained standard wording covering all aspects of the agreement they were presenting for her work as a freelance author. When Skye came to the paragraph containing details of the financial arrangement she had to stop. Her eyes stared in utter disbelief. "I don't believe it," she stammered. Her fingertips curled over the edge of the pages, feeling clammy with dampness. She stared down at the paragraph again, mouthing the words, "Three thousand upon receipt of the signed contract and three thousand on receipt of the finished manuscript." And there was still more... "An additional thousand if the manuscript was in their hands within three months from the date of the contract."

"Six thousand dollars for four months of writing and a thousand extra if I can do it within three!"

Skye leaned back. She hadn't really thought about money when she had sent off the manuscript, only wanting a chance to write. This was proof that she had the talent to be a writer, or at least someone thought so. As she stared at the letter she felt happiness like she had never before. She reached across her desk, grabbed a pen, and carefully signed the contract, placed it in the enclosed return envelope, and positioned it carefully in her out basket. She sat for a long time in silence, still trying to convince herself it wasn't a dream. Something truly wonderful was happening to her. For the first time she began to feel her confidence rise and all doubt of her ability was gone. She could and would be successful, and it was what she wanted most out of life. The clock on her desk clicked away and still she sat there leaning back against the chair. It wasn't until she awakened did she realized she had fallen asleep. It was after eleven o'clock in the evening!

Skye felt more rested than she had in days and was much to excited to go to bed. Besides, she wasn't sleepy. Her body, stiff from sleeping in the chair, caused her to move slowly over to the cabinet where she kept the masters of her computer programs. It took a few minutes, but finally she found what she wanted. Through most of the night she sat working her way through the program functions. Every now and then she wrote something down on a pad beside her as she tried out the features supported by the program. She stayed at it until her fingers began pressing the wrong keys and her neck and back ached from being seated in one position for such a long time. Then and only then did she shut down the computer, flip off the lights, and turn in for the night. She never heard Hank come home that evening.

CHAPTER 13

While Skye weeded through her work, Hank was caught up in his own thoughts. Even as mad as he was at Skye, Hank knew he should listen to her, but realizing this only made him madder. Skye seemed to have a knack for knowing all the right moves and when to make them, but he couldn't give her the satisfaction. Lately she had stopped nagging him about going out and looking for side work or finding a job on his own, yet just like she had this time, she managed to put in a dig now and then and he felt he could count on hearing her complain again. He only had his unemployment check and that wasn't even half of what he had earned as an electrician. How in the hell did she expect him to pay their finances with that! He knew that Skye hated to fall behind on the bills and that was the reason she asked him for money or suggested he find a job. But he paid union dues for just that purpose so why not let the union bosses earn their salaries. As for side work, sure it was out there for the taking, but if he started up, he'd have to continue even after he landed a new assignment and he wasn't about to work around the clock.

Yes, Skye was the one with all the suggestions, the one who seemed to get her kicks out of working around the clock. If only she'd give up the business and go back to being a secretary, he thought. Seeming to forget all the problems they had gone through, Hank silently wished he had the old Skye back. But that wouldn't happen in this lifetime and he knew it.

Hank had thought this through since he had shut the door and walked out after their last argument. His wife was an exciting woman, but damn it--she pissed him off and the only way he could get her attention was to start a quarrel. Why couldn't she say, "Hank, I understand jobs are hard to come by and I'll help as much as I can."

Why did she always have to act like she wore the pants in the family. She was still a beauty, but too strong-willed and determined for his taste.

While he continued to think through his marital problems he soon tired of it. Hank, not one to let anything bother him for long climbed into his van and directly was heading down the road.

It was still early in the day but feeling like he deserved it, Hank pulled into the Circle Bar which was quick becoming one of his favorite hangouts because he could relate to the clientele. There were lots of places he liked to frequent, especially the strip joints, but lately he seemed to have lost interest. Lately he liked being noticed and at the Circle Bar he found that without seeming to try to, he drew to himself all the available attention and interest in the same way a magnet collects paper clips. Most of the patrons he now knew by sight if not by name, except for the big man with the odd dreamy eyes who now came over to his table.

"You look like you could handle some company, 'bout now," the stranger said as he seated himself across from Hank. Hank showed no interest either way as he surveyed the man seated across from him. Neither one spoke and that was fine with Hank as he had a lot on his mind. He would have let the silence ring on forever but the stranger finally spoke.

"My name's Samuel," he said. "I've seen you in here before, but never looking so out of it. You're down, aren't you?"

Samuel was obviously looking for someone to waste some time with and since that was all he seemed to have these days, Hank decided to oblige him.

"You might say that, Sam my man, but I always come here when I feel I need some freedom, and that is more often then not lately."

"Problems at home"?

Immediately Hank was on the defensive, not willing to put his personal business out in the street. He gave Sam a long look before taking a sip of his drink and thinking maybe it would do him good to talk. Besides, the man was a stranger and who better to discuss it with than someone who knew nothing about him or his personal matters. So he said, "You guessed it."

The big man looked thoughtful, as if pondering his next question. "You must be married."

"Right again, and have been for some time now. Until I got married I had only myself to contend with and it was always a private wrestle between what I chose to do and what I should do. Nobody else much entered into it until I got married. Everything changed then and I can't say it was for the better."

Hank sat quietly as if thinking about something. He was beginning to feel the results of the beers he had downed in his van and this first stiff drink at the bar. It wasn't that it showed outwardly to anyone, but he knew it was making his tongue loose.

This was not lost on Sam who continued to stare at Hank, trying to figure out what was on his mind. Already Sam was quite sure this was going to be easy. He was good at reading people and right now he sensed this was a man who would be needing his help. He wasn't sure he could pay, but Sam wasn't worried about that just yet. Collecting what was owed him was never a problem when you got the money up front. Besides if this pigeon wasn't buying he never had trouble finding another. A smile that was more a sneer was on his face as he thought about his money. He had collected plenty of it with out much difficulty over the years. No doubt he had an eye and ear to recognize when trouble was brewing and a knack for getting that business to come his way. Finally he remarked, "I know where you're coming from, son."

"Yeah," Hank said, "I think every married man has been there one time or another."

"True enough. I've been there myself, but the difference is that not every man is willing to take the extra step to get himself out of the dilemma like I did."

Hank's brow wrinkled as he tried to make meaning out of Sam's words and unable to do that said, "What do you mean, get a divorce?"

"Well, that's one way to look at it," Sam responded with a shake of his head and a look that showed his annoyance before continuing. "Every man talks about freedom," he said gently, seeming to draw upon that sure source of personal knowledge again. "But they don't really want it." He paused. "No, that's not entirely true. Half of them do, but don't know how to go about freeing themselves. So what they settle for is maintaining an illusion of freedom in front of their wives and friends. It's a compromise, and as long as they can have that they tell themselves they're happy." He stopped talking again, then carefully added, "But divorce can get damn expensive."

Sam now sat pensively staring down at the table before picking up his drink and taking a sip. He then continued.

"You see, there is always a battle. Whoever wins, the other one loses and both want to be winners. You understand what I'm saying?"

Hank was unsure how he should answer. He looked around the bar and catching the eye of the bartender, nodded his head. Soon there were two new drinks on the table. Hank picked his up and quickly downed the contents while Sam studied him closely. After a while he knew Hank was his for the picking and was not surprised by his answer.

"Maybe," Hank said with uncertainty. "What you mean is that even if I were contemplating a divorce I'd still have to fight for freedom because she'd somehow have me by the nuts when all was said and done."

"Now you're catching on. That's why," Sam said with a twisted smile, "I wouldn't stop any man from killing his wife. If he came up and asked to borrow my gun, I'd give it to him, because I could sympathize with his wanting to put an end to his misery. That's if I thought he was serious, I'd want him to have it. If he was busting my chops I'd want to call his bluff." Sam raised his hands and spread them out on either side of him.

As if taking this as a signal, the bartender came over to the table. "See you've met Sam," he said as if introducing his best friend. "Wait until you hear some of the conversations he starts in here," he added with a snicker. "Eh, Sam?"

Hank was really under the influence of his drinks now and missed the warning look Sam gave the bartender. He wanted to hear more but he had a feeling Sam considered this matter private and would not speak while the bartender was in hearing distance. So Hank picked up his empty whiskey glass and handed it to the bartender. "I'll have another."

Hank leaned back in his chair and lit a cigarette, drawing hard. He stared around the bar at the rest of the patrons. Several looked at him in recognition before returning to what they'd been doing. But there was something in their eyes that Hank couldn't decipher right away. He had the feeling that even though they were too far away to overhear what they'd been talking about, they knew. As he finished checking out the place, his eyes came back to Sam and he felt as if this man could say anything, absolutely anything, and no one would disagree. He didn't know why he felt like that and it seemed weird somehow, but he was sure he was right and he had to admit he liked weird. It made him attentive and gave him the same sensation as when he was in battle in Nam. In all honesty, the man was quite ugly and looked like he had faced a battle himself. Hank wanted to snicker but thought better of it. He said to himself, "Just relax, and have a good time on Skye." That made him want to laugh but he held back. Skye would hit the ceiling when she got the bills this month. But what could she do but fume. Besides she was making his life miserable so he might as well repay her in a way that would hurt the most! Anytime he wanted to he could draw against that card and she could do nothing about it. It was in his name. As for worrying if she'd pay the bill, well, that wasn't worth even thinking about. Skye would pay because it was instilled in her to pay anything and everything that had a balance on it. This put Hank in a more jovial mood.

"Well, Sam my man, I know what I want, I'm just biding my time. I can do what I have to when the time comes-- that's a fact."

"Sure you can," Sam said. "Sure you can. But you can do it a whole lot easier, and save yourself a heap of trouble, if you check it out with someone who knows how to go about it."

"Are you saying that I should consult with you, first"?

"I didn't say that, but like I said before, I wouldn't refuse a friend."

Hank tried to appear calm though inside he was keyed up and tired of this roundabout conversation. He wanted some straight answers now that he was interested, but something told him the conversation was ended--even before Sam got up, shook his hand, and walked away like nothing had happened.

He sat alone again, contemplating the conversation until he became bored. Since ten in the morning it had been looking like early afternoon, but the day was creeping by and he was weary. He again looked around the bar and noticed that Sam was nowhere in sight. He let out a sigh, got up, and being careful to control his steps, he put on his coat as he walked toward the front door. He stepped out to the parking lot for a breath of fresh air, inhaling deeply until he was once more in control.

He drove away concluding that a man could just take so much in one day and he had his fill. From the Circle Bar he went to pick up a paper to read while he downed a couple hamburgs at McDonalds, only as he stared at the headlines, his mind was elsewhere.

Sometimes it all seemed like a fantasy. He had actually thought that marrying Skye would be the start of something wonderful. Before they'd met he had been barely able to support himself. Skye came along and helped him get through school so that he could pursue his dream of becoming an electrician. Now he made more money than he ever dreamed possible and he should be happy. He should have captured the respect of his wife too. It had all seemed so safe. Husband, wage-earner, father--right on down the line, all the duties and offices laid out for him. Only the marriage turned sour.

Why did Skye have to ruin it by sniffing out ways to earn substantially more than he could? Even though she had never said it, he knew it was true. She made sizable deposits in their joint checking account and paid most of the bills without his help. It was dangerous for a woman to earn more than her man. Very dangerous and condescending too. Why couldn't she be content with being a secretary and work regular hours like regular people? Why did he ever give her the go ahead to start up her own business in the first place?

He thought about the problems in his marriage. It had been great before she became so independent, before she had started up the computer business, before their son Scott had moved out of the house, just before....

Why did it have to change? The last four years had really gotten out of hand. He could still be working a regular job if he felt like he was needed. Hell, he had held on to his last job for ten years and it hadn't been that bad. Only now, why should he even try? Where he came from the man was the breadwinner and the woman was dependent on his resourcefulness, not her own.

Tiring of this train of thought and no longer feeling like driving around or stopping at any place in particular, Hank headed home.

CHAPTER 14

Hank sat in the family room wondering what to do. Should he pursue her, pursue the issue or should he just let it all go? It was an enigma, a crazy, unreal enigma and he had no answers. After a few hours he was again bored with his surroundings and got up from the couch to pace around before decisively climbing back into his van. Before he knew it he was back at the Circle Bar.

It had happened so gradually that it did not seem to be happening at all. One moment he was seated at the bar berating the complicated state of matrimony along with the other patrons. It was really comical when he thought back on it now. It was like an unspoken rule of thumb. No matter how much it hurt, make it seem as though it meant nothing. Every one played the game and followed the rules. Or did they? Maybe to them it didn't matter. Maybe he was the only one crazy enough to want to hang on to what he had. But they didn't have Skye. They didn't have a woman who could turn their life around and mold them into someone important. Because of her he had been a man of purpose, with a job, a home, and a family. And he was no fool. No, he knew that without her he would be nothing because without her he had no purpose in life or a reason to do more than eke out a living. But in order to play the game right, Hank knew better than to say too much or to show how much his marital situation bothered him. No one wanted to know exactly how he really felt.

There was noisy laughter in the barroom followed by the nodding of heads as if everyone understood exactly, that is everyone except the bartender. But then that was understandable. Bartenders went to school to learn how to be good listeners and sympathize with their patrons. It was their job to share the burdens on his customers' shoulders and not add to them. So while everyone else laughed, cajoled and told similar tales, Oscar stood at his post with a sympathetic expression plastered on his face.

The banter continued, but soon Hank grew weary of it. He looked around and suddenly Samuel appeared at his elbow.

At first Hank gave him a nod and turned back around. Was it his imagination, or did he catch a worried expression on Oscar's face. He looked closer. Finally he decided it must have been the booze because now Oscar returned his gaze, raising his eyebrows as if asking him what he wanted. Hank ordered another drink.

"Here, I'll pay for that."

Sam reached across the bar and handed Oscar a bill. "Bring me another, too."

Hank didn't know how to react as he turned to find himself staring into the ugly face of Samuel. He started to say something but lost his words as he stared into eyes that seemed to know everything. They were eyes that seemed to see right through him though they were barely open. He wasn't aware of any motion on his part until he found himself seated at a table. Samuel sat directly across from him now.

Hank shook his head in a vain attempt to clear the cobwebs that had accumulated from so much booze. He had downed quite a few Wild Turkey Manhattans and probably should go home before he made a fool of himself. But there was something in Samuel's stare that held him, the same something had him spilling his guts and Samuel never said a word. Hank heard himself letting all his anguish out and he could not stop himself. It was so unlike him to lay his misery at the feet of a friend, let alone a stranger. And Sam who he had chanced to meet only one time before, was still a stranger.

But it was himself he heard, voicing the pain he felt inside. After a while he had to admit he felt better and it got easier. He actually felt elated, as if the responsibility was no longer his but Samuel's to contend with. It was a strange sensation to say the least, but there was no other way to characterize it. It seemed that once he liberated himself, the rest was in this stranger's hands.

Though Samuel remained quiet, his expression seemed to say he felt Hank's pain. And this was what Hank needed and craved most. Someone who understood and would not judge or belittle his pain, because it was real. The pain hurt deep in the pit of his stomach and pressed like clamps around the back of his head. Hank had swallowed three more Wild Turkey Manhattans in succession as he continued to bare his emotions. Finally exhausted he leaned back in his chair and stared into Samuel's face, an ugly face that only a mother could love, he thought to himself as he watched Samuel's expression. For an instant he thought the ugliness had disappeared as Sam attempted a look of sympathy. Hank opened his mouth to say more, but found he was depleted. He had said it all and must have said it well because Samuel's words were right on.

"Yeah, my friend, I understand what you're going through. You want everything to stay intact and the little woman wants out. It's the worst situation to be in my man, the worst. Right now you're thinking how selfish she is for not even trying to understand you when you've been putting up with her nagging, never pleased attitude for so long. You want to scream in her face to stop being so selfish and admit that she's had it good. But let me tell you my friend, it gets old fast. I can tell you I had it up to here," Samuel said, placing his hand up over his head, "before I finally put an end to it." He paused as though seeing the day of his freedom, then added scornfully, "Yeah, I sure showed her all right." He paused again. "I worked my fingers to the bone at two jobs to support her dumb ass until I finally saw the light."

Oscar found excuses to step out from behind the bar so that he could catch a word or two of the conversation at the far table. He wiped off tables, emptied ash trays, and the bits and pieces of conversation he heard sent shivers up his spine. Evil was brewing. With determination Oscar walked over to the table, planning to stop the matter before it went too far. He stared first at Hank, immediately sensing he was three sheets to the wind and prime bait for Sam's manipulation. Then he made a mistake by allowing his gaze to meet Sam's eyes. He could feel in the intensity of Sam's eyes a threat that kept him at bay. Instead of giving Hank a warning he found himself saying, "You guys ready for another drink?"

Samuel relaxed his expression knowing the message had been received. He didn't appreciate anyone interfering in his business and now that it was apparent Oscar knew better, he raised an eyebrow at Hank. Hank responded with a shake of his head.

"Yeah, set us up again," Sam said.

Oscar turned as if to leave, then turned back around, noisily clearing his throat before he spoke.

"Hey Hank, remember what you were telling me at the bar?" He wasn't sure Hank could remember anything that had happened more than five minutes ago, but he had to take a chance.

"What? Oh, sure, about me sending the little woman packing. Yeah I remember."

"Well, I just wanted to tell you I know how you feel, but the best way is not to fight it. It all comes to this sooner or later. Even I'm paying alimony and child support up my ass. You get used to it and before you know it, you'll be off the hook."

Hank misjudged Oscar's purpose as a friendly attempt to ease his pain. He nodded his head in his direction as if agreeing with him, but he did not. His situation was entirely different. He didn't fear paying alimony or child support. No, his fate differed in that he didn't want to let her go, and if it came to that he'd never let anyone else have her.

"Well, when do we get our drinks?" Samuel interrupted.

"Sorry, Sam, just wanted to tell Hank that. I'm getting them now."

"Good. Very good." Sam said harshly, then added even more harshly, "Oscar?"

Oscar turned shakily around recognizing the tone of voice as dangerous to his health. "What, Sam?"

"Let me give you a piece of advice for the future. If you want to be a good bartender, it's best to keep your problems to yourself. Understand?"

Oscar slowly nodded, his muscles tightening as he saw the piercing look again.

"Well, are you going to get us our drinks or do I have to get them myself?"

Slowly managing a slight grin he tried to get back on the good side of Sam. "Nah, Samuel, two drinks on the house, coming up."

They were seated at a table near the back, sitting slightly in the shadows. Hank had wanted the seat facing the door, but Samuel took it before he could move around the table, so he ended up facing the back of the room with nothing to draw his attention away from Sam. Once Oscar left, his eyes were drawn back to the man.

"Well, my friend, I can see things aren't getting any better for you on the home front. Thought about our last conversation?"

For a minute, Hank wasn't sure what Samuel was talking about, but then he remembered. It must have been on his mind all along. Hank stared at Sam and felt a twinge of envy, like the strippers might feel when they encouraged the men watching to place their hard earned money in their skimpy outfits. Sam was the man with all the answers and he was the pawn awaiting instructions from the master. But he also felt scared.

As Hank fought to make sense of his crazy feelings, Samuel was deep in thought, his eyes half closed as if thinking back and realizing he was picking it up again fast. It was like a different universe, and when you were out of it for a while you forgot it was there and almost had to learn it all over again. It was so easy to put it aside and forget it, then when it first came back it shocked you a moment. Now he realized he had missed being part of that universe as it was as much a part of him as breathing. He needed to be in the action again and the opportunity was right before him. He had performed many shady deals, but it had been some time since the last opportunity presented himself to settle a marital dispute in his manner. Samuel opened his eyes to look directly at Hank. He was positive the man was his for the taking.

"Well my man, what will it be. You can ask for my help or do it on your own and face the consequences."

It was Hank's turn. Hank was the one on the stand as Sam waited for his answer. He could just say, forget it. Pretend he had blown it all out of proportion, but what would he gain? Would it all be honkey dory, or would he end up watching Skye walk out of his life and into the arms of another? He couldn't handle that and if it took drastic measures to keep it from happening, he'd do it. Hank looked around the room, but no one seemed interested in them. A final sweep of his eyes and they came to Sam's face. "Okay, tell me what to do."

CHAPTER 15

On Monday morning Skye flipped on the light switch in her office, turned on the computer and then headed for the coffee maker.

At ten the first call came into the office. She scheduled the appointment then jotted down the details she needed to refresh her memory. At eleven a few walk in jobs were delivered by clients who needed resumes polished that she had prepared earlier. She took the time to complete these quick assignments and sent them on their way. It wasn't until after one she was finally able to start on the first of the big projects due that week. This was to be the pattern of her week.

***

Tuesday, Wednesday, Thursday raced by with Skye busy from early morning until late at night. All thoughts of Hank were forgotten. There was just so much she had to contend with that had already reached the critical mark. She kept reprimanding herself for taking time off earlier, then, remembering how enjoyable it had been, was not sorry she had.

There seemed to be no end to her workload and each morning as she showered and readied herself she began to feel like she had finally gotten in over her head, but she couldn't bring herself to refuse that next client or turn down the next job. She was like a person on a mission, trying to surpass what she knew as her level.

Her memory and organization were her salvation. Mentally she anticipated interruptions when scheduling her clients and, along with being able to judge the time for completion quite accurately, she was still managing to meet her deadlines, but there was not a moment to spare.

On Thursday morning she had put the finishing touches on the last of the three projects delivered by the clients she now believed were sent by Mr. Maglioni. Satisfied with her accomplishments Skye sat back sipping a cup of coffee. She barely remembered what had been typed as she had found these jobs to be in perfect order, not requiring her concentration as she entered them into the system. Now all that was left was the editing. A glance at the clock told her that she had plenty of time before her next appointment which was scheduled for three in the afternoon.

Skye picked up the first report and began reading through it, not really showing interest until she came across the name, Samuel Stillman. This was the job dropped off by the well dressed real estate agent, Paulette Locke. She sat up now, with renewed interest as she read through it, a funny sensation coursed through her body and remained with her until she forcibly read it to the end. Strange. She couldn't help wondering how it all fit together. But there was still more she needed to review. With apprehension she set the job aside and picked up the next one.

It was the job for Mitch Cayman, the young, good looking attorney. Again she got the same sensation when she came to the name of Samuel Stillman. With effort she forced herself to read through it, reread it again until she was confident there were no errors. Oddly she was anxious to get to the last one that had come from the private detective, George Palma. He had showed up with his job shortly after she talked with Mitch Cayman. Not much different from the other two, George had offered her a substantial amount of money and the same turnaround time as the other two. Now as she looked over the papers, halfway through she found herself saying, "Samuel Stillman, again!"

Skye forced herself to pay attention to the wording, the contents giving her the same uncanny feeling. Finally when she was done she allowed herself to dwell on what was going through her head. "This is no coincidence. Somehow all of this is connected, and I don't understand."

Skye was puzzled as she again turned to the first job, telling herself she needed to review the layout and the words for accuracy, but really wanting to try and find the key. She went over the other two, but still couldn't quite make the connection, or maybe she was afraid to. Decidedly she stopped trying to figure it out. Her only concern should be that the work she had done was performed correctly and accurately and she knew this to be true. Carefully she placed the papers neatly in their respective folders and set them aside.

Skye drank several cups of coffee during the process of trying to forget the contents of each folder, but never got the relaxing feeling that she usually managed from that amber liquid. Her mind kept turning back to what she had read but the real connection still evaded her. It just didn't make any sense, but something did. Now she was sure how these clients had came to her door. These new clients had been sent to her by Maglioni. That was the only thing that she was positive about.

Her eyes were drawn over to the corner of the room where her unopened briefcase rested. Slowly she got up from the chair and walked over to the briefcase. Hesitantly she picked it up and carried it over to her desk where she again sat, staring at it without making an attempt to open it.

"So many new faces, so many new jobs," she said in a whisper. Had they all been sent by Maglioni? No, she doubted that. Only the three that seemed connected had been sent by him. The other new clients were 'normal'. She let out a shaky laugh over her choice of words.

She tried to calm herself and relieve some of the spooky sensations that came over her as she dwelled on the matter. Hadn't she hoped that by doing the job for him she would get new clients? "Yes," she said, "so quit being so stupid."

Skye sat up straighter in her chair and reached down to retrieve her purse. She pulled out the key to her briefcase and placed it in the lock. Inside were the envelopes and the next assignment that Mr. Maglioni had given her. The one that was due next week. Ignoring the envelopes for the time being, she picked up the folder and opened it. She began to read, her expression showing her surprise. It wasn't what she expected at all. The papers contained facts about a man named William T. Taylor and not Samuel Stillman. She was just about to close the folder when she noticed the name, Evangeline Stillman.

"Stillman", she said dumbly. "Evangeline Stillman". She read a little further and knew this was the name of the wife of Samuel Stillman. Another name mentioned in the report was a Peter Stiles. Skye began to read the report with renewed interest. There was a lot of information concerning the Taylor guy that she ignored, as she was interested in finding out about the woman and the man, Peter, who turned out to be her boyfriend. When she finished reading she sat back, suddenly feeling somewhat relieved. From what she learned from this report, she was now convinced that the man, Samuel Stillman, was innocent. Feeling uplifted, Skye read on. Mr. Maglioni's client was innocent of murder and a Mr. August Pelegrino was the one suspected of murdering Samuel Stillman's wife and Peter Stiles. The report told how this man, August, had an affair with Evangeline. Evangeline ended the affair and started messing around with the younger man, Peter. August, the report stated, had hounded her for months, watching her every move until the day he caught them together. In a jealous rage, he had broken into the house, took one of Samuel's guns, which he kept in a unlocked cabinet, and shot them both.

It was very convincing and as she leaned back in her chair, Skye was convinced that this was what actually had happened. She could feel the relief flow through her body. Somehow knowing the guy Stillman was innocent made her feel much better.

By the time her three o'clock appointment arrived, Skye's mind was trashed from all her concentration. She had to rub her eyes, strained as they were by all the reading, and then forcibly lift her exhausted body out of the chair to greet the client. When she opened the door to let Paulette in, she no longer felt fatigued.

Paulette Locke entered wearing a Christian Dior black suit with a simple white shell under it. She looked like a picture out of Vogue with her red hair done in a mass of curls that framed her perfect features. Everything about her demeanor was perfection. She even wore accessories that enhanced the color of her hair and skin! And her makeup was applied perfectly. Skye found herself complimenting her while apologizing for her own haphazard image.

"You look fantastic in that suit, Mrs. Locke."

"Why, thank you," Paulette said with a perfect smile that displayed a mouth full of gleaming white teeth. As she looked over the report Skye had completed, Skye tried to smooth her dress and let a hand come up and pat her hair. When Paulette finished, she raised her head to look directly at Skye. Skye managed a sheepish grin, feeling like the poor relative and sensing she looked every inch the part.

"You do great work. From the looks of this job, we're going to be seeing a lot of each other so I'd like you to call me Paulette. This is wonderful and I approve of the changes in wording you made."

"Thanks," Skye said self-consciously, still comparing herself to the woman. She hadn't taken much time to dress this morning. She wore not only a simple green knit dress, but an old one. She hadn't taken the time to put on any jewelry, and had dabbed her face with a little makeup. After the day she had put in she was sure her hair was in disarray. Yet it was too late to think about that now. She couldn't help wishing thought that she had at least taken the time to put on some lipstick.

Paulette, having finished reading the transcript, opened her briefcase to place it inside. She removed an envelope and handed to Skye.

"For services rendered," she said with an enchanting smile. "Here's the money we agreed on and may I add, you earned every penny of it."

"Thank you very much."

"Well, I have to dash, but I'll be in touch, Paulette said. Then Skye was showing Paulette to the door, wishing she could have talked with her a while longer. They had barely reaching the top of the steps when the door bell rang again. It was George Palma. He nodded at Paulette as she pushed past him and then turned his attention to Skye who smiled and lead them into the office.

Skye moved behind her desk and produced his job.

"Can I get you some coffee," she asked.

"No, I'm find." He took the folder and sat down on the chair in front of Skye's desk. Skye following his lead, lowered herself into her office chair and waited.

George nonchalantly reviewed the contents of his report, gave her an approving nod of his head before handing her an envelope, much like the one given to her by Paulette. A quick thanks and he was scooting out the door.

Seated again behind her desk, Skye leaned back and stared at the envelopes. She was about to open the one from Paulette when she was interrupted by the phone.

"Hello, Skye Sanders speaking."

It was a call from a new client who wanted to know when it would be convenient to stop by and discuss a job she needed completed. Skye took down the necessary information and agreed on a time next week. She blocked an hour on her calendar then quickly turning back to the envelopes in her desk, picked them up and stock them in her top drawer. There was still a lot she needed to do. She'd take care of the envelopes later.

Two hours later Mitch Cayman arrived and Skye found herself thinking he was beautiful. From head to toe he was the picture of flawlessness. When he reached the top of the steps he unbuttoned his coat and let it glide down his arms, easily catching it and tossing it over the rail that ran along the side of the step well.

"Let me hang that up for you," Skye said, practically stuttering.

"Oh no, it's all right where it is, but thanks, dear."

Calling her "dear" just made it harder for her to compose herself and attempt a more professional attitude. She wondered if he had the same effect on all the women he came in contact with and decided he must. He was the type of man who could make a lasting impression even if he was in ragged jeans, wearing a Bill's sweatshirt, with his hair uncombed. She managed to stumble behind her desk and sit quietly while he read over the transcript. She could tell he was as thorough as he was handsome. He concentrated, his head down and his lips slightly moving as he read word for word. It gave her a chance to look at him without his knowledge until finally she had to look away and busy herself with objects on her desk. He made her heart thump until she thought there was no way he couldn't see it beating against her chest. When he lifted his head, she was ready.

"This is great! I am very pleased with the results. You did a magnificent job, Skye."

It flustered her more to hear him praise her and Skye had to swallow before she spoke.

"I had to do very little to the job, really. It is almost verbatim of what you gave me. I didn't see any need to make any major changes, just a word or two here and there."

"Well, he said," looking directly into her eyes, "not only are you a very capable and beautiful woman, but modest. I like that!"

Now she was fidgeting in her chair and trying very hard to focus. It seemed like forever before she managed to thank him for his compliment. When he handed her the envelope their fingers touched and she felt her heart flip over. She could hardly walk him to the door. Then he was gone.

She sat on the steps for a moment remembering every detail of him before finally going into the kitchen to fix herself a soothing cup of coffee. She would be so embarrassed if he had mentioned her obvious fascination with him and was thankful he had the common curtsey to overlook it. She hadn't been discreet enough to feel it had gone unnoticed. She sipped her coffee as she sat behind her desk until she was again in control and her feet were in contact with the earth.

Now she had five envelopes and without checking the three new ones, she could tell by their thickness they were filled with cash. She started calculating. Two thousand from Locke, twenty three hundred from Cayman, thirty three hundred from Palma and the two envelopes with twelve hundred each from Maglioni.

"My God. I'm sitting here with ten thousand dollars in cash." The words rushed out of Skye's mouth. Quickly she looked around as if someone might hear her. To convince herself she was indeed alone, Skye got up and walked out of the office and into the family room. She opened the door to the garage. Hank's van was gone. Yet she still wasn't convinced as she walked through the whole house checking each of the rooms. That done she was finally satisfied she was indeed alone and returned to the office.

Skye wanted to take a breather before getting involved in another project, but toyed with the idea of making a trip to the bank. She was talking about ten thousand dollars in cash! The banks were closed now, she realized and she couldn't fit that stack of bills through the automatic teller machine! But she didn't want to have that much cash laying around the office. She thought about it and then forced herself to relax. For now all she could do was lock it in her briefcase until tomorrow morning when the bank opened. She reached into her desk drawer and gathered up the envelopes there to add to the one she had just received. The feel of the envelopes and knowing what they contained caused a shiver to go up her spine as she moved quickly over to her briefcase. With shaky fingers she opened it and placed the envelopes inside before going back to retrieve the key and locking it. With that done, she let out a small sigh of assuagement.

As she tried to fixate on her next job, her mind kept returning to the cash. She had never made such a large deposit before and especially not in cash. If the idea of having this much cash made her wonder, what would the cashier at the bank think? She needed some advice, she reflected, and immediately Adam entered her mind.

Skye picked up her office phone and dialed Adam Snyder's office, praying he would be in. She sighed with relief when he picked it up on the second ring.

"Hello, Adam Snyder speaking."

"Hi, Adam, this is Skye."

"Well, I was just thinking about you. It's been sometime since we've had a good chat."

"I know it has, but I have a problem and need some professional advice," she said hesitantly.

"Well, what is it I can help you with, Skye?" Adam could sense the urgency in her voice.

"No, before I tell you, listen to me. I expect to pay you for some legal advice. Is that clear?"

"I'll not hear of it. We're friends and friends help each other. So if there is something I can do, don't insult me by asking for a charge. You hear me?"

"Okay, dear friend, okay. I get the message."

"Okay. Now that we understand each other, what is it you want?"

"Well, I've been paid a substantial amount of money in cash and I don't know how or what I should do."

"You call that a problem! I call that luck. I wish my clients would pay me in cash. I can't tell you how many bounced checks and unpaid bills I've got laying around here."

"I'm serious, Adam. I'm talking about ten thousand dollars in cash."

There was an uncomfortable silence on the other end of the line before finally Adam spoke.

"Did I hear you right? Someone gave you ten thousand dollars in cash?"

"Well, yes," quickly she added, "but it was four people, not one person."

Adam leaned back in his chair. A worried expression covered his face.

"Skye, what are you doing over there? You're either under charging me or something is going on. Now you've got me worried."

Skye didn't speak right away, instead she tried to decide just what she should or could say as she wasn't about to lie to Adam. Careful not to disclose names or the contents of the work, she replied.

"I recently got a large job from a big law firm in town. Actually I got two jobs from them. When I delivered the first, the second was handed over, paid in advance, along with the first job. It was legal work, quite extensive and the client set the pay. Not me." She paused before going on.

"As a result of that work, three other individuals were sent with similar jobs, again quite large. I don't know why, but each of these people paid me in cash. Again setting the price on the job. All I know is that they considered the work very confidential, an imposition on my time and wanted to pay me handsomely for my services."

Adam was not convinced, but he knew Skye would not knowingly get involved in any shady dealings. If something was going on she was innocent. "Skye, can you tell me the clients' names."

"You're a lawyer, Adam, you answer that."

Adam thought about it carefully because Skye was his friend and he did not want to put her in a compromising position. He was afraid to answer hastily. He might advise her one way because he wanted to protect her and he had to pull himself back and think about the legal action.

"Skye, giving me the names is not a breach of trust, but the contents of the transcripts would be."

"Are you sure, Adam?"

"Yes, I'm sure."

Skye gave him the names then waited for his reply.

"Well, I only know one of those names; the Maglioni fellow. I think he's trustworthy or tries to be and I guess if the other three were sent by him, it's okay. It just blows my mind to fathom them paying that much, but I do know Angelo has money and for him to pay thousands in cash wouldn't surprise me. He doesn't worry about write offs for taxes like I do," he added with a slight hint of sarcasm. "He has the money to make his own."

"Well, what should I do."

Adam went on to explain to Skye as much as she hated to keep the money around, he would advise her to make three smaller deposits over the next two months so that no more than five thousand went into the bank this month and the balance she could deposit at the end of the next month. As he didn't want to add to her stress, Adam didn't bother to go into detail on the bank policies of large deposits, especially in cash.

"You mean I have to keep this around here that long?"

"You asked for my advice, Skye and that's what I would suggest."

"But why?"

"It might cause suspicion since you're a small business and you made a large deposit of that amount at one time. It would be less noticeable if it was spread out over several months income, is all."

Skye deliberated the matter and decided she'd have to take his advice.

"Okay, thanks, Adam, but one more question. Where should I keep it in the meantime?"

"Do you have a safe deposit box?"

Skye had completely forgotten that she did.

"Yes, I do. Should I put the balance in there until I can deposit it?"

"You've got it, Skye."

"Thank's Adam, that's a load off my mind. I owe you for this." She grinned. "I mean I owe you a dinner."

Adam hadn't heard her slip as he was too busy looking at the names he had written on the pad. He was going to do some checking on these people before Skye got in too deep. Something was going on and he was going to get to the bottom of it.

"Adam, did you hear me?"

"What? Oh yes, I accept your offer for dinner. Just give me a call when you have the time to wine and dine me."

Skye hung up feeling much better. She trusted Adam and knew he had given her good advice. It was nice, she thought, to have people in high places to help her out when she needed it. It was nice, she continued, to just have someone to talk to. Finally she let out a sigh then polished off a couple more small jobs before working on the bigger ones that had come across her desk. When she tired of this she pulled out her manuscript and worked some more. Exhausted, Skye finally called it a day.

CHAPTER 16

It was Friday and Angelo Maglioni sat in pensive diligence awaiting the arrival of the team. Everything seemed to be falling into place rather nicely and if the final reports were on target he'd have nothing to worry about. The case was in the bag. He wanted to win this case, so much so that he had devoted most of his time and energy to doing just that. If it all came together, Samuel Stillman would appear to the jury as a man unjustly accused.

Angelo paused in reflection. A frown masked his handsome features as he pondered the issue. The easy part was proving that Samuel was a law-abiding citizen who had suffered the loss of his wife while having to deal with the allegations of those who would like to see him behind bars. The hard part, the element that stumped him now was transforming the man to fit the image. He knew from meeting Samuel that his appearance and manners would have to be altered drastically if the case were to be made foolproof. He looked every inch the conniving crook.

How to take the hard, ugly face of Samuel and turn it into the face of a man who had been wronged by society. That was the pressing issue. How to smooth his rough edges so that the jury would recognize him as the man presented in the case. That would be a step above a miracle. Yet it had to be accomplished. No matter what it took it would be established.

He smiled as he again rehashed the details that had already been called in to him. If all had been handled as thoroughly as he now presumed, there was no need to worry. He had his best people on the job and if it came to plastic surgery to finalize the deal, well it was not beyond him.

Angelo's bliss waned as he tapped the end of his gold pen against the top of his desk remembering the events leading up to his sanction of the litigation. It had not been by choice that he was now acting as Samuel's lawyer. Back when Samuel had first walked into his office and sat ominously swearing he would submit to anything Maglioni deemed necessary, if it would allow him to walk away a free man, Angelo had taken one look at the man and knew he was guilty. Samuel was guilty of the crime, but Angelo expressed no malice. He would defend him, but he would do it with caution. He was a successful and respected lawyer because he was not only an excellent lawyer, but an honest one. This was not the type of case he usually took on, but because of the opportunity it afforded, his hand was forced. Learning that the prosecuting attorney was William T. Taylor made the difference. With a defiant expression he swore he would get even.

In a few minutes he would receive the final reports that would either clinch the case or put success out of his reach. He had every reason to feel confident that he would win and finally settle the score between himself and Taylor. His face glowed with anticipation.

The intercom buzzed, jolting Maglioni out of his reverie. He didn't respond right away, instead he paused for a moment to calm himself. Just thinking about Taylor had an adverse affect on his personality. Finally he pressed the intercom button.

"Yes."

"The people for your one o'clock meeting are here, Mr. Maglioni."

"Show them in."

Angelo prepared himself by placing his hands on the desk with his left hand clasping his right thumb and his body sitting erect in his chair. The people who would soon join him were friends who owed him favors. Not the typical run of the mill type friends, but friends nonetheless. He had contacted each one individually so they had no ideal they would be joined by the others. He smiled to himself wondering what they would be thinking when they realized they were all together.

Each one of them was superb in their field. He knew that because he had called upon their services in the past. Now, for the first time they would be working together. Again he smiled as he thought how each had taken on the challenge without question. How each had agreed to abide by his wishes, not asking or expecting anything in return. He knew them well. He also knew they would perform their respective jobs as though their lives depended on it. He could think of no one better equipped to meet the tasks he laid before them.

Now, as he waited, he allowed his eyes to travel around the room as if savoring the moment. He was sure he had done the right thing by not inviting Frank Jaffe to join them. Jaffe's job, as he knew it was to watch the house of Mrs. Sanders. He was to record information on anyone who came or went from the residence as well as keep track of Mrs. Sanders whereabouts at all times. That would mean he would be watching this entourage as well as they came and went from the residence. Maglioni had his reasons for not filling Jaffe in on all the particulars. He did not fully trusted the man. He also had his reasons for not inviting him as part of the assembly. In this way he assured himself that Jaffe was indeed doing his job thoroughly. As for the people who were invited, well he just hadn't felt it essential to tell them.

The door opened and the entourage filed into his office. Paulette Locke, Mitch Cayman, and George Palma had each been chosen for their own specialty. Angelo stood up and began shaking hands while his secretary went over to open the door on the far side of his office to show the group into his private conference room. When the last entered, Angelo moved toward the room to take his chair at the head of the table, waiting until the secretary brought in the coffee and the tray of assorted pastries before silently departing. He remained still while his guest served themselves. He listened for the outside office door to close. Finally the moment of hope had arrived.

The atmosphere in the room seemed thick and sweet with mystery. He could feel it and from the expressions on the faces around the table, it was obvious they felt it too. He took his seat and began the meeting.

"Well, each of you know why you've been asked to this meeting, so let's get started.

Each person present sat up straighter. Maglioni began.

First let's get the introductions out of the way. He turned toward Paulette. "This is Paulette Locke." The two gentlemen nodded in her direction.

Maglioni paused for a second, watching the suspense rise. Slowly he allowed his gaze to fall on Mitch. "This is Mitch Cayman," then moving his eyes away from Mitch said, "And here we have George Palma." He allowed the group to acknowledge each other before going on.

"We have a lot to cover so let's begin. He again turned toward Paulette Locke and said, "Paulette, will you be so kind as to share your report with us."

Paulette smiled at the group then suddenly took on a more businesslike expression as she removed the papers from her briefcase. With a slight turn of her body in Angelo's direction she began.

"Mr. Maglioni, I'm happy to say I have met with success in addressing the issue of obtaining a residence and property for Samuel Stillman." She paused as if in reflection then added, "I did run into a slight problem with getting the dates changed on the deeds so that it would appear that Samuel has been the property owner for sometime, but like you said, your man Sal Posner came through for us there. If anyone were to go back and check the records they'd find that Mr. Stillman has been the owner of his home at 1720 Penfield Road since mid-1980 and the four-family dwelling at 792 Rutgers Street has been in his name since early in 1972."

Angelo could hardly hold back the urge to go over and hug this precious woman as he thought how pertinent this matter was to winning the case. Looking at her now he was surprised when he realized she had more to add.

"To add extra credibility to our client, I have Samuel shown as a live-in landlord at the Rutgers Street until purchasing the Penfield property." The surprise expression on his face did not go unnoticed as Paulette seemed to gloat.

Angelo rearranged his expression and smiled. He hadn't expected this. It was a clever maneuver on her part that would hold a lot of validity in court. He watched as Paulette laid the top page of her report aside and with a confident expression, continued.

"For all intents and purposes, our man is an outstanding member of the community. Not having all the necessary contacts at his current address to establish him there, I went back to the Rutgers area and found just the type of people needed to complete the picture. If anyone were to ask around the neighborhood they would learn that Samuel has been a member of the Rutgers Street Property Development Committee since 1973, a contributor to the Episcopal Church remodeling foundation, and an outstanding member of the congregation."

At this point Paulette hesitated again before going on.

"There's a slight problem that you need to be aware of, Mr. Maglioni, just in case someone decides to snoop around. The minister is not part of the plot to build Mr. Stillman's image. I chose the church because of its large congregation, figuring that no one would question his name on the membership list. And he does appear on the membership roster now. It seems quite logical to assume that with such a large congregation, the minister does not know or recognize each of his parishioners, at least this is what I must rely on."

Another pause while Paulette seemed to be toying with yet another notion.

"I would not suggest considering the minister as a character witness because he can neither account or discount the fact of Mr. Stillman being part of the congregation. To eliminate any suspicion, I purposely chose the year of 1970 to add him to the roster. Around that time the church had a fund raiser for an addition to the previous structure and at that time many new names appeared on the past roster."

Paulette remained standing, one hand laying on top of the page in front of her, while her other hand moved from her side to an almost parallel position.

"Well, that's about it. Unless anyone has any questions, I have nothing further to report."

Paulette looked around the room, allowing ample time for any response, but none came. Carefully she placed the sheets of paper back in the report folder, closed it and then walked to the head of the table to lay the report in on the table in front of Mr. Maglioni.

"Here's the finalized report with names, address and all the details you need to move ahead on this issue, Mr. Maglioni."

"Thanks, Paulette. You've done an outstanding job. I can't think of anything you haven't already covered." He smiled then added, "It's a very thorough job indeed."

As Paulette returned to her seat, each of the men took the opportunity to congratulate her on an excellent job. Graciously she acknowledged their compliments then settled in her chair.

"Mitch, will you go next?" Maglioni said once Paulette was again seated.

Mitch stood up and made eye contact with each person in the room than began his presentation in flawless diction.

"I have established three witnesses that will swear in court that at the time of the shooting of his wife and her alleged boyfriend, Mr. Stillman was seated with them at the Popeye Restaurant on Manitou Road. As a further guarantee I have convinced the owner and two waiters that worked that shift to maintain the same premise."

He gave Mr. Maglioni time to digest this statement, before proceeding.

"I managed to get Mr. Stillman another automobile, more suited to his new station in life. I hesitated to purchase a brand new car, but instead settled on a later model in excellent condition that seemed more appropriate. The title for the automobile as well as the papers have been filed appropriately. I contacted someone on the inside of the Motor Vehicle Bureau who with a little financial coaching was able to match the purchase date with the dealer to reflect the transaction taking place in 1984. Our man purchased a 1982 Lincoln Continental as a used automobile in 1984. The car is currently at a local garage whose address is stated in the report and will be ready for pick up by Mr. Stillman any time during the following week."

Angelo marveled at the confidence of young Mitch. The man spoke with authority and commanded the respect of each person in the room. And rightfully so since there were no loopholes, no unfinished points of contention to examine. He had not only delivered a faultless report, his total investigation was impeccable. What fascinated Angelo was the fact that Mitch could have made it on his handsome face and gracious manners alone, but surprised people by being one of the best lawyers around. He could see by looking at the others they were impressed. Mitch was as good as he was good looking. He was very good indeed.

Maglioni watched as all eyes followed Mitch as he walked over to hand over the folder to Mr. Maglioni. He seemed to not notice all the attention he was getting, nor did he wait for any thank you from Maglioni. Not wavering he walked back to take his seat again.

"Thank you Mitch. Fine job," is all Maglioni said.

"Well, its now your turn, George. What have you to report?"

George Palma remained seated with a dog-eared folder on the table in front of him. He loudly cleared his throat and then proceeded with his report.

"Well, I snooped around and managed to dig up some real dirt on all three of our proteges. Outside of establishing the connection between Mrs. Evangeline Stillman and Mr. August Pelegrino as lovers, I had to do a little more homework, 'cause you see the little wife has her own personal rap sheet. She's been busted for prostitution three times. The last time she was held for eight hours in the county jail before someone bailed her out. That somebody was Mr. August Pelegrino himself. Aware of this, I dug deeper and found out the connection. Not only was our man Pelegrino her lover, but also served as her pimp. And that's not just an insinuation on my part. There is enough proof to support it in the report."

He stood as if waiting for applause, and when none came the disappointment was apparent on his face. He continued.

"So, where was I? Oh, yes, Evangeline also was picked up several times for shoplifting and there is one time back when she was a teenager she served 30 days in the juvenile hall for taking a joy ride in a car that she nor the driver owned. The details on the records at the hall are very sketchy so it would be easy to say she was an accomplice and it couldn't be disproved. What makes it real sweet is that all these incidents of confinement took place in a small remote location that no one ever heard of. Chances are this will all be a surprise to the prosecuting attorney. I doubt that he'll even get wind of them until it's presented in the courtroom. That tie in with Mr. Pelegrino will add a lot of meat to our case against him, 'cause now we have him as her lover and her pimp."

Though the delivery left a lot to be desired, the contents, Angelo had to admit was very impressive. George had presented him with a choice of angles to pursue during the trial and Angelo agreed with George that the prosecuting attorney would have no knowledge of these details. He couldn't wait to hear the rest.

"Do you have anything else, George?"

"Sure Mr. Maglioni. I have the little woman witnessed at several hot spots for prostitution here in Rochester. Though there is no real evidence to substantiate it, she may have been practicing her old profession again. I have eye witnesses lined up who swear to her not only being in the area, but dressed in suggestive clothing that fit the picture of a run of the mill street walker."

Again he paused as if waiting for a pat on the back, then slowly he continued to share his findings.

"As for the boy-man, Peter, he has been in trouble with the law since he was twelve. He was locked up for drugs at the age of thirteen, car theft when he was fourteen, purse snatching at seventeen and replays of them all up until his death. I have copies of the rap sheets in this folder here, also copies of transcripts and reports written by some cops and psychiatrist. It's all here," he said patting the papers gently as though it were a baby. "It's neatly typed and ready for use."

George sort of loped over to Angelo with the well-used folder in his hand. On looking through the contents Angelo saw that some of the sheets were wrinkled, making the folder appear thicker than it was. Further in the package he found other sheets flipped sideways, flopping over the ends of the folder. But it didn't manner one bit as he smiled sincerely into George's face while the man stood waiting for approval.

"Well done, George, well done."

"Thank you Mr. Maglioni, thanks."

As George headed back to his chair he knew that what he had managed to uncovered sounded like he had been at it night and day since the time he received the assignment. Well, that was fine with him. He was not about to let anyone in on his secret. No, it was nothing that needed to be said at all. It had been luck that he happened upon an old roommate of Evangeline Stillman, then known as Evangeline Winters. Patty Mason was more than willing to fill him in on her ex-roommate's sordid past and afterwards it took a few calls and he had all the incriminating evidence in his hot little hands. Yeah, it had been a stroke of luck, but wasn't luck what really separated the mediocre from the best? When he finally sat back down, he had a look of satisfaction on his face.

Maglioni slowly got up from his chair and stood at the head of the table.

"Well, I must say, I am impressed." He paused to allow his words to sink in. As he looked from one face to another, he saw the expressions change to that of relief. "All of you have done an outstanding job and I appreciate the effort you have put into the project. I know how hard it must have been to gather all the information and make all the arrangements that we have heard here today and I can't tell you how much I appreciate what each of you has managed to accomplish. Excellent job, just superb! Thanks again."

Faces beamed at him as he concluded and he showed his respect for their ability by an appraising smile.

"Well, if that is it, I have only one more request. I would like to have each of you return here next Friday, shall we say at three o'clock?" Angelo watched as George, Paulette and Mitch shook their heads, agreeing to the date and time.

"Well then, please stop by my secretary's desk before you leave. I left an envelope for each of you with her. It's just a token of my appreciation for a job well done."

Angelo Maglioni continued to stand as slowly each of the members of the group rose from their seats. Mitch Cayman was the first to push back his chair, then walked behind Paulette's to help her from her seat. George Palma was the last to vacate his chair. Angelo shook each hand as it was extended to him and had a few final words of praise for each of them. When the last one had left, Angelo straightened his tie, and ran a hand along the sides of his hair before turning to follow George out the door of the conference room. He continued to smile as he turned for a final salute before proceeding through the door of his office. When the last one exited, Angelo closed his office door.

Maglioni stood at the door a minute or two as if in deep thought then slowly moved across his office until he stood before his desk. His brow furrowed while he continued to concentrate on the meeting. He had a substantial amount of evidence laying on the conference room table. As if to assure himself, Maglioni reentered the conference room and picked up the folders that had been placed on the table. He carried them back to his office and laid them on his desk, patting the top with his right hand. If all of this was organized and handled in a proper manner he could hypothesize there was more than enough here to win the case. At this moment all odds were in his favor. Slowly pure pleasure washed over him as he said aloud, "Yes!"

In the meantime Paulette, Mitch and George were still positioned in the front office. Lisa Caldwell, finishing up with a caller, hung up the phone and smiled at the group.

"I apologize for the interruption," she said with a smile as she efficiently closed the folder before her, placed it on the side of her desk and reached into her top drawer. She pulled out three envelopes.

"Ms. Locke." Lisa reached across her desk, an envelope in her hand. She smiled as Paulette walked over to receive the envelope. "Thank you for coming," Lisa added. Slowly her gaze moved to the top of her desk and she retrieved the next envelope. "Mr. Palma."

George approached the desk trying to hide his excitement as he reached out to take the envelope. "Enjoy your day," Lisa said with a smile.

Again Lisa reverted her attention as she picked up the final envelope and with an obvious appraising smile said, "And finally, Mr. Cayman."

Mitch ambled slowly across the short distance to Lisa's desk, an enchanting smile on his face. "Thank you, Lisa, he said with familiarity in his voice. "It's always a pleasure to see you." Not hiding her admiration, Lisa smiled shyly.

Lisa continued to watch as Mitch walked away, her eyes only on him as he moved toward the closet, waiting for George, then helping Paulette slip into her coat, before finally getting his and tossing it over one arm. He hesitated a moment then turned around to look at Lisa once more. "Take care, Lisa." He turned back around and walked slowly out the door.

CHAPTER 17

After three days of billable production time that ran from the wee hours of the morning to very late at night, Skye began to see an ease in her work load. She had literally become a hermit trying to keep one step ahead of the scheduled work. Each day seemed to meld into the next with no change in her routine. It was work, work, work with her concentrating only on the business. She didn't allow herself to answer the home line when it rang, only concentrating on calls coming into the business.

By the start of her third morning visual signs of stress appeared in her mirror image, but outside of camouflaging with makeup, she paid no heed to the warning that she was working too hard. Even though clients dropped in throughout each day, she became overwhelmed by a feeling of isolation. She didn't dare break from her routine for fear of falling behind, yet she wished for entertainment that would alleviate the pressure of each day. The need for companionship followed her each night as she finally allowed herself to climb in bed, fully exhausted, but being so keyed up she could not rest. When she was finally able to sleep, it was not the restful type of sleep she so desperately needed or desired.

On Wednesday when she dragged herself into the office it was a brilliant day. It turned the view from the office window into a breathtaking scene of greenery with a golden glow. The house was quiet, and the hum of its silence was unbearably mournful, shadowing the beauty outside as she moved about the kitchen. As she prepared a pot of coffee, Skye toyed with the idea that maybe it was time she considered hiring someone to help out, but by the time she stood sipping her first cup of coffee, she knew she couldn't do that. Her clients expected their work to be completed by her, at least the ones that she was working on now. Maybe when she got work from some new clients she could consider it, but not now.

This seemed to depress her even more. She poured a second cup of coffee, resigning herself to the fact that she had only herself to depend on now. With leaden steps she carried her cup into the office and began working through till she was finally on the last of the pre-scheduled jobs.

By then Skye had finished off two pots of coffee. A faint nausea rose to her throat, and she pushed her final cup away. "Too much coffee," she said to herself. Too many pressing thoughts were finally getting the best of her. Moving her head around on her neck, she attempted to clear her mind before continuing with the final project. When she was finally able to concentrate again, she started right in until she had the job completed to her satisfaction.

Skye moved her hand to the appointment book on her desk. There was nothing else that required her attention today. She was just about to get up when the phone rang. At first she told herself not to answer it, then surrendering Skye reached over to pick up the receiver.

"Hello, Skye Sanders speaking."

The caller introduced himself.

"What can I do for you?"

Skye reached across her desk and grabbed her pad to take down notes. From her experience it was easy to surmise this was a simple project. When the caller was silent, Skye reached for her appointment book, flipped ahead through the pages, selfishly determining she needed some time free. Speaking into the phone, she gave the caller an appointment at the end of the following week and held her breath.

"That's fine Ms. Sanders. I'll bring the job over then."

Slowly letting out her breath, Skye smiled and concluded the conversation.

Skye leaned back in her chair feeling guilty for putting the client off like that, but only a little. She allowed herself to totally relax. Her head nodded as she smiled, realizing she was free. She had finally made it to the end. Her work was up-to-date and there were no appointments scheduled for pick up. Amazingly she had time for herself.

For the first time in days Skye allowed herself to repose. She sat back in her chair and let out a deep breath, her thoughts no longer focused on work. She had to do her aerobics, she thought, wondering if her joints that felt inflexible could actually move fluidly again. As if to test them, Skye pushed her chair back and put her legs out straight in front of her. She lifted them up and then lowered them again. She tried flexing her elbow and moving her head around on her neck. A tired smile turned up the corners of her mouth. She could still move her body, yet she made no attempt to get up.

Skye sat idly in her chair. She turned her head to look out the office window with a weary smile spreading over her face as she congratulated herself on her accomplishments. Shadows crept into the corners of the room but she didn't notice because her eyes had closed. When she awakened the first thing to warrant her attention was the darkness. She had fallen asleep. "Well so much for exercising," she said to herself.

Her muscles ached as she slowly got up, remembering to turn off the computer. She walked across the office to make sure the office door was locked, then walked through the house to lock the ones in the family room. Satisfied all was secure, she retraced her steps, turning off the lights until she was in the bedroom. That evening she slept soundly and if she dreamed, she remembered nothing.

On Thursday Skye was up bright and early even though she had no reason to be. For a moment she stood looking in the mirror. She looked refreshed and happy, and felt it as well. Quickly she began to dress as she thought about having a breakfast of vanilla yogurt, crushed strawberries, maybe a nice croissant and fresh squeezed orange juice. Skye was ravenous which was unusual.

In the kitchen she began making a pot of coffee while still contemplating the breakfast spread. While the coffee perked, she went over and took a look in the refrigerator. "Well, that settles that," she said finally realizing that she hadn't gone shopping in weeks. She closed the refrigerator door, and got a mug from the cabinet, and walked over to pour herself a cup of coffee.

"Can I have one too?"

Skye turned, startled by the sound of a voice other than her own and saw Hank standing in the doorway to the kitchen. She looked at him, opened her mouth to speak, closed it, opened it, closed it again. Finally she composed herself.

"Sure, help yourself," she said a little harshly, failing to cover up her irritation at being caught off guard.

It was easy for Hank to see in her eyes what she was thinking, and it made him angry. But he had something to say and she was going to listen to him if he had to tie her up. Trying to appear as though he hadn't noticed the tone of he voice, Hank sauntered over to the coffee maker and poured himself a cup, wondering just how he was going to say what he had to say. He dropped his hands suddenly, a movement Skye detected as she now sat at the table watching him. He turned around and said, "If you're not too busy, can you spare me a minute?"

Her first inclination was to say no, but something stopped her. "Matter of fact, I'm not." What is it?"

Hank watched her with the concentration of a snake. "I wanted to apologize for the other day."

Arduously covering up her surprise at this request, Skye silently wondered what he had up his sleeve. It was not like Hank to apologize for anything and he was definitely not one to change actions suddenly. She had to admit she was curious, but doubtful. It was rather like paying to see a horror film that you wanted to see yet also was a little leery about being scared out of your skull. Skye was not totally convinced of his sincerity so she said, "We both said what we felt needed to be said, so why apologize."

Looking at him closer she thought he looked drained, or was he hung over? It didn't matter either way because she wasn't falling for whatever trap he was setting now. She was coming to her senses, knowing that In the past when Hank wanted to apologize he did only because he had a request. It was his way of getting what he wanted. Skye prepared herself. "What is it you want?"

Hank knew before she spoke she wasn't taking the bait, but that didn't bother him. He knew her well. He had to keep Skye from becoming suspicious and the best way was to play on her sympathy. He gave it another try.

"Skye, I don't know what comes over me. I try to be nice, but it never ends up that way."

"You can say that again, but let's just forget it, okay?"

Hank gave her a look of frustration, one of those count-to-ten looks and gave up. She wasn't falling for the sympathy routine. He stared at her, wishing he didn't have to play this game, but knew he was going up against a stone wall. He'd just have to take his chances.

"Hank, is there something else?" The irritation was back in her delivery.

He felt the urge to tell her, yes, but hesitated, surprising himself at what he was thinking. Instead of his mind being on his real objective he was thinking he couldn't exist with this coldness of hers anymore. In reply to her question though, he said, "No, that was it."

Skye looked down, then looked back at Hank. This was her opportunity. What better time to bring the matter up, she thought.

"Wait a minute, Hank. There is something I've been wanting to tell you."

Remembering too vividly the indifference she had demonstrated, he was taken off guard. He had been on his way out of the kitchen and now turned back around, wondering if he might still turn the matter around. He hesitantly looked at Skye. He was a little shocked to see that her whole demeanor had changed. Skye's expression was no longer one of irritation, but more... happier. Not knowing how to take this, Hank only shrugged his shoulders, walked over to the table and sat down.

They sat at the table together. When Skye began to talk, Hank watched her face closely as he waited for her to speak.

Skye picked up her cup and took several sips of her coffee before she looked over at Hank. When she spoke, it was as though she were telling a story.

"I saw a TV show once where a friend asked this woman why she remained married to her husband. You see, she was so obviously unhappy. The woman said that sometimes she thought she had become such a go-getter because of her husband who kept her on her toes, that she was afraid if she were without the pressure, she'd sit down somewhere and never get up again. And do you know what the friend said?"

Hank raised his eyebrows.

"The friend said to the woman that she'd never know until she tried."

Hank looked puzzled which was exactly what Skye had hoped for. She knew she had his attention. She continued.

"That's where I'm at now. I think it's time I tried." Skye paused. "Hank, I can only speak for myself, but somehow I feel that you are to the same point I am. I am tired of being miserable and tired of seeing you that way, too. I think that for both our sanities we need to put an end to the relationship." She paused, took a deep breath and uttered, "Hank, I want a divorce."

Sweat glossed his brow as she stared in his direction. He suffered an agony of helplessness, minutely shutting his eyes as he ran the back of his hand across his forehead, then opening them as he placed his arms on the table, clenching and unclenching his fingers.

She had spoken the word so flat and without noticeable feelings as though it was no more than a mere request for an extra napkin or a clean fork "Jesus, a drink would be good about now," he said silently to himself.

"What the hell do you mean,"

Skye dropped her eyes to her coffee cup.

"You know what it means," she said. "It means I can't take living with you anymore. It means its over." She lifted her eyes and repeated herself, "Hank, I want a divorce."

"Why the hell are you telling me this now? Why!" He said it accusingly as he tried to find some method of removing the sting of her confession. Skye had someone else and was now ready to turn her back on him. Yes, that had to be it. The thought increased his rage as he glared in her face.

"Who is it Skye? Tell me who you're whoring around with!"

"Why can't you accept the truth Hank? You know I haven't cheated on you once in this marriage. If there's been any cheating going on it's been on your side. I should think you, of all people, knew I wouldn't take this forever. It shouldn't come as any surprise."

Hank reeled back and swung his fist down on the top of the table. Skye reacted by jumping back in fright. He stood up and paced around the room until finally turning to scowl in her face.

"Shut up!" he barked, pointing a finger straight at her nose. "Shut up!" He towered over her, leaning dangerously near.

Skye didn't have an inkling of what to expect as she watched in frozen silence, having a hard time keeping the fear from showing on her face. At that moment she was scared, no terrified, as she watched him seething with anger. She thought, "I've pushed him beyond the limit."

Incensed now beyond reason, Hank felt only the hate that had been chillingly submerged for so long as it tried to erupt in a wild rage that frightened even him. He had to get away. He headed toward the stairs, then his body became rigid and he turned back around to face her.

"So, you want a divorce," he said between clenched teeth. "Well, you can have your damn divorce." He then turned, quickly descended the steps and disappeared into the family room. Soon she heard the sound of him opening and closing the side door. In the silence that pervaded the kitchen now, she heard the garage door going up on it's hinges, the sound of him gunning the motor of his van and finally complete silence. Skye knew he was gone.

She sat huddled and shivering, reaching out to clasp the coffee cup occasionally, with eyes riveted straight ahead. Her mind was a total blank while her heart pounded heavily in her chest. Slowly she began taking deep breaths, allowing the air to escape through her pursed lips until she felt her body relax and her breathing return to normal. When her brain began to function she realized what had just happened. "Oh my god! He agreed to the divorce!"

It took a moment for it to sink in and when it did she didn't fool herself. He had been angry and chances were it would come up again. Only now she began to wonder about something else. She had been so caught up in the opportunity to finally tell him, she had let something else slip by her. Hank...coming to her...apologizing? That wasn't his way. What on earth had possessed him to apologize for his actions? Hank had to be up to something, but what was it! She got up from the table and walked into the office to look out the window. It was not right. Something was wrong.

Outside across the intersection sat a black Lincoln, the person inside looking directly over at the house. When he saw Skye standing at the window, he slumped down on the car seat. A cigarette dangled in his mouth and the coffee in the Styrofoam cup spilled over his hand from the motion. He stayed low and continued to stare up at the window until he realized she wasn't looking in his direction. Feeling less noticeable, he sat up and continued his surveillance.

Skye moved back from the window now remembering something else. When Hank had asked to talk to her he had a strange expression on his face, almost as if he regretted something. She continued her reverie. Hank was not one to regret anything he did, yet that's how she had read that look. She thought about it some more only couldn't come up with anything. Finally she gave up trying. All that mattered was that she had taken the first step and could proceed with the divorce.

Skye suddenly felt calm and in control of her destiny, something she hadn't felt in a long time. "Too long," she said aloud, "and I'm going to enjoy it."

***

While Skye was patting herself on the back, Hank drove the van with the grim determination of an Indy-500 racer, taking curves and lane-changes in robot like fashion. His rage was so complete his mind was unable to deal with anything but his anger. He had no idea where he was headed or what he'd do when he got there. He had been so enraged he forgot his main purpose for talking with Skye and he failed to see the car as it sat idle at the intersection watching the house.

CHAPTER 18

The moment she entered his office at two o'clock on Friday afternoon, Skye could sense a difference in Mr. Maglioni's attitude. He seemed expansive, proud of himself in a way that differed from before. From his ultraconservative dark blue suit, to his crisp white shirt and subdued blue tie, his demeanor was almost gay. He seemed totally relaxed as she was ushered into his office, offering her a seat and then a cup of coffee, which she accepted.

"Well, Mrs. Sanders, you look refreshed today."

His statement added to the puzzlement and she chose to smile kindly before opening her briefcase and handling over the job she had completed.

Mr. Maglioni accepted the manila folder and sat down behind his desk to look over its contents. His head was down as he pored over the transcript that she had worked diligently on and Skye spent the time looking around his office.

There was a large window behind his desk that looked out over the renovated area of the Genesee River walkway, and from up here on the ninth floor of the building, the water looked clear and sparkling. As her eyes moved inside she noted the leather bound books against the far wall behind his massive desk. There were pictures stationed everywhere, expensively framed and lighted. Most certainly some were originals, maybe all. The floral print drapes that were pulled way back were of a heavy brocaded fabric that made the atmosphere homey, as did the matching fabric on the couch and loveseat and the thick beige carpet on the floor. Everything seemed to blend well in this office, a living room-type environment that had obviously been designed by a professional. Skye was wondering what an office like this would cost when Mr. Maglioni spoke.

"Mrs. Sanders," he said with admiration in his voice, "you've done a marvelous job again."

"Thank you, Mr. Maglioni."

"Do you have any questions?"

Skye looked steadily in his eyes, thinking, boy did she have questions, but only said, "No, none that I can think of."

He smiled saying, "Good, very good." Then as an afterthought added, "I guess I don't have to caution you, there is a loyalty between a lawyer and his clients that is a sacred trust. Even if I wanted to share something with you, I might be required to decline to answer."

At first she only stared at him, feeling like a puppy who has just been whipped and can't understand what he did wrong. Simply she replied, "Yes, I do understand."

Something in the way he looked at her made her suddenly feel an urge to get the hell out of his office, yet she sensed she hadn't been dismissed.

"Mrs. Sanders?" he said imploringly.

"Sorry, I was just trying to figure out how to thank you for the business you've been sending my way. I really appreciate it."

"No thanks is necessary. If I didn't think you worthy, I wouldn't have sent them. It's hard to find someone to handle confidential work properly and it would be selfish of me to keep you a secret. But I do expect to be given first consideration for the jobs I give you. Can I expect that?"

Skye smiled sweetly, aware that she had confirmation on one point. "Of course you can."

Mr Maglioni stood up and came from behind his desk. "Well, if that's it, I have another appointment."

Following his lead, Skye stood, glad the interrogation was over and happy to be dismissed. "Well, thanks again, Mr. Maglioni."

She turn, preparing to leave.

"Oh yes, Mrs. Sanders, I left another job with my secretary. Please stop by her desk before you leave." Mr. Maglioni came from behind his desk.

"I'll do that." Skye gathered up her purse and briefcase, shook his hand and walked out the door.

She moved down the hallway to the front office only to find Lisa was not at her station. "Darn," she said under her breath, anxious to leave. Having no choice, she found herself waiting for Lisa to return. Idly she looked around, noticing several people in the outer waiting area which was lined with cut glass that distorted her vision. Skye could make out a woman with auburn hair, wearing a green suit, but she could not see her features. Next to her sat a man in a black suit, white shirt and red striped tie. The two seemed to be deep in conversation with each other. Across from where they were seated sat a nondescript man, his face hidden behind a magazine.

"Ms. Sanders?"

Skye turned around to see Lisa standing at her desk.

"Hi, Lisa," she stammered apologetically, feeling like she had been caught eavesdropping. "I was just waiting for you."

"I'm sorry Mrs. Sanders. It's just been so hectic today. Would you mind waiting a few minutes longer while I show those people into Mr. Maglioni's office?" As she spoke she pointed toward the waiting room.

"No, I don't mind. Not at all. Go ahead and take care of them, and I'll wait here."

Skye busied herself with looking around Lisa's area which was also richly decorated. She turned her body slightly and watched as Lisa's image became distorted when she entered the waiting area. She heard Lisa say something to the occupants of the waiting room, but wasn't paying close attention. As she continued her observation she saw all three of them rise from their seats. Well, Skye thought, at least she could get a look at the visitors.

As they came from behind the glass, Skye felt her anxiety heighten, recognizing them as her three new clients. Lisa ushered George Palma, Paulette Locke and Mitch Cayman in her direction. She tried not to stare as they approached her. She acknowledged their, glad to see you, and hellos with a false smile plastered on her face. As they proceeded pass she found herself wondering why she feel this way. She had no reason to be surprised by their appearance since she knew they had been sent to her by Mr. Maglioni. It seemed logical they should be here. So why was she be surprised to see them here? Yet, watching them as they disappeared into Maglioni's office, she felt apprehensive and again concerned with the idea she was part of something illegal.

When Lisa returned to her desk with an apologetic look on her face, Skye was able to give her a reassuring smile. She managed to stand still waiting while Lisa searched her desk.

"Ah, here it is Mrs. Sanders."

Skye reached out and took the folder from Lisa and before she had it in her grasp, an envelope fell to the floor in front of her.

"Oh, I'm sorry Mrs. Sanders," Lisa said. Skye saw Lisa lean down to retrieve the thick envelope. "Here, this goes with the folder."

Her hand shook as she accepted the envelope and slipped it into the folder. Trying to appear in control she laid her briefcase on the chair beside Lisa's desk, concentrating diligently as she carefully opened the locks and thrust the folder inside. When she looked up, Lisa was smiling.

"Have a wonderful day, Mrs. Sanders."

"You too, Lisa."

Skye turned and was finally on her way toward the office door when she heard a voice behind her. "Skye? Skye Sanders is that you?"

She turned hesitantly around, her eyes searching for the owner of the voice. Over near the filing cabinet next to Lisa's desk stood a man with a face that was vaguely familiar.

"Skye, its me, Fran Russo. Remember? We met at that small business luncheon meeting and you gave me your card. Remember? You set up my resume for me."

Slowly it came to her. Yes, she remembered. He had come to the meeting hoping to find a job as he had just graduated from high school. He had talked to her for sometime and she had suggested that he get his resume in order and had given him her card. He called her the next day and after talking with him realized that he was interested in law. She suggested that he consider getting a job in a law office and that he might want to consider going to college if he was serious. Obviously he had taken her advice. Yes, she remembered. She could feel the fear slowly draining from her body in the company of a familiar face. Skye started to walk over to Fran, smiling in recognition.

"Of course I know you," she said, all thoughts of making a speedy exit forgotten. "What are you doing here?"

"I could ask you the same thing."

Skye laughed at that, the feelings of apprehension returning. As they began talking, she was able to forget once more. Fran said he had just finished up his junior year at law school. He told her he had taken her advice and had worked at odd jobs at several law offices, this being the latest. He explained that he was just a gofer right now, but he saw potential once he received his law degree. Then, realizing he had been talking about himself for some time he asked, "And what about you. What have you been up to?"

"Oh, mostly the same. I've been working hard. The business is growing by leaps and bounds. I can't complain."

"Well, Skye, I'm not surprised. I still remember how thorough you were when you helped me with my resume. Most people would have just typed up the resume and not bothered to find out all the details. You really showed an interest in me and helped clear up some questions that I had. Anyone that can take the time to show interest in their clients like you demonstrated, well, that goes a long way."

"Well, thank you Fran. What a nice thing to say."

"Well it's true. I owe you for helping me get my life on track. Most of the people I spoke to at that meeting didn't want to give me the time of day. But you did. "It's true," he added as he saw Skye shake her head in denial. "It's definitely true. You were the one who offered to help while everyone else was trying to act like they were too busy to spare a moment."

"Well, thanks but I wouldn't short change yourself. Look at you, going for your law degree. That's just wonderful. I think you will make a wonderful lawyer."

"I hope so because I'm paying too much to end up any other way," he said his eyes dancing with excitement.

"Oh, look at the time!" Skye said as she glanced at her watch. "I hate to break this up, but I've got to get back to work."

"Of course you do. I'm sorry I held you up so long, but it was just so good to see you. Are you planning on coming back this way any time soon?"

"Matter of fact, yes. Mr. Maglioni is one of my clients." She paused then added, "I have to deliver this job next week around one o'clock." Skye smiled mischievously. "Tell you what. I'll let you buy me lunch."

There was an uncomfortable pause before Fran answered. "Well, I'd like that but I don't know right now. Mr. Maglioni has this policy about clients... Tell you what, I'll check it out and let you know. Can I call you at your office?"

"Sure," Skye said as she shuffled through her purse to find a business card to give him. "I can usually be reached at this number. Call any time."

The feeling of wanting to get out of that office returned. "I best be on my way."

"I'll call you, Skye."

Skye nodded, managed a quick, "Goodbye" before moving swiftly to the door. It wasn't until she finally slid behind the steering wheel that she felt safe. That was weird. Why on earth had she felt unsafe? No one had threatened her or made her feel any way accept welcomed. Yet, she couldn't deny her feelings just the same.

Skye was carefully backing up when she noticed a man seated in his automobile who was looking in her direction. That uneasy feeling grew as she tried to ignore the stranger. She pretended to be checking both ways, while she attempted to get a better look at his face, but he was looking off in another direction when she was close enough to look through the windshield of his car as if paying her no concern. She had to laugh as she continued to back out of the parking space. She was really getting paranoid. What did she expect? This was downtown and people were always coming and going out of parking lots so why should it faze her? It just so happened this man had probably just gotten into his car too. It was also likely that he just happened to be looking in her direction. With a shrug of her shoulders she backed the rest of the way out of the parking lot, shifted the gear and drove to the attendant's bay. She paid the fee and soon was on her way home.

CHAPTER 19

Angelo stood behind his desk, watching as Lisa chaperoned the group into his office.

"Thank you, Lisa, that will be all."

"Yes, Mr. Maglioni," she said as she walked over to step through his office door and pull it gently closed behind her.

Angelo smiled. "Please, take a seat. This won't take long."

Mitch was the first to sit down, choosing the chair closest to Maglioni's desk, he seated himself and smiled confidently. George Palma and Paulette followed suit, taking the chair nearest them. When they were settled, Angelo began.

"Since we met last, I've had a chance to review your reports thoroughly and do some checking around." George shifted in his chair, anticipating what was coming. He relaxed when Maglioni continued. "I think it is in our best interest that we have Samuel Stillman under constant surveillance. The man is not to be trusted." The group shook their heads in agreement as Maglioni looked at them. He continued. "Also, there is another matter that I want to discuss. I've been doing a lot of thinking and want to solicit your ideas and any help you can offer."

"Excuse me, Angelo, but if you are wondering about our chances of winning, I would like to go on record as stating we have an excellent case. With your ability and our findings, I think you'll win. There's no doubt in my mind"

"Thanks Mitch, I respect your opinion, but it's not the case that worries me. It's the man himself, and more precisely, his physical makeup. In all honesty he looks like a killer."

It was Paulette who spoke next. "You're right, Mr. Maglioni. I was thinking about that too. He could use some rework, but it'll be quite a piece of work."

"Good, Paulette, because I thought of you when this matter came to mind. I'd like you to take charge of the man, make sure he establishes himself in his new life, looks and acts the part. You might need to befriend him and try and soften up his rough edges. Would you do that for me?"

"I'd be glad to." It was obvious she was pleased to be considered for the project. Her aspect changed. She sat up taller in her chair with an air of importance.

"It's not an easy assignment. I've met the man and he is not a person you'd want to be near for any length of time, but if anyone can do this, it's you." He paused in reflection. "I'm open for any suggestions you might have." He added, "And I'm giving you complete charge as well as offering an open mind to any of your suggestions."

Paulette smiled. "Don't worry, I'll be sure to come to you to finance the miracle."

There was light laughter that seemed to put everyone at ease. They had all seen a picture of the man and knew what she was up against.

"George." George's head turned in the direction of Angelo.

"Yes."

"I'd like to assign you the task of watching Sam. He's been going out a lot lately and I want to find out what he's up to, if anything. If he does anything suspicious, goes anywhere he shouldn't or gets your detective instincts up in arms, you are to report it immediately to me. Do you think you can handle it?" Adamantly, George shook his head yes.

"Now, before you say so, let me tell you that from what I've learned, he's coming and going at all times of the day and night. It's going to mean a lot of leg work and little sleep." He again paused. "Do you still want the assignment?"

"Sure. I'm used to that. Never found a person that was being tailed to be a homebody, at least not the type I've been assigned."

Again laughter permeated the room, this time with more enthusiasm.

Now it was time for the big assignment, the one that was most important to him and his case. It was so important to him, that he wanted to discuss it in private. He looked at the group, his eyes falling on Mitch who sat confidently, not the least bit perturbed.

"Well, I think that just about covers it for now. You have your assignments and if there aren't any questions, the meeting is over."

"Excuse me again, Angelo. Is it all right if I say something before we leave."

"Sure, what is it."

"I'd just like to stress to each of you that we need to keep it in mind that we are only aware of what we have uncovered. We don't know what the prosecuting attorney managed to find. Predicting the outcome is an iffy business from that standpoint and no more of a guarantee than gambling or playing the stock market. After years of being in court, I have learned to stop trying to second guess the opponent, but rather to keep my eyes and ears open for any new evidence that might come my way. I learned that from the master." Mitch turned and looked directly at Maglioni as he spoke his final words. "What I wish to impress upon you is to not let your confidence get in the way of your competence."

Maglioni looked around the room. He could tell from George's expression he was puzzled.

"I agree with Mitch and I couldn't have said it better. We have a strong case, but it benefits us more if we can even make it stronger. I support his contention that we should continue to dig for more information that will support or case."

Satisfied that they were all on the same wave length, Maglioni added, "Well, if that's it, we can adjourn." George got up from his chair, followed by Paulette. As Mitch started to join the other two as they made their way to the door, Maglioni stopped him.

"Mitch, I'd like you to stay behind. I have something I'd like to discuss with you, in private."

Maglioni's request surprised both Paulette and George, though it was noticeable on their faces. Side by side they continued toward the door to the office, opened it and closed the door behind them. Maglioni waited until the door was shut before he returned to his chair.

"Mitch, have a seat." He waited as Mitch came back and reclaimed the chair he had occupied. "Mitch, I appreciate the fact you haven't questioned why I took on this case. I feel I need to share more with you than I wanted the others to know. The reason I am getting involved in it at all has to do with a man named William T. Taylor. Do you know who he is?"

"Sure, he's the District Attorney."

"Right. Mr. Taylor is going to be my opponent on this case."

Mitch sat attentively. He not only listened to Angelo, but also observed what appeared to be an expression of hate cross his face. He had been surprised when Angelo had told him he was taking this case, and now he was more surprised by learning that the District Attorney also viewed the case with interest. He was anxious to hear what Angelo had to say.

Angelo stood up. He walked over to look out the window before he began to speak. "A long time ago I had the chance to meet Taylor, back when we were both starting out in the legal profession. Taylor, then like now, was the prosecutor while I was the defendant, only that time for a man named Michael Zorreli. Does that name ring a bell with you?"

"Yes, I know the name and the case you refer to. Zorreli was being tried for washing mafia money. He was found guilty and sent to jail. But that was a long time ago."

"Yes, seventeen years to be exact. He won, but the case was not his most important triumph. He set out to destroy me and he almost did. I was the one who was on trial that day and not Zorreli. When he couldn't prove his case, he went after me as the son of Angelo Maglioni II and I became the victim. Zorreli went to jail, but my sentence was even harder. It had taken time for me to be recognized as a separate entity from my father and his business and in the aftermath of that case I had to start all over again."

Maglioni turned around to face Mitch. "Do you know what it does to a person to be unjustly accused for no other reason than someone needed a scapegoat? It builds and builds inside you until you choke on it. My hands were tied. Even though I was not working for the mafia, the man was my father and I would not denounce him in public."

He rubbed his hands together, looking as though he were somewhere else at the moment and not at the head of a prestigious law firm. Mitch, seated across the room could feel his pain. He wanted to say something, but for the first time in his life he didn't know what to say.

"Over the years I tried to put it behind me. It got easier once I had succeeded in turning the tides. I wanted a firm such as this. I wanted respect and the right to prove I could live a normal life. I thought I had gotten over the matter. And then this had to happen."

Maglioni walked over to his chair and sat down. He looked directly into Mitch's eyes.

"I have a taste for revenge and I'm not proud of it. My methods of handling this case is not totally legal and I know that, but I am up against the shrewdest man I've ever met. He will stop at nothing. He uses the law to his own advantage and not to serve the people. Taylor is what I always called a gutter fighter. There are no rules, no guides to follow and he can kick a man even after he's down. That's his game and something tells me he hasn't changed. Just as I reacted to his name appearing on the case, he most likely responded in like manner. I counted on that. The only reason for him to prosecute the case is either there is something in it for him, or he's remembering too." Mitch started to say something, but Maglioni interrupted.

"Wait, there's more. When my name appeared in print as defending Samuel Stillman, I hadn't even been approached. I assumed Samuel must have informed them I would be his lawyer. I don't know where Samuel got my name or why he chose me. When he came to my office, I told him I would have to think about it. Somehow he must have taken that to mean I would defend him and it was put in the record. It was a week after the announcement that I made up my mind to defend him. I came to that decision when I saw Taylor's name as the prosecutor."

"You don't have to tell me all of this Angelo. I'm helping because of our friendship and I don't need any explanation. Really! That's a private matter and lawyers are allowed that, you know."

"Yes, but lawyers also owe loyalty to their associates in practice. You are not only a good lawyer, but a respected one too and I would be adverse to not let you know what you were getting into."

Mitch sat up in his chair as it finally dawned on him. Angelo had been right when he said he knew very little about the case, but he knew enough to know that something wasn't just right. He had always admired Angelo, saw him as a respectable lawyer too and he would do whatever it took to help.

"Listen, Angelo, you don't have to explain anything. Like you said, I am a good lawyer and I knew there was more to this case than met the eye. I'm in it and I want to stay a part of it. I trust you and your judgment enough to know that whatever you do it will be handled in a fair and just manner."

"I wish I could promise you that it will, but you have my word that I will stay within the bounds of the law. Defending a guilty man is part of an attorney's job, but that does not extend to trying to take the man and make whatever changes needed to have him appear innocent." He raised his hand to silence Mitch. "No, I know what you're about to say. Sure, dressing him up so he looks more believable in court is okay, but giving him a life that never existed is beyond the confines of the law."

"Like you said, skating on the outskirts. But what you're doing is not going to hurt anybody. Samuel Stillman could have gone with another good attorney and been proven innocent. Besides, we're only assuming he's guilty. There is no proof except that he had a motive and seems capable of the act. Who knows, maybe what we're doing will rub off and make him into a law abiding citizen."

Maglioni almost smiled. "Well, I just wanted you to know, that's all. Now, I need to ask if you want to do another assignment for me." He paused before adding, "Remember, you are under no obligation and can say, no. I'll understand."

"What is it?"

"I want you to see what you can learn about Taylor. See if you can find out what he's up to with this case. Anything. The least bit of information can help."

"I'll do it."

"Are you sure?"

"Listen, I have never forgotten what you did for me, either. I was nothing to you and you took me under your wing. I could never have afforded law school and you paid my way and after I graduated, you gave me my first chance to practice. You are a good man Angelo and whatever you decide to do I'll be right there with you, and not because you asked me to."

What looked like tears filled Angelo's eyes now as he stared at this man who looked so much like his wife, Kay. She was gone now, taken away from him by the man Taylor. He loved her and understood what she was going through and why she wanted the children to be protected from the scandal. It had been hard for him to sign the papers to let her change the children's' last name to Cayman, her maiden name. It was like signing away his life and everything that meant something to him. If it had not been for her brother, Mitch, he might not have made it.

Mitch was just a kid then. It was hard to label him his brother-in-law. It wasn't until Mitch was grown that he told Angelo that Kay supported his decision to come stay with him. He had always liked Angelo and Kay had understood. It was Mitch who had shuffled between the two of them making the arrangements so that he could see his kids and make sure that Kay was doing all right. If anybody owed someone, it was him. He owed Mitch his life.

Angelo cleared his throat. "Well, that about covers it Mitch. Do you have any questions?"

Mitch stood up. "Just one."

"What is it?"

"Don't let this get you down. Everything will be fine. I know it."

Angelo smiled and then Mitch was gone.

CHAPTER 20

The next morning when Skye entered the kitchen she was surprised to see Hank already seated at the table. As she walked to the sink she noticed the coffee was already made. She turned to look at Hank. There was something about the way he sat, his shoulders slump and his hands holding a newspaper that he didn't put down even after she entered the room. As she watched, he kept the paper in front of him, reaching out for his coffee cup without looking up. When she said good morning, he still didn't look at her.

For a moment she thought he might be trying to hide his anger, that he was still enraged she had asked for the divorce, but as she studied his posture she felt that wasn't it. Still, she knew he was angry. As she continued to study him she felt as though he was hiding something--something he knew she would like to be in on. Why she felt that way was beyond her comprehension, but that was exactly the message she got.

Skye stood at the sink watching, half expecting him to speak and when he did not, she left the room. When she returned later, dressed for the day, she was shocked to see him in the same position. Carefully she masked her feelings. She didn't want him to know she was puzzled by his silence. With all the years she'd spent living with him, acting, pretending every moment, she should be an expert at covering her feelings, but she wasn't too sure.

He continued sitting at the table, still hiding behind the newspaper, yet he had to know she was there. She couldn't keep silent any more.

"Hank, what's bothering you?" she said with worry. "If you want, you can say that you asked me for a divorce and I'll support you on that. I didn't mean to hurt you by what I said. I just thought it best to get it out in the open."

"Skye," he said firmly, "I don't want to hear it. Right now that is the least of my problems." With that he left the room, without so much as turning to look at her.

Stunned, Skye continued to stand by the sink wondering what was on Hank's mind. It had to be the divorce because she could think of nothing else that she had done or said that would have him acting so strange. Hank, passing up an opportunity to make a snide remark or start an argument was something to worry about.

As the day wore on and she didn't hear the door open or close, she knew something was definitely on his mind. Skye was only slightly surprised when she found him standing at her office door.

"Come into the kitchen Skye, I need to talk to you."

Skye didn't hesitate. Quickly she got up and followed Hank into the kitchen. She pulled out a chair and sat down then waited, for him to speak.

"I'm sorry to intrude on your privacy," he said sarcastically, "but this is important."

More than a little curious, Skye ignored his tone and said, "Well, what is it?"

"The union phoned yesterday while you were out and told me they had a job." His tone was flat and somewhat depressed.

"Well, isn't that good news?"

Hank didn't speak right away, instead he seemed to fidget; something else strange to his normal demeanor.

"The job is in New York City and I'm to start this Friday." He looked down at his hands, then looked up. "I'll have to live there."

A fresh paroxysm of excitement took hold of her as she stared into his face. With Hank out of the way she would be free to get the divorce underway without worrying about his whereabouts. Ever since she had told him she wanted a divorce she had the feeling he was watching her. Not that she had caught him at it, but it seemed he had been hanging around more than he used to. She was careful to hide the exhilaration in her voice.

"Did they say how long the job would run?"

"Yes. It's slated for six months."

"Well, are you going to take it?"

Hank raised his head and looked at her. "How can I? I don't have the money to go to New York, or a place to stay."

Skye thought for a moment and then said, "I have a cousin there. I could give him a call and see if you could stay with him until you find a place."

"You really want me gone, don't you?"

"It's not that. It's just that we could use the money," she said trying to sound convincing.

"Well, how to you expect me to get there?"

"I have some money I could give you to get there. That's not a problem."

Hank looked surprised. "I thought you were broke. You kept asking me for money when you knew I didn't have it, and you had money stashed away?"

"No!" she said quickly. "It's not extra, but I do have some money to get you there. I put money aside for the bills each month so I'll have it when they are due. I could give you that money."

Hank seemed to be mulling it over. "How much do you have?"

"How much do you think it'll take."

"I don't know... I can drive up so I'll need gas money and money for food." He paused as he worked on a figure. "I don't know. But I am not about to go there with a few hundred dollars in my pocket!"

Skye's first reaction was to say, forget it, but she held back. She had more than a couple hundred and enough to more than take care of the bills. Just how important was it to her to have him out of the way? She decided it was very important. Taking a deep breath and ready to respond to his obvious interrogation, she made the offer.

"Would five hundred be enough?"

Hank stared at her with amazement. "Where did you get five hundred dollars?"

"I told you, I saved it up from the jobs I've been doing. Do you want it or not?"

"Yeah, that would not only get me there, but also pay for a hotel room until I get my first check."

"I thought we decided you would stay with my cousin."

"I don't want to put anyone out. I don't know this cousin of yours and would rather not impose if I can help it. Besides, you're not sure I can stay there anyway."

"No, I won't be sure until I call."

"Well, don't call."

"But..."

"I said, don't call."

Skye decided to leave well enough alone.

"Okay, I won't. Is there anything else?"

"You seem awful cooperative. Is it because you want me out of your hair?"

She was going to deny it, but decided not to. "Maybe it will be better for the both of us if we had a little space. It would give us time to think."

Hank's eyebrows went up, but he didn't say anything. Inside he wondered what she meant by that. Maybe, he thought, she was questioning her decision to get a divorce, but he didn't ask.

"Well, I..." He tried again. "When can you give me the money?"

"Is tomorrow soon enough?"

"Fine."

Hank pushed back the chair and left the room while Skye remained seated thinking. Finally she pushed back her chair and went to work.

The days passed quickly and before she knew it, it was Thursday. Hank had come to her with his hand out the day after their talk and she had given him the money. He was in and out constantly after that, preparing for the trip. At least that's what she thought, and that's what he wanted her to think.

***

There were a lot of loose ends to tie up and he had very little time in which to do it. Hank used pay phones to take care of matters. He made several more calls to make sure everything was being handled. As Oscar was getting very nosy of late, Sam had advised against meeting at the Circle Bar, so he gave Hank a number to call.

"Sam, this is Hank."

"Yeah."

"Something has come up."

"What."

"I've got to be out-of-town for a few months, but I don't want any of this to stop."

Sam hesitated. "Listen, I might need to get in there and I can't unless I have a key." He waited for Hank to speak.

Hank had expected this, but even though he had hired the man, he didn't trust him. Definitely not enough to give him a key to the house. Yet, what else could he do? It was too late to find someone else now and besides who else was there. He had no other alternative.

"Okay, fine, but how do I get the key to you?"

Sam didn't realize he was holding his breath until now. He moved his mouth away from the phone and let the air out of his lungs. He could taste the adventure in front of him and the thought that it might be pulled out from under him now when he was so close to capturing that old feeling had scared him. Now he relaxed and tried to think. Finally he had it.

"Hank, do you know where the Pussycat Lounge is downtown?"

"Yes"

"Well, meet me there in an hour with the key." And Hank?"

"Yes?"

"Don't forget to bring some money with you."

"Okay, I'll be there."

Hank made a stop to have an extra key made. He next made several more stops to gather up some equipment he needed for the job at the house. While he was at the store he decided to ask for some help.

"Can you tell me where I can get a good video set up?"

"Sure, but I need to know what you want it for," the salesman said.

Hank had to think before he spoke, not wanting to make the salesman suspicious. "Well, I want one that can tape a pretty good range. I need to make tapes of rooms in my house for insurance purposes."

The salesman stood thinking about this while Hank looked to see if he was the least bit suspicious. He didn't seem to be. When he finally looked up, Hank smiled.

"I think what you need is more along the lines of a camera then a camcorder so I would suggest you go over to Maynards. I think they might have something for you."

After thanking the salesman, Hank was on his way to Maynards and after talking with the salesman there, was satisfied that the video camera would do the job. He pulled out his American Express card and made the purchase. Sure he had everything he would need, Hank headed for the Pussycat Lounge.

***

He didn't see him at first, not till Sam raised a hand to signal him to the table. Hank put his hand in his pocket and took out the key as he walked over to the table.

"Wanna have a drink on me," Sam said.

"Sure. Make it a Wild Turkey Manhattan."

"I could have guessed that," Sam replied with what was as close to a smile as he could muster. Hank watched as he signaled for the waiter and neither man spoke until the drinks were on the table.

"Well, do you have something for me, Hank."

Hank handed Sam the key. "This goes to the entrance door near the driveway which is the best one to use."

Sam took the key. Once he had it in his hand he looked at it, noticing it was new. "Did you try this in the door."

"Yeah, it works."

"Okay, now give me the layout of the house. The more detailed the better."

"When you enter that door you will be in the family room which is furthest from the bedrooms of the house. All the floors and stairs are carpeted except for the kitchen. When you enter, walk all the way to the other end of the room and on your right will be a door leading to the garage, on the left will be the stairs going to the lower level. Turn toward the stairs and take the ones on the left leading to the lower level. When you go down those stairs, turn immediately to your right and you will be facing the electrical closet where all the stuff is installed."

"Okay. How long are the tapes?"

"I've used six hour tapes so it will mean they'll need to be changed at that interval. I want them to run all night; just in case..." He didn't finish.

"I'll need to know her schedule. If I need to get in there during the day, how will I know when she's out."

"That is a problem. Skye is in most of the day, only running out to make deliveries or run errands, but these last few days I have been watching her closely. Usually around eleven or three she'll leave the office for a half hour to an hour. She'll work late in the office, but is usually so busy you can sneak in without her knowing. She goes to bed around eleven some nights, but mostly its after one when she turns in. You'll have to watch for that. You'll be able to tell as her office is right in the front of the house on the main floor, behind the kitchen. Just watch for the light to go out."

"Maybe you'll need me to watch the house?"

"No!" Hank said quickly. "No, I mean I have someone already doing that.

"Why didn't you ask me?"

Thinking quickly, Hank responded, "You cost too much."

That seemed to satisfy Sam.

"Okay, that's good." Sam had it all in his head as he listened to Hank. "What about the rest of the layout, just in case I run into any problems, it might be helpful."

"Sure. Let me see. Downstairs as you go down the steps there will be a door in front of you. That's the den and a room we don't use much. You can only turn right at the bottom of the stairs and you will be in the rec room. Over to the left of it is a small kitchenette that we use for a bar." He paused trying to get his bearings before he continued.

"As you walk through the rec room and pass the bar the door on your left will be the powder room. A little past that, there are louvered doors behind which is the water heater and the heating system for the house. Walk down a little further and you will be in a small hall; off to the left is a spare bedroom and on the right is my son's room. You won't have to worry about him as he is away at college. Those two rooms are not in use now."

Hank again paused as he tried to picture the upstairs. "Now, back up the stairs will take you to the landing that is before the kitchen. Walk up the two stairs and you'll be in the kitchen. Across the kitchen on the left will be her office. Remember that there are only wooden beads strung at the door and if you go in there she might see you."

"A second string of wooden beads are at the other doorway. There's steps going down to a tiled foyer there. That is at the front door entrance. The hallway at the end of the kitchen leads to the bathroom on the left, laundry room across on the right, and a spare bedroom directly ahead. The bedroom that she'll be sleeping in is the door to your right."

His mind continued to work trying to make sure he had covered everything. "That's it except that the master bedroom is over my son's bedroom. I don't see any reason why you'll need to go in there, but in case you do, it's good to know that."

"Yeah, that sounds sufficient. So, if for any reason she gets up and starts checking around, I can hide in the den or in that bar area."

"Yeah." Hank remembered something. "In the den there is a big closet where she stores her supplies. That would be another area to hide in, if she happens to be wandering around."

"Well, that's it man. I should be all right. The only problem will be to get in and change the tapes. I can't promise you I'll be able to make the switch on time each day, but you have my word I'll give it a hell of a try."

"Oh, yes, I almost forgot. I picked up a video camera this afternoon which I don't exactly know where to install just yet."

"Well, what is the most logical place. Her office?"

"I thought about that but that room is on the front of the house, I don't think that she'd do anything suspicious in there."

"What room is the most secluded? That would be the place."

He pondered the question and finally knew. "The rec room downstairs, of course. The windows have roman shades on them that are usually down so that the light doesn't interfere with the big screen TV down there. I could install the camera there and I bet if she's up to anything, that's the room she'd chose."

"Well, then that's where it needs to be. I'll check that too for reloading. Anything else I should know?"

"No, I think that's it."

They had finished their drinks and Hank made the first move to leave.

"I'll be taking off Friday morning so that's when you need to begin. Don't forget to check with the tail before you go in. I don't want her to get suspicious or it will all be for nothing. She has asked me for a divorce and I figure something is going on. There has to be or she wouldn't have asked me. I think she has somebody, but so far I haven't found out anything. Neither has the tail I put on her. But something is up and I'm going to find out."

Sam stood up. "Well, maybe so, but in any case you might get something that will help if you don't want to end up financially embarrassed for the rest of your life. Woman say one thing and always do another. So even if she said she'll be easy on you, don't take it as fact. Got that?"

Hank shook his head, thanked Sam for the drink and left the bar.

The time until his departure was busy trying to get the equipment installed when Skye was not around. He ran into several problems along the way, but a quick call to one of his buddies that was up on surveillance equipment helped him out. When Thursday morning came, everything was in place.

***

On Thursday morning he was a little surprised to find Skye in the kitchen filling a thermos with coffee, and even more shocked when she opened the refrigerator and handed him a bag with donuts and sandwiches.

"Here, you might get hungry on the way."

"I didn't expect this."

"I didn't say you did. I just thought that it would save you from having to stop and eat."

"Yeah, it's a long drive and I appreciate it."

Skye walked to the garage and watched as he put his things into the van, then stood by until he climbed behind the wheel.

"Well, I guess I'm all set," he said.

"Guess so," she responded.

"I'll call you when I know where I'll be."

"Okay."

She felt self-conscious through the exchange and was relieved when he finally started the engine. He rolled down his window.

"Skye?"

"What is it?" she said, walking over to the van.

"I love you. Whether you believe it or not, I do love you."

She was too shocked to say anything as she stood watching him back out of the garage. She didn't move even after the garage door slid back in place. It was the last thing she expected him to say. When he was headed down the road, she finally went back into the house.

Skye walked into the kitchen and poured a cup of coffee. It seemed strange knowing Hank was gone and would not be coming home that night. Even though he spent as little time as possible around the house, he usually slept there and even though they rarely spoke to each other, she knew wasn't in the house alone. Only now she was really alone and it felt kind of odd. She went into the bathroom and started getting ready for the day, still trying to get used to the fact that she was really alone.

The office phone rang and Skye scurried to answer it. As she said, "Good morning, Skye Sanders speaking," she moved behind her desk. Her head bobbed up and down as she grabbed a pencil and jotted notes on a pad, replying, "Sure, I can see no problem with that. What? No. That's fine. Thank you. Goodbye." When she hung up, she was no longer thinking about Hank or solitude. Her mind was on her work.

Shortly afternoon she stood in front of the printer looking over the job she had just completed. When the last sheet came out she ripped it off and took the pages over to her desk to finish the review. A smile of satisfaction spread over her face as she put the pages into a folder and labeled it. She checked her calendar and realized she was at a good stopping point.

Skye got up and went over to open the office window, aware that it was a beautiful day. She felt a warm breeze blow into the room, carrying the aroma of freshly cut grass. Spring was here, she thought as she stretched, her arms going up over her head. She liked the spring; the green grass, flowers and the trees adorned with leaves. But most of all she liked the idea that summer would soon be here. Summer was indeed her favorite season. She turned and walked back over to her desk to sit in front of the computer.

Skye filed the job she had completed and pulled up the household inventory she had been working on whenever she got a chance. The rest of the afternoon she moved around the house, updating the data until she was satisfied it was as accurate as it could get. Next she started working on her personal budget sheet, totally engrossed with the project until her eyes had trouble focusing.

It was then late afternoon--early evening almost--that peculiarly quiet and gentle hour hovering between the end of the day and the impending nightfall. Skye sat back in her chair and rubbed her eyes while she waited for the printouts. She felt a chill, and walking across the room, she went over to close the window.

It was dark outside now. She started to turn around when something caught her eye. There was a car sitting across the intersection with the inside light on. That seemed strange. She stared, trying to make out who was in it, but it was too far away. The car was dark on the outside, probably blue or black. That was all she could make out as she peered out at it. She continued to look in that direction, feeling uneasy. Why was it sitting there. Suddenly the light inside the car went off and she jumped back in fright. Had they seen her? Worse yet, were they watching her? Quickly she moved away from the window and went over to her desk. She picked up the phone and started dialing Adam, changed her mind and placed the phone back on the cradle. She was being silly. The person had probably lost their way and pulled over to look at directions. Yet somehow she didn't believe that. Hadn't Hank acted funny? Could this be what he was hiding? She wouldn't put it pass him to have someone watching her. After a while she let the matter drop. The car was not that big a threat. If they were indeed watching her they could watch all they wanted. She wasn't doing anything wrong. But just to be on the safe side...

Skye moved through the house making sure the doors and windows were locked. When she returned to the office she went over to shut off the computer and close the office for the night.

The evening was ahead of her as she sat down in the family room and turned on the television set, then went into the kitchen to fix herself something to eat. When she returned, a movie was just starting and she decided to watch it. It had been quite a while since she had the time or the desire to sit in this room and she quite enjoyed being able to do it without being interrupted by Hank. Soon she was engrossed with the story.

Headlights shown into the room. Skye looked at her watch. "Who would be stopping by at this hour," she said as she got up and pulled the curtain back. It was the same car, she was sure of it as she watched it back out of the driveway, go to the intersection and turn right. Not being familiar with cars she couldn't tell it's make or year and being dark she wasn't sure of the color yet still she was positive it was the same car.

Skye started to go into the garage to see where it went, but instead found herself checking the locks again. When the phone rang she jumped and when she went to pick it up there was nobody on the line. That started the tiny tingles of fright to flow through her body until she found herself breathing heavy with panic.

Skye sat back down on the sofa. "Stop it," she said trying to calm herself. People were always turning around in their driveway, so why should it scare her now? But no matter how she tried, she knew this was different and something was wrong. A chill went up her spine. "Somebody's walking on my grave!" she said frightening herself even more. She tried to again get interested in the movie but she was too jumpy. Finally she turned off the television set, and purposely leaving the light on, went into the bedroom.

Skye moved slowly getting out her nightgown and taking it with her to the bathroom. She was just about to close the door when in a panic she went around making sure all the doors and windows were locked. They were, yet she still had this weird feeling and did not feel safe, so she left the bathroom door open while she took her shower. Finally she was ready for bed but instead of going into the bedroom, she found herself walking back into the kitchen. She flipped on the light and then went back to her room. For the next forty-five minutes she stared at the clock until finally she was able to fall asleep.

CHAPTER 21

The next morning when she awoke the incident came back to her and she had a hard time putting it out of her mind. She was able to calm herself by her decision to call Adam if the car was there again that evening. As she hurried to get ready, the matter slipped to the back of her mind.

She was in and out all day, running errands and picking up supplies for the office. At one point it dawned on her that Hank hadn't called, but then she put the concern aside. When she was finally pulling back into the garage for the last time, she sat behind the wheel and let out a sigh. She had been running at full speed all day and it was catching up with her. She was exhausted. She opened the car door and walked to the back to open the trunk, removing packages, and after three trips, she finally closed the door.

The house seemed so empty and still as she walked through the rooms until she was in the kitchen. The knowledge that she was alone, really alone, settled in uncomfortably. On impulse she went into the bedroom, put on some exercise clothing and went downstairs to work out. When she finished she felt much better and went to take a shower. It was then she made up her mind what she'd do.

Dressed, Skye went into the office. On impulse she looked out the office window and seeing nothing, went back to her desk and checked her calendar again. There was nothing on it until the middle of the following week. Her time was her own. She grabbed her purse off the chair where she had tossed it and began rummaging through the contents until she found her address book. She placed it on top of the desk and sat down, staring at it for a moment before picking it up and turning to the "Z" section.

Before her were names of lawyers that she had written down. She stared at them, remembering how she had marked them in after talking with her friends who had gotten a divorce. Some of the names were over ten years old, all written down in the back of her address book as she secretly accumulated them over the years. Next to each lawyer's name she had scribbled the name of the friend who had used him or her for their divorce and now as she stared at the list she knew she had a starting point.

Skye leaned back in her chair with her eyes closed. She had to figure out what she wanted to say before she made any calls. Suddenly her eyes flew open. "Damn it," she said, remembering what she had been told. She threw the address book across the room, her eyes ablaze. These lawyers were used to go for the throat, and that was not what she was planning on doing. Hank may resort to violence and even stoop to having her watched but she wasn't going to play it that way. She had enough dealings with lawyers to know the type these friends had chosen. They would be telling her what she should do and not ask what she wanted from the divorce, which was little or nothing. She paused, wondering if maybe she could still use the list and then decided against it. Her eyes glanced at the thick yellow pages of the telephone book. There had to be a zillion lawyers in there. That could take some time. Yet she was convinced that the friends who had bragged about their divorce, had found a cut throat lawyer that had taken their mate to the cleaners.

"Well, Miss Smarty, what now?"

Skye reached over for her coffee cup and took a sip. "Ugh," she said, as the cold liquid went down her throat. She grabbed the cup and carried it into the kitchen where she absently emptied it into the sink and poured a fresh cup all the time thinking about her problem.

There were her lawyer clients, but none of them were divorce lawyers and neither was Adam...

"That's it!" she said out loud.

Quickly she went back into the office and picked up the phone. She listened to the rings as she sat impatiently waiting until the ringing finally stopped.

"Hello?"

"Hello, Lillian? It's Skye."

"Skye? How are you?"

"I'm fine Lill. How's your family?"

"Oh, Skye, the girls are growing like weeds. You'd hardly recognize them now. Remember how Tanya was always so feminine? Well, she's a real tomboy now. I can't get her into a dress to save my life. And Tiffany is just the opposite. She's the ribbons and bow type and has to have her clothes just so. I can hardly keep up with them or their personalities as it seems to change from one day to the next."

"That's nice," Skye found herself saying as she tried to sound interested. The girls were all Lill had now and she would go on and on.... She forced herself to add, "It's hard to believe how fast they grow, isn't it?"

"Isn't that the truth." The line was quiet until Lill said, "I'm sorry Skye, but I get carried away when I talk about my girls." Again there is silence.

"Skye? Aren't you going to say anything?"

She hadn't been listening, just waiting until Lill finished and now she was embarrassed.

"I'm sorry Lill. I have a lot on my mind."

"Well, are you going to tell me or do I have to play twenty questions?"

She didn't know how to ask her. Lill hadn't wanted the divorce and Skye wondered if she was opening a can of worms. Yet she had to ask.

"I need to ask you something, Lill." She waited for the right words to come and when they didn't she blurted it out. "What was the name of the lawyer you used for your divorce?"

So much for tact, she thought as she waited, holding her breathe and hoping she hadn't upset her friend.

"Skye? What's going on?"

"I'm going to divorce Hank and I am sorry, but I didn't know how else to go about this. I hope I didn't upset you."

"No, it's all right dear. I'm glad you called. It's been almost five years now and I'm pretty much used to the idea. Just hang on a minute. I know I have his name written down somewhere."

Skye listened to the sounds on the other end as Lill shuffled around in search of the information. Finally she was back on the line.

"Got a pencil?"

"Yes, I'm ready."

"The lawyer's name is Mr. D'Angelo and he works for the firm, "Johnson, D'Angelo and Smith. Got that?"

"Yes, go ahead."

"The number is, five-four-six, seven-seven-one-eight."

"Thanks Lill. I really appreciate it."

"Sure, honey, I understand. You just take care of yourself and call me if you need me."

"Bye."

"Bye. Skye, don't forget. You call me."

As Lillian placed the phone in the cradle she said, "It's about time."

Skye didn't replace the phone, but instead pressed the button until the disconnect sound came over the line. Quickly she dialed the number. She counted three rings before the phone was picked up.

"Johnson, D'Angelo, and Smith. Melanie speaking. Can I help you?"

"Hello, this is Skye Sanders. I'd like to speak with Mr. D'Angelo, please."

"Are you a client of Mr. D'Angelo's, Mrs. Sanders."

"I beg your pardon?" She paused, the words finally making sense. "I mean, no. I got his name from a friend."

Why so many questions, she wondered. All she wanted was to talk to the man, not give the secretary her complete dossier.

"Is he in?"

"Yes, he's in Mrs. Sanders. Can I have the spelling of your last name, please."

Trying not to sound annoyed, she spelled, "S-A-N-D-E-R-S." She couldn't help adding, "Just like it sounds."

"Thank you Mrs. Sanders, I'll connect you now."

"Well, its about time," she said as she waited. A few seconds passed and she heard a man speak.

"Hello, Mrs. Sanders, this is Mr. D'Angelo."

"Hello."

"I understand you wanted to speak to me?"

"Yes, I'm sorry. I'm trying to find a lawyer to handle my divorce. I got your name from a friend."

"Well, that's what I'm here for. What can I help you with?"

"Everything," she said. I don't know exactly how to proceed from here."

"Okay. The first step will be to have you come in for a consultation. It's free," he added if sensing her next question. "When can you come in?"

"Anytime. The sooner the better."

"Well, let me see... It looks like I have one o'clock on Thursday of next week free. Is that good for you?"

"Yes," Skye said with enthusiasm, not expecting an appointment that soon.

"Well then, I'll see you Thursday at one o'clock."

"Thank you, Mr. D'Angelo. I'll be there. Should I bring anything with me?"

"No, not for the consultation, but if you decide to have me represent you, I'll need to see your marriage certificate, and birth certificates of you, your husband and any children, along with a lot of other details. But we can get to that later."

"Okay. Well, thank you again, and I look forward to meeting you."

After she hung up the phone, Skye felt better than she had in months. Out of curiosity she went over to make sure she could put her hands on the information he had mentioned. She found everything she was looking for in the file cabinet, set aside for the home. Everything was intact. Satisfied she sat down in front of the computer and turned it on. She waited while the system came up and began typing, her fingers moving swiftly. Finally she stopped and began reading the words on the screen.

"I want the divorce to be handled in a fair and equitable manner with Hank and I sharing all monies and expenses equally. That is with the exception of monies I have earned from the business. I will consider a fair percentage, but not share fifty, fifty on any business income or property. As I compromise I would be willing to take on the responsibility of our son's education with Hank paying a lesser percentage. I also will not ask for any alimony payments. I want to sell the house and any furnishings that neither of us want for personal use. I... " She couldn't think of anything else. Carefully Skye worded the details so that the lawyer would have no trouble deciphering her meaning on how to handle the divorce. She studied the file for a long time, making sure she had covered everything that needed to be considered. And when she could think of nothing more, she saved the file. It was then that she realized she was crying.

She had spent the last twenty years or so trying to face the bleak prospect of living out the rest of her life with a man she didn't love or respect. He had cheated on her, used her as if she was a piece of furniture and she had allowed it. He had controlled her whether she liked to admit it or not. And now, the realization that she was finally putting an end to it all, had her weeping with joy.

Just then the familiar ring of the office line bought Skye back down to earth. With a swipe of her hand across her cheeks, she was back in control. She talked for a long time with the client and finally they decided they'd have to meet.

"Ms. Sanders, I don't want to put you out, but is it possible for you to come to my office, say tomorrow at noon."

Skye didn't make it a practice to set up her meetings outside the office unless she couldn't help it and this Mr. Walker seemed quite adamant about her going there. "Sure, no problem," she said trying to not let the irritation show in her voice. "That will be fine. I'll need directions."

"Well, it's quite easy. You know where the Genesee River runs along Front Street?"

Skye thought for a moment. "Yes. Are you in the Front Street Office Building that faces the river?"

"You've got it. I have an office on the fourth floor. The room number is 403."

"Okay, I'll see you at twelve noon tomorrow."

"Yes, and thank you, Ms. Sanders."

The conversation was ended and Skye closed the file on the screen. The phone rang again. Again she sat listening as the caller explained what they needed. It continued to ring throughout the rest of the day until she was forced to get back to work or find herself pushing to meet deadlines.

Skye leaned back in her chair, finally confident she was back on track. Placing the job she had just completed into a folder she realized she wasn't tired, so pulled out the computer book which was now near completion. She finished off the last few pages, looked them over carefully, then decided to call it a day. She forgot to check to see if the car from the night before was sitting at it's post.

***

In his office, Mr. Walker picked up the phone and dialed a number.

"Hello?"

"Hi, Dan, can you talk?"

Dan looked around the room to see if he was alone. "Hang on a minute." He said this before laying down the phone and walking through the house. Janet was no where to be seen. As he walked by the staircase he heard her voice upstairs and knew it was safe. He went back to the phone.

"What's up?"

"Well, she fell for it. She'll be at my office at noon and I'll try and keep her here for an hour."

"Thanks," is all he said before placing the phone back on it's base.

***

Skye again found she had trouble falling asleep. She tried counting sheep but still she was wide awake. She got up and went downstairs to the den to search for a book and finding one that was not a horror story, she returned to her bedroom. She read until she drifted off. Suddenly her eyes flew open. She looked over and saw it was two in the morning. Frightened and wondering what had caused her to wake up, she finally remembered the nightmare and it now came back to her again.

It was evening and she was walking along the banks of the Genesee River, not as it was today, but like it must have been a long time ago. She trudged along the banks walking very slowly with her head down when she heard a voice. Looking up she saw a young man with a very pale complexion, short, curly hair, dark trousers and a white shirt walking beside her. At first neither spoke to the other, but she found it hard to remain silent and finally started a conversation. When she asked him where he was going, he merely pointed down the road. Skye thought the man might be a deaf-mute and pursued no further conversation.

They continued to walk side by side for the next twenty minutes or so. The man pulled out a cigarette and offered her one. She refused. She turned back around and looked straight ahead trying to figure out what to say to this man who had suddenly become her companion. Finally she turned to try and talk to him again.

There was no one by his side. The young man had silently vanished. But that could not be, as she had distinctly heard his footfalls beside her.

She turned around, looking in every direction but could find no sign of this silent companion. She was so confused by the disappearance she headed straight for the nearest building which turned out to be a local bar, she quickly ordered a glass of wine to steady her nerves.

The bartender looked at her and seeing she was unnerved, asked if anything was wrong. Skye immediately began talking, her words falling over each other in her haste to get it out. A man several stools down came over and started asking her questions until finally saying he had the same experience.

She looked at him with surprise and though something told her not to ask, she did. She needed to know if he knew the man. His reply shocked her even more. The man whose name was Pete had been killed during the building of the canal over a hundred years ago.

Her breath came in gasps as she tried to force the dream away She tried to control her breathing as she lay curled up in a ball and finally she succeeded. What had made her dream this, she wondered as she hesitantly reached over to pick up the book that lay opened on the bed. No, that it wasn't the culprit. Then it came to her. The call she had gotten. The man had mentioned his office was on the

Genesee River and she had somehow held that in memory. She also knew where the story came from. She now remembered reading something similar some time back when she was interested in learning about the area. Now, with her nerves already raw, the story had come back to her.

She started to get up but decided against it. She had to get some sleep if she was going to take care of what she had to do tomorrow. She just had to sleep. These dreams, nightmares or whatever label was applied, were coming frequently and it worried her to no end. What if she was losing her mind? As far as she knew there was no cure for bringing one's mind back. No vitamin or mineral to swallow that magically gave all your faculties back. Hopefully this was a temporary situation caused by the stress she had been under, or it might be that her sub-conscious was trying to warn her of something. But what?

"Stop it!" she said out loud. "You're driving yourself crazy." Skye looked around the darkened room, frightened by everything her eyes fell upon. She held her breath as if to be soundless so that nothing could find her. She held it so long that when she had to release a big noisy exhale filled the room, then slowly she started breathing in and breathing out slowly until she was finally breathing normally again.

From all the excitement her heart beat loudly in her chest and refused to calm. It took a lot of concentration on Skye's part to finally succeed in lowering her heart beat. By that time she was exhausted and closing her eyes she fell into a deep sleep. She didn't wake again until the next morning.

CHAPTER 22

Hank had driven out of his driveway by eight o'clock that morning, but he didn't turn onto Interstate 90 to begin his trip to Long Island until sometime after eleven. First he swung by the neighborhood restaurant to say goodbye to a special waitress and put a hot breakfast in his belly. After lingering over coffee until the bank opened, he went to break down the large bills that Skye had handed over to him. Next he pulled into Wegmans and purchased a half case of beer, some soft drinks and crushed ice. In the parking lot he placed a thin layer of ice in the cooler he had put behind the driver's seat, followed by the half case of beer. He covered this with more ice and then added the soft drinks, followed by the rest of the ice. He made a final stop over at the Circle Bar only half expecting to find Sam and when he didn't, had a quick beer and then was on his way.

He was beginning to have second thoughts as he drove down Calkins Road pass his street. His uneasiness heighten by the time he turned left on Middle Road heading toward LeHigh where he would pick up the thruway. He tried to convince himself he had done what needed to be done, but that didn't help so he tried not to think about it, only failed to make his head cooperate. It didn't bother him so much about what he had done, but whether or not he could trust Sam. He could tell from the last time they met, the man was like a time bomb waiting to go off. He either was anxious to get into the house or, possibly his frame of mind was caused by something else that had nothing to do with Skye.

Hank paused trying to take his mind off the matter, but was able to master that feat as he thought, when it came to woman, the man had a really warped and perverted attitude. The next deliberation that crossed his mind, petrified him. Sam was a man he didn't trust.

In all honesty he actually wouldn't put it pass him to assault his wife and yet he had given him the key!

Hank's face tightened as unpleasant visions passed through his head. He visualized Sam taking advantage of Skye and he broke into a cold sweat, realizing that if this were to happen, he would be too far away to help her. The last thing he wanted was for any man, including Sam, to lay a hand on Skye in that way.

His mind far away, Hank barely heard the horn being pressed frantically by the driver he started to pull in front of as he tried to change lanes. Quickly he swerved his van back into the right lane, just in time to avoid the crash.

"Wait a minute," he said to himself as the danger passed and he drove down the thruway. "Wait just one fucking minute! He had paid Sam to perform a services for him, only after he had checked him out. "Well...." He stalled. He hadn't really done much checking. Just a question here and there, done with extreme care so as not to upset Sam. Besides the people who knew him, who's to say they could be trusted! No, he wasn't going to lay a guilt trip on himself. He had to believe that what he had done was going to work out as planned because he had no other alternative. He had instructed Sam on what he was to do very explicitly. "Explicit pay for explicit services," he said lightly. "Yeah," he surmised, he could trust Sam to do only his job, because Sam was the type of man who would only do what he was paid, in advance, to do.

That seemed to alleviate his indecisions and he felt much better when he added, "Now if Skye were to somehow put Sam in a threatening position, he would not put it past the man to do her in." If that were to happen then it was her own fault and there was no blame in it for him. He didn't like that idea much but settled his nerves further, thinking Skye was afraid of her own shadow so the likelihood of her doing anything that smelled of danger was remote. He decided it best that he just forget any reservations he might have and maybe forget about Skye altogether. She obviously had forgotten about him. But that was easier said than done.

Why did she have to always act so superior, like she was the one who wore the pants in the family, he asked himself. Yeah, why was that? She was always sitting in front of that damn computer of hers and thinking she could support them on her own. She seemed to forget the money he made when he had a job and it wasn't really that long ago. It was her attitude that made him lose the job in the first place. He could have stayed on if he wanted, he was a damn good electrician and the union knew it. But why bother? She made him feel useless, always trying to be so high and mighty.

Sure she was smart and had proven she was capable of making good money. Hadn't he given his okay to start up the business? He wouldn't have done it if he thought she couldn't handle it. But she had obviously forgotten that it was his money that helped buy the supplies she needed to get started. It was his name that got her the loan to purchase the new equipment when she had outgrown the old. Did she think about that? Probably not.

What really gnawed away at his conscious most was the kidding he had to take from his peers. More than once he had to shut up some bastard who insinuated she supported him and wouldn't he like to be in his shoes. Well, he wouldn't have to take it much longer. He would be making good money again and just let her come with her hand out. He would get great pleasure at throwing it all in her face.

Hank's features were distorted with his anger. But under the anger he knew he was hurting because there was no way he could convince himself he was better off without her. He had known when he met her she wasn't his type, but he had determined he was going to change. Compared to before, he had changed quite a bit. Only, Skye had wanted much more... Hank pounded his fists against the steering wheel and it was all he could do to keep from crying. He couldn't let her go. He loved her and if it weren't for her he'd still be wearing that damn security guard uniform and going nowhere. He thought he had enjoyed his life and even fooled himself into believing he was doing okay, but she opened his eyes.

Hank relaxed feeling the anger subsided as his mind drifted back. He wiggled in the seat until he was in a more comfortable position, stretching his long legs out in front of him as the cruise control kept the car in motion. She was so sweet back then...

***

"Skye, I can't hang on to a job because I hate what I'm doing. I didn't get a chance to go on to college so I'm limited in what I can manage."

They had been seated at the kitchen table and experiencing one of those rare moments when they were actually able to discuss something rationally.

"Well, do you know what interest you?"

At first he couldn't think of anything but eventually a picture entered his mind. He recalled working summers doing odd jobs at his uncle's electrical shop. He started out just cleaning up the sites while the electricians did the real work. Slowly his uncle allowed him to become more involved with the profession as he could see the shine on Hank's face each time he watched the electricians do their work. When he felt he was ready, his uncle let him put in a light switch following his verbal instructions. After that his uncle had allowed him to do more and more of the electrical work until he was doing almost everything that the trained electricians did. Hank felt like he had died and gone to heaven. It was power... That was the only way he could describe the feeling that came over him. He had the power in his hands and at anytime, at any point he was careless, the power could switch back to it's owner. His uncle drummed it into his head that he must respect electricity. Electricity could do good, or it could turn and snap the life out of you. But there was more that interested him... Money. To do something that gave him such a high and get paid more than he ever dreamed of was like taking candy from a baby. Finally he knew what to say.

"I want to become an electrician!"

From that stated fact, Skye had made it happen. She worked two jobs while he worked one during the day and attended classes at night until he graduated.

***

It was too much for him. His eyes grew so foggy he could barely see the road. He tried to force himself to stop thinking about it. He turned up the volume on the radio and concentrated on the music that seemed to vibrate off the walls of the van. His head started pounding and his mind kept rewinding until he couldn't stand it much longer so he finally turned the volume back down and reached for the map. He was still on Interstate 90 and had covered the distance between Rochester and Syracuse. He figured he was now somewhere between Syracuse and Utica.

According to the black line he had drawn he should continue on Interstate 90 through Utica, Amsterdam, Schenectady and Albany.

His first turn off would come once he passed Albany. At that point he had to look for Rte 87. Keeping an eye on the road, Hank glanced back and forth reviewing the map and noted he would be switching on to Rte 84 just before Newburgh. He looked at his watch and saw it was just after one o'clock and decided this was as good a time as any to pull over and eat.

Hank moved the van over to the shoulder and shut it off. He reached behind his seat and grabbed the bag that Skye had packed for him and open the cooler he had stocked before leaving Rochester. Hank dug down in the ice to where he had placed the half case of beer and took one out. Once he had everything set up for easy access, he started the van and pulled back out on the thruway. He devoured two of the sandwiches, finished off the donuts then reached back to get another beer. When he finished his second brew he reached back again and did so repeatedly.

Hank felt fully reposed as he continued to drive with the cruise control set at 60 miles per hour. He had started out going 65 and 70, but lowered the speed while he consumed nourishment. Now ready to adjust his speed again, his glance fell on the chronometer that he had set before beginning his trip. It showed 270 miles!

"Damn," he said. Hank leaned over and reached into the glove compartment to retrieve the mile listing he had compiled.

"Damn, damn, damn," He said. According to his calculations, he should have turned on Rte. 87 some fifty miles back. He started to pull over to the shoulder of the thruway, then pulled back on. Up ahead was a U-turn area. The traffic wasn't that heavy as he glanced around, looking for any official cars. When he was confident he wouldn't get caught, Hank barreled down the road, turned right at the U-turn area and was heading back toward Utica again. By the time he reached the exit that would take him to Rte. 87 he was two hours behind time.

Once he was going in the right direction, the strain of realizing he had missed his mark was removed and he reached for another beer. There was a little over a hundred and fifty miles between here and the next turn off which would be prior to Newburgh, he thought. He drove steadily putting the miles behind him as he absently grabbed another sandwich, telling himself that once he reached Rte. 84 he would look for some place to get a hot meal. He kept his eyes on the road and his mind clear as he continued down Rte 87.

"Damn," he said when he finally remembered to check his gas gauge. He had to find a service station fast. As luck would have it, Hank saw a sign up ahead advertising gas and food just up ahead. He stopped, filled the tank and wasting no time, was back on the road.

The hours seemed interminable as he pressed down on the accelerate, switching from lane to lane, trying to make up for lost time. Shortly before seven o'clock he saw the first sign alerting him that he was nearing Newburgh. By seven fifteen he was turning on Rte. 84. He pulled in at the first place he came to that offered a good meal.

Hank entered a small diner and walked over to the first empty table. Outside of himself, he counted five other people in the place. He didn't have to wait long before a waitress came to take his order. While he waited for his food, he glanced around at the other people seated in the diner. At two of the tables, what appeared to be husband and wife teams, sat talking quietly across the table. Quickly he averted his eyes to let them settle on the tables that were occupied by a lone individual. He felt more comfortable realizing he was not the only one without a companion. When his meal came he ate quickly, left money and a small tip on the table. Then he was back in the parking lot and climbing into his van.

He turned back onto Rte 84 , heading east. After driving forty miles the route switched to head south toward Brewster. Hank picked up the mileage chart again. According to this he would be switching to Rte 684 once he passed through Brewster. He had covered almost 400 miles.

"What I need is a real drink," he said. Not wanting to stop and lose any more time, he only toyed with the idea, but his thirst got the best of him. Keeping his eyes pealed he drove looking for another exit and when it came into view he steered the van down the exit ramp, turned right and drove down the road in search of a bar. He had no idea where he was or did he care. He was not lost, just unfamiliar with the area in these parts. The one thing he did know was every town had a bar or two--every town. All he had to do was find it. He stayed on the main road and kept looking out on his right, then his left. After he had gone a little over a mile, he was rewarded.

The place was empty when he walked.

"Can I get you something?"

"Yeah, fix me a Wild Turkey Manhattan." He leaned forward on the bar, then added, "Make it a double."

While he waited he surveyed his surroundings. It was a dump. As he slipped his body onto a bar stool he thought, Skye wouldn't be caught dead in a place like this. She hardly ever drank, but thought she was the authority on alcoholism. She was always complaining about how much he consumed. Sure he drank, he did it to relax. He drank to give himself the courage to face each day. Everybody did. Him an alcoholic! He was far from that. The bartender set his drink down in front of him. Hank reached into his pocket and got out his wallet.

"That'll be two and a half."

Hank opened his wallet and shuffled off three bucks. "Here, keep the change!"

Quickly he picked up the glass. He held it up in the dim light and stared through the liquid. The room looked a lot better, he thought. He slowly moved the glass down until the rim was at his mouth. He tipped the glass, took a small sip, then a larger one. Before he knew it the glass was empty, except for the ice cubes.

"Want another?" The bartender stood in front of him again.

He did, too. He wanted more than just one more, but he couldn't do that. He still had a long way to go.

"No, I'm fine," he lied as he hopped off the stool and started toward the door.

"Well, maybe... Do you have bottled beer?"

"Yeah."

"Well, get me four bottles of Coors, unopened. I'll take them with me." On his last check, he had noticed his supply was getting low and he really wasn't interested in the soft drinks. Not knowing where there was a supermarket, or wanting to stop again, Hank assumed it best to take care of this matter now even if he had to pay more.

When the bartender deposited the bottles in front of him he paid, made his way through the door and was back in the parking lot. Hank unlocked the driver's side and climbed in. Carefully he turned around in his seat and placed the beers in the cooler. With the lid back in place he turned the ignition on and drove back down the highway until he saw the entrance ramp that would put him back on Rte. 84. Soon he was on his way again.

He drove feeling the loneliness of the stretch of road ahead. To cover up the quietness he played the radio loudly for company. But that, the drink at the bar, nor the beers helped to alleviate the solitude sensation that had overcome him. He saw the sign marking his passing of Brewster some forty miles after he left the bar. He continued to drive noticing the sky as it darkened and caught a glimpse of the sunset on the horizon. He was turning on Rte. 684 at nineteen minutes after eleven.

Hank was exhausted by now and only wanted to get to his destination so he could get some sleep. He leaned forward in the driver's seat and opened a window to let air in, hoping it would keep him awake. He drove steadily, his eyes alert for any signs that appeared. He managed to make the right turns at the right place, passing through White Plains, Yonkers and then the Bronx before crossing the East River. He was now in Long Island . At Queens he stopped long enough to fill the tank and verify his directions with the attendant. He found the 495 expressway without any trouble. He was finally in Jericho.

By the time he reached the city it was after one, the next morning. He was already thinking about the added depression of checking into a motel room alone. Though he hadn't slept with Skye for some time, he hadn't gone without companionship either. Women found him attractive and he wasn't against sleeping with someone other than his wife. She was the one who had forced him out of the bed, but she couldn't force him to live a life of celibacy. That was one of the many things that she accused him of that he had to admit he was guilty. He had slept with other women, but only when he couldn't get what he wanted at home. Thinking about this now, Hank decided that once he got settled in he'd go to the motel bar and find someone who wouldn't find him repulsive. He knew he was a good-looking man and he could be very charming when he wanted to be.

That thought brightened his spirits and he drove less irritably through the streets, checking the map frequently that the Union had given him until he found the address he was looking for. When he finally pulled into the parking lot of the Sanford Arms, he was so stiff and tired he could barely climb out of the van. It looked quite expensive but there was no way he was going to look for another place. He had driven a total of 580 miles and had been behind the wheel of his van for almost sixteen hours, with the exception of a few quick stops.

The hotel was as impressive on the inside as it was on the outside. He stood in the lobby looking around before carrying his bags up to the front desk. He rank the bell.

"Yes, can I help you?"

"Sure. I'd like a room."

The desk clerk pushed the registration book in front of him and waited while he filled in the background requested. When he finished, Hank laid down the pen and watched as the desk clerk turned the book back around so he could read it.

"Mr. Sanders, will that be a single or a double?"

He started to say, single, but changed his mind. "A double, please," he said as politely as pie.

"Will you be staying alone or are you expecting someone."

"No, I'll be staying alone." He could barely stand up, his legs wanting to buckle under him so he leaned on the counter.

"How many nights, sir."

"Well, I'm not sure right now." He thought for a moment. It might be possible that he'd hear of a better place once he met up with the rest of the men. "I'll pay for two nights now."

He handled the transaction as quickly as possible then asked about room service and the desk clerk said he could arrange something for him.

He thanked the clerk by handing him a folded bill.

"Thank you, sir. Here's the key. Would you like help with your bags?"

"No, that won't be necessary, thanks."

He could barely put one foot in front of the other as he walked unsteadily to the elevator, a bag on either side of him for balance. Gratefully the elevator door opened and he took it up to his floor. He got out and started walking down the long hallway, checking the room number on the key and stopping to insert it into the lock once he reached his destination. When he opened the door he was impressed with what he found, but too tired to enjoy it as he quickly headed for the bathroom to take a hot shower. He didn't bother to dress but instead took his robe out of the suitcase. He then placed a call to the front desk clerk to order a bowl of chili, extra bread and crackers.

After he hung up the phone, Hank laid on the bed feeling comfortable now, though still very tired as he glanced around his room, noting there was a television. He started to get up, then saw the remote on the bedside table. "Thank God," he said with a groan. He clicked until a western was on the screen and reclined enjoy it. There was a knock on the door.

"Yeah, who is it."

"Room service, sir."

Hank got up and slowly walked over to let the waiter in. He watched as he laid out the spread on the table in the room and then gave him a large tip.

"Thank you, sir!"

He smiled as he closed the door then quickly went over to the table, gathered up the food and took it over to the bed. He ate hungrily while he watched the movie.

"Ah, this is the life." He felt important as he leaned back against the headboard with the remains from his meal resting on the end table. He reached over and picked up the phone again, this time to place a wake up call for five am. He was to report to the job site by six.

It wasn't long before he got up and taking off his robe, pulled back the covers and climbed into bed. The TV continued to play as he drifted off to sleep. His desire for companionship had fallen by the wayside.

***

He was stunned into wakefulness by the phone ringing excessively on the end table. Slowly he reached over, still half asleep.

"It's five o'clock."

"Yeah, thanks."

Morning had come too soon. Hank had to force himself out of the bed and moved sluggishly readying himself for work. As he slowly swung his legs over the side of the bed he could feel the strain of sitting in one position for so long and the beginnings of a headache from the booze he had consumed. He sat on the edge of the bed and reached over to retrieve his suitcase. Digging through the contents he found what he was looking for and carried it with him to the bathroom. "First the aspirin, then the shower," he said as he stared at his reflection. He downed three aspirin then reached for the handles in the tub. When the water was the right temperature, he climbed in. When he climbed out he was feeling much better and quickly managed to finish his morning rituals. Just as swiftly he left the room, locking the door behind him and was on his way to the lobby. He walked over to the desk clerk and handed him the key, then made his way to the parking lot to climb into his van. Soon he was on his way.

He arrived at the site on time to stand around with a bunch of other men who were waiting for their identification batches. Hank, still slightly hung over from the drinks down, was not feeling very chipper and did not look forward to spending time standing in line. But there was nothing he could do about it as he shifted from side to side, demonstrating his impatience. He was startled when someone tapped him on the shoulder.

Turning around he faced the culprit.

"Sorry, I didn't mean to startle you. Look's like this is going to take some time." the man who had tapped him said. "Are you from here?"

"No," Hank replied, glad to have something to occupy his time.

"Neither am I. I'm from Jersey. Where are you from?"

"Rochester, New York. You probably never heard of it."

"No, I've heard of it," the stranger said. " I thought there were a lot of jobs there."

"There used to be, but lately they've been scarce."

"By the way, my name is Pete Draper." Pete tapped the man in front of him and then said, "This here is Joe Beecham and the man in front of him is Jim Sampson. We all rode up together."

Hank shook hands with the men. "Where are you guys staying?"

"Nowhere just yet. We drove up this morning and figured we would drive in each day, but we're not sure now. We talked with some of the other men who have been on the crew for some time and they said that the last thing we would want to do would be to drive any distance when we get off. He said they've been working long hours and the work is damn hard on the body."

"I've never done it, so I don't know," Hank replied. "I got a room at the Sanford Arms Hotel, but it's quite expensive and I'll have to check out other places."

They talked amongst themselves as the line started to move. Hank found he liked them. They were okay guys. They found they had a lot in common so Hank wasn't surprised when Pete said, "Tell you what, Hank, if we decide to stay in the city, we can all get an apartment together. That would save on our living expenses."

"Sounds good to me. I'm in."

The line started moving along quite rapidly and soon they were climbing into assigned trucks that would take them to the job site. No time was wasted in putting them to work, which turned out to be the most strenuous job he had ever done. He was working for a cable company in the Brookville area that was in the process of laying new cable. All day he was on his feet, pulling wire off of huge reels. The more experienced men were climbing poles and making the connections for the service while the newer men kept feeding them the lines of wire.

By mid-morning Hank was sweating profusely, his clothes clinging to his body as he continued to force the wire to roll off the reels. They worked all that morning with only a half hour break for lunch. He hadn't thought to bring food with him and was too tired to search for a place to get some. He was grateful when Pete and his friends shared what they had brought. Before he had time to digest his food, it was time to get back to work.

Hank thought the day would never end. They worked, too tired for words now as they continued to lay the cable. Hank wished he had worn lighter clothing or at least thought to bring something to change as sweat stains appeared on the front of his shirt, under his arms and around his neck. He could feel it trickling down his back making him uncomfortable. When he thought he couldn't walk another inch or tug another cable, the day finally ended. Silently the men climbed into the vans supplied by the contractor. Hank looked around and spotted Pete, but didn't see the other two men. When they arrived at the office site in Jericho, the men started piling out of the vans. Hank waited for Pete and together they walked into the building.

"Did you see Joe or Jim," Pete asked.

"No, I was about to ask you the same question."

"Well, they ought to be here soon. Let's wait outside, though. I'm so hot I can hardly breathe in here. I could use some fresh air."

Hank nodded and they walked back outside to wait. Soon Joe and Jim walked up to them.

"Man, they sure know how to pack us into those vans." Joe said as he sauntered over.

"Yeah, ours was overloaded too." Pete responded.

"Well, are we ready."

"Yeah. I think so. Why don't we split up. I'll ride with Hank and you two follow in the truck."

"Fine with me," Joe replied. "I just want to get to where there's a shower. I'm sweating profusely."

"We all are." This was said by Jim who had made the arrangements. As Jim walked with Hank to his van, Pete and Joe moved away to climb in Pete's truck. As they climbed into the vehicles all Hank could think of was taking a hot shower and climbing into bed. Soon they were on their way with Hank driving and watching to make sure the truck was behind them.

"Listen, why don't we plan on checking out places once we get to my motel?"

"Sounds great, but first I want a hot shower and some food." Hank replied.

They pulled into the parking lot of the hotel. Joe and Pete were right behind them and pulled in next to the van. Slowly, their bodies feeling the strain of unfamiliar work, the men climbed out and started toward the entrance to the building. No one spoke.

They stood in the hotel lobby looking out of place with sweat visible on their clothing and mud caked on their shoes. Hank could tell by the expression on the desk clerks face this was not the clientele they were used to, but he ignored their surprise stairs as he moved toward the front desk with the other three in tow.

"My friends and I are going up to my room to clean up."

"Will they be staying in the hotel?"

Hank turned around. It was Pete who spoke to the clerk.

"Sure, what's the cost for the night."

"It's eighty dollars a night," the clerk said smugly.

"Wow, that's steep, I don't think I have that much on me." The other men nodded in agreement.

Hank, only thinking of how great a hot shower would feel about now, quickly announced, "Listen, I'll put it on my American Express and you can settle with me later."

"Are you sure about that? I won't be able to pay you until I get my first check," said Pete.

The others nodded in agreement.

"Sure, no problem. I haven't got much on me either, but I can put it on the card.

"Thank's Hank, we'll pay you back," they said in unison.

Hank turned back around to face the clerk. "Do you have another double next to mine," he inquired.

"Let me check."

Hank waited while the clerk checked. Shortly the clerk came back to the front desk.

"Yes, I have one just across the hall from you."

"We'll take it."

Hank settled up with the clerk and then slowly turned around, feeling his body being overcome with aches and pains.

"Let's go," he said to the men. "Do you want to get your stuff before we go up?" He inquired.

"Sure. Once I'm comfortable, there will be no moving me!"

Painstakingly, Joe, Pete, Jim and Hank went back out to the truck and carried in their bags. As they rode up in the elevators they decided to have Joe and Jim share the other double and Pete would move in with Hank.

"I don't know about the rest of you, but I could sure go for a beer."

"Yeah, me too," Joe chimed in.

"I think we all could, but don't you think we ought to clean up first?"

"You're right." Then on hearing Joe groan, Hank added, "Come on old man, you can make it."

They arrived on their floor, the bags seeming to weight a ton as they traveled down the hall way.

"I'll make a call down for the beer. Pete, you can take your shower while I do that. I hope everyone likes Ginny."

"I can't speak for the rest of you, but I'd drink a pitcher of panther piss about now and enjoy it."

The men started laughing. As tired as they were, a good laugh was in order and it took little to get them started. They laughed so hard their sides ached. When Joe's stomach growled loudly, they laughed more until tears rolled from their eyes. They could hardly contain themselves as they stood in front of the doors to their rooms trying to put the key in the lock.

In the room, Hank stood by the bed, feeling too dirty to sit down. He picked up the phone and started dialing while Pete placed his suitcase on the table and rummaged through it getting out a clean set of clothing and his toiletries. Soon he was on his way to begin his shower.

Across the hall Joe was just stepping out of the shower feeling refreshed. He passed Jim who was wasting no time to begin his. Joe puttered around then decided to go down to lobby to get a newspaper. When he returned to the room, Joe was dressed and ready.

"Let's go see how their doing," Jim said.

"I'm ready. I just went to get a paper so we can check out the rentals."

With the newspaper in tow, the men locked the door and knocked on the one across the hall. Pete let them in.

I've got a newspaper we can check for rentals in the area."

"Good thinking on your part, Joe."

Soon Hank joined the others. There was a knock on the door.

"Who is it."

"Room service."

While Hank went to let them in he could hear the other men sigh with relief. Pete walked over to remove his suitcase from the table and placed it on the floor, then they waited while the beer was set up on the table. Hank slipped the man a five and then walked with him to the door. Pete, Joe and Jim didn't wait on ceremony as they poured the beer into the glasses. Once everyone was settled, Joe opened the paper and started looking through the want ads.

"What do you want to eat," Hank said.

"Something quick", was the reply.

"Pizza?"

"Sure. What about a sheet with pepperoni, extra cheese and sausage."

"You're on! But let's get peppers and black olives too."

"That okay with everyone?"

The response was unanimous. Hank went over to the phone and placed the order. While they waited, Jim read out loud the rentals that seemed appropriate for their needs. When the pizza arrived, they quickly dug in and in no time it was history.

Lounging back with their stomachs full and a fresh glass of beer, they started making decisions on where they would move. Several times they placed calls to the front desk to find out about street locations and several hours later they had two that looked promising.

"Let's go see them after work tomorrow."

"Sure, anything you say, Hank. All I want to do is climb into bed and get some sleep."

"Yeah, me too. I'm so tired I can hardly chew," Joe whined as he tried to finish the last bit of pizza in his hand.

"You can say that again. The only way I got through mine was sheer starvation. My stomach was hitting my backbone." While he talked, Jim tried to stand up and demonstrate for them, but his legs were so weak he fell back into his chair. They all started laughing and the laughter kept their mind off their bodies that were now stiffening.

"I don't know about you guys, but we need to finish this beer before I pass out. I'm so tired I can hardly move."

All the men nodded. They lifted their glasses in a toast. "Down the hatch."

"I can't keep my eyes open any longer. You guys have got to go."

"You pushing us out Hank?" Jim said with fatigue slurring his words.

"Take it any way you want to, but say goodnight."

"Goodnight. Meet you in the lobby at five thirty."

"Damn, did you have to say that!" Hank said jokingly. "Don't forget to call down for a wake up call", he added as he closed the door behind them.

When Hank closed the door, both himself and Pete wasted no time climbing into the bed. Hank barely had the energy to turn off the light before walking over and pulling the covers down so he could fall into the bed. By the time he settled in his, Pete was already asleep. For once Hank was thankful he was sleeping alone, he sprawled out and soon joined Pete.

The night passed quickly, it seemed, when Hank heard the phone ringing next to his bed. He reached over to pick it up.

"Yeah."

"It's five am, Mr. Sanders."

"Thanks."

He fumbled in the dark trying to place the phone back in its cradle and wanting to turn over and go back to sleep, but he didn't. His legs were stiff and his gait clumsy as he made his unsteady progress across the room to the bathroom where he stood for a time looking in the mirror before finally getting his body to function. A quick shower and shave and he was back in the room to find Pete waiting his turn.

"Five o'clock comes mighty early." Pete mumbled as he passed by Hank.

"God, you can say that again."

While Pete was in the shower, Hank finished dressing. He called across the hall to make sure Joe and Jim were in the process of getting ready. The phone rang for some time before it was finally picked up.

"You guys up?"

"We are now." Joe said sleepily. "Take that back," Joe added as he saw Jim coming out of the bathroom. "Jim is."

"Well, hurry up. We'll meet you in the lobby."

Pete and Hank were the first to arrive downstairs. When the other two joined them, they had already checked with the front desk for a restaurant that would be open at this hour. Once they were all together, they went out and climbed in their vehicles. Hank again lead the way as they pulled out on the street and soon were seated, having coffee and a breakfast of eggs, sausage and fried potatoes. They ordered sandwiches to go and another cup of coffee to take with them. Hank put it all on the American Express card.

"Ah, good, very good. I feel prepared to face what's in store for us now. Breakfast and lunch is my treat. Thanks for sharing with me yesterday."

"You didn't have to do that, Hank."

"I know. I wanted to do it."

"Well thanks," Pete said.

"Yeah, thanks a lot," Joe and Jim chimed in as they climbed back in to head toward the jobsite.

They barely saw each other all day. At lunch time, the only one Hank was able to locate was Jim. He didn't have any idea where the other two had been assigned.

"I don't think I can take much more of this," Hank said.

"I know where you're coming from, man, but just think about the money. Keep your mind on what they're paying you and it'll be easier to go through the torture."

"You're right. Besides, what other choice do we have."

They seemed to have barely sat down on the ground so they could eat when it was time to get back to work.

"Here we go again," Jim groaned.

"Catch you later."

By the end of the day, Hank knew there was no way he would make it through three months of this tortuous labor. He was so exhausted, his muscles strained to the limit and his body unable to follow his simplest command. At lunch he had eaten, but was way too exhausted to enjoy the food, now all he could think of was the unlimited work that still laid ahead. This, he thought, was more physical than the exercises he had to do for basic training. But finally it was over for another day.

"Hank, you still up to checking out the apartments?"

"No, but I will," he responded to Pete's question.

Joe and Jim had joined them and were waiting when they walked into the parking lot.

Hank leaned against the building wall for support while they discussed plans before rushing to the hotel to shower and change clothes. They decided to eat after they had seen the two apartments. When they were on their way out, the desk clerk stopped them.

"Gentlemen, can I see you for a moment?"

Hank walked ahead to the front desk, reaching into his pocket for his American Express card as he went, pretty sure he knew what was coming.

Trying to make casual conversation, the desk clerk started, "Good afternoon, gentlemen. Are you enjoying your stay?"

Four heads bobbed up and down.

"Well, we're glad to have you here." He paused as if hesitate to make his next statement. "Gentlemen, I was wondering if you plan on staying tonight. We're really booked up and need to know when the rooms will be available.

"Well, quite honestly, we don't know for sure," Hank replied, silencing the others. "But we should have a better idea this evening."

"That will be find, Mr. Sanders. I hope you don't take offense to my asking."

"No, not at all. We understand. We'll be able to tell you more when we come back this evening."

"Thank you, Mr. Sanders."

"We will be staying tonight. Here's my card. You can put the charge for the extra room on this." He paused, then remembering added, "And you may as well include the charges for last night's food and beer."

The desk clerk smiled. "This will only take a minute."

With his card back in his pocket, Hank joined the others, explaining as they went out the door to go check out the two apartments. By now, they were all anxious to figure out less expensive living conditions and were not picky about what they ended up with. Just so long as it was reasonably priced. Their one objective was to have the location as near to the job site as possible. Outside of that, they were ready to settle for anything.

The first apartment was worse than expected and they left feeling despondent that they would find the same situation at the next. They had chosen the two because of the prices and were beginning to think that maybe they'd have to settle on a higher price. This apartment could barely be called that. It was really a large room with four cots posing as beds, a stove and refrigerator and a closet for a bathroom.

As they drove silently to the next address that was located in the same neighborhood, they weren't too optimistic as they passed through the area. It was all run down and filthy. They turned on the street were the next apartment was located and were immediately surprised to see an improvement in the neighborhood. The houses seemed better kept up, not luxurious by any means, but promising. As they climbed out to inspect the place, they all had their fingers crossed.

They rang the bell and were welcomed by what seemed to be a nice elderly man who explained the apartment was the other side of the house. Together they followed him as he walked them to the door and unlocked it.

It was two floors, all newly painted The furniture was old, but in good shape as they glanced around. As they followed the man, who introduced himself as Mr. Henderson, they were pleased. It had three bedrooms, livingroom, bathroom, and kitchen. Mr. Henderson explained that the sofa in the livingroom converted to a bed as well. Before they adjourned to Mr. Henderson's side of the building, they were in agreement. The price was right and it could be rented by the month. It was in walking distance to the job site which meant they wouldn't have to worry about the expense of parking in New York City. It was really to good to be true.

"We'll take it."

"Fine," Mr. Henderson said. Let's fill out the papers."

When the papers were completed, Hank handed them to their new landlord.

"When do you want to move in?"

"Well, can we plan on this weekend."

"No problem. I'll need a deposit and the first month's rent."

"Sure, how much will that be?"

"Twelve hundred dollars in all."

Pete tried not to grimace as he heard this. He asked if they could discuss this alone and Mr. Henderson nodded and left the room.

"What do you think," Pete asked no one in particular.

"Well, I can put it on my VISA. We get paid next Friday." Hank said, thinking out loud. "You guys can pay me back then for the hotel expenses and then we'll have the rest of the month to settle on the apartment cost."

"I don't see any problem with that," Pete said. "How about you guys?"

"No, I can manage that," Joe said.

"Me too."

"Okay, that's settled."

Hank walked over to the door that Mr. Henderson had walked through and called, "Mr. Henderson, we've reached an agreement."

Mr. Henderson gladly accepted Hank's VISA and after running it through the machine, placed the receipt in front of Hank for his signature. Once the financial arrangements were out of the way, they shook hands.

"Welcome men. I hope you find the apartment satisfactory."

"I think we will, Mr. Henderson."

"I'll expect next month's rent on the first."

"That will be find."

With nothing left to do, Joe, Pete, Jim and Hank left and went off to find some place to eat. They stopped at the first McDonalds along the way and once their trays of food were in front of them, no one spoke.

They were ravenous as they bit into their hamburgers and pushed french fries into their mouths. With just the crumbs remained, they talked about their good fortune in finding the apartment and how much easier it would be to handle their expenses with the rent split four ways. They considered the savings of being able to eat in and being in walking distance to work and they agreed they had been lucky.

"Well, this calls for a celebration!" Joe said to the group.

"What did you have in mind?" Pete asked.

"I know," chimed in Hank. "Since we'll be living here, why not check out the bar we passed on our way. I believe it's right on the corner."

They were all in agreement, their fatigue forgotten for the moment as they left the van at McDonalds and walked down to the bar. It was called The Frog Pond. Upon surveying the premises they recognized a few guys from the jobsite and went over to join them. They had a couple drinks apiece before finally walking back to get the van and drive to their hotel.

For the first time, Hank felt bad about putting so much on the American Express card, but he really had no choice. The money Skye had given him would have to hold him until next Friday and that was a long ways away. He sent the others up to the room while he went to the front desk.

"Sir," Hank said. "We've found an apartment."

"I'm happy for you," was the response.

"We can move in on Friday, so if you can tell me how much we owe, I'll pay it all now."

"Certainly. I'll just be a minute."

While Hank waited he thought about putting it on the VISA then rejected the idea. The VISA was only in his name. If he put it on the American Express he was sure Skye would have to help him pay it. He told himself that he'd give her the money as soon as he had it so it wasn't that big a deal. Yet the amount was quite a bit and it would have to be paid right away. What if he needed the card again? All this went through his head while he waited. When the desk clerk returned, Hank handed him the American Express card, sure it would get paid and glad he wasn't going to be there when Skye got the bill.

CHAPTER 23

Hank hadn't called. That seemed to be on her mind all day as she handled her work. Several times she scolded herself, knowing it was just like Hank to pull a stunt like this. Say he'd call and then decide to let her sit back and worry. Yet, she was admittedly a worrier and wondered if everything was going okay. She placed a call to the Union.

"Hello, this is Mrs. Sanders. I am inquiring about my husband. Do you know how I can reach him?"

"Mrs. Sanders, do you know where your husband is working? What job site?"

"Yes, he's working for a cable company in New York City. That's all I was told. If he mentioned the company name, I forgot it."

"Well, give me your husband's name and I'll check around and call you back."

Skye left Hank's name with the receptionist and when she hung up the phone she felt a lot better and found the matter move to the back of her mind as she worked throughout the rest of the day.

She was tired when she finally decided to call it quits, feeling not only achy from sitting so long, but her stomach was screaming for food. She hadn't eaten all day. She shut down the office and went searching through the refrigerator for something to eat, realizing she had used most of what was left to fix Hank's snacks for his trip.

That thought made her angry. The Union hadn't called back and she still didn't know if he were alive or dead. Why didn't he extend her the same courtesy she had extended to him in helping him get ready for his journey? But she knew the answer. He wasn't the type to wonder if anyone was worried about him, and why should he think that she'd be worried, especially with the way things were between them!

She managed to put the matter aside while she got herself some crackers and opened a can of soup. She found herself wondering about Hank again as she carried the food into the family room where she sat the dish on the tv while she turned on the set. Retrieving her food, she moved over to the couch and sat eating and watching the news. When she was done, she carried everything back into the kitchen, cleaned up and was on her way back to the family room when she decided to check her calendar.

Skye went into her office and flipped on the light, for the first time realizing it was getting late. Chances were that she'd not hear from the Union now. She grabbed her calendar and looked at the following day. Her shocked surprise showed on her face. She had almost forgotten!

Penciled in on Thursday at one o'clock was the name, Johnson D'Angelo and Smith. It had come up on her so suddenly she had almost forgotten that her appointment with the lawyer had been scheduled for the following day.

"How could I have forgotten!" she mused, upset with herself. Getting around to finally call a lawyer had been a stepping stone in the right direction and here she had almost forgotten all about it! She put the calendar down and realized she was shaking. This was a big step she was taking, she thought to herself, but one she had to take.

The idea scared her, but she didn't know why. She wanted the divorce and wanted it all to be behind her. This was the first step in making it happen. So why did it frighten her?

Skye turned off the light and went back into the family room. There was a movie on, but she paid no attention as she continued to think about the upcoming meeting. What would she say? What would he ask? She had no idea. She got up again and went into the kitchen. Standing my the sink she continued to work through the next day, wondering about it and how such a matter was handled. After a time she forced herself to stop worrying and got a glass of water before returning to the family room to sit and stare at the tv screen. At eleven thirty she turned the television off and leaving the light on, went back through the kitchen and into the bedroom where she undressed and climbed into bed to fall into a troubled sleep.

***

The first thing Skye sees when she enters the lawyer's office is Hank. He sits in an oversized burgundy leather chair in front of the lawyer's desk, turning to look at her with a sense of confidence as she enters. "Hello, Skye," he says easily.

"Hank?" Her hands smooth the front of her most expensive suit to hide the shaking of her hands. He shouldn't be here, she thinks while trying to stifle the urge to run from the expensively furnished room. Who had told him about her appointment, anyway? All this goes through her head before the lawyer addresses her.

"Come in Skye. Please take a seat. I've just been talking with your husband." A knowing smile passes between them.

"I just bet you have," she says under her breath. "Oh, and what has Hank been telling you?" she says in a voice coated with sarcasm.

"Now Skye, calm down and stop acting paranoid. The good man and I are old drinking buddies." Seeing the surprise on her face Hank adds, "Yes, I do have friends in high places that I meet for a drink now and then." He looks at the lawyer who shakes his head, agreeing with Hank.

Skye looks from one to the other, her face frozen with anger. Well isn't that just grand. I have chosen a man to represent me who is best buddies with my husband. Isn't that just my luck.

"Well, shall we get started. First, I would like to stress that we'll accomplish more if we all act like civilized adults. I think we should begin..."

"No, wait a minute. First I'd like to know why Hank is here. I don't want him here.."

"Now Mrs. Sanders, he's here because the matter concerns him also. He's here because you think you want a divorce."

I think! Did he actually say, I think I want a divorce.

Brokenly she says, "I want him out of here, now!"

"I'm in charge of this proceeding and you are sitting in my office and you will listen to what I have to say. Is that understood?"

She screamed and screamed, holding her face between her hands. And she kept on screaming.

***

Her eyes flew open. After a momentary look of horror, she lay back on the pillow. She was soaked with perspiration and the bed covers were twisted around her body, hampering her movements. She shifted back and forth until finally she was able to loosen the envelope of coverings so she could sit up. She tucked her knees up against her chest.

Skye felt as though she couldn't breathe, her throat closing as she managed to get out of bed and open the window a bit. She stood there taking deep breathes, clutching her neck with her head raised, sucking in air until she was revitalized and calmed.

"You're crazy, you know that! You're a real basket case!" She attempted to laugh, only it came out funny and far from convincing as she again sat up in bed with her knees clutched tight against her. Slowly she unfolded her body and slipped out of the bed one more time. She moved slowly, flipping on the hall light as she made her way into the kitchen. She removed a glass from the cabinet and carried it to the refrigerator where she pushed it against the water dispenser on the door until she had a full glass of water. She took a big gulp, feeling the pain of the chilled water as it went down her throat .

She was very dry as she finished the glass of water and fixed herself another before going back to her bedroom. She lay down under the covers wondering. Was this a premonition of what was to come or just a silly nightmare. She didn't have the answer. Her body calmed on it's own as she thought how silly she was acting. She knew she had been dreaming and there was no reason to assume something as insane as her dream would happen. Hank wasn't even in town and that, plus the fact he had no way of knowing what she was up to made her even more sure she was acting paranoid. A calmness settled over her then and she turned on her side, allowing herself to relax until finally she drifted off to sleep, not waking until the alarm went off the following morning.

***

"Damn," he said when he finally felt it was safe to come out of the closet. That had been a close one. Sam stood for a moment listening intently before he allowed himself to step into the den. There he remained, with ears perked listening for a sound of danger and when it didn't come, he walked boldly across the floor and back to the utility closet. Not wasting any time he finished changing the tapes in the wiretaps that Hank had set up, then went into the rec room to complete the job.

All was still in the house while he worked. He opened the video camera and removed the tape, anxious to get out while the getting was good. That had been a close call. He had heard the screaming and that had set him on his heels, forgetting his bearings and running in the wrong direction before finally remembering the closet, off the den where he moved swiftly, but silently to the door. Turning the handle ever so gently so he could stop if it let out any sound, he finally managed to get the door open and stepped inside.

It was dark in the closet and he had to lift each foot up carefully then slowly place it down in the over packed room of supplies. She had a lot of stuff stashed in a small area, he thought menacingly, as he proceeded careful not to knock anything over. Finally he was able to move cautiously forward. When he was in as far as he could get he knew that if she happened to come down and open the door he was a sitting duck as there was nothing to hide behind. He cursed himself for not taking the time beforehand to check the closet out.

He had remained there, afraid to turn on the light. He had heard her footsteps as she walked across the floor upstairs and kept hoping she'd not decide to come downstairs as, in his haste, he had left the closet door open. He barely allowed himself to breathe as he crouched down among the boxes of supplies that left his head sticking above them. He was afraid that any movement would send off an avalanche of stuff that would surely alert her and he wasn't prepared, at least this time. When he finally heard her footfalls going back in the direction of the bedroom he held his breath, not moving until the silence continued. He had to make sure she was really retiring for the night before he dare leave the closet.

Now all he wanted to do was finish his job and get out of there, but he had to do something first. He went back into the den, opened the closet and turned on the light. What he saw was several boxes piled on top of each other. Off to the left were shelves with smaller boxes of pens, erasers, paper clips and staples. He looked toward the back as he moved into the closet. As he leaned over the stack of boxes that he had crouched behind, he saw that the wall jutted out to the left. Quietly he lifted boxes, shuffling them around so that his pathway would be safe. If this happened again, he could hide by flattening himself up against that wall. Satisfied, Sam carefully turned off the light in the closet and then reentered the rec room. He looked over at the utility room checking to be sure he had indeed closed the door, then he silently proceeded up the stairs.

He was like a lion stalking his prey, his feet falling precisely in the center of each step and lifting up slowly so as not to make a sound as he made his way up. Just before the landing he froze, listening carefully for the least little sound before stepping up, turning to his right and making his way across the family room to the front door where he moved the curtain back to look out.

Everything seemed quiet. The lights were out in all the houses that he could see through the window, but he waited a bit longer. He moved the curtain back and reached in his pocket for a lighter which he flicked on and held up momentarily before moving it back out of sight. He watched. Nothing. He did the same thing again. There it was.

The car across the intersection blinked it's headlights, then all went dark again. That was the signal it was okay to come out. Sam turned the knob and let himself out. He moved swiftly down the street until he was back at his car. Not until he climbed in did he allow himself to breathe normally. As careful as he had been, he neglected to notice another car that sat watching the premises.

CHAPTER 24

The next morning Skye woke trembling with nostalgia and a touch of fear. From the moment she woke she had a strange sensation of something not being quite right. Try as she did, she couldn't shake it. Her only anodyne was work and Skye immersed herself in it totally so that she had no time to think about anything except work before the appointment with the lawyer. She pledged not to let some dream set her off on a tizzy as she worked non-stop until it was time to get ready for the appointment.

It was a warm spring day outside and Skye decided to dress appropriately, choosing a beige skirt that was softly full, and a silk blouse open just enough so as not to appear matronly. Her auburn hair was worn down and slightly curling around her face. Her choice in clothing and hair style gave her the appropriate effect of being a serious person. It also served to flatter her green eyes. On a whim she clasp a gold chain around her neck, added a pair of sensible size earrings and a spray of perfume. When she was done she glanced with open admiration at her reflection before she finally left the house.

It was a lovely day for a drive. Skye turned on the car radio and tried to forget her nervousness about the meeting facing her. She felt as though she were floating, soaring as she drove down the familiar streets of her neighborhood and on to the expressway. The scenery turned from interesting to bland as she sped along the open road. She tried to thing about her schedule and when that failed, what she needed to pick up at the grocery store, but was only able to think about her own uncertainties. Would she be staying in that house? Almost certainly not, for Hank would hardly agree to that after she had left him. So there would be a new place to prepare. Should it be around here where she had established herself, or would it be better to move to another area of the city? She couldn't supply an answer. And then there loomed the larger, ominous problem; the severance itself. She had no experience at all with the law. How exactly did one go about this divorce thing?

It felt as though a swirling cloud of doubt had descended around her, becoming more menacing as she continued. The ideas going through her head only increased her worry until she found herself wishing that a genie would appear and release her anxiety by the granting of one wish. She wish it was all over!

The expressway curved to the left and Skye barely managed to guide the car without going over into the next lane, occupied by other fast moving vehicles. That put her mind on her driving as she realized this stretch of the expressway was unfamiliar to her. She was not often in this part of town, she thought as she watched out the window to observe the names of the streets. She was able to recognize a few, but wasn't sure when her exit would appear so she watched until it was safe to move into the right lane. Two exits down she saw the street she was looking for and at that precise moment a cloud passed over the sun, and she thought silently. "God, help me."

She saw the building ahead and turned on her signal. Bright color spring flowers were planted in front of the red brick office building, lining the sidewalk. Skye admired them as she sat in her car thinking. The truth was, she was afraid. How was it that she, determined to do this, was so scared? She did know the answer. She didn't want to face life alone. She wasn't old, but not that young any more and she knew she didn't want to live without love. She tried to shake the feeling. "I'm forty-two, and I have my business, a level head on my shoulders and enough determination in my soul to make it." That seemed to suffice as she finally climbed out of the car and entered the building.

The building was one of several, set up to resemble a small community. Inside the lobby was a billboard with names and floors. She walked over and studied it for a moment before walking over to the elevator that arrived immediately to take her to her destination. She found herself wishing she had chosen her black suit instead of the simple ensemble she now wore. When the elevator opened she walked nervously to the glass door stenciled Johnson, D'Angelo & Smith. She stood in the hallway, composing her face and took a deep breath before finally entering and walking up to the receptionist.

"I'm here to see Mr. D'Angelo."

The blonde young woman who sat in the reception area had been painting her nails. Skye knew this before the lady started blowing on her fingers, because she could smell the polish. The woman carefully inspected each of her nails before raising her head to smile radiantly at her visitor. And with a slight apologetic expression she managed a more professional demeanor.

"I have an appointment with Mr. D'Angelo," Skye said, feeling a little put off having to repeat herself. As if to emphasize her statement, she quickly glanced at the nameplate on the desk and added, "Ms. Washington."

Myrna Washington, as a name, didn't seem to fit the blonde whatsoever. The name had a professional air of matronly experience that this young woman seemed to lack as she shifted her gaze over to the appointment book on the corner of her desk. Skye watched as she picked up a pen, careful not to smudge her freshly painted nails, and crossed off the name, before finally turning back to Skye.

"Wait here, Ms. Saunders, while I go tell Mr. D'Angelo you've arrived."

"Excuse me, that's Mrs. Sanders."

"Sorry," Myrna replied meekly as she got up from her chair. "I'll only be a minute.

Skye watched her progression. Myrna was wearing the tiniest leather skirt imaginable with what was at least three-inch heels. She walked with a flounce that had her long shining hair bouncing with each step she took. Skye thought of a lot of things she would like to tell this woman about proper office attire and had to hold her tongue when Myrna finally motioned her over to the door.

She didn't know what to expect as she stepped across the threshold of the lawyer's office, but was pleased to see it looked as it should. There were law books behind the desk, a large picture window that let in a lot of natural light, sensible furnishings and the type of furniture that she had seen in Mr. Maglioni's office, just not as impressive. Her survey was interrupted by Myrna.

"How do you take your coffee?"

Ignoring the fact she hadn't been asked if she wanted any, Skye replied, "Black will be fine. Thank you, Ms Washington." Her attention turned as she heard a deep baritone voice addressing her now.

"Well, we finally get a chance to meet, Mrs. Sanders. Please have a seat." Mr. D'Angelo motioned toward the chair in front of his desk and suddenly Skye recalled who had been there in her dream.

"Are you all right?"

"What? Oh, yes, I'm fine." She gave her host a smile as she reached out to shake his hand before she sat down. Mr. Pierce D'Angelo moved back behind his desk while she observed that he was quite tall, probably around six foot, three. He had a slender frame, long thin fingers like a pianist, and a sincere smile. His complexion was dark giving the impression he had been visiting the tanning booths or had just recently returned from a vacation in the sun. He sported a well trimmed moustache over his thin upper lip, and that as much as his aquiline nose gave a stern look to his rather pleasant face. The greetings out of the way, he was all professional now as he addressed her.

"Mrs. Sanders, can you tell me a little about yourself and your marriage. I need to get a feel for the situation so I can determine how to best serve you."

"I don't know what to tell you."

"Well for starters, why do you want a divorce?"

"I want a divorce because I am unhappy with my marriage."

"Okay, that's a start. How are you unhappy."

Skye thought for a moment before answering. "I no longer love my husband, and we haven't lived like a married couple for a long time. He sleeps in one bedroom while I occupy another. I just don't want to continue living like this any longer."

"How long have you been married?"

She dreaded that question, but knew it was surely going to be asked. Taking a deep breath she replied. "We've been married twenty years. It'll be twenty-one years, the end of June."

The lawyer leaned back in his chair, his eyes focused on Skye. "That's a long time."

"I know it is, plenty of time to know exactly what I want out of life." Her words came tumbling out. "I have tried to love him, understand him, but I just can't. He is an enigma that cannot be solved. One minute he acts like anybody else, the next it is impossible to figure what planet he's from. He goes into moods, drinks heavily and treats me like a possession instead of a human being. I have had enough, and don't want to be married to him any longer. She stopped to take a breath before continuing. "Living with him is like being on a roller coaster that keeps going round and round and never gets anywhere. Nothing I can do will ever change that and I want off!"

"Well," Mr. D'Angelo said, "That's a pretty interesting summation of your situation."

Is that all he can say, Skye wondered as she stared with surprise. "Mr. D'Angelo, I'm here because I want to divorce my husband."

"I know that Mrs. Sanders, and I'm here to help you. Do you have any idea of how you want the divorce to proceed?"

"What? I don't know what you mean," she said bewildered.

"What is it you want out of this marriage?

"Oh, yes, I just want what's mine. I don't want alimony, I mean, maintenance is what you call it now, I think. There's no need for any child support as our son is twenty-one years old. If I can count on Hank for anything it will be to continue to help our son through college. No one needs to push that issue."

"Well, that seems pretty thorough, but what about your home. Have you given that any thought? I assume your son grew up in your home and you might want to stay there so that he has a place to stay when he comes to visit. You need to look to the future and not just the present when you make a decision for a divorce, especially since you've been married so long."

"I've thought about it from a future perspective as well. We have debts that need to be paid off and selling the house will clear us of any debts so that both of us gets a fresh start. And that's what I want, a fresh start. I can't do that living in that house. I detest the house and I don't want any part of it. As for my son, I'll always have a place for him to stay."

"Maybe we should think this thing through again. You are putting yourself out on the street and starting anew without any support from your husband of twenty years? That's not a sane alternative unless you have money stashed away to take care of all your needs."

Skye had to stifle a laugh. Sure she had a stash, quite a big one that would keep on building as long as she was capable of running the business. Trying for a serious demeanor, she sat up straighter in her chair and carefully replied.

"I understand you are only looking out for my best interest, but I am an adult and I have a business that will support me just fine. I want you to handle the divorce as a fair and equitable settlement. We sell the house, pay off the debts, and then split the proceeds."

Silence loomed in the room and Skye found herself fidgeting in her chair.

"Mrs Sanders, you've come to me to represent you and I want to represent you in the best way I can. I think you need to reconsider your position." Seeing her personification changing, he quickly added, "For your own sake. I've handled a lot of divorces and I know how wanting to sever the ties can take precedence over the future, which is why people seek legal advice. This is a very trying time for you and I want to make it less trying later on down the road."

"Listen," Skye said impatiently. "I know I want a divorce. I want it to be quick, painless and uncomplicated. Whatever that means from a legal point of view is how I want you to proceed."

"Your mind seems to be made up, Mrs. Sanders." She could hear the disagreement in his voice, before she knew what she was doing, she reacted to his last statement.

"Yes, it has!" Skye got up from the chair and walked over to Mr. D'Angelo's desk and extended her hand. "I want to thank you for your time and patience with me."

Mr. D'Angelo looked at Skye, shocked. "I want you to understand I have listened to all you've said and I would like to represent you."

"I appreciate that."

Skye managed a little smile before turning to walk out of his office, wondering where to go from here. When she finally climbed into her car there were tears of frustration in her eyes and she laid her head on the steering wheel. She stayed like that for sometime before putting the matter aside and backing out of the parking lot. She'd just have to find another lawyer. As she drove by the lines of parked cars she thought she saw one she recognized, but she was too upset to take a second look.

Back on the expressway she realized she was no further ahead than when she first got up this morning and that upset her tremendously. She had waited for this one appointment with this one lawyer, only to have it come to naught. Even more upsetting was that she would probably run into a lot of others that felt the same way as Mr. D'Angelo.

Skye sighed deeply, trying to quiet her emotions so she could think clearly. She still needed a lawyer and she was not in the mood to wait another week for an appointment. There had to be someone out there who would listen and do as she asked and she needed to find him, or her. She needed to find that lawyer now.

Skye was surprised to find herself pulling into her own driveway. Without hesitating she climbed out of the car without pulling it into the garage, and headed toward the family room door, already searching her purse for her key. Fumbling, she couldn't seem to get the key in the lock. Finally, she managed to seat it and entered, feeling impatient to begin.

She wanted to start making phone calls but forced herself to think the matter through. So, what do I do? When she couldn't come up with anything, Skye reviewed her alternatives. She could call all the lawyers she scribbled down in the "Z" section of her address book or start calling from the list in the phone book, starting with "A" until she found someone. Both seemed time-consuming and with no guarantee on finding the lawyer who would follow her wishes.

Skye stood there in the family room for fifteen minutes until she resolved there was only one sure fire method to use right now and that was to contact the friends who went through a quiet divorce. That at least seemed to offer some guarantee--the individuals had settled for a hushed, if not fair divorce, and the lawyer might be one who would listen to her demands.

Now the problem was how to go about getting what she needed. If the friend didn't want to talk about their divorce back then, what made her think they would talk to her about it now? "Darn," she said. "Must I always make myself feel defeated before I begin!"

That got her going. Skye walked into the kitchen, stopping to heat up the last of the morning coffee, pouring it into her mug and placing it in the microwave. Then when it was ready she carried it into her office to sit at her desk.

She looked pensively off into the distance, hesitantly wondering if she was doing the right thing. Shaking it off, she picked up the phone and started dialing the number of Sue Walker. It rang only once before the line was picked up.

"Hello."

"Hi. Is this Sue?"

"Skye?

"Yes, it's me."

"How have you been?"

"Just fine. And you?"

"Just the same, nothing new to report."

"Sue, I need to ask you something."

"Sure, what is it?"

"I hate to ask so bluntly, but I don't know how else to do this." Skye took a deep breath then plunged ahead. "Can you tell me about your divorce and the lawyer you used."

Silence. Skye reprimanded herself thinking; so much for tact.

Sue was taken aback, not hurt, but surprised by the question itself. She wanted to ask Skye what had possessed her to bring this up now, some five years after the divorce, but as she listened she could hear Skye breathing. It sounded like the breathing exercises you do to relax yourself. No, Skye wasn't up to questioning. Pulling herself together, Sue responded.

"What is you want to know, exactly?"

"Anything you want to tell me."

"Well, the lawyer got me the house, full medical coverage, alimony, support for the kids. The whole nine yards."

Skye let the news sink in and found herself not wanting to take a chance.

"Thanks Sue, you've been very helpful."

"But, Skye..."

"I'll call you back later, okay?"

"Okay, but..."

"Talk to you soon." Skye hung up the phone.

Can't expect everything on the first try, she said to herself and started dialing again. She waited for Barb Sartin to answer.

"Hello?"

"Hello Barb, this is Skye."

"Well, how the hell are you?"

Barb was a talker, and she knew not to get her started. She ignored the question and dropped the bomb shell.

"Barb, I want to know about your divorce."

"What?" Barb was lost.

"I'm sorry, Barb, but I just need to get some information quick. Please, can you tell me how your lawyer handled your divorce?"

Barb was astonished by the blunt request, but a bell went off in her head. Skye was going to do the big "D" finally. Well good for her.

"Barb," Skye said impatiently.

"Hold your horses and let me catch up," Barb responded lightly. "My lawyer was a dreamboat to say the least. Under different circumstances, I might have made a play for him. But you don't want to hear that. You want to know if he was a good lawyer. He was. He had me actually enjoying the divorce. I walked away that day feeling like my ex had gotten just what he deserved for all those years of misery." Barb laughed. "Nothing!"

Strike two, Skye thought.

"Well, thanks, Barb..."

Barb interrupted. "Skye? If you want to call him you're going to need his name and number. Don't be in such a hurry!"

"No, not right now. Listen, I'll have to call you back, okay?"

"Sure, but..."

Again, Skye rudely hung up the phone as she whispered, "Sorry, Barb."

She could feel the frustration growing as she looked at the last number left to dial. Stephen Jenkins, her friend, her last hope she thought as she looked at the name. If this didn't pan out, she'd have to think of another alternative. Slowly she dialed the seven numbers. It rang once, twice, three times before the connection was made.

"Hello?"

"Stephen? This is Skye."

"Oh, hi, Skye. Can you hold on a minute?"

Before she had a chance to answer, she could hear Stephen talking to someone in the background. She prayed silently, "Please let this be it, please!"

"Sorry, Skye. I hate to be short, but I'm pretty busy here. If it's not urgent, can I call you back?"

"I'll be quick, Stephen." She inhaled. "Can you tell me about your divorce?"

"Quick, you said, well I must agree with that!" He had to prepare himself after the shock of her blunt request. "That is some question to be quick about. I wish I had time to ask some of my own, but, here goes. His name was Mitchell Cayman. He's a straightforward kind of guy, real pleasant, quite likeable and a good listener. I mean he listens to what you have to say and asks questions, then he does what it takes to get you the kind of divorce you're looking for."

Stephen paused, then adds, "Is that enough, Skye?"

Skye was still working on the lawyer's name, Mitchell Cayman, Mitch Cayman. Could it be the same person? Cayman wasn't a real common last name, and both named Mitch!

"Skye, come on, I haven't got all day?"

"What? Oh, yes, that's exactly what I wanted to hear. Thanks."

"Wait a minute, don't you want the phone number."

She was pretty sure she wouldn't need it, but said, "Okay."

"Hang on a second."

While she waited she flipped to "C" on her office directory and looked down to the name, Mitch Cayman.

"Here it is, Mitchell Cayman, four-six-seven-one-two-one-two?"

"Bingo!"

"What did you say?"

"Oh, nothing, Stephen, but I'd better let you go so you can get back to what you were doing."

"Not so fast. Promise you'll be in contact later and ready to give me some details?"

"Of course I will, now get back to work!"

Skye leaned back, smiling. At that moment she was sure her search was over. Not only that, but also she felt confident she would be successful in persuading him to see her soon, possibly even today. The name could have been a coincidence, but the phone number, never! Stephen's lawyer was the man she had been working with on the transcript job. "What luck!" She said joyously.

Still gazing at the phone, she said, "Mitch Cayman." She visualized him sitting behind a desk and a shiver went down her spine. "Jeez, pull yourself together!"

She snatched the phone from the cradle, punched buttons hurriedly. Twisting the cord and biting her tongue she forced herself to turn her mind elsewhere as she waited.

"Mr. Cayman's office, Stephanie speaking, how can I help you?"

The pleasant voice of the receptionist seemed to run the words together.

"Hello, this is Skye Sanders, an associate of Mr. Cayman's. May I speak with him, please?"

"Can I tell him what this is concerning?"

This time she was patient and not because she had gone through the routine before. "Sure, I would like to discuss my divorce with him."

"Oh, I see." Skye could hear the identifiable sound of someone flipping through cards and she decided to save her some time. "Stephanie, I'm not a client of his, yet, but I'd like to talk to him if he's available."

The sound stopped. "Sure, just let me check for you. The name was Skye Sanders?"

"That's right."

"Please hold the line, Mrs. Sanders."

There was a click, followed by the melody of a love song playing in the distance. She played the memory game, trying to guess the singer and the name of the song while she hung on the line.

"Mrs. Sanders, this is Mr. Cayman."

"Hello, Mr. Cayman. I don't know if you remember me..."

"Sure I do. Nice looking redhead, about five-four, five-five, with green eyes and unbelievable skills in preparing transcripts. Am I right?"

There was merriment in her voice as she complimented him on matching the face with the name.

"Well, is there a problem or is this a social call?"

"Well, I need a lawyer and I'd like to see if you have time to handle a divorce."

"Whose divorce are we talking about?"

Skye answered truthfully, "Mine."

"I see," Mitch said thoughtfully. "Well then, would you like to set up an appointment to come in, Mrs. Sanders?"

"Today?" she said meekly.

"It's short notice, but let me see."

The line remained open and Skye could hear the sound of him buzzing his secretary, his voice as he asked her to check the calendar, and his okay as he disconnected that line. "It looks like I do have some time available today. Can you be at my office by three?"

A smile spread from her mouth to her eyes and they radiated. Her eyes filled with tears and she could not answer right away. Very low, she finally replied. "Thank you. Thank you, Mr. Cayman. I'll be there at three."

"Do you know how to get here?"

She looked at the address on his card. "Sure, I know exactly where it is."

"Fine, I'll see you at three then."

She thanked him again and was about to hang up when he spoke.

"Don't hang up, Mrs. Sanders," he said with amusement. I'm going to put my secretary on the line so you can give her some information. It'll save us time, later."

"Okay."

Again the music replaced the voice, then she was connected to the secretary. She patiently answered the questions she asked and gave the spelling of her name, the address and the phone number before finally putting down the phone.

Although her heart was still pounding, she was beginning to recover and take command of herself when the phone rang. She picked it up.

"Computer Systems Unlimited. Skye Sanders speaking."

There was no reply.

"Hello, this is Skye Sanders."

Still silence. Skye seemed unconcerned as she allowed her gaze to fall on the window and she got up from the desk to stretch the cord so she could glance out. The sun shone brightly, twinkling off the hood of the car sitting directly across the intersection. She started to look away but something stopped her. Carefully she put the phone down and moved cautiously closer to the window. She stood to the side so that she couldn't be observed from the street and stared hard. She could see the man now. He had on a baggy shirt and was undoing the top three buttons, most of his skin was the color of spoiled milk. Strands of white hair adhered to his pasty, moist forehead. The face below was long and sallow, wide and flabby. He had white eyebrows and his eyes were staring directly at her window. She took several steps to the side. Slowly she moved across the room and picked up the phone. "Hello?" Again there was no reply, shaking, she hung it up.

The paranoia set in. She fought hard to keep from shaking and slowly calmed. Then the feelings came back again. She wrapped her arms around her body and attempted to laugh, to compose herself, only she couldn't see it as humorous. The man was watching the house. Why she did not know, but there was no doubt he was watching. With effort she forced herself away from the window and back to her desk. Was he just watching the house, or was he watching her? There was one way she'd find out.

Quickly Skye walked out of the office and into the bedroom, now sure she'd have her answer as she prepared for her appointment with Mr. Cayman. The day was bright and she carefully considered what she would wear, using this as a method to keep her mind off the car. Dark red? No, that would do if it were raining, but it was sunny. Maybe a soft blue would be best. Yes, she said to herself as she reached into the closet and began gathering her clothes. When she was finished dressing, she examined herself from the tips of her matching blue heels to the auburn cap of her shining hair, and was more pleased with herself than she had been in a long time. The tension she felt seemed to enhance her features in a way that was quite appealing. She was still frightened, but the activity of getting ready and the anticipation of seeing Mitch Cayman were overpowering and kept her mind off the situation she had encountered.

A short while later, alone in the kitchen, Skye wondered if he was still out there? She walked to office window, careful to remain unseen and peered out. He was still there. She moved back, turned and looked at the clock on the stove. It was time for her to leave.

She was now visibly shaking again as she walked through the kitchen and into the family room. She was about to open the door when she stopped, retraced her steps and walked to the hall closet to put on her London Fog raincoat. Then she was making her way to the door, checking to make sure it locked before going over to climb into her car. She reminded herself not to look across the intersection.

She backed out of the driveway slowly, pausing at the intersection and heading down her street to the main thoroughfare. She made a left turn onto Calkins, then another left at the light on East Henrietta Road, checking in the rearview mirror at each turn.

He was there, right behind her at a safe distance, but obviously following her. "Okay, keep calm."

She managed to get every light on East Henrietta Road as she made her way to the entrance to the expressway, heading north. At the light before the turn she again caught the light and she sat making up her mind. She was being followed, but she still didn't know why. She knew she didn't want whoever it was to know her destination, toying with the idea that they were spying on her at Hank's command. When the light changed she shot onto the expressway. The traffic was gummy and ill-tempered all the way to Route 490 East and she had a hard time switching lanes in an attempt to lose her pursuer. She kept an eye on the rearview mirror as she drove faster than usual, speeding ahead of cars and switching lanes just in time to make it off the exit of 490.

She chanced another look in the mirror and couldn't find the car, but she was afraid to slow down, continuing to drive as quickly as she dared. When she finally turned off on Monroe Avenue she was sure she had lost him and as luck would have it, she managed to get through the light. Down Monroe, past the public library, the filling station, and passing through the neighborhoods, gave her immediate recall, such as follows a flavor or scent. It brought back the memory of where she had her first apartment, over on Averill Avenue. She had moved from there into the apartment on Union Street where they lived when she and Hank first got married. Hank was a security guard back then, going to school at night to become a private investigator while she worked at Xerox Square. And suddenly it seemed to her that all these memories were somehow linked in ways that she couldn't fathom, that these things had their origin in one place, one time.

The feeling was still with her when she came to the Inner Loop with no sign of her pursuer. She made a right onto the ramp and soon was heading toward downtown. By the time she pulled her car into the parking lot, she had to force herself to drive to the back before entering an empty space. Her heart was pounding in her chest so hard now she could hardly breathe.

Relief and disappointment mingled as she tried to calm herself. In one way she had to know, she wanted to know, but in another way, she dreaded it. Finally she was able to climb out of the car and enter the office building. Once inside she stood for a moment and watched each car that pulled in after her. No car resembling the one she had seen earlier. She continued her surveillance until she was sure she hadn't been followed, and then she turned to check the board for Mitch Cayman's name, climbed the two flights of stairs to the second floor as a precaution and because she felt the exercise would do her good.

When she opened the door to the office, Skye turned around looking for a place to hang her coat. She jumped when she heard a voice, seeming to come from no where.

"May I help you?" The receptionist, noticing Skye's reaction quickly adds, "I'm sorry, I didn't mean to startle you."

"No, I'm sorry, I'm the one who should apologize. I'm just jumpy today. Stephanie, isn't it?"

"Yes. You must be Mrs. Sanders?"

"Yes, I am."

"Why don't you hang your coat here," she said pointing to a door on her left, "and I'll go tell Mr. Cayman you've arrived."

Skye smiled at Stephanie, and placed her coat on a hanger in the closet. She nervously ran her hand down the side of her dress, glad Stephanie hadn't shook hands before she had a chance to wipe the nervous sweat from her fingers. She sat on one of the leather benches in the waiting area and picked up a magazine, pretending interest, while she glanced around.

Vegetation abounded in flower pots, on the three end tables in the reception area, and trees seemed to grow out of the forest green carpet on the floor. The wallpaper was a splash of colors that blended with the cranberry-colored leather benches. Stephanie's desk, directly across from the waiting area, was of dark wood with two similar, dark wood side chairs. The area was much smaller than that of Mr. Maglioni's, but just as impressively decorated.

Skye glanced at the desk plate and saw that Stephanie's last name was Elling. Just then, Stephanie came into her vision as she walked toward the waiting area. Skye watched noting Stephanie had light brown hair, flecked with blond, her skin was a rosy pink, peeking over the high collar of her Kelly-green suit that was buttoned all the way up to the neck. When Skye looked down, she was glad to see that Stephanie's skirt length was just below her knees.

"Mrs. Sanders, if you're ready, I can take you back now."

With a smile, she rose from the bench to follow Stephanie down the short hall to Mr. Cayman's office. She opened the door and stood aside while Skye entered.

"Thank you, Stephanie."

A smile was her reply. Skye looked across the room and watched Mitch Cayman as he came from behind his desk, walking up to her with his hand extended. Nervously she ran her hand down the side of her skirt again, than reached out.

"Hello, Mrs. Sanders, it's a pleasure to see you again."

"Thank you."

"Please, have a seat." Mr. Cayman pointed to a winged back chair that sat close to the front of his desk. Skye sat down, making sure she smoothed the back of her skirt before doing so. Once she was seated, Cayman moved back behind his desk and sat down. His movements were graceful as he kept his attention on Skye.

"Can we get you some coffee?"

If she ever needed a cup, it was now, she thought as she shook her head yes.

"Stephanie."

"Sure. It'll be just a minute." Stephanie closed the door quietly.

"Now, Mrs. Sanders, how have you been?"

"Just fine... No, not fine. I've been okay."

Mr. Cayman's eyebrow raised as he studied her face. "You look a little flustered, maybe I should offer you something stronger."

She could tell he was joking with her. "No, I'll be all right, but I think I have something I ought to share with you." Skye paused. "It may or may not be connected to the divorce..."

At that moment Stephanie entered the office and moving proficiently, set up the table with a decanter of coffee, cream and sugar. Patiently she proceeded to pour two cups, graciously carrying one over to Skye, then setting the other on the desk in front of Mr. Cayman. She performed the duty in silence and when she was done, without a word, turned a round and walked the expanse of the office to the door. Skye watched as she reached behind her and drew the door closed.

Mr. Cayman picked up his cup and with a nod in Skye's direction she continued.

"Let me start at the beginning." With ease she told him that she had been married for twenty years and was disappointed with her marital situation. There were problems that wouldn't go away. Her decision to end the marriage hadn't happened suddenly, but had been maturing for some time until she was finally ready to do something about it. She wanted a divorce, but not because she wanted to hurt Hank. There had been enough hurt during their marriage. All she wanted was to clear up their debts, sell the house and what furnishings neither wanted, then split the income equally. They had one son who had just turned twenty-one. She was confident that Hank would continue to help her with his college expenses without any pressure.

No maintenance, no child support, just a clean severance of the relationship, handled as quickly as possible.

Skye's confidence grew. She had said exactly what she wanted to say. There had been no change in Mr. Cayman's expression, which had her assuming he was not going to disagree with her decision. She waited.

Mitch cleared his throat. "So, sell the lot and keep the cash. No strings, no ties; nothing that would force a connection between you and your husband."

"Yes, I want to make a clear, clean break. In this situation I won't be cheating my son because he is grown and has a good relationship with his dad. For myself, I will take nothing except what's left after the bills and mortgage are paid off. I'm sure you already know I am capable of making my own living from the income of my business." Skye hesitated. "That reminds me. I see the business, the equipment and my car as my private possessions and want them to remain as such."

Mitch shook his head. "Do you know Mrs. Sanders, you are incredible? I can't decide what to think about you."

"I will take that as a compliment, but could you call me Skye?"

"Yes, if you will call me Mitch?"

"Agreed," Skye said smiling.

Mitch looked at Skye so long and hard that she wondered whether it was admiration or pity. Finally sensing he was making her uncomfortable, Mitch smiled.

"I'm sorry, Skye, but I've never had a client like you. But then, I'm not surprised as I thought you were quite unique when I first met you."

Skye only smiled in return. She waited as Mitch pulled a tablet in front of him before looking up to inquire. "I'm going to need some additional information Skye. Where is your husband staying?"

"Well, he still is living in the house, sleeping downstairs in one of the spare bedrooms. It's a large house so we're not always running into each other. But right now he's working in New York City on an extended job."

"Well that gives you some space, assuming your husband is not in agreement with your decision."

"He isn't, but there's nothing he can do to stop me. Is there?"

"Quite frankly, no. Nothing legal, that is." He added the last, hoping Skye would not question him on his meaning until he had a chance to gather other details.

"What you appear to be asking for in a divorce settlement, does not allow your husband any method to delay the proceedings. Whatever happened between the two of you is a personal matter." He seemed to be organizing his thoughts, then added. "Just a brief statement of your reasons for applying for a divorce is all that's warranted."

Mitch asked her a few more questions about the house, the furnishings, and the date of their marriage. All of this he wrote down. "This should be a very simple matter to conclude," he finally said. "The location of your house is good, but from what you mentioned about the size, you may have trouble selling it. The market is good right now so I really can't say for sure." Seeing the puzzling look of dismay on Skye's face, reassuringly he added. "I mean you need to contact a Realtor as soon as possible. The divorce will stem on the sale of the house."

"Why's that?"

"Because this is joint property that must be resolved before the severance. You either sell it or buy your partner out and take sole ownership. That is the only legal matter that needs to be settled before proceeding with the divorce."

"Okay." So what do you suggest I do in the mean time?"

"Well, for starters, we will set up another appointment. At that time you will need to bring your marriage license, birth certificates, a statement of your holdings, to name a few. I have a list I give to each client that helps them prepare all of this. Stephanie will have a package of information ready for you when we adjourn, so make sure you stop by her desk. She'll also schedule your next appointment."

"I'd like to get this going as soon as possible," Mitch.

"I know. What about your living arrangements? Are you both going to stay in the house until after the divorce? A lot of people do it, but it can get sticky once he is aware you are getting the divorce."

"I can handle it." Skye added directly. "Hank is aware I want a divorce. I already confronted him on that point. With luck this job will keep him occupied while I handle things."

"Skye, I don't want to scare you, but people going through the stages of a divorce tend to change. I don't know your husband. He could be a nice guy now, but that could change in a blink of an eye."

"Believe me, Mitch, I know to be careful. Hank has never threatened me with bodily harm, but mentally he has been abusive. I've seen his reaction when he is backed up against the wall, so know I can expect to see need for caution. No, I am not going at this blindly."

"I'm glad to hear that, Skye. If you're careful and try not to get in each other's way, you can probably expect to see the matter to the end without making major changes until necessary. All I ask is you proceed with care and keep your eyes and ears open."

The turn in the conversation reminded her of what she had been about to say at the beginning of their meeting. "There is something that I would like to tell you, though. Today I realized someone has been watching the house. That same person tried to follow me here, but I was able to lose him. I think I've seen the car before. Once before that I can recall. It was parked in Mr. Maglioni's parking lot the day I dropped off a job."

"What do you think, Skye. Do you think your husband is having you tailed?" She could hear the worry in his voice.

"Possibly." She paused. "Really, I don't know what I think right now. I might as well mention this too. I've had calls lately where I pick up the phone and sometimes I know there is someone on the line, other times it seems there's no connection. On two occasions I was quite sure that there was someone sitting across the intersection watching the house I the evening, too. I've been too busy lately to check it out, but I don't think it is the same person."

"Why do you say that?"

"Well, I'm not well-versed on car models, but the cars are not the same. I haven't been able to get a look at the person driving the other automobile. All I know is it is a dark blue or black. I've noticed it only at night."

"Maybe you had better give a lot of thought to staying in the house. That phone bit might mean your line is being tapped. These are not normal situations, Skye, and definitely not something to fool around with."

"What if I get the licenses nu...?"

"No, don't even think of doing that. I'm pretty sure that whoever is having you watched, even if it is more than one person, they are smart enough to not use their own cars. It might be one person that is watching, just using different automobiles."

"I can't move out, Mitch. My business is there. I'm not going to be scared away and have my business fall apart, too. I need the business and my clients expect to find me there. When I'm ready to move, once the house is sold, I will give my clients plenty of notice so I don't lose them."

"It's your choice, but please be careful and if anything, I mean anything at all seems odd, call me night or day. Here's my home phone number." He grabbed one of his business cards from the desk and quickly scribbled down the number, then with a worried expression he handed across his desk. He held tight to the other end as she reached for it. "Promise me you won't take any chances."

"I promise. If I feel the least bit suspicious about anything, I'll call you."

"You might want to consider having someone stay with you, too. Not only because of the situation, but someone who can give you support and keep you company. If you can think of anybody who can do this, call them, Skye."

Skye stood up. "I will. Believe me, I'm not one to take chances. I enjoy life too much for that."

"Okay. Don't forget to stop by Stephanie's desk on your way out. Mitch came over to Skye and they shook hands, his giving hers a light squeeze before she walked out of the office. Skye scheduled the next appointment with Stephanie and was given the material that Mitch had mentioned, then she was on her way. She saw nothing suspicious as she drove toward home, nothing at all. When she pulled into the driveway, the car was again parked across the intersection. What was he doing there? She tried to ignored the fear building inside her as she waited for the garage door to lift and drove in. Then she let herself into the house. What should she do?

***

Paul Angelino was the closest thing to a friend as one could be to a man like Samuel Stillman. As he sat as his post his mind traverse the past.

They had met at the Pussycat lounge some time back when Paul was on the verge of leaving his wife of seven years, and for good reasons. In just that short span of time, the woman had changed into someone he no longer knew. She had been so sexy when they had first met, the type of woman that deserved a second look. But she had turned into a cow and what was worse, she acted like a cow. No longer did she take the time to fix herself up. Not that it would have done any good. Her boobs sagged, looking like pendulums swinging against her rib cage. The waist that use to be so tiny, now blended into her hips that had spread to a ridiculous size with celluloid extending down to her massive thighs. It actually had made him sick to his stomach to look at her.

He could have put up with her if she hadn't acted so uppity. Along with her physical transformation, she became a nag, always asking where he was going and when he'd be home. And money... Money was her biggest nag! She always had her hand out.

As for himself, he wasn't quite bad. His hair was still thick, if not black any more. His face was fuller, but his body was still in pretty good shape if you overlooked the pouch of his belly. He didn't deserve to have a wife like Madeline and he wasn't about to stay with her. When she said she would make him pay if he tried to divorce her, he saw red. When he met Sam, all that changed.

Sam had convinced him that the only way out was his way. At first he had thought it too extreme, but the more Madeline yelled she'd get even, the more he thought it was fair play. He didn't know how Sam managed it, or if the man had done it on his own. He only knew that Madeline was gone and it had been done in a way that to this day kept the cops searching for the killer.

Now as he sat watching Skye's car go into the driveway, he was wondering if maybe he had lost his touch. He was good at his job and it bothered him when he thought that he had been spotted. Then later when he realized he had lost her he began to worry, giving up the chase and returning to his post. There he wondered some more until finally convincing himself that there were other sane reasons why she had driven like a maniac, the least of them being she knew she was being followed. She ran a business and could have been running late for an appointment or something. That might have been why she had been in such a hurry. Besides he hadn't seen her observing him at all, so he wasn't about to jump to any conclusions.

There was a very good reason he wanted to believe this, too. If he thought she knew she was being tailed, he would have to tell Sam. Of all the things in the world he dreaded, telling Sam that he had been spotted was at the top of the heap. The man could act very threatening, especially when someone might have fucked up. After working for Sam several times before he knew that being pulled off the job was the least of his worries. Sam was not the type to hand out such a mild punishment. No, he decided, he wasn't looking forward to having to tell Sam he had lost her. It would be better for his health if he waited. Why jump the gun now.

He leaned forward over the steering wheel, staring at the windows that faced his way. He couldn't see her in any of them. By the time he leaned back he was quite sure he was right. She wasn't spooked, she was just in a hurry to get somewhere. Of course, not knowing where she had gone wasn't good either, but he had been tailing her long enough to know the places she normally went. Outside of that high-society lawyer guy, Maglioni, which raised Sam's eyebrows when he reported her whereabouts, it was the normal run of the mill job sites and supply houses where he spent boring hours waiting for her to get what she needed to get before making her way back home.

He frowned as he tried to figure out where she might have been, just in case he was asked. It had better be as near the truth as possible since he didn't put it pass Sam to do some detective work on his own. As he stared through the windshield he tried to remember where she normally went when she headed in that direction. Most likely it was somewhere downtown, though he had searched every possible place she had gone before down there and hadn't run across her car. But still, she might have been there and he just hadn't seen her automobile.

It was indeed a possibility. The more he thought about it the easier he felt. It was also a greater possibility that Sam wasn't tailing her. He had his hands full with the jobs the man who had hired him had turned over since he was now out of town. Why would he spend more time trailing the woman when he had Paul to do that? Besides, Sam trusted him and had picked him because he knew he was good. So, why worry?

Paul knew why. The damn bugs in the house might have something on them that would make Sam question him about her whereabouts. That was a real threat! If he didn't want to tell Sam, he had better pray that those tapes didn't have something on them that he should know.

But then, there was a way around that too. He looked at his watch. There were several hours before Sam would be due to change the tapes. He knew about wiretaps, knew them well. He had a small recorder in his trunk. He could sneak in there, grab out a tape and play it back and see if he could come up with something. He could do that. But how, or when would he get the time. The bitch was in there now. He couldn't just stroll in and ask her permission to check the wiretaps.

Then he had it. Sam would check with him first before going in the house. It wasn't that big a deal. He could tell him that she had been moving around all night and that he didn't think it was safe for Sam to go in and change the tapes. He might even offer to do it himself later and give the man a break. Knowing exactly how he would handle it put him at ease now and he concentrated on watching the house.

Evening was ascending as Paul continued his watch. Every now and then he would see Skye walk by a window, but nothing more. He leaned back feeling exhausted from all his thinking. As if in tune to his decision, he noticed lights going on and off throughout the house, making him sense she was restless. He hoped it would continue. It would help support his story if the woman was definitely having a restless evening.

***

Skye was too keyed up to get into her work, besides, it could wait until morning. It was now six and she was anxious to get started, wanted to start gathering the information Mitch requested. She walked over and picked up her briefcase that she had placed over by the office window. She placed it on a chair and opened it to remove the forms Mitch had given her. She stood looking them over, then paced back and forth as she reviewed their contents. Walking over to her desk she laid the forms down and then walked to the filing cabinet, searching for the details she needed.

Her stomach reminded her she hadn't eaten, so she laid the papers on her desk and went into the kitchen to fix herself something to eat. Skye placed the food on the kitchen table and went back into the office to get the form, but decided she needed to relax. Instead she went back into the kitchen and picked up her food, carrying it with her to the family room where she turned on the TV and sat on the couch to eat.

She ate quickly, anxious to begin and unable to relax. When she was done she turned off the light in the family room and went back to the kitchen to rinse her dishes and place them in the dish washer before going back into the office.

Skye sat down at her desk and picked up the papers she had accumulated. She could feel the tension settling in as she leaned over her desk. The words in front of her began to blur and she had a hard time focusing. Suddenly she laid them aside. There was plenty of time for this too. Besides, from what she had read on the forms, she had already started working on most of what he wanted and knew where she had filed the rest. She had two weeks before her next meeting with him and that gave her plenty of time. Besides she was too tired to attend to the matter properly.

At first she wasn't exactly sure what was on her mind until she found herself in the den downstairs studying the bookcase. She had found a good lawyer, one she had some familiarity with, but she still wanted to understand the legalities surrounding a divorce. Her eyes swept across the titles on the bookcase until finally they rested on what she was looking for, a book she had purchased sometime ago that concerned most family legal matters. She had purchased it when they were in the process of looking for a house and had found out some interesting facts. Now she turned to the index of the book and ran her finger down the listing until locating the page she wanted. She flipped the book to the section and started reading aloud.

"Divorce ends all the rights gained by marriage. A divorced spouse no longer has the right to sex, support, or a share of the other's estate when he or she dies. Divorce may be granted on demand if both parties agree that the marriage cannot be salvaged, if one party asserts that the marriage is dead and he or she wants out, or if one person asks for a divorce after certain events.

If a divorce cannot be handled out of court, the spouse who is sued has the right to use one of five defenses. One. Recrimination, which is saying that yes, I'm guilty, but so are you. Two. Provocation; saying you drove me to it. Three. Condonation; when one party says you forgave me at the time, so why are you suing me now? Four. Connivance; when one says, you had a share in causing or promoting my misconduct; you just stood by and let it happen, now you have no right to complain. Lastly, Five. Collusion, which is when one party says to the other, you talked me into helping you trick the court so we'd be granted a divorce, and now I've changed my mind.

Where the court is concerned, whether a divorce goes to court or not, maintenance is actually uncommon. Most divorces are granted without maintenance orders."

Skye was a little surprised by what she was reading, and as she read on she could just about pick which defense Hank would choose. But she needed to know more.

"The first step is to obtain a settlement agreement, which must be signed by both parties and be witnessed by a notary public.

As concerns property settlements, they're governed by either of two sets of rules: Separate-property states that each spouse owns everything he or she held before the marriage and acquired during the marriage. Or, community-property where all property acquired during the marriage is considered equally claimed by each partner, with any property prior to the union being returned to the rightful owner during the division of property at the time of the divorce."

Skye found this section extremely interesting and worth remembering when the time came. She browsed through the rest until she came to a section that sparked her interest even more. She continued to read.

"In New York State you can get a no-fault divorce. That is, you need not show that either party was at fault, but only that there has been an 'irretrievable breakdown' of the marriage."

"Irretrievable breakdown." She repeated the phrase, excitement showing on her face. She could just see herself telling Hank they had an irretrievable breakdown in their marriage. It gave her the giggles, which was welcomed after saying the word over and over again. Divorce was a cold, ugly word, and she avoided it. Now she had a new word--well, really a phrase to replace it.

She carried the book with her as she trudged up the stairs and into the kitchen where she stood looking around. Everything sparkled, everything was polished, from the pots to the burnished color tile, from the wet leaves of the African violets to the slick covers of the cookbooks on their shelves. Apples displayed their shiny skins in a glass bowl on the counter top, and a bunch of bananas lay in a wicker basket beside the sink. It came to her that this place was the one room, outside of her office, in the house that held any fond memories. Here she had worked hour upon hour, contented and even singing as she went about the preparations of putting food on the table. Whenever she had a problem, the kitchen was were she came to try and solve whatever was bothering her. Yes, she did like the kitchen. It had become her domain.

For no particular reason she put down the book in her arms and took a cookbook from the shelf. It fell open in her hands to the recipe for chocolate chip cookies, which she had made hundreds of times trying to keep a supply in the cookie jar. They were Scott's favorite even now when he came home he would check out the cookie jar. She kept standing there with the book in hand, a far away look on her face, thinking... thinking.

She must put herself in order, she thought. The past was gone and what laid ahead was the future. That was what she needed to think about now. She needed to begin concentrating on how to handle the business.

A serious expression appeared on her face. She would have to consider sending out notices of her move to a different location. How soon after she found a new location should she start sending out the notices? Would she be able to get a good estimate of the cost of her expenses once she was on her own, so she could plan for that? There was so much that needed to be thought out now. Once she was captured in the process of divorce everything would crash down upon her at once. Now was the time to work on the important matters that would lead to her ability to make it on her own. Again Scott entered her mind. When was the appropriate time to break the news to him. After a moment she made her decision. She'd call him tomorrow and without bias, tell him of her decision.

Skye picked up the legal book again and it fell open, just like the cookbook. She looked down to see a section concerning personal actions and attitudes during a divorce. She started reading again.

"It can't be over stressed, the importance of moving quickly and cautiously during the period prior to a divorce. Once you approach the spouse with your determination and they are uncompromising, the partner becomes so determined to find ways to get even that he will stop at nothing. When this happens, the separation of property drags on for ages, and as a result, so do the divorce proceedings. This not only increases the cost of the divorce, but can develop into a very nasty situation."

"One must not underestimate their spouse. A disgruntled spouse will do everything and anything to halt the divorce. Be prepared for it. One should be careful, pick the opportune time and with an non threatening ambience present the separation papers. Choose a time when you are certain that the spouse will be objective and work with you in making the decisions that are needed to finalize the severance. Join the spouse when they go to have the papers signed in front of a notary and make a backup copy, before the documents leave your hands."

The house was heavily quiet now. She felt the winds of evil blowing over her domain and she wanted to run from them. She stood in the center of the room. All at once the cruelty of fate seemed to invade her space. She felt helpless and that increased her rage. She could feel her face swell, and the veins in her temples beat visibly. She clenched her fists at her side as she walked stolidly into the office. Just inside the door she leaned against the wall, breathing with difficulty. She closed her eyes. There was a huge pain in her chest. She had every reason to believe the words she had read. She knew Hank would not cooperate and would do everything in his power to fight what he knew was right for both of them. What frightened her now was not knowing how far he would go.

CHAPTER 25

Paul had fallen asleep. He was awakened by the pounding on the car window. His bloodshot eyes flew open while his head remained against the back of the car seat until he finally remembered where he was. When he turned and saw the face peering in the window, his first reaction was to jump back in fright, but he recognized the intruder. Feeling aches in every muscle of his body, he rolled down the window.

"Looks like you are on guard my friend!"

"Sam, I just closed my eyes for a minute. It's been one heck of a day keeping up with her." He added, "She's been twitchy all day."

"What's that suppose to mean?"

"I don't know. Going here and there, just farting around all day is all."

"Is she in there now?"

Paul was now fully awake. He remembered his early resolution. "Yeah, but I wouldn't go in there if I were you."

An impatient expression glazed Sam's face. "Well are you going to tell me why not or do I have to guess?"

"Well, she was up late, roaming around the house. I could tell by the lights going on and off. Then it was quiet for a time..." Paul happened to look out the windshield at just that moment. "See what I mean!"

Sam followed the direction of his gaze and saw the light in the window of the den.

***

Inside the house there was not a sound. Skye had stood in the kitchen for some time with her thoughts jumbled. She had forgotten about the light in the den as she worried whether she would be able to second guess Hank. She was sad and very tired, but found her head fill with scattered recollections. Her feet leaden she turned around and found herself in the bedroom. She laid down on the bed, her mind churning and it was as if she were turning pages in a photo album in her head. Their first dinner together, the wedding music, the double ring ceremony, and the blaze of sunshine on the church steps when they came out together... The dark rage of his anger, his fist pounding against the table, and the lamp crashing to the floor. Disjointed thoughts of her life with Hank played through her mind and a sigh came out of her mouth.

The unthinkable was happening, or was about to. Leaving Hank! Just yesterday she would have said in spite of everything that there was always a way to end it nicely. But now knowing the truth in the words she had read, she felt entirely different. A great, unheralded, unexpected change had taken place within her and she was filled with doubt.

Her eyes closed as her head dropped further into the pillow. She was so tired... so very tired. She couldn't think about it now, she'd have to deal with it later.

***

"What the hell," Sam said getting up from his crouched position he had taken by the car when the light went on.

"See, what did I tell you."

"Well, what happened today?"

"I don't know. Maybe she got a phone call that upset her, or maybe she's having cramps or something. How the fuck should I know!"

"There's no way I'll chance going in there now."

Paul didn't have to be hit over the head. "Listen, Sam, I've gotta be here all night anyway. Why don't I try later tonight. That's if she settles down?" he quickly added.

Sam thought for a moment. "If you want to, go ahead, but don't take any risk. Be damn sure she's in bed before you go in, otherwise you can blow the whole thing. Especially if she's been acting strangely." Sam saw Paul shake his head, then not feeling quite right about the situation, hesitantly he added, "Here's the key. I'll be back tomorrow to collect this and the tapes if you can manage to get them. Just remember to be absolutely sure before you even think to try and enter, and if you aren't sure, don't do it. I'll take care of it myself."

"It'll be okay, Sam, you can count on me."

Sam filled him in on the layout of the house and what he needed to do. "You got all that."

"Sure, I'm not stupid, you know. I got it."

"Okay, I'll see you tomorrow. And try to keep your eyes and ears open, will you."

"Yeah, boss!"

When Sam left, Paul sneered. He had pulled that off just fine, thanks to the little lady's help. Now, the bitch had better stay put so he could do his job.

The light was still on in the den. At first that worried him, but after an hour had gone by and there was no change he figured she had the jitters and hadn't bothered to turn it off. Quietly he got out of the car and opened up the trunk. There it was, right where he had put it. He tucked the portable tape recorder under his arm and crept to the side of the car, opened the door and laid it on the seat, then went across the street, keeping a look out in all directions. He stood on the side of the step, listening for any sounds or movements inside or outside and when none came, he turned the key in the lock.

It was a piece of cake! Down the stairs, open the utility closet, remove the tapes, check the camera, and he was safely letting himself out the door again. Paul retraced his steps across to the intersection and climbed back behind the wheel.

"Nothing to it," he said as he fumbled around trying to place the tape into his portable recorder. When he had the it seated he pressed the rewind button. Once it was at the beginning of the tape, he leaned back and relaxed, listening. There was nothing much on the tape. There was a message left by her mother, several disconnected lines, and a call from someone named Mary, asking her to call her back.

Skye's voice filled the interior of the car as she talked on the recording to some people about divorces. As he listened, Paul laughed to himself. Her husband was going through all this trouble to learn information about nothing. He already knew she was getting a divorce or else he wouldn't have hired him or Sam. He figured that what her husband was looking for was some dirt, possibly her running around with someone. Well wouldn't he be surprised.

Now bored, he only half listened until the conversation with Mitch Cayman came on. He sat up with curiosity, listening to the conversation. She had met with this lawyer, Michael Cayman, that had to be where she went. The time she left and the time of the appointment conformed. He continued to let the tape play until it came to the end of the recording where she was reading from some book. Paul listened to the end, removed it and placed it on the dashboard. He looked across the street. Everything seemed quiet enough so he started up the car, turned right at the intersection and drove down to the light. He sat wondering which way to go then he remembered the grocery store on the corner. There might be some pay phones out front. He swung left and drove to the store, looking for a phone booth.

He wasn't disappointed. Taking his time so he wouldn't appear suspicious, Paul walked over to the phone and picked up the telephone book. There was just enough illumination from the parking area lights to allow him to see. He flipped pages until he came to the right section and looked through the listings until he found the name Mitch Cayman. He reached into his chest pocket, found a pencil and a wrapper off of a stick of chewing gum, then wrote down the address. Just as calmly he climbed back into his car and returned to his spot across from the house. Now he was set. He had the address he needed if Sam asked him any questions.

He slid down on the seat and rested his head against the back and drifted off to sleep.

CHAPTER 26

Skye woke feeling as though she hadn't had a wink of sleep as she pried her body from under the twisted covers, then slid out of the bed. She grabbed her robe and slipped it on, turning back around to stand beside the bed, looking down at the disarray that showed she had been tossing throughout the night.

Must have been dreaming again, she thought, but she couldn't remember at first what had caused her to wake sweating and trembling. Then it came to her, the person tailing her, the last thing she read from the legal book... It had all been on her mind when she fell asleep. Her life was changed now, she thought. Irrevocably changed.

She felt something moving from the pit of her stomach as she walked hesitantly as if the floor might evaporate beneath her feet. The sensation took hold of her until she was running down the hallway and into the bathroom.

Skye barely made it before she began vomiting into the toilet. With one hand on her forehead, the other holding on the toilet seat, she heaved and heaved, her stomach convulsing, jerking in its attempt to bring up more. Tears trailed down her cheeks as she leaned forward emptying her stomach. When there was no more left to choke out of her she hung over the bowl with her stomach moving in spasms, waiting until it passed. Finally she was able to get up and move to the sink.

Skye turned on the faucet and filled her hands with water trying to rinse the nasty taste from her mouth. She soaked a washcloth in cold water, then pressed it to her forehead as she flushed the toilet and put the lid down. So much for being in control!

When she finally emerged from the bathroom, all washed and primped, she looked and felt much better. She even walked with more confidence as she moved about the kitchen preparing a pot of coffee. It wasn't until she dared a peek and saw the car still sitting across the intersection, did she slip back, just a little, before managing to gain control again. She thought, if he wanted to fight dirty, then so be it. At least she was now aware of what he was up to. That was something in her favor.

Once Skye was seated at her desk her mind cleared and she began her work with diligence. The phone rang, and with her best professional voice she answered.

"Computer Services Unlimited, Skye speaking."

"Well?"

It took a moment for her to recognize the voice.

"Hi, Stephen."

"Don't 'hi' me. Tell me what happened."

"Nothing yet, Stephen, I just saw the lawyer." She paused. "I am going to let him represent me."

"That's not exactly what I was calling for, but it'll do for starters. I want to know what happened to finally persuade you to divorce that guy."

"It wasn't just one thing. It was everything. I finally decided I didn't have to and wouldn't put up with his baloney any longer."

"Its about time, Love. I've watched you change from a woman who had it all together to a real idiot and finally you're on your way back."

"Yes, I know. I just didn't want to go through any major changes until Scott was grown. And then, well, it was easier not to rock the boat."

"I know, Skye. We all go through that. Wanting to get out of a bad marriage, but putting it off because we're afraid of the consequences. I've been there so I know what goes through your mind. What you have to remember is that you deserve happiness and not be content to settle for less."

"I know, Stephen, it's just so hard to make such a major change without worrying what will happen."

They talked back and forth and Skye found herself wanting to tell him about the man sitting across the intersection, but thought better of it. There was nothing he could do to help except worry just like she was doing. She convinced herself that one of them worrying was enough. She'd keep it to herself. Finally she ended the conversation.

"Stephen, I have to get back to work. Things are starting to pile up again and I don't want to get behind. There's a lot I have yet to do and I need time to concentrate on this divorce thing too."

"Just promise you will stay in touch. That's all I ask."

"You don't even have to ask that, I will."

She hung up the phone and immediately began working. After a while she stopped long enough to listen to the calls that had come in the previous day. There was nothing pressing so she wrote what she needed to know on a pad. The phone rang.

"Computer Services Unlimited."

Listening attentively, Skye said, "That's not a problem. What? Sure. Yes, that will be fine. Thanks." She hung up.

Throughout the morning the phone calls came and she scheduled the work immediately on her DayTimer. By noon she had the next few days pretty well filled. New clients were beginning to come. Not a great many, but enough to make her again think about hiring some help. She was on her way now, she thought and that seemed to brighten her spirits as she picked up where she had left off. The phone rang again.

"Computer Services Unlimited. Skye speaking."

"Hello, Skye?"

"Hank?" It had been three weeks since he left.

"Yeah. I'm sorry I didn't call sooner, but it's been hectic. We've been working double shifts and the work is so strenuous, I have all I can do to just climb in the bed."

"Well, I'm glad to see you made it there. Is everything all right?" Skye tried to sound sincere.

"Yes." There was silence. "I plan on coming home this weekend."

There was a funny sound to his voice that had Skye immediately wondering what was up. She frowned, puzzlement written all over her face. "What's wrong?"

Hank didn't reply right away, but waited, not wanting to sound anxious.

"Hank? Are you still there?"

"Skye, I have a slight problem."

"I gathered that, just tell me what's wrong."

"Well, a couple of the guys couldn't come up with their hotel charges and I had to get the money for them. I charged their rooms on my American Express card."

Skye thought quickly. She moved the phone away from her ear and stared at it as if seeing Hank. He hadn't found the time to call her, or send her any money, yet he had been gracious to some strangers.

"Skye, are you still there?"

"Yes," she said through clenched teeth. "I'm here all right. Why don't you tell me the rest of it."

"I know you won't believe me, but I'm really sorry. At the time it seemed like the right thing to do. They were going to pay me back as soon as they got their check, but then we decided to move into an apartment together and they had to use their money to help pay their share of the security and rent. Anyway, I wanted to tell you before you got the bill."

"Well, that's big of you."

"Skye, I can't cover the payment alone. I'm going to need your help." There, he had said it.

She couldn't help herself. "Why not, you sure as hell haven't been sending money home!"

"I deserve that."

"You bet you do. The object of your going to New York was to work and earn money. Instead you're now calling me to pay your bill for some charity you extended to your new friends. I don't know how you can even form your mouth to ask me for the money!"

Hank was seething now, but he knew he had no choice. She was acting like a real bitch about it and it infuriated him.

"Listen to me. These guys are my family now. If I had been short they would have come through for me. We're all in this together and we have to help each other out."

"Well then, that explains it, doesn't it. Got to support family, don't we!" she said icily. Skye paused to calm herself and then added, "Get the money back from them before the end of the month and your problem is solved."

"It's not that easy, Skye. If I had that choice, do you think I'd call you, knowing how you'd feel and what you'd say? They have a perfectly legit explanation, and just had to put off giving me the money for a few weeks."

"Good. Tell you what. I have a perfectly legit reason to say no! I am not going to help you."

There was a decisiveness in her voice that frightened Hank. He was almost pleading now. "Skye, don't do this. We'll lose the card and mess up our credit. I promise you'll get the money back, and interest if you like. Just don't turn your back on me now. I need your help."

"What about your check? You do get a check each week, don't you."

"Sure I do, but it's expensive living here. I moved into this apartment with three other guys because it was cheaper than living in a motel. We've started shopping so that we can save money on meals, but it can only go so far. It's not like living in Rochester."

"Forget it Hank. I'm paying more than my share now. I draw the line at helping you out with your friends... correction, your family!"

He knew she was not going to give in. "I could have guessed you'd act this way. I don't know why I even bothered to call."

"Frankly, I don't know why, either." As an afterthought she continued. "Are you still planning on coming home for the weekend?"

"You bet your ass I am. That you can count on." His words sounded threatening. Skye hung up the phone without saying another word.

With resolution she tried to return to her work, but it was useless. She was too upset. She reached across the desk and grabbed a yellow pad and began listing a number of points to discuss with the lawyer, one of which was the limit of her responsibilities to Hank. She was about to dial his number, then changed her mind.

Skye leaned back in the chair glancing around the office with distaste. She found the ambiance oddly depressing now. The dark wood-paneled walls, the heavy mahogany furniture, the expensive blue carpet, all seemed ponderous and ugly. The cheerless, dismal effect of it all had her recalling a scene in Wuthering Heights. Nelly Dean telling the story of how Wuthering Heights used to be a beautiful and cheerful place. Her avid listener, Mr. Lockwood, sat within the dark and dismal abode, unable to envision any love or happiness gracing the rooms.

So much like the feelings of Mr. Lockwood are Skye's now as she realizes how much she is apart from the furnishings of this house, and now, even the office which had become her domain. She felt as though she didn't belong here anymore. The feeling crept into her bones and filled her with new determination to end the unpredictable existence of her life. She would no longer be a puppet, dancing on strings, held by one who considered himself to be her master. She was her own master. And her salvation would be achieved through the money she earned from her business.

With renewed determination she was back at the computer, working afresh, determined to not let anything disrupt what she had laid out before her. And nothing did.

***

After he hung up the pay phone, Hank stood staring at it for a long time. Evening was settling in as he stepped onto the sidewalk. What he needed was a drink.

He walked down the street, passed the apartment without stopping and headed for the corner bar, hoping he'd not run into any one he knew. Right now he wanted to be alone. He wanted to drown his sorrows. He was angry and in need of time to think. As he entered the bar, he glared at the man behind the counter, roughly ordering his favorite drink. When it was placed in front of him, he pounded the money on the counter and said, "Keep them coming."

He drank one after the other, letting the amber liquid soothe his body and his mind until he was better able to cope. He realized that it wasn't so much her refusal to pay the bill that got him mad, it was the feeling that she was up to something and he thought he knew what it was. At that moment he believed that Skye was going ahead with the divorce. It made sense! Why else would she be willing to take a chance on messing up their credit.

Hank slowly became aware of the pain growing inside him. He would not let her get that divorce. But how could he stop her? No matter how he tried to convince himself he knew that if she wanted a divorce there was no way he could keep her from getting one. That angered him more. He ordered another drink.

Suddenly his eyebrows raised. What if they had turned up something? What if there was something on the tapes he had planted that he could confront her with and threaten to blab to anyone who would listen. Skye was very susceptible to control if she thought people would think bad of her. She was very protective of her reputation and anything that could smear it might be his weapon to convince her to drop the whole divorce idea!

But he didn't believe it. He didn't believe they would have anything on her, or if they did, that she would care enough to back down. No, that was a wild pipedream. She was stubborn when she had her mind made up and he was sure that she did. She was going for the divorce and he couldn't stop her.

He wanted to cry, but even with this much booze he couldn't, and he found it wasn't helping to ease his pain. Finally he just gave up and left the bar. He walked unsteadily down the sidewalk, barely able to pick up his feet and managing to trip several times on the cracked sidewalk. He hung on to the railing as he went up the stairs and after fumbling with the key, managed to finally let himself in to the apartment.

The place was silent except for the heavy breathing of his roommates. Hank quietly moved through the rooms until he was in his bedroom. He didn't bother to undress, but fell across the bed in a drunken stupor.

He slept hard, tossing and turning throughout the night until the alarm went off, forcing his eyes to fly open. He laid there, listening to his roommates moving about the place and answering when one knocked on his door.

"Yeah, yeah, I'm awake."

"You'd better get a move on, Hank, or we'll be late," Pete yelled as he returned from the bathroom.

"I'm coming."

Hank tried to lift his head, but the pounding sent it back to the pillow. Taking a deep breath he tried once more and managed a sitting position, holding his head between his hands. With a grunt he finally was on his feet and heading for the bathroom.

He stared at his reflection in the mirror. He was forty-five, hardly a ripe old age, but lately he had begun to notice it was taking much longer to pull himself together. He held onto the sink, thinking back to when he could have spent the night on the town, gotten home in the wee hours, caught some sleep, bounced up at the sound of the alarm to shower and shave and be on his way. Now he moved slowly, balancing his head so that the weight was distributed evenly atop his neck. Shakily, he climbed into the shower, letting cold water cascade over his body before finally making it more tepid. He tried to organize his thoughts, but the cobwebs wouldn't be pushed away that quickly, so he gave up for the time being.

He brushed his teeth, looked again in the mirror and decided it would be unwise to shave; it wasn't his blood he wanted to see.

Finally he was putting on his work clothes, slipping his feet into some shoes, but he still had doubts he could make it. Instead of joining the men in the livingroom, he went into the kitchen, and took out the family size can of tomato juice from the refrigerator. He closed his eyes, as if to ward off the taste as he gulped down as much as he could manage without throwing up.

It did nothing to halt the bubbling in his stomach as he finally joined his friends in the livingroom. So much for that theory, he thought. What he needed was a good strong cup of coffee.

"You look like hell!"

"Thanks, thanks a lot... The effort it took to speak was not worth it to him as he grimaced in pain.

"Are you all right."

"Fine."

Hank was silently grateful as they drove to the work site with no one saying a word. He knew they were watching him and wondering what had made him spend the evening drinking until he could hardly stand up, but no one asked. Once they arrived, there was no time for words as they prepared for yet another strenuous day. By noon his mind began functioning again and he remembered his marital predicament. It amazed him to realize that she was on his mind and he couldn't push her image away! When it was time to break for lunch he didn't make an attempt to join the conversation, nor did he eat. Again he felt their eyes skating over him, but he remained silent.

Back at work he tried to get her out of his head but he could not. He didn't want to live without her. He thought of all she handled so easily that he would have to handle himself if she were gone and it sickened him. It was so vividly clear to him that life as he knew it would change drastically once she walked out the door. No longer would there be someone to do the worrying for him and make sure everything was in order. But that wasn't all of it. He knew without a doubt he loved her, and, yes, he needed her.

The day finally came to an end and as he walked toward his roommates he found himself thinking of the marriage vow. What was it they had said? Til death do us part? Well, he thought harshly, if she wanted out, that was his only recourse. If he couldn't have her, no one else could either.

By the time he joined his friends he was smiling and more amiable.

"Let's eat out," he said. "I'm buying!"

***

Skye placed the call to the lawyer. She sat organizing her thoughts while she waited to be put through.

"Hello."

"Hi, Mr. Cayman."

"Please call me Mitch, Skye."

"Mitch? I'm still being followed."

"Are you sure."

"Yes."

"Tell me about it."

Skye told him about the car, letting him know that it was sitting there as she spoke to him. She explained that it was the same man who had tried to follow her the day she came to his office. She gave him a description of the driver and apologized for not being able to identify the car.

"Tell me what you can, then."

"Well, the car is black, quite big. Possibly a Lincoln or maybe even a Pontiac. I just don't know. It's not new, if that helps."

"That's okay Skye. I can find out what I need to know. Don't worry about it."

Skye let out a sigh of relief.

"Well, this seems to change things. Do you think your husband put the tail on you?"

"I'm not sure, but it has to be him. Who else would want to tail me? Maybe since he knew he would be out of town and not able to keep an eye on me, he did the next best thing. Remember, I told him I wanted a divorce before he left for New York."

Mitch listened carefully. He knew that there might be someone else who might have her tailed, Angelo. Since he had her working on the transcripts, he might have someone watching to make sure this Taylor fellow didn't get close to her. It seemed like a possibility. He made a note to check that out. He said nothing about this to Skye.

"Listen, Skye. See if you can get me the license plate on that car. I'll hang on. But be careful and don't let him see you looking."

"I'll try," she said. He heard the sound of the phone as it was laid down, and he waited.

Skye walked over to the window and peeked around the side, but couldn't see the license plate. After a moment she walked out of the office, through the kitchen, and into the family room. She walked over to the television set and leaned across it so that she could see through the window. She saw the plate then. As she walked back to the office she kept repeating it until she was at her desk. She picked up the phone.

"Mitch, the license plate is MWP667."

"Okay, Skye, now I want you to do as I tell you."

"I'm listening."

"Try and think of someone who can come stay with you. It should be someone that will not rouse any suspicion. Can you think of anyone?"

"Not right this minute, but I will give it some thought."

"Okay. I want you to try and act normally, like nothing is happening."

"I will." She remembered! "Oh, I forgot to tell you. I had a call from Hank and he said he's coming home this weekend."

"Well, that just might change things. It might also answer some questions. Since you haven't been threatened in any way, hold back on getting someone to stay with you for now. What I want you to do is see if the tailing stops while your husband is in town. That might mean that he was the one that set it up."

"I'll do that."

"Be careful and don't hesitate to call, night or day, if anything is the least bit suspicious. In the mean time I'll check out this license plate and when you can, give me a call."

"Thank you, Mitch."

"You are entirely welcome."

The conversation ended.

Skye took the time following the conversation to come up with a name. Who would be willing to come stay with her? She kept asking herself the same question over and over again until finally giving up. She'd concentrate on it again, later.

As she sat there wondering what to do, she remembered she had planned to call Scott. Looking at the clock she knew that he would be in his dorm now. She picked up the phone and dialed.

"Hello!"

Skye didn't recognize the voice. "Hello, this is Mrs. Sanders. I would like to speak with Scott?"

"Sure. Hang on a minute and I'll transfer you to his room."

In the time she waited, Skye organized what she would say. Then she heard his voice.

"Hello, this is Scott."

"Hi Scott, it's Mom."

"Hi Mom. What's up."

After asking how he was doing and listening to his comments, slowly and carefully she told him that she was planning to divorce his dad. She tried to assure him that this had nothing to do with him and that as far as he was concerned, they would both still be there for him. She told him nothing about what was happening, only that they had decided it would be best if they separated. When she was done she sat waiting for him to say something.

He didn't speak right away and Skye went through a terrible time of convincing herself he hated her. Finally Scott spoke.

"I thought something was wrong. I could feel it, but I didn't think it had gone this far. Are you sure, Mom. Can't you and Dad work this out?"

"No, there is no other alternative." She couldn't think of anything else to say.

"Well, I love you both and I want you happy. As long as you're sure this is the only thing to do, I'm behind you both."

"Thank's Scott. I knew you'd understand."

Scott wasn't sure he should say what he said next, but decided he owed her that.

"Mom. I have to admit that it isn't all a surprise. I know you two tried to keep your problems from me, but you weren't always successful. I guess I knew it might come to this. I could tell you were unhappy and I have to admit I know Dad can be trying at times."

"I hope we didn't hurt you, Scott."

"No, no Mom. Don't think that."

"Are you going to be all right with this? Do you want to talk about it?"

"No. It's really between the two of you. It bothers me, but I can understand why you feel like you do. Dad's not the easiest person to get along with and I know he's done things to hurt you."

"Scott?"

"What, Mom."

"I don't want you to hate your Dad. It's not entirely his fault. It's both of us. We just can't get along together, is all."

"Mom. I'm not a baby. You don't have to worry. My feelings for both of you will not change. Okay?"

"Okay."

On a lighter note, Skye told Scott his Dad would be in town during the weekend and if he got a chance, to come home. Scott informed her that he would. They hung up then, each thinking their own thoughts.

Skye started feeling the strain of the day as it crept over her body, until finally she forced herself to shut down the office and go to bed.

***

The nightmare woke her, but the dream continued. For a minute after she rose up in fear from her pillows, colorful snatches of the nightmare swam clearly in her mind. There was blood, someone lying face down on the family room floor, but she couldn't see the face. It was more vivid than any vision, it seemed real!

The shadows of the bedroom settled over her and she adjusted her eyes. She tried to get up. The room spun and she had to support herself by holding on to the cover that hung down to the floor at the foot of the bed. When she regained her balance, she went into the bathroom, not closing the door because she was afraid to have to reopen it.

Skye felt personally threatened by the nightmare. The dead body, the blood all seemed to be linked to her. She drew a glass of cold water, drank it, then another, holding the glass with both hands to steady it. Each time she shut her eyes, it all came back as clear as if she had actually seen it happen. Worst of all, Skye felt that if she could turn over the body and look at the face, she would know it at once.

She put down the glass and immediately found herself on the floor, hugging the toilet bowl again as she heaved uncontrollably.

Her stomach hurt, her sides ached, yet she couldn't stop it. She found herself thinking that perhaps there was a meaning to the nightmare that couldn't be defined in rational terms, and then she heaved again.

Finally there was nothing left in her to come up. She shuddered. She was cold clear through to her bones as she managed to get up and rinse out her mouth, then splashed cold water on her face. She returned to the bedroom but left on the bathroom light. She was uneasy in the dark as she stared up at the ceiling until finally drifting off into a troubled sleep.

When she awoke again it was morning. After getting up and in the process of readying herself for the day, she managed to convince herself it had been a dream. Just because she couldn't phantom it's origin meant nothing. Dreams and nightmares did not always have a cause. Putting it in this perspective allowed her to function.

Skye was glad for the work. It kept her mind off of her problems as she delved into it. Throughout the day she thought about Hank coming home and of her conversation with Scott. She reminded herself that she should let Hank know she had mentioned the divorce to their son. It was the only fair thing to do. When she had finished the last of her jobs, closed the door on the last customer for the day, it suddenly dawned on Skye she hadn't talked with Adam in a while. She picked up the phone and made a call to Adam Snyder.

"Hello, Adam, this is Skye."

***

He had been thinking about her, thinking and checking on the names she had given him and was anxious to talk with her about his findings.

It had come as no surprise to him when he found that the clients she had mentioned were connected to this Angelo Maglioni. Just from the little she had shared, that was a given. What he was sure she didn't know was the lowdown on this guy Samuel Stillman. That was a man to be feared even if you were on his side. He had learned through his sources that Sam was indeed being tried for the murder of his wife. Witnesses could prove that he had done the deed. A man of his type would certainly not sit back and lay his life in the hands of his lawyer, or anyone else. No, that type of man would stop at nothing to protect himself.

Though Skye's involvement would not be any kind of a threat, it still had bothered Adam so he had hired someone to watch and see if anything odd took shape. The man had reported to him just the other day that Skye was being tailed. Though he wasn't able to find out who had hired the man, he did have information on him. The man's name was Paul Angelino.

Paul was a small time drug dealer and had been in and out of trouble with the law. He was also known to be friendly with Samuel Stillman, doing odd jobs now and then that Sam sent his way. It didn't take a legal brain to pick it up from there. Adam was sure that Paul had been hired by Sam. He also was sure that Maglioni was not aware of his dealings, but if he were to find out he would put an end to it. After all, Maglioni was out to prove that Sam was innocent of the crime.

In Adam's investigation, he had uncovered a possible connection between this Maglioni and the district attorney who would be serving as the prosecutor for the Stillman trial. The two went back a long time. There was something about a case they had served on opposite sides a long time ago that had caused a rift between them, which Adam was sure was not forgotten by either party. That would explain why a man as prominent as this Maglioni fellow would take on the Stillman case and why Taylor, who was the district attorney, would not send some one on his staff to prosecute in his stead.

Yes, there was a lot going on here and he didn't like the idea of Skye playing even a tiny role in it. He was glad she had called.

***

"Skye, I've been thinking about you."

"I'm sorry, Adam. I know I've been remiss. I promised to take you out to dinner and I am just now getting around to asking if you are available."

"You bet I am. Just tell me where and when."

"I was thinking about tonight. Would you like to go to the Olive Garden and have them gorge us with all that Italian food?"

"You've got a date. What time would you like me to meet you?"

"In an hour and a hour?"

"Sure. I'm just about done here. I can be there."

After she hung up the phone, Skye went to make herself as presentable as possible. Staring at the bathroom mirror, she knew it wouldn't be easy. There were dark rings under her eyes that were puffy, all due to lack of sleep and the bout of nausea she had experienced. As she gazed at her reflection she could see dampness on her forehead that seemed to signify the fact that she was still scared and uneasy. She was used to seeing a reflection that most women would envy. Shiny auburn hair, green eyes, high cheekbones and except for a light sprinkle of freckles, a flawless complexion. Now the person looking back at her seemed somewhat strange and alien. She started working on it.

She splashed handful after handful of cold water on her face and then began the process of giving herself a quick facial. She applied a toner, reached under the sink and grabbed out a jar that contained a mint facial and spread it evenly over her face and neck. She dabbed two cotton balls with witch hazel and held them on her eyes, holding her head back and counting. After five minutes she washed it all off and applied her makeup. A quick glance into the mirror and she saw her old self again.

Skye went into the bedroom and changed her clothes quickly, settling on a pair of red slacks, a Liz Clairborne pullover shirt and no jewelry. She went back into the bathroom and brushed her hair, adding a dab of hair dressing to make it shine. Then she was out the door.

She saw the car following her, but this time didn't try to lose it. Instead she drove carefully toward her destination. She was sure this is what Mitch would have her do. When she arrived at the Olive Garden she found a parking space and quickly climbed out, feeling more frightened by relinquishing the sanctuary of her car.

Once inside the restaurant it took a moment for her eyes to adjust to the dim light. When the hostess approached her, she informed her she was meeting someone and brushed pass her to find Adam. Just as she had expected, he was already seated at a table.

"Sorry," she said apologetically as she slid into the chair across from him, knowing she was a little late.

"Don't apologize. I only just got here myself."

The waiter came over and introduced himself, asking if they would like something to drink while they looked over the menu.

"What would you like, Skye?"

"A glass of Chablis would be nice, no ice."

"Bring the lady a Chablis and myself a Scotch and water."

When the waiter left, Adam turned toward Skye and reached across to lay his hand over hers.

"It's so nice to see you."

"Thanks. I'm glad to see you, too."

They chatted about unimportant matters until their order was taken. Adam had decided he wouldn't tell her until after they had eaten.

Skye acted and felt lively as she laughed at Adam's jokes and allowed the wine to warm her body. She hadn't had a drink in so long she was feeling quite relaxed by the time she finished the glass. But when Adam asked if she would like another, she said no.

They placed their order and while they waited they again chatted, catching each other up on what they'd been doing without touching on the subject that bothered them most. The conversation continued in this manner until dinner was behind them.

Skye pushed back in her chair and sighed. "I haven't eaten this much in a long time,"

"I could tell that. You've lost a lot of weight, Skye. You never were fat, and now you're bordering on skinny."

"Don't pick on me now. I haven't felt this good in months." She said jokingly.

Adam smiled at her, not wanting to affect her mood, but knowing he had to.

"Skye, I think you should have another drink!" He said it more like fact then a choice.

"Why, I'm already feeling relaxed. Another drink would just about put me over the edge."

Adam's expression was very serious now as he looked at her. "Please have one, for me!"

"Sure, Adam." Skye was already worrying. Just by the look on his face she knew he had something unpleasant to say. She waited while Adam placed the order. She sat in silence until the drinks were set in front of them, and then leaned forward as Adam began to speak.

He spoke rapidly as if his life depended on him getting it all out as quickly as possible, and Skye listened. He told her everything, right down to how he felt about what he had learned, and when he was finished he was exhausted from the effort of saying it in a way that would make her realize how serious his findings were.

Skye could only look at him, baffled at first, but as she thought it through, she realized that all that he had said she had felt along the way. Now it was her turn. She told him that she was aware of the tail, and how she had managed to lose him when she went to her lawyer's office. Seeing his expression when she mentioned the lawyer, she went on to explain that she was getting a divorce. She also told him the lawyer's name and that she knew he was connected to Maglioni. That also shocked him as he wondered why she hadn't told him this earlier. He continued to listen now aware that she knew much more than he had given her credit for. When she told him about Stephen giving her Cayman's name, he couldn't hold back.

"Skye, that's stupid. Why would you take a chance like that. How do you know that Stephen wasn't told to give you his name. I don't know for what purpose, but that seems like more than a coincidence to me."

"Calm down, Adam. I told you, Stephen is a friend of mine from way back and he didn't know anything about what I'm been doing or that I've had any connection with the man. I didn't tell him. No, nothing you could say would convince me that Stephen is part of all of this."

She was adamant and Adam knew she would not be swayed. He decided to do some checking up on Stephen without mentioning it to Skye.

"So, are you doing what the lawyer said? Are you acting as if nothing is happening?"

"Yes, I think so. I don't think the man who is following me knows I spotted him."

"What about the house, Skye? Did you think to have it checked out for bugs. If you say that your husband put the tail on you, he may have the house wired for sound!"

"No, I didn't think about that, but you know, you may be right. He took a criminology course a long time ago and just might have thought of that, too. That's if he is the one who put the tail on me." There was renewed concern on her face as she looked at Adam. "What should I do?"

"Would you know what to look for?" He asked doubtfully.

"No."

"Let me think a minute." Skye leaned forward staring worriedly into his face. "Okay, I think I know what to do. I don't want them to get suspicious and it might hamper my investigation of them if they find out my name. I think it would be wise to remove the tape that's in there now. You say he followed you here?"

"Yes."

"I think he's working with this Sam fellow and if I'm right, they may have a key or at least someway they're getting in and out to change the tapes." Adam paused. "Let me think. If I assume they are putting in at least six hour tapes and trying to work around your schedule, it is most likely that they would change it at night when they were sure you had gone to bed. With that man, Paul watching, he can let them know just by the lights going out at night."

Skye interrupted him there. "I've been leaving lights on lately," she said sheepishly.

"I don't blame you for that. I probably would too. They've most likely figured that out as well, but that wouldn't interfere with their schedule. I would conjecture that they would probably be changing the tape around... What time do you normally turn in, Skye?"

"Usually by midnight I'd say. Sometimes by eleven, but generally in that area."

"Okay, then allowing time for you to fall asleep they are looking at around twelve-thirty, one o'clock."

He was quiet for some time. Skye, now unnerved by it all, couldn't wait for him to finish thinking. "Well?"

"Sorry," Adam said. "I want you to go home as if nothing has happened and leave on the lights that you would normally have on. At exactly twelve I will be at the back of your house. If they're watching from the corner you mentioned, they can't see in back."

"I'm pretty sure they are. I haven't really checked anywhere but out front."

"Unless they're suspicious, I don't think they have more than one person watching, so let's assume the back is not being watched."

"But..."

"Don't worry Skye. I'll be careful. I know the area well so I can turn opposite to where he is watching and drive down the road, park and sneak back up. You be there waiting for me and don't turn on any extra lights. The least amount of lighting, the better."

"I will," was all she could muster. The plan laid out, Adam reached for the check to have his hand slapped by Skye, who gathered it up and searched in her purse for the money. "Remember, I invited you out to dinner."

When she had placed the cash on the little tray for that purpose, they pushed back their chairs. Adam grabbed her arm as she passed him, whispering, "You go out first. I'll follow later."

Skye, walking unsteadily and not from the two drinks she had, managed to get into her car and finally was on her way home. Once inside she tried to do exactly what she would do under normal circumstances, go to the bathroom, wash her face and brush her teeth as if nothing was different. When she went into the bedroom she didn't undress, but turned off the light, lying restlessly in the darkness with her eye on the clock. When the hands worked their way to twelve midnight, she got up and went into the lighted hallway. She had left that light and the one in the office on. The rest of the house was bathed in darkness as she moved quickly to the family room. Shortly after she arrived, there was a light tap on the door. Shaking uncontrollably, she walked over and peeked through the curtain, barely lifting the edge with her hand. It was Adam. She let him in.

He put a finger to his lips to silence her as she guided him to the lower level of the house. Adam leaned toward her, placing his hand over her mouth and whispered into her ear, "Where is the circuit box?" Skye pointed toward the utility closet. He pushed her gently to one side, placed his finger to his lips and then opened the door. Fumbling around, he finally found the chain to the light, but before he turned it on, he turned toward Skye and motioned with his hand for her to go over and close the door to the den. He didn't want the tail to see the light come on. When she had it closed, he turned on the light.

It seemed like he was in there for hours, but in reality it was only five minutes before he was again by her side whispering. "I've got the tapes. I put blanks in their place so they won't get suspicious. They've got it set up so that every word you say, any where in this house, is recorded. Is there anything you should tell me?" Skye shook her head, no.

This time Adam led the way, pulling Skye behind him. When they were on the landing he whispered again. "If you need to get in touch with me for any reason, use a pay phone. Any conversations that you don't want recorded, don't make them here. Do you understand?" Again she shook her head yes.

Adam kissed her lightly on the cheek as he let go of her hand. The moon shone through the window now, bathing her face in a silver glow. He could she her very clearly now and he saw she was more than frightened, she was petrified.

Time was running out. He reached down and squeezed both her hands. That brought a weak smile to her face. Then he lifted his fist and lightly brushed it against her chin. She only looked at him as if she were looking at something that was far, far away from where she was now.

If only he had more time! But he didn't. He went down the two stairs into the family room and staying close to the wall, reached over to slide the door open, just enough so that his body would fit through, then ducking down so that his shadow would not show on the family room door, he was soon gone from view.

***

Skye watched. She felt Adam's hand take hers. She felt his chin up motion, but it did nothing to console her. It was like she was watching from somewhere up above, looking down at someone else standing here on the landing and playing a part in the scene. Ever since coming back up the stairs and finding out that the walls not only had ears, but that they could also speak, she had felt herself moving back. It was the only way she knew to handle her feelings.

Now with Adam gone, she was only spurred to motion out of necessity. He had slid the door closed, so leaning over from the safety of the bottom step she was able to put the lock in place. She performed as Adam would actually have wanted her to, but she did because she didn't have the energy to spare, not because she was aware that the moonlight would have reflected her image on the curtains in this room.

When that job was done, Skye walked heavily up the stairs and back to her bedroom. She stood there in the enchanting light cast by the moon and slowly removed her clothing before climbing in under the covers. But she did not sleep. Instead she lay there with her eyes open, at first only staring until finally her mind began to operate on its own.

This couldn't be happening! This was not the way it went in real life, she cried. She moved her head from side to side as if shaking the idea from her head, but it continued. It reminded her that she might not be in the house alone. Maybe at this very minute some stranger named Sam, or that ugly man sitting behind the wheel of that familiar automobile were in here with her now. She pushed back against the bed with the heels of her feet. The covers lifted and fell slightly from the movement.

Now not only were her eyes open, her ears were too, listening to every sound. And there were a lot of sounds to be heard in an older home. Enough sounds so that she wasn't sure exactly what or who was making them, and admittedly she was glad. If they weren't already inside, creeping downstairs to gather their merchandise, they would be soon.

She thought of what Adam had done for her tonight. He had saved her from not knowing that someone was playing back her voice and hearing everything that she had said or done between these walls. Adam had helped her to get even this time but what he had done might cause more problems. They would sit back and hear nothing. Wouldn't that make them suspicious!

She allowed her eyes to close. If they were here, or just entering, or entering five minutes from now, she didn't want to know. At the moment she felt violated, a precious freedom taken away from her and why, she didn't know. Hank couldn't have come up with a better way of making her suffer if he had tried. Nothing could have made her feel more helpless, more out of control of her life than knowing someone else was listening to each and every word she said. But not tonight, or tomorrow, or the next day. Now that she knew, she thought fiercely, they would only hear what she wanted them to hear. That was some sort of control, wasn't it?

She was totally exhausted now. Her mind refused to do any more thinking and shut down. Her eyes that now glistened with tears of frustration could not stay open any longer as her lashes fluttered down and the tears spilled out on her cheeks. But she didn't feel them, her body moving back to the place where her mind had all ready arrived. She was no longer aware of where she was or who she was. It was all gone as her body shut down on it's own accord and forced her to finally fall into a deep sleep.

CHAPTER 27

Hank woke when he heard the soft sound of someone moving quietly pass his bedroom door. Since working the ungodly hours of the job, he seemed to sleep soundly most nights, but woke just before the alarm went off, as if anticipating some joyous day at the beach. It was frustrating to say the least, but it was something he could not change. It came from keeping one ear alert and listening so as not to be up late and find the rest of the guys waiting on him.

Easing out of bed to sit on the edge he felt the first stab of his hangover. They had stayed up late last night celebrating with a case of beer. Hank reached up and started kneading his throbbing forehead. It all started coming back to him then as he realized it was Saturday, the first Saturday since starting this job that they had off. As his mind began to function, he remembered. Due to a lost shipment, they had Monday off. Since they didn't have to report to work until Tuesday morning, they had all planned to go home.

Remembering brought it all back now, the laughing and joking of the guys as their tongues grew loose from all the beer they had consumed, and the conversation with Skye. To pretend with them had been easy as he hadn't told them about his relationship with his wife, but he couldn't pretend to himself that he was going home to a loving wife. At one point as Jim described in detail what he planned to do with his wife the minute he walked in the door, he almost lost it, wishing that his situation had been different, but he had caught himself before he had a chance to say what was on his mind. All the smoking and drinking couldn't bury the feelings that he held inside, because Skye wanted a divorce. But he couldn't drown the sorrow of not being able to take her in his arms and making mad passionate love to her, such as Jim described.

Now as he sat there, his head aching even more, he found he was anxious to get home, maybe not for the same reason as the other men, but he was eager just the same. Sometimes he felt like it was a waste of time to get out of bed and he felt that way now. Life was a scam. The only way he could make it was to cope with everything one at a time. But right now as he anticipated going home it all piled up, and he wanted to just get back in bed. It didn't seem worth it. But he had to know what Skye had been up to during his absence.

He had managed to call Sam twice since he left, but wasn't satisfied with what he heard. As far as Sam was concerned, Skye hadn't been up to anything. He just couldn't believe that. Skye was not the type to make irrational threats and then sit back and do nothing. They either weren't doing their job or Skye knew she was being followed. He was sure she wasn't aware of the wiretaps, but she was too observant to overlook someone tailing her for long.

Hank placed his hands on either side of his body and pushed himself up from the bed. He felt disoriented. And he had all those problems. It seemed easier to stay exactly where he was, climb back under the blanket and forget about it. His head screamed at him as he forced one foot in front of the other until he stood in the hallway of the apartment, calculating the distance to the bathroom door. You can do it, old man, he said, trying to drum up the courage needed to make it that far. He dragged a foot in front of him, his head lowered as he started down the hallway. Just then the bedroom door across from him opened and a haggard, Pete, stepped over the threshold.

"Man, what a night!"

Hank forced his head up and attempted a tired smile. "Yeah."

"How much did we drink?"

"Too much."

He continued down the hall, then disappeared into the bathroom, wanting only to get into the shower, but forced himself to down two aspirins before doing so. It seemed the older he got, the less he could drink without paying for it the next day. It could be age, Hank thought, but most likely it was all the pressure he was experiencing.

The cold water woke him up. He snapped out of his daze, shivering as the chill penetrated his body and took his mind off his aching head. He was sober, but the headache threatened to break down the battlements of his skull as he leaned over to warm up the water cascading over his body. As he washed himself he tried to remember the conversations of the evening, wondering if he had said or done anything that might have his friends alerted of his home situation. But he couldn't think of anything. By the time he stepped out of the shower he was not only confident he had played his role well, but also aware that his head hurt less as he stood in front of the mirror, preparing to shave. When he had washed off the last remnants of the shaving lotion and brushed his teeth, he felt better able to cope with the day.

Hank passed Pete in the hallway as he made his way to the bedroom. By the time he was dressed in a short sleeve shirt, the two buttons left undone at the neck, a pair of casual slacks and his favorite dress boots, he felt as good as he looked. He wandered into the kitchen to find the coffee already made. Jim and Joe sat at the table fully dressed and looking none the worse for wear.

"It's amazing what a hot cup of coffee can do," Jim said.

Joe added to his statement. "That and some decent clothes."

The three men shook their heads in agreement as Hank joined them. He put two teaspoons of coffeemate into his steaming mug and wasted no time taking that first sip. He took several more before bringing the mug down to rest on the table.

"It's going to be a scorcher."

"Yeah, I heard."

"How long will it take you to get home, Hank?"

"If I pull out of here by eight, I can be home by five, five-thirty. That's if I don't make any stops along the way."

"Just in time to get a good home cooked meal, huh?"

"Yeah," he said, trying not to let the sarcasm creep into his voice. The last thing he expected was Skye cooking dinner for him. She hadn't even asked him when he expected to make it home and he knew she didn't care.

Each of the men were silent now as they finished their coffee. By the time Pete joined them they were just getting up to leave.

"Well, don't all run on my account," he said trying to sound hurt.

"I don't know about you, Pete, but I'm ready to get on the road. I can't wait to get home."

"Me too. Just let me pour a cup and I'll take it with me."

Hank stood there watching their excitement for a while, then ambled off to pack a few things. When he entered the livingroom they were all there, ready to leave.

"Well, Hank, have a safe trip and don't do anything we wouldn't."

"You, too. See you back here on Sunday night."

They trudged out into the hall and walked down the stairs to the street together. Hank watched as they climbed into Pete's car and waved before climbing into his van. He was finally on his way. He had just one day to do all he needed before he returned.

***

Already it was getting warm. He checked the clock on the van radio and saw that it was almost eight-thirty now. He looked through the rear view mirror and started to slowly back out of his parking space. He turned his head to look into the side mirror, one eyebrow arched, the lid hovering above his brown eyes, the skin twisting at his neck as he carefully maneuvered the van out onto the street. He was finally on his way, weaving through the side streets until he arrived at the main road that would take him to the thruway. When he checked the time again, it was after nine.

He drove along the thruway, thinking. Just what did he expect to accomplish in one day? His whole life was falling apart and he had one day to change that. He wished that he could hope Skye had changed her mind, but that he knew was no more than a pipe dream. The best he could hope for was that he'd have something to dissuade her from going through with the divorce.

Hank leaned back in his seat, putting his head back and staring out the windshield at the blue sky with a shrewd look on his face. He looked better than he had when Skye had married him. The strenuous labor had left his body taunt and trim, something he had noticed when he had put on his clothes this morning and found they were now too big. He hadn't been in this good a shape in a long time, not since he had left the service. Now as he drove down the lonely stretch of road, he couldn't help wondering if Skye would notice. Maybe seeing him this way would make her change her mind. He smiled as he reached over and turned up the volume of the radio.

A little after one, he felt the first pangs of hunger. He hadn't eaten since last night. He started watching the signs as he drove and pulled off at the next rest stop to get something to eat.

The inside of the building was cool as he entered. In looking around he saw that the place was packed. At first he hesitated, not wanting to waste too much time, but then figured he'd get something to go and proceeded to stand in one of the long lines which seemed to be moving quite quickly. He watched a woman trying to herd her two children who were restlessly running around her. She looked to be in her early thirties, dressed in a pair of well worn knit pants and a pullover short sleeve shirt that was clinging to her sweaty body. She looked tired and drawn.

"Stop it," she said to the kids with little energy. They ignored her and continued their game. She raised her voice slightly and yelled again. "I said stop it or I'll tell your father." When they didn't respond to her threat, she finally gave up.

As he watched a man came up to join her with another child in tow. "What took you so long?" Instead of responding, he quickly grabbed each of the kids as they made their next trip around his wife's body. "There's a table over there," he said, pointing to the far corner of the room, "I'll take the kids with me." That brought a smile to the woman's face that adjusted her features so that she actually looked pretty. He watched as the man planted a kiss on her forehead before shepherding the three kids out of the line.

Hank found himself wondering if he had been right in the first place. When they had Scott, he had tried to convince Skye to have more kids. He had always wanted a large family. He figured that kids were what cemented a marriage and now he thought that maybe if they had more, Skye wouldn't be leaving him now. It hurt to think that way, but he couldn't help wondering if it might have been different. He was certain that with more responsibility he would have worked harder. Responsibility was what got a man going and he just hadn't had enough responsibility during their marriage. Maybe if she hadn't refused to have another kid they could be just like that couple, except that Skye wouldn't be caught dead in that outfit!

Hank was smiling now as he allowed his eyes to look over the people in the restaurant. He saw a young couple standing in the line to his left, waiting their turn at the counter and filling the time by whispering into each other's ears with broad smiles on their faces. Every now and then the man's hand would rub the girl's back sensuously and she would stand on her tiptoes and plant a kiss on his lips, then laughingly draw away as his hand rubbed lower. He felt like he was intruding, standing there staring at them as they petted each other fondly, so he forced his eyes away. Finally it was his turn to place an order.

Hank watched the staff as they moved around within the cramped space behind the counter. Soon his food was in a bag before him and he reached into his pocket and paid, then moved carefully through the throng of people until he was back outside.

The heat hit him immediately and he had to adjust before making his way across the lawn to his van. Inside he quickly turned on the engine, and sat waiting for the air conditioner to cool the inside. He neatly laid out the food on the empty seat, then carefully maneuvered the van out onto the thruway again.

By four it started cooling off. Hank shut off the air conditioner and rolled down the window. The highway sounds filled the inside of the van, competing with the radio which was starting to pick up static. He started searching for another station, wishing he hadn't let Skye talk him out of having a tape deck installed in the van.

"Can't you be satisfied with anything, Hank?" she had asked when he had told her he wanted to buy the tape deck. He could hear her voice, raised in frustration and telling him again what still needed to be paid. The only reason he had mentioned it in the first place was because he didn't have the time to take it in and had finally asked if she would do it for him. Finally he had backed down because he couldn't stand her whining. Instead, he had gone out and purchased a portable tape deck, only in his haste to pack for the trip he had left it home. Now he wished he had it as he found himself constantly searching for new channels.

He welcomed the coolness of the evening as it began to set in. He was hungry again and looked at the clock, realized it was close to five now. He started watching the road, hoping to see a sign that would tell him how many more miles he had to go. When one finally came into view he sat up straighter. Fifty more miles and he'd be at his exit.

That last stretch turned out to be the hardest. The traffic was thicker now as he approached Rochester and he had a hard time switching lanes to get from behind slow moving vehicles. His whole concentration was now on his driving as he tried to cover the distance as quickly as possible. The effort strained him as he moved at a pretty good clip, but not fast enough for his taste. He was already figuring out what he would do when he got there. First, he'd stop over at the Circle Bar and see if he could locate Sam. He hadn't been able to reach him when he had called to tell him what time he planned to arrive so he'd have to play it by ear. Hank didn't know where Sam lived so he hoped Sam would be at the Circle Bar. If he wasn't, he'd just have to check all the bars in town. He had to find him. It started to bother him that he had given Sam a key to the house, but only a little. Right now he had a hard time thinking of it as his house. Besides he had no alternative.

Finally his exit was up ahead. Hank fumbled around in the tray where he kept his change for tolls and with one eye on the road, he used the other to gather up the amount he'd need at the exit. Then he was driving down the exit ramp, sitting in line waiting to pay the fee and then finally on familiar territory.

It felt good to be back in his old stomping grounds as he headed toward the Circle Bar. Familiar landmarks passed by the window and he breathed in the air, suddenly feeling as though he had never left. By the time he turned into the Circle Bar he was relaxed and feeling almost jubilant.

The place was busy as Hank stood just inside the door, taking it all in as his eyes adjusted to the dim lights. He caught a few eyes on him, some he knew and nodded at, others that were strangers as he gazed around hoping to find Sam. After a moment he walked over to the bar.

"Long time no see. Where have you been?"

"Oh, hi, Oscar. I've been out of town."

"Vacation?"

"No, work. I got a job in New York. I just got in. Have you seen Sam?"

"No, not this evening, but he usually drops by around this time. Are you thirsty?"

"Yeah, give me the usual," he said.

When Oscar bought over his drink he stood there for a moment as if wanting to say something, but changed his mind, instead saying, "Enjoy!"

Hank pulled out a stool and sat leaning on the bar. He could feel the fatigue from the long drive catching up with him as he sat there drinking in the familiar surroundings. The clientele had changed, but that was about it. The rest of the place was just as he remembered it. He had finished his first drink and was just starting his second when Sam walked in.

"Hi, friend. Care to join me for a drink." Sam stood by the side of his stool with that funny look that he called a smile.

"Sure." Hank picked up his drink and followed Sam over to a table. He waited until they were both seated.

"So, tell me, what's up."

"Since we talked last, a lot has happened, my friend. I don't know how it happened, but from the last tapes we got from the house, I think the little lady is on to us. I know for a fact she knows she's being tailed. I also think she knows the house is wired."

"No, how would she know that? Why do you think she knows."

"Well, for starters we took out some tapes that I think you should hear. One is her talking to her lawyer and setting up an appointment. Another is telling the lawyer about the tail and giving him the license plate of the car." Seeing the worried look on Hank's face, he added, "That's not a problem. They won't find out much when they check the plates. But that's how I know. That and the fact that the last tapes were just standard conversations and she's been going out to pay phones to make calls. She also has been visiting friends and I think she might be making calls at their houses, too."

Hank had a puzzled look on his face now. "I guess she has figured it out. But how?"

"My man said he was careful, but he must have gotten careless and she caught on to him. As for the wiretaps, I think she spoke to this guy that you will see on the video. Obviously they didn't realize they had been taped. Probably never thought to look for a video set up when they discovered the tapes."

Hank perked up. "You've got her on tape with some man?"

"It's not what you think. They're standing there whispering right in view of the camera. It was while they were taking out the tapes and obviously replacing them with blanks so we wouldn't get suspicious."

"Who's the man?"

"I don't know. Thought maybe you'd know."

"Do you have the stuff here?"

"No, it's back at my place now. I've moved since you left. Has to do with my lawyer who is trying to give me a better image so I can beat this murder rap. Anyway, we could go there and take a look."

"Well, what are we waiting for?"

They finished their drinks and headed out the door. Hank left his van in the parking lot and climbed into Sam's car.

"This is nice. Where did you get this?"

"I told you my lawyer was trying to change my image. He got this for me. Pretty nifty, huh?"

"Sure is."

They drove for a long time, Hank recognized the nice suburban area as they drove along and pulled into the parking lot of a well-kept house and yard. He was impressed, never figuring a man like Sam to live in these surroundings.

"Another perk from my lawyer. It took some getting used to, but I have to admit I like living like this."

They entered the foyer and Sam turned on the light, illuminating a moderately furnished living room. He watched as Sam walked in, looking totally out of his environment, then turned around to face him. "Wanna beer?"

"Sure." While Sam went into the kitchen to get their beer, Hank checked out the place. There was a matching sofa and chair, an array of end tables and on the wall before the large picture window was an entertainment center that contained a 25 inch television, a VCR and a tape deck. He waited, standing in the center of the room until Sam returned.

"Here," Sam said extending a can of beer toward him. He took it and went over to sit on the couch while Sam fished around inside a case that contained tapes. When he had found the two he wanted, he placed the first into the tape deck and set it up. He stood by the unit until the tape had played out and then replaced it with the second tape.

Hank listened carefully. He tried to recognize the voices as he listened to the conversations, but outside of Skye's he didn't have an inkling of the others. But he knew that Sam was right. Skye had seen a lawyer and from the last conversation with him she had obviously spotted the tail. He made a mental note to check around her office and see if he could put a name to the voices. She usually kept all her appointments on a calendar so he shouldn't have too much trouble figuring out the voices on the other end of the line. He'd have to see if Sam could give him some dates and times so he could match it all up.

After that, Sam turned on the television set and placed a video tape in the VCR. He recognized the man instantly as one of Skye's clients. He had seen him in her office on numerous occasions and had spoken to him a couple of times. He also knew the man was a friend, but he doubted he was a lover. Hank didn't think he was Skye's type. From the video image, which was all he had to go on, he was trying to keep her from speaking as he obviously gave her some advice. It was logical to assume he told her to be careful and probably told her to make all her important calls away from the house. He thought he remembered Skye mentioning once that the man was a lawyer. As he stared at the man's image he remembered his name, Adam Snyder. It wasn't much, but at least he had something to go on.

"Well, do you recognize the man?"

Hank started to tell him his name, but instead said, "Yes, he's one of Skye's clients. I've seen him in the office on several occasions.

"So, what do you want to do?"

"Let me see what I can come up with. I don't have to leave until late Sunday or Monday morning. Why don't I nose around for a while and then call you?"

"When?"

"Right now I'd say I'll be in touch by midnight Sunday."

"Okay, I'll be here waiting for your call. Let me give you my new phone number."

After writing down his number and giving it to Hank, he played back the rest of the tapes so that Hank could here them. He then filled him in on what Paul had noticed, which wasn't that much and then the talk turned to Sam and his new life. He bragged about the building he now owned downtown and some of the other things he had obtained from his lawyer.

"Oh yeah, the best part is the lady. You have got to see this looker. A beautiful red head who can make any man drool even with her luscious body covered in all that fancy clothing. I think she likes me. She's been calling and dropping by asking if there is anything I want. Is there anything I want! Can you imagine that. She's real classy, obviously educated, and out of my reach in normal circumstances, but this is not normal circumstances." He said this as he looked around his house with a smirk on his face. "Boy, would I like to give her a toss in the hay!"

Hank, who was busy trying to figure out if there was something he had missed on the tapes was only half listening to Sam brag about his luck. After a while he stood up.

"Going home?"

"Yeah. I've got a lot to do before I take off so I might as well get started. Listen, I'll call you at exactly twelve midnight."

Sam followed him out the door and drove him back to the Circle Bar. He decided to go in for a nightcap, glad that he was going to be able to go home and get some sleep. He'd be off until Hank took off Sunday night and he was going to make the most of that time.

Hank watched as Sam ambled away, wishing he could arm himself with another drink, but knew he had to conserve his time. Quickly he climbed into his van and headed home.

CHAPTER 28

Skye had put in a full day. Except for several trips out to make phone calls, which was becoming a real pain, she was in the office most of the time working non-stop. Between the jobs she had managed to gather all the information she needed to take with her on her next visit to Mitch's office and was finally able to take a rest. In front of her was a folder and she picked up one of the papers and looked at it.

The papers, stapled together, ran for twenty pages listing everything they owned. As she had been advised, she had set a price to each item and was amazed at the final tally, which she flipped to now, estimating how much money this meant if they were able to sell all of the stuff they had no use for. After a while she laid the packet down and picked up another sheet. This one covered all their debts. She had also been surprised at the final figure. Outside of the remaining balance on the mortgage, they owed a lot less than she had anticipated. All her efforts during the past few months had paid off. From the money she had been making, she had managed to put quite an impressive dent in their expenses, which would mean they would end up with quite a nice nest egg after the house was sold.

Skye ran a hand across her eyes, which were tired from staring at the computer screen for so long. She leaned back and closed them as she thought about what she had left to do. There was just as much ahead of her as there had been in the beginning. She hadn't begun to search for a Realtor or check into finding a place for herself once the house was sold. How would she manage to get it all done? She let out a sigh and slowly her eyes opened again. She'd manage it, she thought. She'd find the strength to see this through to the end if it killed her and she'd not give up anything on the way. She'd continue to keep her business running at it's maniacal pace and do whatever was required of her to get this divorce behind her.

Exhausted, but feeling quite proud of herself, Skye pushed her chair back, listening as it rolled across the static protector pad on the carpet. Then, placing her hands on the edge of the desk, she lifted herself out of the chair and walked over to the window. As she looked out at the lovely day that had transcended she felt an urge to breathe in the air. Slowly she reached out and slid the window open.

Skye looked across the street at the neighbor's house and her gaze automatically went further, until it rested on the intersection to the left of her vision. The car sat where it had been since she had spotted it the first time and now it seemed to steal away all her good feelings, forcing her to close the window and step back.

It wasn't fair, she thought. She had done nothing wrong and yet she was being made to feel like a prisoner in this house. Something as simple as opening a window to let in some fresh air was not possible now, since the tail might see her and think she had spotted him. Even making phone calls was hampered. She could not just pick up the phone and have a conversation. No, every time she spoke on the phone, every time she spoke anywhere in this house, other ears were attuned to all that had been said. The worst part was that she could do nothing about it. She had to put up with this violation of her privacy and pretend she knew nothing. Did he love her that much? She wanted to weep for Hank's misery and doomed hopes and for her own splintered dreams, only she didn't dare. That would be one more sound recorded for prosperity.

She moved back across the office and went into the kitchen, wondering at her own question. Did he really love her that much? If it was love that made Hank do this to her was he aware of how she perceived it, or didn't he care. Though she tried, she couldn't suggest anything else that would have him watching her like this. Nothing else made any sense. She could sympathize with his misery because she knew that feeling well. Misery was a knife piercing your body and twisted until you wanted to scream. The only way to relieve it was to find a way to end that feeling. It meant searching your soul until you knew from whence it came and then do whatever your mind suggested that would ease your pain. And she knew that the mind could play nasty tricks, forcing a person to do something that was far from the method that would give them the desired results.

Skye stood at the kitchen sink looking out the window. The pressure was on. She was expected to act normal, make any calls that she didn't want replayed from telephone booths or at friends', and pretend as she climbed into her car, that she was not aware of someone following her. Just how long could she continue to do this without letting the pressure get the best of her. The nightmares were coming more frequently now and for good reason. How much longer before she cracked?

While her life had suddenly become an open book for others to read, magnetic tape of words and voices, Hank's life still remained private. She didn't know or care what he had done or said since the day she had told him she wanted a divorce. It would never occur to her to sneak behind his back and listen in on his conversations. Yet that was exactly what he had done to her. Why should she sympathize with his feelings? He obviously hadn't thought about hers, but there was the major difference between them. She was compassionate, he was not. That's probably the reason why she had felt like she was just journeying through life, waiting for the next event to arrive, the next state, as though she were always positioned somewhere between here and there. Perhaps everyone felt that way when they were getting a divorce.

She had grown thinner since the start of summer through exercising too much, working too long and eating too little. Her face looked thinner and when she dressed she found her clothes drooping from her waist. She noticed it but seemed incapable of doing anything about it. Or so it seemed. Before she had remembered to eat by hearing Hank rummaging around in the kitchen. Now, alone, unless someone asked her over, or took her out, she never sat down to a meal. But that was okay. That she could deal with.

Skye stood there for a moment longer, thinking, the house quiet behind her, tapping the sink with the fingernails of one hand, the other clasping the window sill. Slowly she looked up and exerting her full strength managed to walk back to the bedroom where she stood looking at the bed. She wanted to climb in and sleep, but knew if she turned in this early she would be up and down all night long. Thinking again of the tapes, she thought, maybe that wouldn't be such a bad idea...

A clap of thunder ended her thoughts, and a flash of lightning illuminated the bedroom, and suddenly the lightning outside seemed to enter the room, so that Skye felt energy rise in her body. She crossed the room and pulled up the blinds.

Outside the lightning flashed almost continuously, and when Skye opened the window, the sound of rain and thunder took on enormous volume. The only light in the room was that of the lightning, but it was enough. Even outside she could see the silhouette of each house on the street running behind theirs as clear as if it was day.

***

While Skye stood mesmerized by the storm, Hank entered through the garage door entrance. He stood in the family room listening before moving slowly, very, very slowly, to the landing that led downstairs. He stopped there waiting and listening again, realizing that the storm was a godsend. It would serve as a cover until he finished what he needed to do.

His adrenaline flowed as he continued cautious steps down the stairs. The room below was dark. He moved toward the utility closet, opened the door, reached in and flicked the light on. Then he was disconnecting the wiretaps, while making a mental note to reconnect them before he left. He walked out of the utility room, lifted the ceiling panel just prior to the door leaning into the den. He stood for a minute marveling at the tiny hole that was barely visible, but served as the orifice for the camera lens. He quietly lifted the panel, reached in and pulled out the plug. He had decided on his way home that whatever he had to say to Skye he didn't want anyone else to hear, any movements he made, he didn't want recorded. To keep their conversations personal, he was willing to give up the chance of taping her phone calls, which by now he figured weren't worth taping at all. When he was done, he was careful to turn off the utility room light and shut the door. A glance over at the ceiling tile assured him it had been seated properly.

Hank moved to the bottom of the stairs and again stood listening, and on hearing nothing made his way up to the landing. He paused there, leaning on the railing, and composing himself.

***

Her fascination with the storm had passed. Skye walked down the hallway and entered the kitchen. She reached over and flipped on the light.

She sensed rather than saw him and her pulse quickened. Forcing herself to look across the kitchen, her eyes fell on Hank standing with his hand on the rail. Shocked, she was unable to speak right away, instead she stared at him seeing a grin as it spread across his face and sensing the composed stance as insincere. She could tell he was trying to hid his nervousness. Careful to hid her shock, she took a breath before she spoke.

"How long have you been home?" she asked.

"Just got here," he lied.

They remained at their stations trying to figure out what to say next. Hank seized the moment, attempting to get himself under control. He was shocked by what came out of his mouth. "Do you still care for me at all?"

Skye looked at him unable to hid her surprise, her face expressing--doubt; surprise;

regret until his words sunk in. "I don't know," she said slowly. "What made you ask that?"

"I don't know either," he said matter-of-fact.

She didn't want to talk about her feelings until she felt more in control. Skye quickly changed the course of the conversation.

"How long will you be here?"

She saw his expression immediately change, reflexing his dislike for being the one cross-examined. His mind worked overtime and he began to doubt there was a remote prospect of reconciliation. This angered him. She had been so firm with her decision to get a divorce so why should he hope that she had changed her mind. Now he was angry at himself for asking such a stupid question. No longer in control his feelings showed on his face, only Skye read him wrong. To her, standing across the room, she thought he looked as though she had kicked him in the teeth and she held back from saying anything more.

Hank continued when she remained silent, "We seem to have reached a pause. In our marriage, I mean. Between the acts, sort of."

"I guess you could say that."

"But maybe there are extenuating circumstances here. Maybe all of this is happening because you have found someone else!"

"That's not true." Skye spoke sincerely. She meant to say no more, but found herself talking again. "I've become greedy, like everyone else. It's the modern way. There has to be more to life, but I will never find out if I continue this way."

"Just what is that suppose to mean."

Skye looked at him. She could see the change in his body, which was thin and muscular, his beer belly diminished. He looked tired and undernourished and she felt a rush of maternal feelings. But there was bleakness in her now, and an indifference to him, brought on by all the pain of the years they had shared. Without much effort she relinquished the desire to make it easier for him.

"It's no use," she said, and turned her eyes away realized she was right. This was the same Hank.

"All I'm asking is to simply postpone everything," he said a little too roughly.

"Life doesn't allow postponements." Her voice began to rise, reflecting the rising anger within her. "You can't tell me to put my life on the shelf." She started walking toward him as she continued. "You have been playing dirty, putting a tail on me and wiretaps on the phone. What makes you think that I'd stick around for more of that."

It all came out before she could stop herself, but she wasn't sorry she had said it.

"What are you talking about?" Hank countered as if he had no knowledge of what she referred to.

Skye's eyes were upon him, but he was looking away, and seemed disconnected from his surroundings. It was not just that he was lying; she knew he was. But, while lying, he had retreated deep within himself. She was seeing another facet of this many-sided man. Now there was almost a stillness in him, a certainty. His stare turned inward, and he seemed to be listening to his own falsehoods, with approval. He was so sure, so sure that what he was doing was right, that the splendid end justified any sordid means.

"Don't act innocent, I know what you've been up to."

"So far I am guilty only in intent--not the public eye." Amused, he gestured with his eyes by raising them up to the ceiling and back down as if what she suggested was so farfetched that he thought her quite insane. That look, his denial, his stupid reply, all added more fuel to the fire that burned within her, but she controlled herself. Skye changed the subject.

"Well, how was your trip?"

"The hell with my trip. You are no more interested in how I got here, then you are to see me!"

"Okay, let's talk about what's bothering you first and then maybe I can get some questions answered."

"You want to know what's bothering me? Well, for starters your whole attitude bothers me to no end. You always think you know everything, don't you."

"I'm serious, Hank, if you don't have anything you need to talk to me about, then just be still because I have some questions I want answered!"

Boiling with anger, Hank breathed deeply until he calmed down. He was too heated to discuss the divorce, and definitely not ready to get into what he knew she wanted to talk about, so he chose a lesser concern.

"If you insist, my dear. Let's talk about my American Express bill. Are you going to help me or not?"

"I've already told you that on the phone. No, I am not going to pay it!"

"That's not enough. Tell me why you're not going to pay it!"

Skye pretended not to hear him as she moved over to the sink, opened a cabinet and took out a glass. She carried it with her as she went to the refrigerator and filled it.

"Are you listening to me?" Hank asked furiously, moving further into the kitchen.

"Yes, I heard you." She paused. "In all honesty I would help if I could, but I can't. I just don't have the money," She lied convincingly.

Hank was taken aback. He expected some lame excuse to fire from her mouth, but she had answered in a monotone voice as though it were fact. He believed her, yet he couldn't help staring at her, searching her face to see if there was another reason. He saw nothing.

Skye felt his eyes on her and knew he postulated what she had said. Since she was in a position to be generous, what with most of the finances in control, she added. "I know it gets on your nerves, my nagging about money, but you make bills a real struggle at times. Only this time there is no way I can help."

Hank continued to stare. There was a painful silence. He was distressed and shocked. Then suddenly as she watched, a smile of relief mingled with something she could not decipher, moved over his features. She would have given anything at that moment to know what he was thinking.

"So, Skye, you said, No. You're not going to help pay the bill, and I certainly believe you think you mean it. But I know better. You would no more jeopardize our credit than you would openly insult your best friend. You'll find a way to pay it off, I'm sure of that!" Aside from the oblivious fatigue that had overcome him, and the slight slur of his words showing the affect of the booze, he spoke with confidence.

She couldn't believe what she was hearing! Silence. A changed silence that made Skye and Hank look at each other like strangers. "You seem to have a lot of confidence in yourself, don't you?"

Hank stood there for a second, then smirked, his face filled with luminosity. "Instinct," he replied, then turned on his heels and walked away.

She stood as if struck by his statement. Hank had sounded as though it was an eventuality, and she felt threatened, as if he knew her better than herself. For a moment she tensed with frustration until she faced the truth. Hank was right! Even though she wanted to ignore the bill, she couldn't. She frowned, and then with a breath, relaxed. "Oh hell, why am I getting all in a stew about, it?"

As she allowed the matter to clear from her mind she realized she had been so shocked, so unprepared for him saying such a thing, that she lost track of her own questions. She had forgotten to interrogate him about the ugly man at the corner watching her, even her accusation about the wiretaps hadn't been settled properly. After a while she shrugged. It would all wait till morning.

Skye walked wearily to her bedroom. She picked out a nightgown, grabbed her robe and went into the bathroom. Hot water soothed her; she stood in the shower for a long time trying to keep her mind off of Hank's strange rebuttal. When she finally stepped out, she was yawning. She turned out lights as she made her way back to the bedroom, feeling exhaustion claiming her. Just about to climb between the sheets, she hesitated. She had forgotten to see if the man was still there watching the house. She had a feeling he wasn't, but she needed to know for sure. She walked back into the hallway and went into the spare bedroom to look out.

There was no car parked near the intersection. She opened the window, and leaning into the screen checked all the visible areas outside. Nothing. Satisfied, Skye closed the window and headed back toward the bedroom. As she came through the door, she found herself face to face with Hank.

Skye managed to keep herself intact. "Good night," she said.

"Good night."

CHAPTER 29

Sleep. The increasing anxiety over whether she would get enough made it even more difficult to relax once she climbed into bed. The longer she craved it, the further she came from having what she wanted. She was upset. She had allowed herself to become sidetracked and now she regretted not forcing Hank to admit to all the sordid techniques he had used. And she was afraid that in her present state of mind there would be another nightmare.

Annoyed that she could not settle down, Skye tumbled out of bed and went to the window knowing she had to sleep or she would lose the alertness she needed. She opened the blinds and looked out over at the pool. Moonlight formed dancing shimmers over the surface of the water that helped to soothed her troubled mind. As she gazed outside, her ears picked up a strange sound coming from somewhere in the house. She listened, trying to identify it, only she could not. Finally she backed away from the window, moving silently to the doorway and listened again. The sound was coming from downstairs. She heard voices but so faint she couldn't pick up any words. She continued to eavesdrop, but after awhile decided that it must be the television set. Hank must have turned it on, she thought. He always had it on! The man would die if he didn't have a television set. He preferred it over people. Probably even talked to it when no one was around. Well, she didn't care. It wasn't her problem any more.

Skye began to feel the stress-induced fatigue settling around her. She was completely drained. Certain now that she would sleep, she climbed into bed and just as she hoped, she immediately was overtaken with sleep.

***

Hank had been doing some tossing in turning of his own, except in his case it was due to the desire to be with Skye. He wondered what she would do if he climbed into the bed and started fondling her. Would she be so filled with the need of being loved that she would give in, or would she push him away. He hated being pushed away, yet, he thought, there just might be a chance she would welcome the closeness.

He had continued to think along these lines when he heard the sound of someone stealing down the staircase and entering the family room right outside his bed room. At first he laid there listening until finally he ventured out of the bed, reached up to move aside one of the ceiling panels and removed the gun he had hidden there. He reached down on the floor by the bed and balancing his body, managed to step into his boxers then silently he moved across to the doorway and peeked out. He had to wait a moment for his eyes to adjust to the darkness before he was able to see the figure standing in front of the utility closet door. He knew it was Sam.

Careful, not to startle him, Hank moved silently across the carpet with the gun dangling at his side until he was in whispering distance.

"What are you doing here?"

"Damn," was the whispered response as the shadow form turned to face him and seeing the gun Sam let out a low nervous laugh, then replied, "I forgot. I totally forgot."

Hank just stood there looking into Sam's eyes. "Man, you scared the by Jesus out of me," Sam whispered.

"Sorry," Hank replied, following Sam's eyes as they stared at the gun. "You gave me quite a scare too." Carefully he laid the gun on the top of the pit group before continuing.

"Look, I'd better walk you out." Sam turned as if to leave. "Wait a minute, man." He said, straining to hear any other sounds in the house. When he met with silence, he turned and placing a hand on Sam's shoulder, gave him the signal to start back up. He walked him over to the front door, turned to knob slowly and let Sam out. Before the door closed, Sam turned and said, "Won't happen again."

"I'll call you."

With the door closed and locked, Hank, shaking his head, made his way back downstairs. He paused at the utility closet, opened it and saw that everything was as he had left it. He then walked back into his bedroom, fell into bed and quickly went to sleep.

***

Skye was in the process of making coffee when Hank entered the kitchen. He cleared his throat noisily and the sound caused Skye to turn around..

"Would you like some coffee?"

"Sure."

Hank crossed through the kitchen and headed down the hallway to the bathroom while Skye continued to get the coffee ready. As she moved about the kitchen she was calculating how she would bring up the matter of the tail and the tapes. She was pretty sure Hank was behind it all, but wanted to hear it from his own mouth. She might even get him to tell her why he had gone to such an extreme. When Hank returned, she poured two cups and carried them over to the table. She waited until he was seated and as he picked up his cup, she began.

"Why have you had someone tailing me?"

"What, is someone following you?" he asked innocently.

"Let's don't play games, Hank, I know you set this up."

"What if I did?"

"I'd like to know why."

Hank thought about it for a while and decided to give, but just a little. "I was afraid you'd run out on me, once I was gone."

She wasn't fooled by this, but decided to go on. "And the wiretaps?"

"What about them?"

"Why did you put in wiretaps? Did you expect to catch me talking to anyone special?"

"No, it just seemed like a sensible thing to do. I didn't want you figuring that all of this was yours and come back to find that it was all gone. I was looking after my own interest, you might say."

She could see he wasn't going to cooperate. While she tried to figure her next move, Hank was looking dead into her eyes and thinking... She didn't mention the video. She hadn't found the video tape. After a few seconds, Skye straightened her back. She would not break down or allow herself to get mad! She could not! Forcing herself to concentrate, she went into action.

"You just wasted your money and your time, Hank. I am doing nothing wrong and I don't plan to cheat on you just because I want a divorce. No matter what you do or say, I am going to divorce you and you might as well face it!"

It came out coarse and hard and she found herself changing her tone with him, speaking softer, "All I'm trying to do is make you face facts. I don't..."

"I am facing facts." There was steel in his voice now.

"Are you? I don't think so. I think you figure that if you can get something on me I'll drop the matter. I won't, you know, and you can't stop me. I want this divorce and I will have it!" she said vehemently.

"Oh, you will, will you?"

"Yes."

She looked at him, softening her expression as she sat up straighter. "We're being silly. Ridiculous. We need to discuss this like adults." She paused trying to take the situation under her control again. "I've already talked with a lawyer, which you probably know by listening to the tapes. I've told him to handle the divorce prudently. I plan on selling the house and paying off our debts, and selling the furnishings that neither of us want. Whatever is left we split it down the middle and go our separate ways."

Moody silence. Hank was trying to figure out what to say, what straw he could grasp and use. It was a while before he spoke. "And just how do you plan on going about all this, alone? You need my signature to sell the house!"

Anger flared briefly in her but was quickly extinguished. She closed her eyes, then opened them again. "I know that. Hank, you'll only postpone the inevitable. I don't want to hurt you, I just want a better future for both of us. It won't do either of us any good to fight over this."

He felt defeated with no alternative to take. He saw no hope in getting her to at least talk it over before taking such a rash step, knew at that moment he couldn't stop her. "I'm not up to this right now. I don't want to think about it." She watched as he pressed his hands against the sides of his temples.

"I'm sorry. I really don't mean to push you, but we need to get some things settled. I have some papers made up that I want to show you. Will you look at them?"

The fight seemed to be all out of him now as he shook his head. He watched as Skye got up from her chair and went into the office. He listened, hearing a drawer open and the rattling of papers. When she reentered the room and laid the sheets in front of him he realized he had been holding his breath. He let it out slowly, his eyes on her as she silently slid the chair back, sat down and scooted it up to the table.

Hank kept his eyes averted at first, then finally looked down and started reading, showing no reaction as he flipped through the pages of the household belongings, then on to the page that showed an estimate of the value of the house, until finally he came to the listing of their debts. He looked up, his eyes asking questions before he even spoke.

"Where did you get these figures?"

"Well, for the list of our belongings, I had the original receipts of purchase and figured out an estimate of what we could get for them now. As far as the house is concerned, I called a realtor and asked what houses in this area were listed for and used that figure. The bills, only required a call to each creditor to find out what if any deductions would be applied, if we paid them off before the end of the term."

Hank looked down again as if he couldn't believe what was written. She smiled indulgently, knowing what he was thinking, and sure she was going to get the reaction she had waited for.

"I'm not saying I'm going along with this, but, do you have any idea of what we'll have when this is ... when we sell the house?"

"Yes, I do. If you agree with all of this, we'll have at the very least, twenty thousand dollars to split between us!"

He was speechless, her words ringing in his head, making him forget the headache that throbbed at his temples.

"That can't be right."

"It is, Hank."

He couldn't help thinking what he could do with that kind of money, all at one time. That plus the fact of no debts pressing in on him wasn't too hard to take. Only what she was asking him to give up in order to have it was not worth it. After a minute, Hank got up and walked toward the coffeemaker. He stood idly his head swimming with the idea of being totally solvent, before finally grabbing the handle of the pot and pouring himself another cup of coffee, his mind working all the time. While he fantasized, Skye gathered up the papers and returned them to her office desk, her heart cresting with joy. For the first time since making the decision to divorce him, it had finally come, that surge of relief that she would succeed. All her dedication and hard work would soon allow her to achieve her reward after years of frustration.

She went back into the kitchen, and it dawned on her that this joy stemmed from the confidence she was feeling at the moment. What she had managed now was the easy part because to get there would be an extremely hard task that would require all her energy and know how. Her elation dwindled slightly.

Upon hearing her footsteps, Hank turned around. "Skye, I have to ask you something."

"What is it?"

"Will you at least wait until I am done with this job in New York. Can you hold off until I am back here?"

"When will that be?"

"It's been a month. I only have two more on the contract!"

She contemplated his request. "Yes, I'll hold off until then, but not on everything. I want to be totally aboveboard and tell you that I will meet with the lawyer again and start looking for a good realtor, but I won't go any further than that. In return I want you to think about the part you have to play. You will need to meet with the realtor, too, and there will be papers that will require your signature. I want you to think about that and be ready to cooperate when you get back. Agreed?"

Since there was no reason not too, he said, "Sure."

He started to walk away, but Skye called to him.

"Hank, one more thing. I want you to take the tail off me and remove the wiretaps. You all ready know it's useless, and besides I'm not doing anything that would be interesting enough to record."

Hank had already made that decision. With her knowing she was being taped, she'd not be stupid enough to make any important calls here. As for the tail, he didn't have money to continue that anyway. Only he didn't tell her all of this, instead he said he'd do it.

"Anything else before I leave?"

"No... Wait a minute, Hank. I hate to say it, but you were right. I will pay the American Express bill, but don't take that to mean I'll do it again. I can get the money by finishing up some of the jobs I have. It will mean working longer hours, but I'll do it this time and not because I want to help you out of a bind. I'll do it because I don't want to begin my new life with a bad credit rating." Seeing that "I told you so" look on Hank's face, Skye added, "But I warn you, I can't help even myself if you do this again. I don't have the time or strength to continue at this pace."

Attempting to look grateful, Hank replied amiably. "Don't worry, I'll pay you back, and I mean that." With the situation resolved, Hank left without another word.

***

After the consultation with Hank, it took a while for Skye to calm herself. She felt used and out of control. To change her mood she decided to workout and went into the bedroom to put on her exercise clothes. Downstairs in the Rec Room her mind was on her exercise and not on Hank. When she reached the end of the workout she felt refreshed and better able to face the day. It was Saturday and contradictory to what she had told Hank, she could spend the day any way she pleased. Her jobs were up to date and she already had the funds set aside to pay the bill, or for that matter, any other bills that came across her desk. Financially she was indeed secure, thanks to Mr. Maglioni and his people. After taking a shower, Skye went into the office.

The day passed quickly as she worked on her manuscript. It was coming along better than she expected. At the rate she was going, she could have it completed in the next few months. Then it would be a matter of getting someone to buy it. Engrossed in her project, Skye worked diligently until she found herself tiring. Leaning back in her chair she stretched her arms above her head and got up to open the window in the office to let in some fresh air. Slowly she went back and settled in front of the computer.

The heat made the air as visible as a thin sheet of moire silk. Her hair drooped and the stirrup pants she had put on soon became uncomfortable. She managed to tough it out for a while, but then went to change into a pair of shorts and a tank top, wishing for once she had allowed Hank to install air conditioning. She turned on the ceiling fan in the office, and went over to close the window. She paused in the process, changing her mind. The pungent air, a mixture of blossoms and freshly cut grass helped to remind her that she would have given her life for this heat when she was freezing during the winter, so why shut it out now. Smiling, she went back to her manuscript.

At dinner time she half expected Hank to walk in, but when he did not, she fixed herself a salad and settled in front of the television set, only to find there was nothing on that interested her, so she went to get a book. It was too nice a day to let past, she thought, so gathering up her salad, she opened the patio door and sat on the deck to enjoying the warm evening air as she ate and read, wondering if one day she could hold her own book in her hands and join the ranks of published authors.

She reached the start of the last chapter before laying the book aside and taking a long, deep breath as she looked up at the sky. The sun was setting and Skye paused to watch the colors streak across the sky as it made its way below the horizon. She could hear the faint sounds of water splashing as the kids in the neighborhood made use of their pools. Skye drew her knees to her chest and placed her hands on the top of her thighs. Her heartbeat settled. Her breathing slowed and she found herself wondering what Hank was doing at this moment. She thought about her friends and wondered what they were doing, and then her family, and suddenly she wanted to talk to her mother. She sat up and checked her watch. Her mother would still be up. She went back into the house taking her dish with her. Carefully she rinsed it and placed everything into the dishwasher before going into the bedroom to make the call.

She talked to her mom for a little over five minutes before hearing her mother announce she had to run off to one of her volunteer functions. But she still wanted to talk. Skye then called her sister and chatted with her until running out of conversation, she said her goodbyes. She made one last call and that was to her son, Scott. She talked with him for sometime about school then found herself dodging his inquiries concerning her decision to divorce his dad. She just didn't want to get into it and Scott was able to sense this so he quickly turned the conversation around, asking about her business. When she finally hung up she felt totally relaxed and no longer wondering about Hank. After awhile she decided to call it a day and went to get ready for bed. Hank still hadn't come home. Surprising herself, Skye had no trouble falling asleep.

***

Hank who had set out right after the confrontation with Skye had driven directly to the Circle Bar in hopes of meeting up with Sam. He hung out there for a couple hours, but Sam never came in. After settling up with the bartender, he decided to get something to eat.

As he drove away, Hank decided he was tired of quick food joints and looked for a place where he could get a good meal. The Cartwright Inn came to mind and he decided to check and see if he could get in without a reservation. Driving much slower than usual, Hank found himself wondering what Skye was doing. Was she wondering what he was up to or had she put him out of her mind? He had to start thinking of ways to make her drop this divorce thing, but he could think of nothing he could do or say to sway her decision. Before he knew it, he was at his destination and pulled into the parking lot. Lucky for him, the Cartwright Inn wasn't busy and soon he was seated. When the waiter came, he placed his order and sat looking around the premises until his food arrived. He devoured it hungrily.

Over a last cup of coffee and a cigarette Hank decided he should check out Sam's new home and see if he was there. Checking his watch he noticed it was quite late which made him feel certain he would find Sam at home. After paying for his meal, Hank climbed back into his van and drove the route that he had taken with Sam before.

The empty streets were made lonelier by the darkness. As he drove up Pittsford-Brighton Road, a pair of headlights appeared in his rearview mirror and remained there, constant as the moon. When he turned off on Pine Grove Avenue, a blinking red light appeared over the two white ones. "Just what I need," Hank said to himself. It was a patrol car.

Hank pulled over, switched off the engine, and waited. An amplified voice said, "Out of the car, sir."

He complied, moving slowly, Hank opened his car door and stepped out. A Pittsford police cruiser was nudged up close to the rear bumper of his Van, its brights on, its engine running. He could smell the gasoline, feel the heat from its radiator as it intensified in the warm summer evening.

Hank watched as the driver's door opened and an officer got out, one hand on his hip. He lifted something out of the belt and Hank felt a tingle going through his body. When a flashlight beam blinded him, Hank relaxed and involuntarily he raised an arm reflexively.

"Both hands up in the air where I can see them, sir."

He complied again. The light traveled up and down his body.

Squinting, he said, "What's going on? Did I do something wrong?"

The cop stepped closer, and in the light he could see it was a young white man with a prominent jaw, blue eyes and from what he could glimpse under his hat, baby fine blonde hair.

Not responding to his question, the officer said, "Where are you going, sir?" The beam lowered, illuminating his slacks.

"To a friend's house. Why, is something wrong?"

"What's the name of your friend?"

"Sam", Hank responded questioningly.

"Sam, who?"

"Sam Stillman. He lives down this street."

"What did you say your name was, sir?"

"Hank. Hank Sanders."

"Mr. Sanders, give me your license and your registration."

"Sure, it's in my wallet."

"Pull it out slowly, please."

Hank reached in his pocket and pulled out his wallet. He reached into the front compartment and removed his license and registration, handing them over to the officer.

"Thank you. Now, Mr. Sanders, move to the rear of your car, sir. Put your hands on the trunk and keep them there. I'll be right back.

He took the pose and looking over his shoulder watched as the officer went to his car and pulled out his radio. He wondered what was up, but figured he'd find out soon enough. He heard the cop give his name and license number, talking low into the mouthpiece. Hank watched and listened, wiping his brow were beads of sweat had accumulated, waiting for the officer to return. Finally he heard him reply, "Thanks." Hank continued to listen and watch. He saw the officer reach down and replace the phone, then watched him get out of the car and walk back to where he was standing.

"Okay, sir you're free to go." He handed Hank his license and registration.

"Can you tell me what's going on?"

"Just police business. Sorry for the inconvenience."

Hank put his license and registration back into his wallet, wanting to question the officer further, but thinking better of it. He walked to the driver's side of his van and climbed in. He took his time turning on the engine, the lights, giving the cop a chance to take off first, watching as the police car pulled back onto the road and disappeared around a corner before pulling the van back onto the road. Hank continued up the wondering what had caused the officer to pull him over in the first place.

Sam wasn't home or at least he didn't appear to be. He rung the buzzer several times and quenched an urge to walk around the house. After a while he climbed back into his van and opened the glove compartment. He scribbled a quick note and went back up to Sam's front door and wedged it between the front door jam. Satisfied that Sam would find it, he climbed back in his van and headed toward home. It was too late to return to the Circle Bar or anyplace else. He decided to go home.

***

When he entered, the house was dark and quiet. He turned on the family room light and found the evening paper. Quietly he turned the pages looking for something that might shed light on the encounter with the police car. Something had to be up for them to pull over cars for no reason, but he found nothing. Hank passed over the story.

LOCAL MAN DIES SUSPICIOUSLY

Monroe County sheriff's investigators tonight are searching for a man who shot a city resident through the side of the head sometime yesterday.

Paul Angelino was found dead in a parked car near the Nationwide Warehouse and Storage Inc. store at 171 Clay Road in Henrietta. Mr. Angelino had been shot at close range, and there was no evidence of force entry.

The sheriff's department is concentrating the investigation on someone who might have had some dealings with Mr. Angelino, who worked as a private investigator. So far there are no leads in the case.

Hank laid the paper aside and looked at his watch. It was late. He started thinking about what he had decided earlier. He had to reach Sam and tell him of his decision. On the off change he might reach him, Hank decided to try Hank's number. Keeping his noise to a minimum, he walked quietly through the family room and down the stairs to the den on the lower level. He reached into his pocket and took out his wallet, searching for the slip of paper that Sam had written his number on. When he found it he picked up the phone and started dialing. He was in luck. Sam picked it up on the second ring.

"Hello?"

"Hi, Sam, this is Hank. I've got to make this quick. I've decided to take the tail off Skye and remove the wiretaps so I won't need you anymore."

"Man, what are you doing? I thought you planned on going back to the City tomorrow!"

"I am, but Skye is wise to us now so it won't do any good to continue. She knows she's being tailed and she knew about the wiretaps so there is no way she'd do anything suspicious. Besides that, if I hooked up the wiretaps she would just have that man we saw on the video come and disconnect them again."

There was an uncomfortable silence on the other end and Hank found was getting nervous. "You understand, don't you, Sam?"

"No, can't say that I do. There is always something that can be done. I thought you were serious about this, but I must have been wrong about you. You're giving up, letting the woman take control of your life and you'll pay for it. Mark my words, she'll make you regret this!"

"Maybe, but what else can I do?"

Sam was thinking hard now. He needed the money badly, just in case he needed to do a disappearing act. He was good at smelling out new prospects, but he was in too much hot water already. Besides, every time he got a job like this where the woman was the mark, it made him feel like he was evening the score for the hurt he had suffered at the hands of a woman.

Sam switched his train of thought. He hadn't meant to kill Paul, but the man had made him angry by trying to lie to him when he questioned him about the location of the lawyer's office. Instead of admitting he had been spotted and the woman had managed to lose him, he gave Sam the address. When he asked about the route she had taken and he said he didn't remember, he knew he was lying. That's when he asked, point blank if Paul thought he had been spotted. Paul had looked at him and lied in his face. He said no.

Sam hated liars, especially one who was stupid enough to continue lying after he'd been found out. He had asked him a second time and that's when Paul had said heatedly, "Listen, you mind your business and don't worry about how I do mine." Sam wanted to kill him for that, but meant only to scare him when he pulled out his gun. Paul had reached down and grabbed the shotgun he kept hidden under the seat. When Sam saw the shotgun, he went crazy and before he knew what was happening, Paul fell forward hard, his head slamming against the steering wheel. He had pulled the trigger without even thinking.

There had been blood everywhere! Afraid that someone might have heard the shot, he had jumped out of the car and tried to wipe off his fingerprints before fleeing. He was pretty sure he had covered his tracks, but the car could be traced to him and he knew it. It had been his old car and when Paul said he was having car problems, he had given it to him to use until he could make other arrangements. Now it was only a matter of time before the cops traced the automobile to him and unless he came up with something viable, he'd be under suspicion. Just what he needed with this murder case hanging over his head.

Now Hank was about to cut him off after he had come to his aid when he needed him! Well, he wouldn't allow it. "Listen man, why don't I tail her? She doesn't know my car so she won't get suspicious."

Sam wasn't going to let him off the hook. Cautiously, he said, "Wish I could, but I'm running low on funds."

"Okay, tell you what, I'll take half now and the other have in a couple weeks!"

Afraid to say no, Hank found himself agreeing before he hung up the phone. He sat there for a long time wondering how he was going to get the man off his back without making him mad. He could tell by his voice that Sam wanted the money, and he was afraid what he'd do if he backed down. He'd have to figure out something, but it wasn't going to be easy. Finally he went into the spare bedroom and laid on the bed. He slept in his clothes that night.

***

Skye woke feeling refreshed and she knew instinctively it was because she was not alone. Even if it was Hank, at least she felt safe having him there because she knew if she looked out the window she'd not find someone watching. Only Hank was planning to leave this morning and she wasn't sure what to expect once he was gone. But there was a much more pressing matters to contend with now, she reminded herself as she slid out from under the covers. As her feet hit the floor, she was already planning her morning strategy.

She'd fix Hank a nice breakfast and pack him some sandwiches to eat on his drive back to the city. Over breakfast she'd calmly discuss what she would like him to do so that she could finalize the details to take with her to the lawyer. She needed him to tell her what furnishings he wanted from the house and to let her know of any personal effects he wished to keep. She had already figured that she could have a garage sale and get rid of some of the small things, and maybe take out an advertisement and sell some of the furnishings ahead of time. This way when it got down to the wire, she'd be a few steps ahead in the planning.

Skye went into the bathroom to get ready, her mind spinning with details. Not knowing when Hank planned to leave, she wanted to make sure she had enough time to discuss all this with him. When Hank came upstairs, she was already in the kitchen.

"Sleep well?"

"Yeah." He walked by her and went into the bathroom.

Skye rushed about fixing his favorite breakfast. She filled the coffee maker and then made sausage and eggs, toast, and home fries. She was so busy she didn't hear him behind her and jumped at the sound of his voice.

"What's all this," he said.

"Oh, that was quick", she said trying to compose herself. "I thought you might like something to eat."

He was hungry and the smell of the food only emphasized it. She watched as he hurried downstairs to get dress. By the time he returned, breakfast was on the table.

They ate in silence. Skye, not one to eat meat and not really hungry, nibbled at a slice of toast, giving him time to relax. When his plate was almost empty, she watched as he wiped his toast in the pool of egg yolks and sausage drippings, and decided the time was right.

"Hank, one of the things I need to tell the lawyer is what you plan on keeping. Do you know what you don't want sold?"

He thought for a moment. "I thought we decided to hold off until I got back."

"Yes, but I told you I was going ahead with meeting with the lawyer. I'm not going to finalize anything, just maybe have a garage sale and sell some of the things we don't need."

"Well, I don't know right now."

She tried another tactic. "Listen Hank, no matter what, we know that we need money and we're going to have to sell the house. You said it yourself! The money you are earning is needed for living expenses and you don't have much left after paying for gas, food and rent. If we continue this way, we'll end up losing the house and neither one of us will get anything out of it. I can cover the mortgage, and the expenses a while longer, but eventually it'll have to go, so why not make sure we don't end up losing everything."

That seemed to make sense to him. "Tell you what, I'll think about it while I'm packing and let you know before I leave. Okay?"

"Sure, that's fine."

They finished in silence, each caught up in their own contemplations until Hank pushed back his chair. "I'd better get a move on."

"I'll fix you some sandwiches to take with you."

"Thanks."

Skye rinsed off the dishes and put them in the dishwasher and then started making the sandwiches. When everything was in order, she went to get a legal tablet from the office and waited for Hank.

Hank moved slowly, gathering up his things, already wishing he didn't have to leave. There was so much on his mind. The thing with Sam and now Skye pushing him to make some decisions. He was not in the mood to make the long drive with all this bothering him, but he had no choice. He tried to concentrate on what it was he wanted and at first he wanted everything. Finally he knew what he'd tell her. Dragging his suitcase he went back upstairs to get it over with.

Skye smiled at him, trying not to appear too anxious as she waited for Hank to break the silence. He, on the other hand, had decided to wait for her to broach the matter. After a while Skye determined she'd have to make the first move.

"Have you thought about what you want?"

"I guess so."

"Well, tell me so I can set the items aside."

He quickly gave her a list of things that he thought he wanted. The list was small.

He watched as Skye wrote down his choices.

"Listen, I'm not sure what I want. If I think of anything else, I'll call, so don't move to hastily." He knew he was stalling and figured she did too, but she said nothing as she stared down at the list. Then looking up she questioned him. "Hank, you didn't mention any furniture."

"I don't want any of the furniture."

"But you'll need things to furnish an apartment. Were you thinking about that?"

No, he wasn't thinking about that, he couldn't think about that. "I don't want any of the furniture," he said. If I need anything, I want it to be new. If I have to start out all over again, I'm not taking any reminders with me."

She could tell he meant it and didn't push. She changed the subject. "What time do you plan on leaving?"

"Are you anxious to get rid of me?"

"No, it's just a question."

Hank looked at his watch. It was eleven o'clock. If he left now he could be back in the City by seven; at the latest, eight. That would give him time to settle in and get a good night's sleep before reporting to the job site. "I should take off now," he said.

Without a word, Skye got up, went to the sink and filled a thermos with the leftover coffee. She gathered up the bag of food and followed Hank out to his van. She stood by the driver's side while Hank put his suitcase in the back before coming around to the front of the van. She handed it all to him once he was seated behind the wheel, shocked when he grabbed her hand.

"Listen Skye, I did what you asked. The wiretaps are off and I let the man know he is not to follow you."

"Thanks, Hank."

"I've done everything you asked so can I ask you something?"

"Yes, what is it?"

"If you get the least bit suspicious, anyone following you, anything at all, tell me you will let me know?"

"Why, is there something wrong?" she asked nervously.

"No, but I'm not sure, so I want you to tell me you'll call me first. Okay?"

"Okay," she said hesitantly.

"One more thing. Don't say anything right now, but think about it for me."

"What?"

Hank was squeezing her hand now and she felt the pressure and tried to pull away only he held her hand tighter. "If we sell the house and the furnishings we will eliminate one of our biggest problems, the bills. Will you think about that. Maybe without the pressure of the bills, we can make a go of it again. At least we could try."

"I..."

"No, don't say anything now, just promise me you will give it some thought."

"Okay, I'll think about it, but..."

"Good. That's all I ask."

He released her hand and turned the key in the ignition. Stunned, Skye stood watching as he backed out of the garage and onto the street. When his van crossed the intersection she finally made her way back into the house.

She felt tormented. All she wanted was some peace. All she wanted was to be left alone to do what she had to do. She was frightened. She could feel her own mortality, feel it as surely as if it were fragments of ice melting in her hand. Hank had spoken with genuine concern and that frightened her. Why was he cautioning her in this way? At that moment she was positive the matter had some how gotten out of his control.

CHAPTER 30

George Palma called Angelo at four o'clock on Monday and gave him a detailed synopsis of his findings.

"Mr. Maglioni's office."

"Put me through to Mr. Maglioni?"

"May I ask who's calling?"

"Tell him it's George Palma."

Mr. Maglioni's voice came over the line. "Yes, George, what is it?"

"You're not going to like it."

"What is it?"

"I've learned something very interesting about this Sam Stillman."

"Such as?"

"You know that woman you had us take our transcripts to?"

"Yes," Maglioni replied, worry already apparent in his voice.

"Well, it seems that Stillman has put a tail on her. Don't ask me why, but he had some guy by the name of Paul Angelino, watching the house."

Maglioni tried to remember where he had heard the name before. Then it came to him, he had read about the man, Angelino being shot. Why would Sam be interested in Skye Sanders? That was the question he couldn't answer.

"George, it's important that you find out what Stillman is up to. Check out his hangouts, follow him, do whatever you have to do to, but find out. You understand?"

"Sure, Mr. Maglioni. I think I know where to start. I'll get back to you as soon as I learn something."

"Good. But be careful, don't let him catch on that you're asking around or following him. And, by the way George, in case you didn't read it, that man, Paul Angelino, he was killed the night before last. We've got to find out before the cops do whether Sam had anything to do with it. While you're at it see if you can get anything on that, too,."

He hadn't known. George was not one to sit down and read the paper unless he was looking for something specific. From all he had learned about Stillman he was pretty sure there was a tie. Not only that, but if he wanted to remain among the living he'd have to move cautiously. He had been taken aback by the news of Angelino's death and was slightly embarrassed that he hadn't known. From here on he'd have to keep his eyes and ears open and the sooner he finished the job, the better he'd feel. George decided to get to work.

"I'll be in touch."

As soon as he hung up, he went to get the paper and started looking through it quickly. He came across the story and read it carefully, taking in the details, carefully putting himself in Stillman's shoes and trying to determine what hadn't been uncovered. He sat for a long time with a blank stare on his face as he concentrated on Stillman and what might be his next move. Finally he decided his first objective would be to stay one step ahead of Stillman and to do that he needed to trace him down. If he kept in front of him he should be okay.

George had a pretty good idea of the type of places a man like Stillman hung around. He had been checking up on guys like him for some time now so it would be easy to find him. Though he hadn't exactly met the man, from all the information he figured he would be easy to identify, but what bothered him was not knowing the hidden characters who might be involved. What if he misread Stillman and the man found him out and had him followed by one of his low life comrades... He put the thought aside. He'd have to depend on his sharp instincts if he wanted to stay alive and he'd need to feed that instinct with information from people that knew Stillman. Quickly he prepared to leave and shortly was on the road, stopping at every beer joint that Stillman frequented and engaging in conversations with the patrons and bartenders. It was a starting point. After cautiously asking questions at several places he ended up at the Circle Bar.

***

"What can I get you?" Oscar asked as he stared at the stranger.

"A whiskey and make it a double. I need something to calm my nerves."

He watched as Oscar went to get his drink, hoping his words would lead the bartender into a conversation. He was in luck.

"Something bothering you, friend?"

"Yeah, just had a fight with the Missus and could use something to calm me down. You know how it is."

"Yeah, we've all been down that road before."

"She made me so mad, I'd a killed her if I hadn't left."

"Yeah, sounds familiar. Want to talk about it?"

"Talk about it, hell, I just want to forget it!"

Oscar started to walk away, but turned back as George started talking again.

"I'm not going to let her get away with it. No, I'm going to do something about it before she gets it in her head she can cheat on me and not face the consequences. Hey, bartender, know anybody who could help me teach her a lesson."

He hadn't heard the man come in and jumped when he heard a voice behind him.

"You've got problems at home, my friend?"

George turned on the bar stool and looked into the ugliest face he had ever seen. The man who sat next to him had a nose that was bulbous and filled with pock marks. There were all sorts of battle scars on his face. He had seen a lot in his days, but this man had obviously been through it all. As George continued to observe him he noticed the man's eyes were mere slits and he could see gook piled in the corner, making him immediately lower his eyes. He then found himself staring into a mouth of blackened teeth and thinking, "When had he last seen his dentist?" There was nothing even remotely attractive about the man, George found himself thinking. His body was large and flabby, his hair unkempt, his clothes haphazardly laid on his body. As he raised his eyes to rest on the man's face, George started to say that's none of your business, but something in the man's face made him swallow those words.

"Yeah, but nothing I can't handle," he said in an uncertain tone, then turned to face Oscar again.

It wasn't hard to decipher the look on Oscar's face as he stood there as if carved out of granite. George sensed immediately that Oscar was frightened, but what was it exactly that frightened him. Was it George's remark or just the appearance of the stranger. For a moment George thought that Oscar wasn't going to answer him, then he heard Oscar say quickly, "No, I don't know anyone like that."

George could tell he was lying but before he could question him further, the man behind him spoke again.

"If it's help you want, my friend, why don't you join me at the table and I'll help you out."

"Sure, why not." As soon as the words came out of his mouth, George wished he could take them back. He had enough problems already and to get into another one was just stupid, but it was too late now. George laid some money on the bar, picked up his drink and followed the man to a table.

"What's your name, friend?"

"John Sexton," he lied.

"Well, John, tell me your problem."

"And who would I be telling?"

"The name's Sam. Sam Still... He started to use his real name but thought better of it. Instead he said, "Sam Stillmaucher."

George couldn't believe his luck. Careful not to show recognition he tried to keep his expression blank. No doubt this was Sam Stillman. Now that he faced the man and had the name he could put it together. The man standing before him was indeed Sam Stillman, older than the pictures he had come across, but definitely the same person. He had been thrown at first, but now he was sure. All he had to do was handle it right and he'd have the details he needed.

As he looked at the face across the table, he cautioned himself to be careful. The man had killed his wife, her lover, and now possibly this man Paul Angelino. If he wanted to keep his life intact he had best play it canny. He worked up a story in his head and then shared it with Stillman. He was careful not to over do the details as he explained the situation to Stillman, careful not to sound phony or let his face reveal anything but animosity for the woman he so cleverly created. When he was sure he had said enough, he sat back with a look of distaste written on his face.

"Well, what is it you'd like to have done?"

"I want to scare her enough so that she'll know she can't get away with it. Got any suggestions?"

"Sure."

George waited, then realized the man needed some prompting. He reached into his pocket and pulled out a roll of bills. He laid two fifties on the table. When Sam reached over to pick them up, he slapped his hand over the money.

"Not so fast my friend," he said mimicking Sam. "First I need assurance that you know what you're talking about. You know, something to prove you can earn this money."

Sam lowered his head and thought fast. "I'm working on a case right now. Following this woman who is giving her man a hard time. Told him she wanted a divorce."

George stared into the ugly face, careful not to show too much interest. Now he knew why he was following her, but he still didn't have the rest of the facts he needed.

"So, you're following her. What of it?"

"Had some wiretaps and a camera installed and gave them to the husband."

"How did you do that?"

"Can't tell you all my business, friend. Just take my word for it."

He tried another angle. "If you're still on that case, how can I be sure you have time for mine?"

"There's always time. I have friends to help out when the situation arises."

That answered his other question and gave him the opportunity to alleviate any unknown characters. That was if he could trust the man...

"Well, if I hire you, I want you to do the job."

"Fine, I'll do it."

Again he pressed with caution. "Are you a private detective, or something like that?

"No," Sam said honestly.

"Well, I need to hire a real private detective, too. Know anybody?"

"I did, but... Forget about a private detective, shit, what you need done I can handle it with no problem."

It wasn't a confession, but enough to convince George that Sam had killed the Angelino fellow or had arranged to have him killed. It sounded logical and he was one to credit logic. Besides, he usually was right when he reached an assumption. He had all he needed to know.

"Well, Sam was it?" Sam nodded. "Well, then, what I'll do is give you this money as a retainer, you might say. I'm going to think about this and then let you know. Where can I reach you?"

"I come in here often enough. When you make up your mind, just come looking for me and we'll deal."

George pushed back his chair, not worried about the money since he'd get it back from Maglioni twofold when he told him what he'd found out. He shook Sam's hand and headed for the door, making sure to look at Oscar one more time before he left. What he saw on Oscar's face clinched it. The man showed fear for him and looked as if he wanted to say something only he didn't dare. As he made his way out to the parking lot he knew if he needed more information, Oscar would be the one to talk to. With the right approach, Oscar would melt and having dealt with people like him before, he knew how to get the bartender to talk.

As George walked out to his car, felt he already knew a lot about this man Sam, and what he knew frightened him. There was no doubt in his mind this was a man to fear. Anyone who was willing to stick his neck out for a stranger had to be mad or crazy even if they did it for financial gain. By the time he reached the parking lot he was confident that he was on target and glad he'd not have to deal with Stillman again. He drove away deciding he'd call Maglioni, first thing in the morning.

***

As soon as he knew he'd find Maglioni in his office, George made the call. His secretary answered again and with annoyance he answered her inquiries before being connected to Maglioni.

"Hello, George. Don't tell me you've got something already?"

"Yeah, I do. And I got it from the horse's mouth, you might say."

"Okay, fill me in."

George told how he was about to question the bartender when who should come in but Sam himself. After making up some story he was able to get Stillman talking and had found out that he was tailing Ms. Sanders at her husband's request. He added that they were in the process of a divorce that she was initiating and her husband obviously was trying to curtail it by whatever means possible. He added that in further questioning him he had mentioned getting in contact with a private investigator.

"Stillman was uncomfortable when I mentioned it, even started to say something about having one, but didn't any longer. I'd say that was as close to a confession as anyone could get. He either killed the Angelino guy himself or had him killed."

"Did you get anything that would tell you why he'd do that?"

"No, but putting two and two together I'd say that Angelino must have messed up on the job he was doing for Stillman. Maybe to us it might not warrant killing him, but after meeting the guy face to face, I'd say that it takes very little to make him kill. He didn't appear to be a man who had any respect for life, if you know what I mean."

"I tend to agree with you. Just from meeting with him a couple of times, I got the same feeling."

"So what now," George said hoping he didn't have to deal with Stillman again.

"Just sit tight. You did a good job, and fast too. When you get a chance, stop by my office. I'll leave an envelope with Lisa."

"Thanks, Mr. Maglioni. Do you want me to do anything further?"

"Yes, keep following Stillman and report back if you find out anything else."

George sat back on his sofa, his ego boosted by the conversation. He wasn't elated by the news he'd have to tail Stillman, but he could handle it. Maglioni had been impressed and when ever Maglioni was impressed he'd be generous. George decided he would celebrate. Getting up from the sofa, George went into the bathroom and shaved while he made up his mind just what he'd do. By the time he entered his bedroom and put on a pair of his best slacks and a stiffly starched white shirt, he knew. He placed a call to his friend, Lilly and asked her if she'd join him for dinner. When she said, yes, he made the arrangement.

George whistled as he drove to Lilly's house, which was no bigger than a small apartment. Lilly was someone he called when he had a hankering for sex and she usually obliged. She was his type of woman. Right now he had an urge to show his manhood. He pulled up in front and blew his horn. In less than a minute, Lilly was walking out her front door, careful to lock it before opening the passenger side of the car and climbing in beside George. He pulled the car out onto the highway and proceeded toward the Hampton Inn. with a smile on his face as he complimented her on her low-cut red dress and she fingered his crotch in appreciation. Yeah, she was his type of lady all right. When they arrived at the Inn, he acted the gentlemen, taking her elbow and guiding her up the steps until they stood before the hostess stand.

"Two for dinner."

"It'll be just a minute. Would you like to wait in the bar?"

George looked at the bar which was visible from the lobby. The crowd was two-deep with stand-up drinkers, and all the booths were occupied. He didn't like standing in crowds and preferred to drink sitting down.

"No, we'll wait right here."

Lilly was in a very good mood and he found he actually enjoyed her chatter as she told him about her boss making a pass at her and the fact that she had been wondering why he hadn't called. They were in the midst of whispering obscenities in each other's ears when the hostess approached them.

"Your table is ready, sir." They stood and followed her to a small table, set up against the window. There wasn't much outside to see, but it was classy anyway. A waiter walked by and George stopped him.

"Can we have a couple drinks?"

"Sure, what would you like."

"A vodka gimlet for the lady and I'll have a whiskey, straight up."

When the waiter was out of hearing distance, George leaned over and said. "I really like that dress!"

"You already said that. It's really nothing special, but what I have on under it might interest you more."

"What's that?"

"Perfume," she giggled.

Their drinks arrived and Lilly picked her's up and took a big gulp. Liquid dribbled down her chin and she giggled again when George handed her a napkin.

"Ooh, I'm so sloppy. I almost ruined my perfume."

They laughed and were still laughing when the waiter came to take their orders. Again they made love talk and when their food was placed in front of them, Lilly ate her food suggestively until George was so hot he couldn't wait to get her home. As soon as he could grab the waiter, he got the check and paid for it.

They drove through the warm summer night with the windows rolled all the way down. From time to time George looked over at Lilly's blonde hair blowing in the gentle breeze and he licked his lips in anticipation. By the time they arrived at her house, they practically ran up the walk and once the door closed behind them, they were already ripping at each other's clothes. They didn't waste time going into the bedroom, instead dropped down on the living room carpet. He pressed himself against her naked body, heady from the drinks and the smell of her perfume. He ran his tongue across her nipples until they hardened, then slid up her body to place it in her mouth.

George gyrated his body against hers, feeling her gyrations as she pushed even closer. He raised his knee and pressed it high between her legs and she clung to him. He moved his hand down between their bodies and he whispered in her ear, "Ah, Lilly, you feel good."

He tried to hold back longer, but he could feel her insistence as they rolled on the floor, switching positions until he thought he would burst. He pushed her down and climbed on top of her, plunging deep, undulating, their bodies in tune with each other. All the built up passion exploded and she yelled out in ecstasy.

He rolled over on to his back and stared up at the ceiling trying to catch his breath. He heard Lilly getting up and leaving the room, but he remained still. She returned with a jug of cheap wine and they sat, naked on the floor, drinking until the bottle was empty.

"Will you stay the night?" she pleaded.

"No, I've got some things I need to do in the morning."

He could sense her disappointment as she watched him put on his clothes, then as she opened the door, she whispered, "Call me?"

"Sure. Get some sleep."

He stepped out and drove home, conscious of the fact he had had way too much to drink. When he was back at his apartment, he managed to park the car without mishap and weaved his way up the stairs. Once inside he forced himself to undress and climb in bed.

He woke up realizing his tongue hurt. He'd bitten it and there was an odd taste in his mouth. He was lying on his stomach, his arms flung out on either side of him. He managed to life his head and open his eyes, but just barely as he felt the pain shoot through his body. A face peered down at him and he thought, he knew that face, and he knew the voice.

"Thought you could fool me! John Sexton my ass," he heard Sam say viciously. "Can't seem to find the little woman either. I don't know exactly what you're up to, but I do know you work for a mutual friend. The name Maglioni ring a bell with you?"

George gaped, eyes wide in fear, unable to say a word.

"Well, Maglioni won't be able to help you now my friend because you won't be able to tell him." There was a ugly grin on his face as he moved it closer to George's before backing away and walking silently toward the front room. George heard the door close behind him.

He tried to raise his head, but he couldn't. He tried to remember how many times he'd been stabbed. Was it three, maybe four times? He tried to laugh, thinking it could have been worse. But it was bad enough because he knew he was dying. He had no strength at all; it had all drained out of him.

He thought bitterly, what an idiot. How could he have been so careless? It felt like thousands of ants were crawling inside him, stinging and biting as they moved. He was scared, his body floating in the darkness before he sank down until he was away from the pain, away from everything.

CHAPTER 31

Adam Snyder sat with his third cup of coffee in front of him, trying to dissuade himself from making a call to Skye. He had hoped she'd have contacted him by now, but she hadn't. He waited throughout the morning and when no call came in, he finally figured he'd chance it. He could do the night route again and remove the evidence, but he had to talk to her. He picked up the phone and called her office.

"Computer Services Unlimited, Skye Sanders speaking."

"Skye, this is Adam. Are you alone?"

"No, not this minute, but hold on, please."

He could hear her talking to someone in her office while he listened on the line. After what seemed like hours, but was no more than five minutes he heard Skye's voice as she said, "I'll walk with you to the door." Soon she was back on the phone.

"I'm here, Adam. I just had to shoo a customer out so I could talk with you. By the way, I've got some good news. No more wiretaps, we can talk freely."

Puzzled, he asked, "Are you sure?"

"Yes. Hank came home over the weekend and we talked. He agreed to take the wiretaps off and remove the tail. I checked to be sure he did it and as a precaution I checked each morning to see if anyone had come in and reconnected them. They're off. For once Hank kept his word."

"That's good news, but I have some bad news to tell you."

She immediately pulled herself up straighter in her chair. Tension coursed through her and she could barely manage to say, "What is it?"

"I hate to say this, but I'm glad you're scared because you need to be. You need to be scared and careful at all times. I don't know the whole deal, but the man that was tailing you was named Paul Angelino. You read the papers faithfully so you know that there have been stories about his death."

Her eyes grew big with fear. She had read the story and all the ones that had followed. The man had been killed, less than four miles from her door. She waited for Adam to continue.

"Anyway, Paul Angelino had been hired to watch you by a Sam Stillman. That's the man who is going to be tried for the murder of his wife and her lover, the name that you've been bombarded with in those transcripts. Skye, Sam was hired by Hank to put the tail on you and he is not a man to fool around with. I'm sure if Hank even told him to stop, he'd only do it if he had a mind to. It's all too much of a coincidence if you ask me. All these people are connected and you are a sitting duck in the middle."

"But why? I didn't do anything, so why is this happening to me?"

"I know you did nothing, but maybe Sam doesn't know that. I'm being honest with you, Skye. I'm scared for you. It's the innocent ones who always end up getting hurt and I don't want that to happen to you. I want you to do two things for me."

"Anything, anything, just tell me what to do."

"First, as soon as I hang up I want you to call your lawyer, and tell him all that I told you. Second, I want you to start thinking seriously about someone who can come and stay with you. Promise that you'll do that?"

"Yes, I promise."

"And Skye, I'm going to be watching you. I'll be checking to see if anyone follows you when you leave there, and pass by at night to see if anyone is watching the house. Try to limit your trips as much as possible and be sure to ask who it is before opening your door. It's very important that you do this. I know you have clients coming and going, but unless you know them, don't open the door. I think you're pretty safe during the day, but I don't want you to take any chances. If you see, hear, or get a funny feeling about anything, call me. Got a pencil?"

"Yes, I've got one."

"I'm going to give you my car phone number, my home phone, and a phone of a friend of mine. I want you to call all the numbers until you get me."

"I will," she said meekly.

"Are you ready?"

She jotted down the numbers and checked them as Adam repeated them a second time.

"Okay, now try and act like nothing is wrong. I know that's not easy, but try real hard and don't forget to call your lawyer."

Skye shook her head up and down and then remembering she was on the phone, said, "I will."

"Bye, Skye."

"Bye."

She hung up the receiver and picked it immediately back up. She dialed Mitch Cayman.

"Good afternoon, Mr. Cayman's office."

"Hello, this is Skye Sanders. I need to speak to Mr. Cayman."

The secretary recognized the name and immediately buzzed her boss, informing him that Ms. Sanders was on the line.

"Hello, Skye."

"Hello, Mitch, this is Skye Sanders."

"I know that all ready."

Skye laughed nervously. "Sorry. I'm just so shook up."

All concerned now, Mitch asked, "What's wrong Skye."

She told him everything. About the tail, the wiretaps, Hank coming home, the call from Adam and his suspicions. She tried not to succumb to fear as she related the details of the man who had been watching her, but by the time she finished she was shaking.

"I can understand why you're so upset, Skye, but it won't do any good for you to lose your head. You said the wiretaps are off and you haven't seen any signs of anyone following you?"

"Yes," she said.

"Okay, now Skye, I think Mr. Snyder gave you some good advice and I want you to follow it. Let me take care of the rest. Will you do that for me?"

Again she replied, yes, not knowing what else to say and reluctantly hung up the phone. She sat in her chair, the house abnormally quiet. She could hear the clock in the family room ticking.

One hour passed, two, then three and Skye hadn't moved a muscle. It grew dark outside, and the light from her office lamp cast shadows in the corner, but she wasn't aware of them any more than she was aware the sun had sunk below the horizon.

The office line rang, but she didn't answer. It rang several more times, but she let the answering service take the call. In the family room the home line rang and she ignored it. Hour after hour she sat there in a daze until a knock at the door shook her back to reality. Slowly she got up, unaware of what she was doing until the knock came again. She dragged her body into the family room, pulled back the curtain and peeked out. She saw her neighbor, Selma Johnson standing on the step.

Reflectively she drew back, her breath coming in gasp as she recalled the nightmare she had witnessed with her eyes open, that strange haunting nightmare that revealed Selma taken over by some apparition. It was only after shaking the cobwebs from her head that she realized it was only a stupid vision, not something that had actually happened. She managed to smile and just as Selma lifted her hand to knock again, she opened the door.

"Hi, Selma."

"Hi, Skye, are you all right."

Puzzled, she said, "Sure, why?"

"Well, Hank called our house. He said he had called both the home and office lines and got no answer. He asked me to come and check on you."

"Yes, I'm fine." Quickly she conjured up an excuse. "I was so busy working, I just let the service take the calls."

"Are you sure?"

"Sure, I'm sure. Don't I look all right?"

"Frankly, Skye, you look like you've just seen a ghost."

It took all her will power not to laugh in Selma's sweet face. "I guess I'm tired and jumpy. Your knocking did give me quite a fright, knowing how late it was."

"Well, if you are all right, I'll go back and tell Hank. He said he needed to talk to you so he'll probably call back."

"Thanks, Selma. I'm sorry to have bothered you, but tell Hank I'll be here waiting for his call."

Skye closed the door and watched until Selma was across the street before she allowed herself to burst into laughter. "I look like I've seen a ghost," she howled. She laughed until her sides ached and went into the kitchen to get a glass of water. When she had drunk half of it, she sobered and was more in control.

The phone rang and Skye picked up the extension in the kitchen.

"Hello," she said as she stretched the cord so she could sit at the table.

"Hello, Skye. What's going on?"

"Nothing, didn't Selma tell you I was letting the service take the calls while I finished a job."

"She told me, but that's not like you. You always answer the phone when you're home."

"I told you, I was busy. Remember I mentioned that I would have to put in extra hours to pay your American Express bill? Well, that's what I'm doing." It was amazing how easily she was able to come up with yet another lie, and so quickly. But it wasn't a big lie, just a little one.

"Okay, I got the picture," Hank said irritably.

"Selma said you needed to speak to me, Hank. What's up?"

"I'm quitting the job and coming home."

Too stunned to attempt an answer right away, Skye remained silent.

"Skye, did you hear me?"

She came out of her reverie, looked across the room at the far wall with a sour expression. "Yes, I heard you. Are you going to tell me why you quit?"

"You said it yourself. I can't handle much more than my own expenses here. So, after thinking about it I figured it wasn't worth it. I called the Union and they've arranged a replacement."

"Do they have a job for you."

He hesitated before retorting. "No they don't, but I plan on checking around myself."

Catching the harshness in his voice, she said, "Hank, I didn't mean anything by that, it's just a shock is all."

"That's not how you sounded. Sounded to me like you were dreading my return."

"Listen, I don't want to argue. When will you be home?"

"I'm going to leave in the morning."

"Well, I guess I'll see you sometime tomorrow."

"Guess so."

Hank hung up the phone first, wondering if something had happened and Skye wasn't telling. He was depressed and anxious. He did not like what he saw when he looked plainly at what he had done. The truth struck him harshly. He had acted very stupidly and now Skye was in danger. As soon as he admitted it, he knew that was not his real intent. All he wanted was to make Skye change her mind and not go through with the divorce. That was all, but somewhere along the line he had been sidetracked, believing that there was no hope had made him act irrationally.

It had been easy to think that he wouldn't let anyone have her if she left him. Very easy indeed, especially since Skye wasn't giving an inch. But the scheme was to first try forcing her hand, find something that would give him a leg up in the situation, but it wasn't happening that way. He had gotten in with what Skye would call the wrong crowd and now circumstances were getting out of control.

Hank sighed deeply. What brought him up short was his acute consciousness of Skye and the magnetic draw he felt whenever she entered a room. During that weekend home he had been intensely aware of her presence and strong physical urges had him wanting to pull her into his arms and feel her body close to his. The only thing that held him back was his fear of rejection. He couldn't handle that.

Well, he thought, what's done is done. At least now he'd be able to be there and able better to take control of the situation, and maybe if he played his cards right, make Skye change her mind. Yes, quitting the job was the right move. The right move indeed.

Later that evening, Hank laid on his bed in the apartment looking up at the ceiling and wishing there was someone to console him. He was remorseful, but so tired that he soon fell asleep.

He bent down and kissed Skye deeply, feeling her body close as he enveloped her in his arms. She cuddled securely against him. Placing a hand under her chin he raised her face to his and found her mouth again. He kissed her with fervor, Skye returning his wild, impassioned kisses while one hand stroked the nape of his neck, sending chills down his spine.

His blood raced, his heart thundered in his chest, and desire was rampant in him. He had to have her. He brought his lips to her breast, his hands moving down over her stomach until his fingers were entwined in the hair between her thighs.

Hank awoke in a cold sweat, his jockey shorts clinging to his wet thighs. As he glanced around his surroundings he realized he was in bed alone, far from home and that he had been dreaming. He was afraid to close his eyes again. It seemed so real and he knew he was hard. He wanted it to be real, wanted to hold her in his arms and feel her body respond to his touch. Why couldn't it be like it was before? What could he do to make all the bad times disappear and have her in his arms again. "Oh, Skye," he whispered. He wanted it so bad...

Finally he got up from the bed and quietly went into the kitchen. Taking a beer out of the refrigerator, he sat alone, polishing off one beer after the other until finally he hobbled to the bedroom and laid down. Reminiscing was strenuous exercise, and fatigue had enveloped him. He was too drunk to do much else, and finally slept fitfully.

***

At first Skye was upset by the news. Hank was coming home. That would mean that she'd have to proceed cautiously with her plans to finalize the divorce. For a half an hour, maybe longer, she sat at the table thinking about it until something clicked in her head. "That won't be so bad," she said aloud. "It might even be a good omen."

The house was quiet and mournful as she remained at the kitchen table. It was easy to think. She realized that having Hank around would be protection, in a sense, and she wouldn't have to find someone to stay with her. Since she had told him her plans, she could continue openly, maybe even faster since he'd be around to sign the papers. Maybe it was a blessing in disguise.

Skye stretched, feeling better once she had eased the tension in her neck muscles after sitting stiffly for so long. She felt a surge of strength, as if she possessed the power to do anything, to bear anything, to solve whatever problem came up. Yes, it might be the best news she had thus far. After talking with Adam she had to admit having Hank around might be the best news yet. She continued her reverie trying to decide how she should move from here. Every now and then she would stretch to ease the stiffness of her joints and then return to concentrate on her next move.

It was after midnight when Skye finally pushed away from the table and stood up. As she moved down the hallway to the bedroom she had convinced herself that she would be able to handle the details that needed to be handled. Hank had solved the need for her to find someone to come stay with her and through all their differences, she was assured that Hank meant her no harm. After all, all she was trying to do was give them a good start. Hank knew that, she was sure, even if he did not portray that he knew. It might work out better this way with him feeling like he was a part of the decisions being made and not learning about them second hand. In all truthfulness she didn't fear Hank or doubt that he wouldn't hurt her physically. If she were right, everything should move along nicely from here on out.

CHAPTER 32

At eight o'clock the next morning, while Hank was doing a good impression of waking in his apartment, Skye was already seated in her office with her second cup of coffee. By nine o'clock Hank had managed to march into the shower and a few minutes after, dressed and began packing. Skye was by that time dialing her lawyer to inform him Hank was due home. And at noon when Hank finished his goodbyes and started the first leg of his journey home, Skye was on the threshold of receiving some good, most unexpected, news.

***

There was a knock at the office door. Skye, engrossed in thought, didn't hear it. She was editing a short article that one of her customers had dropped off the previous week. The section she was on needed something to support the author's statements, but she couldn't figure out exactly what to add. She found herself reading it again...

Many a poet has downplayed the subject, casting doubt that the word "love" had a place in the English language. I at least admit it has a place; even will go so far as to say my antagonistic viewpoint results from a one-sided love affair.

I had openly admitted that I had felt love at one point in my life, only to see it dissolve before my very eyes. Isn't that proof of what I am saying? Love is more a thing of the moment, than a lasting feeling.

The knocking, became more insistent. Again the sound didn't register as Skye tried to organize her mind. So engrossed in the article, she continued to try and figure out what was needed to support the author's claim. She had read something, somewhere...

It escaped her as she strained for remembrance until finally she had it. Quickly she got up from her chair and hurried down to the den to grab The Complete Works of Shakespeare. Flipping the pages as she rushed back to the office, she turned to Twelfth Night. Her eyes quickly scanned the words until she found what she was looking for and she read it out loud.

What is love? 'tis not hereafter;

Present mirth hath present laughter;

What's to come is still unsure:

In delay there lies no plenty;

Then come kiss me, sweet and twenty,

Youth's a stuff will not endure.

Feeling quite proud of herself, Skye made a note in the margins for the inclusion of the lines.

The knocking, now more a banging, made Skye jump into awareness. Quickly she hurried to the office door and peeked through the window. Standing on the front porch, with an irritated expression on her face was Paulette Locke. Skye reached down and turned the door knob.

"Good afternoon, Ms. Locke," she said, stepping aside as Paulette slipped by her.

"Skye, I was about to give up. I've been knocking loud enough to wake the dead!"

She had never seen Paulette any way but composed; now, standing in front of her looking slightly shaken Skye felt responsible for her discomfort. "I'm sorry. Truly I'm sorry. I didn't hear you knocking until just now. I hope you weren't out there long. Sometimes I get so involved, I shut out everything."

"It's okay. I must admit I was upset at first," Paulette stated as she found herself calming, "But I'm more relieved then anything now. When you didn't answer after the second knock, I checked the garage and saw your car was here and when I walked pass the window I could hear sounds coming from inside. I guess I was concerned about you. I thought something might be wrong."

"No, I'm fine, just a little hard of hearing when I get into my work." She paused and studied Paulette's face. "Come on in and have a seat. Can I get you a glass of water?"

"Thanks, that would be nice. It's really hot out today!"

Skye excused herself and went into the kitchen, she returned with the water and handed it to Paulette. She stood in front of her for a moment before going behind her desk to sit, then facing her said, "What can I do for you, Ms. Locke?"

"Call me Paulette, Skye. I like my friends to call me by my first name."

"Sure, Paulette. I'm sorry. I know you asked me before to call you by your name. I just forgot."

"Oh, don't worry about it. I forgive you." Paulette replied kidding after seeing the serious expression on Skye's face. It's just been such a trying day, is all." She paused and then a look of remembrance appeared on her face. "I almost forgot why I stopped by. I have these papers I need your help on. This damn project has me boggled," she said not looking up from the papers that she had removed from her briefcase.

"Well, let me see if I can help."

Skye came from behind her desk and walked over to stand behind Paulette. She looked down at the folder. She watched as one of Paulette's tapered fingers guided her eyes to a section on the page.

"You see here, where it has all the details of the area? Well, it's like that throughout the document," she said in an exasperated voice. "I am no expert when it comes to writing down technical directions. I was wondering if you could go through this and add whatever you think is needed. While you're at it, take out anything that doesn't make sense."

Skye came back from behind the chair now and taking the papers from Paulette scanned over the contents as she stood at Paulette's side. After a moment she said, "Yes, I see what you mean."

Paulette continued to look frustrated. "Skye, I guess I'm asking if you can just redo all the sections that deal with directions!"

Skye smiled, "It doesn't look too complicated. I've got a city guide that I can use, and along with road maps, it shouldn't be too much trouble to clean it up."

Paulette said as she placed the balance of the folder in Skye's hands and watched Skye carry it with her as she moved to her chair and sat down. "Can you, really? It's such a mess!" She said exasperated. Skye continued to flip through noting the areas of concern, then looked at Paulette. "Yes, don't worry, Paulette. I think I can handle this for you."

"Oh, you're a life saver, Skye. I knew if anyone could help me, it'd be you. How long will it take?"

"I don't know right offhand. It's not something I do regularly."

"Well, it doesn't matter, really. Do you think you can do it in a week, two weeks?"

"It shouldn't take any more than a week."

"Fine, the job is yours. Do you have a fee in mind?"

"No, like I said, this is not something I've done before. Let me look it over again." Skye again went through the pages trying to get an idea of how long it would take.

"Listen, don't worry about it, now. Whatever you charge is okay with me. Just to get it off my back is worth a bundle. We can discuss it when you've finished."

That out of the way, Paulette relaxed against the chair. "Skye, you don't have any coffee made, do you?"

"Yes, I have a pot going in the kitchen. How do you take it?"

"Two creams."

Skye went in the kitchen and poured them both a cup. She turned around with the cups in her hand to find Paulette standing behind her.

"Let's take a break, Skye. Can we sit out here."

"Sure," she said a little puzzled as she sat the cups on the table and pulled out a chair.

"This is nice. I've been rushing around all day. Between my regular work and this extra assignment that is just blowing my mind, I need a break."

"If you need help, I'm willing to give you a hand, Paulette. All you need to do is ask."

"Oh, you don't know how I wish I could turn this project over to someone. Can you imagine trying to turn a swine into a swan? You probably can't, no one could. But lets forget it. I don't even want to think about work now. How are things with you?"

"What?" Her question caught Skye off guard for a moment. She had liked Paulette from the minute she had met her, but they had only talked business up till now. She was at a loss for words.

"Skye, what didn't you understand? I asked you how are things going with you?"

She could see that Paulette wanted to relax. "Everything is fine," she said, but even to her own ears it didn't sound convincing.

"No, honestly, Skye. I really like you and would like it if we could be friends. I'm usually in such a hurry I don't have time to sit and chat, but for once in my life I'm going to just relax. My work keeps me so busy all the time, I don't socialize much, but lately I've been thinking about changing that. Did you know I used to be married?"

"No, I didn't know that."

"Well, I was. I used to have a normal life. One day I came home and my husband was packing his things. He said he was tired of trying to make an appointment to talk with me and had it up to here!" She lifted a well-manicured hand up above her head. "At first I was shocked and hurt, wondering what I had done wrong and until recently I never did understand. But for some reason I've been thinking about it a lot lately and realized that I haven't allowed time for much of anything that didn't deal with my work. I deserved to lose him."

"I'm sorry," Skye said sincerely.

"Oh, don't be. I'm not. I don't think we were right for each other. We kind of fell into marriage before I knew what it was I wanted."

"And what did you want?"

"Good question! I guess what I wanted was to have a chance to concentrate on me. I came from a large family and never felt like I had time for myself. First it was helping my mother with the other kids, then the next thing I knew I was married and dealing with my husband's concerns. After the divorce I found there was more time for me, but I thought it was work I craved, only now I think it's friendship, something I hadn't given myself a chance to develop." She seemed to be thinking about what she had said. "But enough about me. Tell me about you."

Skye took a deep breath. "Work wise everything is just fine, but personally, well, that's another story."

Paulette looked concerned. "Why, what's wrong? Want to tell me about it?"

Skye didn't respond immediately, but figuring Paulette had talked freely, decided to open up. "I haven't been happy with my marriage for a long time. Sort of like you, I kind of fell into mine, too. I kept putting it off and putting it off until a few months ago I made my decision and asked Hank, that's my husband, for a divorce." She looked across the room at nothing in particular and then added. "I guess I was afraid at first, but after awhile I realized that I wanted happiness and decided to go ahead and chance it."

"What were you afraid of?"

"I guess being alone. But that doesn't matter that much anymore. I just want some peace and a chance to enjoy life. I can't be happy married to Hank. I also didn't want to end up losing the business I've built. It took a long time to get where I am now and I didn't want to rock that boat, so to speak."

"You won't have to lose the business, Skye. You probably have a lot of loyal customers and they'd understand. No one holds a divorce over your head. It's too commonplace for that."

"I guess I do have loyal clients," Skye said more to herself than to Paulette. "I know they won't turn their backs on me, but we're planning to sell the house and right now I don't know where I'll be going. That and whether I can get settled permanently right away has me worried. I can't expect clients, even loyal ones to traipse around until I finally settle."

"How soon are you talking, Skye?"

"Well, I've seen a lawyer and he's in the process of preparing the paperwork, but before anything can be finalized I need to sell the house, the furnishings and find a place to live."

"Are you upset by all this? I mean do you want the divorce?"

"No, I'm not upset. It's what I want, I know that. It's just that there is so much involved that it makes my head spin."

"You know I can help you out on one point. I'm a real estate agent and if you'd like, I'll handle the sale of the property for you. I can also help with selling the furniture. I have contacts that handle household sales and can put you in touch with someone who will guide you through that tedious process. I can also help in finding you a place to live, if you'll accept my help."

"Oh you don't know what this means to me. My lawyer... You know him, it's Mitch Cayman, is handling the divorce. Anyway, outside of the papers that I need to get Hank to sign, the next big project was to get the house sold. Not until all of our possessions are sold or accounted for, and all of the joint debts are cleared, can I move ahead with the divorce."

"Worry no more. It's as good as done. Paulette looked around her. "This is very nice, Skye. You shouldn't have any trouble selling it. What is the square footage?"

"Twenty-five hundred."

"You're kidding."

"Come on cleaning day and work with me and you'll know it's a fact," she laughed.

"Can I see it?"

"Sure."

Skye led Paulette through the upstairs rooms first, reciting the names as they moved along: "Spare bedroom, master bedroom, master bathroom, laundry room, kitchen, and the office which used to be the living room."

She guided her to the steps and they went down. "Den, rec room, kitchenette converted to bar, spare bathroom, spare bedroom, our son's room."

They started back up the stairs and Skye turned to her right and they descended the two steps. "And this is the family room."

"What's through that door?" Paulette said looking in front of her.

Skye walked over and opened the door and led Paulette into the garage. "Two, car garage." She walked to the center and pulled the chain that hung on a trap door. Cautiously she pushed Paulette gently to the side as the steps unfolded. "Full attic over the garage."

Paulette looked in Skye's direction. "Sure, go ahead up." When Paulette was again standing beside her she said, "This is a wonderful house. How can you give it up?"

"Believe me, it's easy."

They walked back into the kitchen. Paulette turned to Skye. "Skye, from what I've seen this is a well laid out house. There's so much room, lots of storage space, and it's well decorated. I have to be honest though, we may run into trouble finding a buyer who is looking for a house this size, but that's the only problem I can foresee. It's perfect for a large family."

"Oh, yes, I almost forgot, there's an in ground pool and deck out back."

Paulette got out of her chair and went to the window, and Skye followed her. "The sliding glass doors off the family room lead to the deck." She added as they looked out across the back yard.

Paulette stood, running figures through her head. "Skye, I'm going to bring some papers back for you. If you're serious, I'll have someone come out and take measurements, but I would guess you could get somewhere in the range of ninety thousand for this property. It's a corner lot, well treed... Newly sided?"

"We had vinyl siding and vinyl windows put in about six or seven years ago, so it's not that new."

"Take me through again, I need to make some notes."

Skye walked her back through. On this second trip, Paulette had her open up the louver doors downstairs which housed the water heater, and furnace, then the utility closet. When they returned upstairs she prepared to leave.

"I'll be in touch, soon. I have enough now to work with. I'll call before I send someone out to take the measurements."

"That will be good. I'm a little leery of strangers walking around the property lately. This is not a mutually agreed upon divorce and Hank has hit me with some surprises."

"Don't worry, I'll definitely call first. I know how it can be. I was married once and went through this, only I kept the house. My ex put me through some changes, but we all survive in the end. Just keep your chin up."

"I will. And Paulette? Thank you."

"You're entirely welcome. It's me that should be thanking you though. I'm going to earn a nice commission!"

As she walked with her to the door, Skye thought the commission she'd earn was pennies to this woman who dressed like she just walked off a magazine cover. She had a feeling that Paulette Locke had plenty of money and was only doing this more as a favor than for the income.

After seeing Paulette out, Skye found it easier to work. Her mind seemed freer, uncumbered with the pressure of figuring out how to handle her personal matters. She worked through the day.

CHAPTER 33

William Taylor sat behind the District Attorney desk, pensively working through the case before him. As yet he had been unsuccessful in making any headway. Even using his best staff members, he had nothing. He knew the man was guilty, but it would take proof to put Samuel Stillman behind bars and thereby prove to all the world he was the better lawyer. But his real purpose was to defeat Mr. Angelo Maglioni. That was the challenge he put before himself.

He slammed his big hand down on the marred desktop. "Asshole used me for fucking bait!" That was how he felt and he couldn't shake it. No way would someone of Maglioni's stature take on this case, except to even a score. Should have ripped his lungs out and tossed them at the cameras after that last time, he thought remembering how frightened he had been when he discovered after the conclusion of that case so long ago he was being followed. He recalled the time he came home to find his apartment ransacked and other little incidents that ate at him now. He knew Maglioni was behind it, though he swore he hadn't done anything. Well someone had, just the same and Maglioni was the one who would pay.

Another second of confusion, then insight hit. Revulsion followed a moment later. His hard brown eyes shifted as he rose a few inches in his chair, stared straight ahead, then started laughing. "Nothing like adrenaline to make the mind glow." He leaned over and pressed the intercom button on his desk.

"Yes, Bill?"

God, didn't the woman ever learn. How many times had he told her to address him as Mr. Taylor when they were in the office!

"Patricia, get me Daniel Malone on the phone."

He leaned back, a smirk on his face. Patricia's voice came over the intercom.

"He's on line one, Bill."

"Will you stop calling me, Bill. The name is Mr. Taylor during office hours. Got that?"

"S-o-r-r-y," she said emphasizing each letter.

Taylor released the button and picked up the phone.

"Daniel, my friend, how's it going?"

"Just fine, Bill. I was surprised to get your call. Got something for me?"

"You bet I do. This may be your ship coming in," he quipped. "How fast can you get to my office?"

"I'm as good as there."

Taylor hung up the phone.

***

Daniel stared at the phone for a moment before placing it back in the cradle. It had been quite some time since Taylor had initially called him and he had been wondering what was going on, but reminded himself that ever since Bill landed the District Attorney job, he was well set for help. There was plenty of staff to do his leg work. That's why it usually surprised him when he did get a call from him.

He himself had amassed an impressive amount of clients, managed to keep busy and be the sole support of his family. And he had a wonderful family. Thinking of them now, he remembered he had promised Janet he would go to the grocery store with her. He went to find her now.

Janet was sitting at the kitchen table going through her coupons. Dan stood in the doorway and watched her for a while, wearing a pair of old denim jeans that hugged her body tightly. Her hair was a mass of curls tumbling around her shoulders as she hunched over the table. He could picture her face with fresh makeup, the heart-shaped face he had woken up to so many mornings. Still beautiful, still desirable.

Finally he stepped directly in front of her to catch her attention. Even then there was a delay before her eyes met his and she finally stopped, placing the file of coupons aside and looking into his eyes. She gifted him with a sweet smile.

"Hi, hon, I know I promised I'd go to the store with you, but I've got to go out for a while," he said with sincere regret.

Janet, used to the nature of his business, knowing it popped up unexpectedly and that he couldn't tell her much about his cases, was not upset. They had been married almost twenty-five years and to this day she tingled when he walked into the room. They were still lovers and every day she counted her blessings. She loved him so much.

In the beginning, Janet had thought that the overwhelming physical feeling they had for each other would diminish after the children came, but instead it grew stronger. Dan was the best father, the best husband that any woman could wish for and he was all hers.

Janet got up from her chair and walked into his arms, then jokingly said. "Honey it's all right, I understand. Even I'd rather pierce my whole body with needles then face the long lines at the grocery store!"

Dan turned her face up to his and kissed her passionately. He could feel her body moving closer to his, feel her tongue searching through his mouth and he had to pull away. "Whoa, baby, if you keep that up neither one of us is going anywhere!"

Janet smiled and took one step back. "When do you think you'll be back?"

"I don't know, but I don't think this will take long. I need to get some details on a case that's being turned over to me by the District Attorney."

"Oh," Janet said sounding impressed. "Is that William Taylor, the same man you used to do work for in the past?"

"Yeah, one and the same. Since he got elected, he's had enough staff to handle most of his leg work. I was kind of surprised when he called, but he's thrown work my way before and I want it to continue. He's a good contact."

"Well, take your time and don't worry about me, I'll push my own grocery cart just like all the other wives in town."

"Oh, sweetie, I'm sorry. I did want to go with you."

"I'm just kidding, Dan. I'll walk you to the door?"

A final kiss, a pat on the fanny, and Dan was finally out the door. Janet returned to her coupons.

***

"Daniel Malone to see you, Mr. Taylor."

"Send him in."

Dan entered the office. Taylor came from behind his desk to give his old friend a hug. "Nice to see you again, my friend."

"Thanks. Nice to see you too. I was surprised when you called. With all this," he said holding his arms out to the side, "I can't imagine why you still call me. I take it you've got something you want me to do?"

"I called because I have a job that no one can handle like you could."

"Fill me in."

Taylor passed the papers on the Stillman case across his desk for Dan to read. While he read, Taylor concentrated on his approach.

"This seems cut and dried to me," Dan said.

"Yeah, on the surface that's exactly what everyone thinks. Take it a step further. Think about Angelo Maglioni, the only son of Maglioni, the mafia guy. Why would a rich, prominent lawyer like him take on a case like this?"

"Good question. Got any answers?"

"Only one that I can come up with on the spot."

"And, what's that?"

"He saw my name on the papers and jumped at the chance to even the score."

Dan was well aware of the past run-in between Taylor and Maglioni. Matter-of-fact, he had been hired by Taylor to watch his back after he had told him he was being tailed. But that was a long time ago. Surely a man like Maglioni had better things to occupy his time than to pull up an old grudge. Besides, he had managed to repair any damage done to him.

"Taylor, I think you're being a little paranoid, here."

"You think so? I don't."

"Okay, tell me what I can do."

"There's a lot you can do. First I want you to find out all you can about Samuel Stillman. I have names and address I can give you to help you get started. Keep an eye on him and if he does anything suspicious file the information."

"Okay. Anything else?"

"Yeah, I don't know if you read it in the papers, but a shady undercover detective named Paul Angelino was killed recently. See if you can find out if there is any connection between him and Stillman. I want you to check every lead you uncover and report everything, right down to how many times the man takes a piss. Then in your spare time I'd like you to nose around and see if you can find out any details on how Maglioni is going to fight this case. He has to have an angle because he can't win it any other way, and he's not the type of lawyer to fight a losing battle."

"Did you say, in my spare time? Checking up on the Stillman guy is a full time job by itself. Besides, I don't know if I want to touch that last part. A man could end up dead, putting his nose into a lawyer like Maglioni's business!"

"Dan, you're the only one I could trust to ask that. You are the best private investigator I know. You're smart, cautious and not afraid of hard work. I know it's asking a lot and I'm willing to double your hourly rate for the whole package deal. Does that change your mind?"

Dan couldn't refuse the offer. He'd not be able to take on any other jobs if he decided to do this for Taylor. To get double his rate made it hard to say no.

"Well, Dan?" Taylor was getting impatient.

"Okay, I'm on the case, but I will need a copy of the case papers, the leads you offered, and whatever else you've got. Right now it looks like I'll be spending my days and nights in the street, but maybe what you have and what your men might have overlooked will help me get to the bottom of this and still have time for my family."

Taylor didn't say a word, just went behind his desk and starting pulling out folders. When he had everything in a heap he pressed the intercom button.

"Yes, Mr. Taylor."

"Patricia can you come in here a sec. I have some files I need duplicated right away."

In a few minutes Patricia came through the front door of the office. She was wearing a thin black, silky shell top tucked into a tight black mini skirt with very high heeled shoes. Her lips were red, eyes glossed with heavy eye shadow. She looked more like a hooker than the secretary of the District Attorney. She paused, smiled at Dan and then went over to Taylor's desk to gather the files he handed her, frowning as she did so. "Will that be all, Mr. Taylor?" she said in a mocking voice.

"Yes, that's it for now. We need these right away."

"Why, of course." She smiled, but the tone of her voice let Taylor and Dan know she wasn't thrilled. As she leaned over to retrieve the folders, Dan couldn't help glancing at her long legs, that seemed to go on forever. Her skirt, if you could call it that, was barely covering her, and bending at the waist threatened to reveal more exposure than he cared to see. Quickly he lowered his eyes to his lap to stare at his pad. Finally, with the folders juggled haphazardly in her arms, Patricia left the room.

"Dan, let me just briefly summarize what the files contain."

Taylor talked while Dan jotted notes on his pad. Every now and then he examined Taylor's face as he continued to flood him with details. There was no time to concentrate on the data as his pencil flew across the pad. When Taylor finally stopped speaking, he continued writing until he had every piece of information written down. He looked over his notes quickly, making sure he could read them, but not too worried about the contents. What he had scribbled on the pad was more or less a checkpoint to use in reviewing the files.

"Well, what do you think?"

"Don't know. I need time to go through the files before I'd chance an opinion." Secretly he knew a lot, but didn't think he should say anything at this point. From the last assignment and the information he had gathered from Skye, this case might become a personal matter, but he wasn't sure of that now, but something told him that from the standpoint of his marriage and the case he would have to be very careful.

"But do you think you can come up with something?"

After a slight pause Dan sighed and addressed Taylor. "Yeah, probably, but clarify this for me. You mentioned that you thought there was a connection between this Paul Angelino and Stillman. Why?"

Now it was time for Taylor to reflect. He raised an eyebrow and thought for a moment. "Well, it's an assumption on my part. In the files is a report that mentions a connection between the two men. Stillman and Angelino go back a ways, but most recently Stillman had Angelino spying on his deceased wife. There may be nothing, but it's worth checking out. I only learned about the connection when one of my men mentioned that Stillman had been seen talking to Angelino. What made me suspicious was that my man who had been following Stillman, said that Angelino had been parked late at night at an intersection in Henrietta. Stillman had gone up to the car and Angelino had let him in. They sat there for some time and then Stillman got out and walked across the intersection and let himself into a house that sat directly across from where Angelino was parked. Seems to me that the two were up to something which ended shortly before Angelino was found shot. That and the fact that the police report on Angelino's death states that there was no signs of anyone breaking into his car leads me to believe Stillman might have had something to do with his murder."

Dan's face showed his interest. "Where was this?"

"Now that's the strange part. The house that Angelino was watching belongs to a man named Hank Sanders. He has no record, just an ordinary Joe. He's known at the Circle Bar; a place that Stillman frequents, but outside of that, there doesn't seem to be any connection. As far as I know, the men don't even know each other!"

Dan tried to hide is surprise at the mention of the name Sanders. At that moment he knew he was right. He would have to make a decision on just what information he could share with Taylor. Either that or get himself between a rock and a hard place. He made a quick note on his pad, wondering to himself. All he said was, "Is the address in the report?"

"Yes. Got any ideas?"

"No, but I don't want to leave any stone unturned."

They were interrupted by Patricia returning with the files. Dan watched as she went over to Taylor and deposited her load on the top of his desk.

"Thanks, Patricia, that will be all."

They both watched as she slowly moved across the floor to the door. Just before she stepped over the threshold she turned around. "Oh, by the way, the copies are in the binders." With a slight smile and an exaggerated twist of her hips, she disappeared behind the door.

"Thanks!" Taylor said before the door closed. Dan could hear the surprise in Taylor's voice, as if shocked by her efficiency. He knew he was!

"Any more questions?" Taylor asked.

"No, that just about covers it."

Dan picked up his notepad and slipped it into his briefcase. He took the binders that Taylor handed to him from behind the desk and tucked them under his arm, then shifting his load, he extended his hand.

"I'll be in touch."

"Dan? Thanks. I know it's a lot, but I have confidence in you."

Dan only smiled, turned and let himself out.

***

After the exchange, Taylor felt better than he had since first seeing the Stillman case. He could remember that day in minute detail that was as clear as his memory of the first time he had come in contact with Maglioni. When he had browsed through the papers and seen Maglioni's name he first saw red, then felt the surge of triumph flow through his body as he realized this was a chance to get even. Now as he sat back he was relieved to have someone like Dan doing the legwork and was sure now that he'd finally get somewhere. Dan was the right choice! Dan was a friend that owed him. The best of all contacts to use in a situation like this. He had helped him over the years, putting him in touch with the right people and using him to investigate his clients when he was practicing his profession on his own. Dan knew the situation between himself and Maglioni and would use foresight in helping him achieve both his goals--to win the case and finally put Maglioni in his place.

He could feel the stress easing as he leaned back in his chair with confidence. As far as he was concerned, Dan was the best damn detective in the business. He sat there enjoying the ambience, then leaned forward and pressed the intercom button.

"Yes, Mr. Taylor?"

"Patricia, come into my office, I'd like you to take a letter."

"Sure, Mr. Taylor," she said sweetly. With a wide grin on her face, she reached into her purse and pulled out her makeup bag. She freshened her perfume, reapplied her lipstick and just before she opened the door, ran her hands down the sides of her tight skirt, laughing silently knowing that all her vain attention would be unnoticeable when she returned to her office.

***

While Taylor fondled his secretary in his air-conditioned office, Dan was on his way out of the building. When he opened the door that led to the street, the heat of the day hit him smack in the face. Adjusting the files that were too bulky to place in his briefcase, he finally managed to free a hand and loosened his tie. He moved slowly down the steps and onto the sidewalk, his mind on the assignment. When he finally climbed into his car, he turned on the engine and sat waiting for the air to cool. In the interim he looked at the last note he had written, unanswered questions feeling his head.

What did a man like Stillman have in common with the Sanders? Even though he knew little about Skye's husband, he was quite certain that him being the obvious connection would in this situation prove to be a blind alley. There was more here than met the eye. But finding the answer to that question was what bothered him most about the whole case. The only other alternative was that Maglioni had Stillman watching the house, but that would be a stupid move on Maglioni's part and from what he knew of the man, he was far from stupid. He sat deliberating with his eyes staring straight ahead trying to make sense of it all and when he could not he reached into his pocket and pulled out a small notebook. He flipped through the pages until he found one that was blank, then stared at it for some time. Finally, taking a deep breath he began to jot down random notes.

The Sanders house being watched by Angelino.

Janet mentioning her friend Skye told her she was getting a divorce.

Skye revealing her new clientele.

Hank Sanders out of town.

Stillman talking to Angelino.

Angelino shot in the head.

Slowly his mind started working and he began to see the puzzle slowly coming together. He reminded himself it was just a theory, but one that he should check out. He looked at the notes again as if doubting the validity of his conclusion, then closed the pad, slipping it back into his shirt pocket. As he shifted gears and backed out of the parking space, there was a smile on his face. He was pretty sure he knew the connection.

CHAPTER 34

It was after nine in the evening when Hank finally pulled into his own driveway. It had been a long, boring drive home and he was glad to finally reach his destination. He pressed the garage door button and waited as it moved up the tracks, already thinking about Skye. He missed her and right now all he wanted to do was get inside and maybe have a chance to talk this whole business out. Maybe if he handled it right, he could get her to change her mind, or at least agree to hold off for a while. No matter what, he had to try.

Finally he pulled the van into the bay and climbed out. He stood there in the stifling heat of the garage stretching his body, then walked to the back of the van to gather up as much of his things as he could handle in one trip. With his hands loaded he walked to the garage door entrance, and setting down his load, put the key in the lock and let himself in.

The family room was dark and quiet. He stood a moment waiting for his eyes to adjust, then walked over to the far wall and turned on the overhead light. That's when he heard a familiar sound coming from the lower level. Skye was playing one of her Jane Fonda tapes. He stepped on the landing and slowly went down the steps, trying to be quiet so he didn't disturb her.

There she stood, her eyes staring straight ahead at the television as she mimicked the moves on screen. She bent to the left, her arms moving symmetrically overhead with her body, then all shifting to the other side as she leaned right. She had on a purple leotard outfit that showed off her firm body as she gyrated to the music and he stared lustfully. As he continued to watch he began to notice how thin she had gotten. She had never been heavy, and now as he watched her he saw she was thinner than he ever remembered her being. So was he, but he had been doing strenuous work over the past few months. As if sensing she wasn't alone, Skye turned around.

"You gave me a start," she said. "When did you get in?"

"Just now."

He watched as she picked up a towel she had laid on one of the bar stools. "How was your trip?"

"Not bad. It just took me longer to get going than I planned. Had to settle up on the apartment and say my goodbyes. You know how it goes."

Skye didn't respond, just stared intently at him. She liked this easy going conversation without raising voices or poking fingers.

"Have you eaten yet?"

"No," Skye responded, realizing she hadn't taken the time to eat all day.

"Want to go get something to eat?"

Hank asking her out! That came as a surprise. Careful not to show her astonishment at his suggestion, she pondered the matter, started to say it was awful late to be going out to eat, then changed her mind. It was awful late for her to be here exercising too. "Sure, what did you have in mind?"

He couldn't believe his luck. "I'm starving. Let's go out and have a sit down meal somewhere!"

"I don't know..." She was beginning to wonder what he was up to.

"Come on Skye, I'm just asking you to go eat with me, is all. From the looks of you, you haven't had a good meal in a long time."

She couldn't disagree with that. She knew she had lost a lot of weight, what with the worry and the stress from working day in and day out. What could it hurt? She wanted the divorce to be amicable so she should oblige. "Okay. Just give me time to clean up."

"Sure. I'll unpack the van and clean up a little, too, so don't rush yourself."

Skye watched as Hank went back up the steps, then went over and stopped the tape. She then went upstairs to take a shower and dress. When she walked into the kitchen, Hank was waiting for her. Her mind recalled the warning of her lawyer, "Remember, he's not the same person you knew, and you should be careful." She started to back down, then decided it didn't matter one way or the other. They could be here together or out in public. She put a smile on her face. "I'm ready," she said, "Just let me grab a sweater." Soon she was following him out to the garage.

Hank slid in behind the wheel, pulling the door shut in the same motion and then pressed the garage door opener. He watched as Skye climbed up into the van, settled herself in the passenger seat, then reached over and pulled the door shut. He had to control the urge to laugh as her motions reminded him of that Lilly Tomlin character, the one where she is this little girl sitting in an oversized chair with her feet dangling over the edge. When Skye was finally settled in, he began backing out of the garage and they were on their way.

"Where are we going?"

"I thought maybe Mr. Domino's Steakhouse over on Jefferson Road. I haven't been in there since it changed hands and I could go for a nice juicy steak." Then remembering, he quickly added, "They probably have seafood and chicken, too."

Skye, glad to be out of the house, only shook her head in agreement as she rolled down the window. It was a warm night and she enjoyed the feel of the air flowing into the van as they drove down Calkins. She watched the houses as they passed, outside lights flooding the yards and the scent of roses filling her nostrils. It all seemed so peaceful, so normal. By the time they reached the restaurant she was relaxed and ready to enjoy herself.

They pulled into the parking lot and she opened her door and stepped down to join Hank who stood waiting for her at the back of the van and they walked in together just like any other couple. Inside they were met by a blast of cold air and she shivered noticeably, then gratefully placed her sweater over her shoulders as the hostess came to show them to a table.

"Two for dinner," Hank said politely.

She watched as the hostess reached behind the desk and pulled out two menus, then they followed her to the table. When they were seated she placed a menu in front of each of them, and with a smile said, "Your waiter will be with you shortly." She then left them alone.

Skye picked up the menu immediately and was absorbed in making a decision, while Hank looked around the room. He reached in his pocket and pulled out a pack of cigarettes, pulled out one and lit it, then looked over at her.

"See anything you like?"

Before she had a chance to answer, a waiter appeared beside their table.

"My name is Ken and I'll be your waiter this evening. Can I get you something from the bar?"

"Yes, I'll have a Wild Turkey Manhattan. Skye, what do you want?"

"A white wine."

"Chablis?" Ken said and Skye shook her head.

They sat in silence, then Hank asked her again. "What are you having?"

"I think I'll try the broiled chicken dinner," she said.

"I'm going to have the New York strip steak," he said firmly.

They sat like strangers, neither one speaking. Sky fingered her napkin, then unfolded it and placed it on her lap. She adjusted the utensils, stared down at the placemat, then lifted her eyes to look around the restaurant. The room was done in pinks and burgundies, the lighting dimmed, giving the interior a romantic feel. There were quite a few patrons seated at the tables and she studied them, allowing her glance to move when one happened to look her way. It was obvious that it wasn't such a late hour to be dining, just late for her.

When their drinks arrived, she ran her fingers along the side of her wine glass, then lifted the glass and took a sip, her eyes meeting Hank's.

"How is it?" he asked.

"Fine."

She felt uncomfortable and was glad when the waiter returned. "Are you ready to order?"

The question and answer session began.

"I'll have the New York strip steak," Hank replied.

"How would you like that, Sir?"

"Well done."

"Would you like mashed, fried or baked potatoes?"

"Baked."

"Sour cream?"

"Yes."

"A vegetable or salad?"

"A salad."

"What type of dressing? We have..."

"Ranch," he interrupted, not giving the waiter a chance to continue.

"Will that be all?"

"Yes. Skye?"

She placed her order, and made her choices. Then they were alone again, neither one knowing what to say to the other. When the salads arrived they immediately picked up their forks, but that's where the similarity ended. While Skye used her knife to cut the vegetables into fork size portions, Hank dumped tons of salad dressing on his and dug into the bowl pulling up half the salad and popping the load into his waiting mouth. The silence continued while they both ate, avoiding eye contact. The salad plates were removed and their dinners were placed in front of them. Skye picked up her fork, only to find she wasn't hungry. She toyed with the food, then cautiously looked over at Hank who was busily pouring steak sauce on his meat, reaching over and grabbing the salt and then the pepper without even tasting it before loading it up with seasonings. Happening to catch her eye, he smiled shyly.

"I know what you're thinking," he said. "I should taste it first."

"You really should," was all she said, but it wasn't what she was thinking. Her thoughts were more along the lines of his lack of table manners. She had sat across the table from him at home and witnessed the same scene, but not in public. Usually he showed more culture on the rare occasions when they were dining out.

He put down the pepper and started carving up the meat on his plate. Skye could only watch with irritation. So many times she had watched as he seasoned his food without first tasting it until she never bothered with seasonings any more. That part was normal, but at least he use to eat in public like he had some manners. She sighed then picked up her fork, forcing herself to eat and ignore her table partner. She had just sliced off a portion of chicken and placed it in her mouth when she looked over to see his eyes on her. Skye lowered her empty fork.

"See Skye, just as easy as you slice that chicken, you're cutting up our life. That's exactly how I see what you are doing." He paused waiting for his words to sink in while she sat, her jaws rigid with the piece of chicken laying somewhere in her mouth, too shocked to chew.

As if sensing the reaction his words had on her now, Hank continued. "Go ahead, chew it up. What you don't eat they'll throw down the garbage disposal and it'll finish it off for you. Gone and done with just like you want our life together."

Skye had an overpowering urge to spit it out. Slowly she reached into her lap for her napkin and brought it up to her mouth, hoping no one was watching her, that no one would suspect what she was doing. She had to get it out of her mouth. She could feel her stomach heave as she reached across her plate for the glass of water and took a big gulp. The water rushed all at once to the back of her mouth in one giant lump that brought tears to her eyes as she tried to force it down her throat.

Shock was written all over her features as she dabbed at the tears that now spilled from her eyes and ran down her face. Her eyes fixated on Hank and she could find no words to say in her defense.

There was a self-righteous expression on Hank's face as he watched Skye try to gain some composure. It was an unrehearsed score and the results were right up there with his best retorts, he thought. His eyebrow raised as if he were saying, "Gotcha", then he lowered his head and began eating. He ate, ignoring her as he popped each fork full into his. He ate until his plate was empty, then took the bread and removed the last traces from his dish, while all she could do was stare in silence. Finally he looked directly into her eyes.

"What's wrong with you?" he asked innocently.

"Don't do this, Hank."

"Do what?"

She didn't reply, instead she picked up the water and drank again, careful to not overload her mouth.

Hank looked at her plate, the food untouched, and for the first time he felt contrite. He hadn't meant to upset her, hadn't planned it at all. It had just happened. Now that he had finished savoring his triumph he regretted his words. He just wanted her to know how he felt about her throwing him away after twenty one years of marriage! Why couldn't she see what she was doing to him? Why didn't she care? The waiter came by and he ordered two coffees without asking Skye if she wanted a cup. He kept his eyes averted as he lit another cigarette and tried to figure out what to do next. Should he just let the remark stand, or should he apologize? He drew deeply on his cigarette before he spoke.

"I'm sorry, Skye. Go ahead and finish eating."

"I'm not hungry."

"I said, I'm sorry," he said meekly.

The coffee arrived. Skye picked up the cup and drank, and when she felt more in control, she forced herself to think rationally. Hank hadn't planned to shock her and she was pretty certain he had hoped to cajole her into giving him another chance. At least that's what she had sensed when he had asked her to join him. He was probably just as shocked as she was by his words. It was also likely that she wasn't going to be able to stop him from discussing the divorce without creating a scene. If he wanted to get into this now, she'd have to oblige him.

"Hank, if you have something to say, go ahead and say it and lets talk about it sensibly."

"Okay. I don't want a divorce!"

"I know you don't, but I don't understand why you're fighting it."

"I think we should give it another go. You've said it before yourself. You've told me on countless occasions that the pressure of the bills were making it impossible for us. Well, if your figures are right, there will be no bills. I'm not against selling the house and getting ourselves out of debt, but we should at least see how it goes after that before making a decision to split."

"It's more than the bills, Hank."

"No, I don't think we know that for a fact and I don't think you can be so sure without at least giving it a shot," he said adamantly.

Skye felt the urge to argue the point but waited until she was calm before she spoke. "Hank, we don't have a marriage. We never really did. We got married too fast and for the wrong reasons, and now it's time to put an end to it. I know how you feel. Having to start all over again is not easy for me either, but it's what's best for both of us. I just want us both to have a chance for some happiness."

"I am happy."

"Maybe you think you are, but you're no happier than I am with the way things are. Paying our bills is only a small part of it, Hank, and I think you know it too. Throughout the marriage you've gone elsewhere to try and find happiness, so you can't tell me you are happy. You're only fighting it because it wasn't your idea. Give it time and you'll know I'm doing what's right for both you and me."

"Skye, please."

She looked at his pained expression and couldn't help feeling sorry for him. The fact that she felt she was just as much at fault for the problems with their marriage didn't make it any easier.

"You haven't once asked me how I felt about the divorce. I don't remember you saying even, let's discuss it. All I remember is you're telling me you wanted to leave me and then asking me to pick out what I wanted to keep from our marriage. Why can't we take this in steps, get a separation and see how it goes before we make a final decision?"

Skye sat pensively, listening to Hank and remembering that the lawyer had said they needed to draw up separation papers, have them signed and then he could proceed with the divorce. Of course, the papers were no more than an agreement on what to do with their possessions, but Hank might not know that. It might, she thought, be a way to get him to put his signature to the document and then willingly sign for the sale of their house.

She had to be firm or end up going through all of this again at a later date. Sure, she didn't want to hurt him and didn't relish tricking him into doing something, but what other alternative did she have. She couldn't think of any. Right now she had his attention and she'd be a fool to not take advantage of it. All she had to do was say the right words and hope for the best. It would make it much easier.

"Hank, in order for the lawyer to draw up any separation agreement, it'll mean that you'll have to decide on what to do with the household furnishings and the sale of the house. We can do that, proceed with the sale of the house and then take it from there."

Hank sat up straighter in his chair, listening closely now. She was willing to forestall the divorce if he was willing to cooperate. "Tell me what you want me to do and I'll do it."

"Okay, tomorrow we can start going through the papers I showed you that listed the things we own and what we owe. We can start there. I've talked with a Realtor and I can call her and set up an appointment for us. We'll probably have to sign some forms to authorize her to go ahead with the sale, then it's just a matter of waiting."

"Fine. You just tell me what to do and I'll do it. All I ask is that in return, you at least give me a chance. I can change, Skye, and I want to change. Just don't ask me to rush ahead on something this important and I'll promise to be cooperative."

She wanted to continue the charade but she felt guilty as they walked out of the restaurant. By the time they were pulling into the garage she regretted letting him believe she was giving him a second chance. By the time they entered the family room she had to come clean.

"Hank, I know what you're thinking. You think I am agreeing on a separation to give us both time to contemplate the next move. I guess that's what I wanted you to think, but I can't do that to you. The separation papers are no more than us agreeing on what to do with the house and the furnishings. No more. In all honesty, those papers need to be signed to begin the divorce proceedings."

He was livid. At that moment he hated her. He stood in the room wanting to avenge himself, punch her in the face, shake some sense into her, do something to let her feel his anger. His fist clenched and unclenched by his sides and he stared at her, his face distorted. Finally he forced himself to walk pass her and went downstairs.

She couldn't move! She had seen the raw anger in his face, sensed the passion that flowed through him as he stood angrily in front of her, and she again remembered what the lawyer had said, "Remember, he's not the same person you knew, and you should be careful." At that moment she wanted to run out the door and hide, go somewhere he'd never find her. Because she knew now he had been pushed beyond his limit. Why couldn't she have left well enough alone, let him think what he wanted to think? But it was too late to speculate now, too late to do anything but move quickly toward severing the relationship.

Skye managed to make her body move through the family room. She walked as if the weight of the whole world was on her shoulders. In the bedroom she closed and locked the door, afraid that Hank might come up to find her, then slowly undressed and climbed into the bed. She lay for a long time staring up at the ceiling and listening for any sounds until she finally fell asleep.

CHAPTER 35

Hank lay on his bed in tortured silence, his head throbbed with the words she had spoken. He could feel his heart racing and it crossed his mind that even at his age one could have a heart attack. Just how fast could a heart beat before it gave up, he wondered. The pounding filled his ears until he had to prop himself up against the headboard of the bed, wait a moment, then slide to the edge. Slowly he tested himself by pushing himself up with his hands, then standing with his weight on his feet. When he felt secure he tried taking regulated steps until he stood in the rec room. He thought to himself, I need a drink!

Standing with his feet encased in the thick shag carpet, he waited for his eyes to adjust to the darkness, then walking with less effort now, moved over to the bar, flipped the light switch and pushed in on the cafe doors. The pounding had stopped.

Hank searched through the cabinets until he found what he was looking for, then got out a glass and filled it halfway with the whiskey. His hand shook as he brought the glass up to his mouth and took a big gulp. He started coughing, feeling the liquid as it cruised down his throat. He leaned on the padded bar edge, hacking until finally the spasm stopped. This time he took a small sip, then another, continuing until the glass was empty. He filled it again.

The effect was slow in coming, but after three, maybe four glasses he could feel the whiskey taking control of his sense. He was recovering. He knew this because his problem no longer seemed unsurmountable; he could handle it.

Skye had forced him into a state of physical shock. His mouth had gone dry, his palms were still wet, and the audible drumming of his heart were summoned by stress. He stood quite still, not moving from the support of the counter with his mind thinking clearly. She would not get away with it. She would pay. Somehow he would make her pay. But how?

Hank moved forward placing his full weight on his feet while continuing his deliberation. He would get revenge for his suffering and make her life a living hell if it was the last thing he did. The marriage hadn't been one big picnic for him, but he wasn't trying to bail out. Hell, he knew her people hated him and probably helped instigate her decision to leave him. Well he would show them all. He was not some one to take anything lying down.

Faintly dizzy now, he struggled through the swinging cafe doors, walking cautiously with the wall for support until he was back in the bedroom. He fell across the bed and in a matter of minutes fell into a deep sleep.

He was in Vietnam again. Somehow he had become separated from the rest of the company and stood terrified in the midst of the deadening silence of the jungle. Desperately he meandered chaotically in search of coverage. He heard the rifle shot, then the breeze as the bullet soared past his ear and suddenly the jungle was alive with sound. Birds screeched and flew into the air above the trees, and the sound of dry leaves cracking seemed to come from all around him. He turned to the left, then the right, trying to identify the location, then instinctively dropped down on the ground, stomach first, and rolled under the foliage, certain that this was the moment of his death.

Silence again transcended and he saw the sunlight glimmer off something in the tree ahead. He squinted, trying to see while his mind attuned to the vision and suddenly he knew it was a sniper. Slowly he inched forward, concealed by the thick foliage, aware of the sound of his body moving across the bed of dry leaves. He touched his side with the rifle he dragged in his right hand and felt a sense of security as he continued to inch his way across the ground.

His body was clammy cold, wet with the sweat that trickled from his pores. As he bent his knees slightly to push himself forward, he felt the tremble in his legs. He was petrified, afraid the Vietcong would hear the rustling of the leaves and search him out.

Finally he was less than twenty feet from the tree. He looked up. The figure crouched in it's branches now totally visible, no longer distorted by the reflecting light. He lifted his rifle, aimed and fired.

Again the jungle reacted with sounds while he lay sweating profusely with leaves stuck to his body. His ears perked as he stared up, but no indication came that his bullet had hit its target.

He held his breath and waited until the sudden sound of a rifle falling to the ground beside him forced the air from his lungs. He raised his eyes and let them follow the form of the man plunging to the earth like a rag doll, while his rifle slowly lowered with the plummeting figure.

There was a look of contempt on his face as he stared down at his assailant, his rifle posed for action. He lifted the butt of the gun up as he ran his face along the inside of his arm to wipe the sweat from his face and into his eyes.

The body laid still on its bed of leaves, yet he felt his fingers tighten around the trigger again. He stood stock still, not moving as the gun recoiled and the insensate kick of the butt careened into his shoulder causing white lightening pain to travel down his arm. He felt nothing.

He stood godlike staring into the eyes of his victim, feeling a sense of power until he was finally able to move. He turned and walked away.

Hank woke, his body bathed in sweat, his mind totally disoriented as he twisted on the bed. He was home, he was in his bed at home, he kept repeating to himself until he finally came to his senses. It had seemed so real, as if it were all happening again and the scene stayed with him long after he had awakened.

He stared up at the ceiling while his mind and body calmed, and that's when it came to him. Suddenly he knew just how he would get even. He half rose, blood pushing to his face, his chest now a block of ice and sweat dotting his body, feeling like a zillion insects coursing down the length of him.

It was still dark. He eased himself off the bed, turned on the light, then went to the dresser and randomly pulled out a pair of jeans, a shirt, socks and underwear. Quickly he put on the clothes, slipped his feet into a pair of loafers and went walked through the rec room. At the foot of the steps he stood and listened and hearing no sounds, started up the steps. At the landing he again paused, waiting, making sure it was safe before he quickly went down the two steps into the family room and over to the garage door exit. He twisted the knob slowly with both hands around it and stepped through, flipping on the light as soon as the door closed behind him. He walked over to the cabinets on the far side of the garage and stooped down, searching through the bottles and cans until he found what he was looking for.

In a matter of minutes it was done. A sneer planted itself on his face as he moved back to the door, making sure to turn off the garage light before he let himself back in. Silently he went back to his bedroom and climbed into bed. This time he slept peacefully throughout the night.

***

When Skye woke the next morning her first thought was of the previous evening. It seemed strange knowing she was not alone anymore, that Hank was somewhere in the house infuriated by her admittance and no longer seeking her favor. What had possessed her anyway. She was lucky to be alive, she thought, remembering the look on his face. Hank could have gotten his gun and what would she have done then? But he hadn't. It would be best if she was more cautious in the future.

She continued her train of thought and knew she had a right to be scared. She'd just have to be careful she told herself. She couldn't allow herself to worry about what he might do, just not provoke him further. Besides it wasn't like she was powerless. She had power, yes indeed she did. She had made a foolish move, but it was done with and there was nothing she could do about it now. "So now, what", she asked herself as she stared at the ceiling. She must act now and put it all behind her before it was too late. Too late? She wondered what she meant by that, but after a while as she forced herself out of bed and put the matter aside.

As she stood in the shower washing her body she felt as though the alarming transition from past to present had her caught up in a melodrama. She had to work, she had to be careful, she had to keep her eyes and ears open, and along with all this, she had to be calm. Skye sighed deeply and then leaned over and turned off the water. She stepped out and dried herself, then went about finalizing her morning routine. She was in the midst of making a pot of coffee when the phone rang.

"Oh my god," she said as she ran into the office, glancing at the clock as she went by the stove. She remembered she had a nine thirty appointment. It was now nine o'clock! Quickly she moved across the carpet until she was in front of her desk. She leaned over and picked up the phone.

"Good morning, Skye Sanders speaking."

The caller identified himself and then went on to explain that he had to cancel his nine thirty appointment with her. "Can I reschedule?"

Letting out a sigh of relief, Skye said, "Just a second, let me get my appointment book."

Skye scrambled behind her desk and pulled the book in front of her, flipping quickly to the month and checking through the dates.

"Is Thursday of next week good for you? I can be free around two, two-thirty."

"No, that's not good for me. Can we make it for Tuesday of the following week?"

Skye looked to the date and saw she had some time. "Okay, lets make it Tuesday at one o'clock if that's okay with you."

"That will be fine."

"Well, then, I'll see you on Tuesday."

She no sooner hung up the phone and it rang again. When she finally finished with the caller, she leaned back in her chair, took a deep breath and went to the kitchen to pour herself a cup of coffee and carried it to the office. If this was any sign of how her day would transpire, she couldn't waste a minute. She turned on the computer and while it beeped into life, she grabbed a piece of scrap paper and jotted down some quick notes as reminders. No matter what, she told herself, she would call Paulette and ask her to start the process for the sale of the house and later this afternoon she would keep her appointment with the lawyer. She sat the pad aside and started on the first job.

***

While she worked, Hank stumbled into the kitchen. He could hear her pounding away at the keyboard and the sound echoed in his throbbing head. He moved slowly across the linoleum floor, each step making his head ache all the more. He reached into the cabinet and pulled out a cup and started to fill it, then changed his mind and went to the refrigerator. He pulled out an open container of tomato juice, but instead of pouring it in the cup, he drank straight from the can. After that he made himself a cup of coffee.

The clacking of the keys in the next room angered him. He hated that machine, hated how it had come between him and Skye. She felt more for that damn computer than she had ever thought of him. He chastised himself for paying a role in helping her get started in business. He could feel the tension grow and afraid of making his head ache even more, he forced himself out of the kitchen and into the family room to enjoy his coffee in peace.

As he sat there, wondering how he'd fill the day, an idea came to him. Hank got up from the couch and went over to the phone. He dialed and then waited for the connection.

"Local Union 86, Brenda speaking."

"Hello, Brenda, this is Hank Sanders. Can I speak to Mr. Ames."

"Sure, Hank, I'll put you through."

He heard the click as the call was being transferred, then Mr. Ames came on the line.

"Hello Hank, I was just thinking about you."

"Hi, Mr. Ames. I guess you heard; I left the job in New York."

"Yes, my secretary told me you called and then the job site called to verify it. Don't worry about that, though, we've all been there. You can't expect to like every job assignment and from my understanding, this one was more like slave labor." There was silence and then he continued. "Ready to get back on the roll again?"

"Yes, I thought I'd stop by this afternoon and sign up for work."

"That will be fine. Stop in when you can." Mr. Ames hesitated. "I have to tell you, work is slow coming in and there are quite a few men on the bench. Why don't I have my secretary prepare papers so you can at least collect unemployment until something comes up?"

"Thanks Mr. Ames. That'll help a lot."

When he hung up the phone, Hank felt a little better. He leaned back, resting his head against the back of the couch with his eyes closed until the pulsation stopped. When he opened his eyes he got up and turned on the television set, but he wasn't watching. He busily concentrated on his next move if the first should fall through.

Hank realized he was getting hungry and looking at his watch he saw it was almost noon. Ignoring the sounds coming from the office, he moved around the kitchen fixing himself something to eat. When he was done, he didn't bother to clean up or turn off the television in the family room on his way out the door.

***

In the office Skye worked frantically. When it was nearly one in the afternoon, she was more than ready for a break. Her body was stiff from sitting in one position. Skye stretched her arms over her head and slowly made her way into the kitchen.

There were crumbs on the counter, the mayonnaise and mustard sat uncapped on the counter top. She started to yell out, "Hank", but stopped herself. She stood in the kitchen listening and hearing nothing, moved silently across the floor until she was at the top of the landing. Slowly she walked down the step into the family room and saw that the room was empty. "Where is he", she said to herself as she walked to the door to the garage and opened the door.

Her car sat all alone in the garage. Hank's van was gone. "Whoa", she said out loud, feeling the tension of her body being released. She turned on her heels and made her way back into the office where she called Paulette.

"Hello?" An unfamiliar voice rang in her ears.

"Hello, this is Skye Sanders. May I speak to Paulette Locke."

"Sure. Hold on for a minute."

"Skye, how are you?"

"Just fine, Paulette." She didn't have time for amenities. "I want you to proceed with the sale of the house."

"Fine, Skye. You have great timing, the person who handles the surveys is standing right in front of me. I can have him there this morning if it's okay with you."

Skye thought for a moment, wondering how Hank would react to someone walking around the property. Then she decided it didn't matter. "Yes, that will be fine. Do I need to do anything?"

"Just let him in when he finishes outside so he can measure the interior."

"Thanks, Paulette."

"Don't mention it. I'll call you when I have everything ready and we can go on to the next step." She hesitated. "Skye, I took it upon myself to check out some places for you. I have several that would work out just fine. One even has an office already set up on the lower level with a private entrance. You might want to see that one first."

"Sounds interesting, but price is going to be a factor. I may find I have to move slowly and settle in an apartment until I can afford a house."

"I took that into consideration beforehand. I'm telling you that this one is a steal. I'm pretty sure we can work something out. But don't worry about that now. That'll come later."

"Paulette?"

"Yes."

"I remember you mentioning you had the name of someone who handled household sales. I'd like to get in touch with them now. Do you have the information available."

"Got a pencil?"

"Yes." Skye wrote down the name, phone number and address of the individual. Her hand moved rapidly across the pad as Paulette dictated to her."

"I don't know how to thank you, Paulette. I wouldn't know where to start if it weren't for you."

"You already have, Skye! You were very sweet to me when I needed to talk to someone, and then there is the commission when we sell the house. I think that's payment, wouldn't you agree," she added humorously."

"Yes, I do agree".

"Now, don't worry about a thing, and keep your chin up."

"I'll try. Goodbye, Paulette."

"Bye, Skye."

With that out of the way, Skye felt much better as she turned again to the work on her desk. There was a persistent knock at the door.

Still engrossed in what she was doing, Skye absently got up and opened the office door. No one was there. She heard the knock again and realized the sound was coming from the family room door. Carefully she locked the office door and hurried into the family room.

"Caution, remember to be cautious Stupid," she said as she entered the family room. Precociously she peeked through the curtain and saw a stranger standing on the door step. Not having a chain on the door, Skye raised her voice and through the closed door said, "Can I help you?"

"I'm the surveyor sent by Ms. Locke."

Quickly Skye opened the door and let the surveyor in. "I'm sorry, sir."

"That's okay. Can't be too cautious these days. I need to get some measurements."

Patiently Skye showed him through the rooms, responding to questions and waiting as he took his measurements. When he finished, she saw him to the door and thanked him before returning to the office to sit again in front of the computer.

At two o'clock she finally was at a good stopping point. Skye turned off the computer and went to get ready for the appointment. She rearranged her hair, gathering it up into a ponytail, then refreshed her makeup. While in the midst of assembling the household information, for Mitch Cayman, she decided to kill two birds with one stone and added the finished project for Mr. Maglioni to the pile before placing it all in her briefcase.

"Oh my god!" she cried, seeing the envelope. How could I have forgotten!" Laying in the bottom of the briefcase was the money. It had completely slipped her mind. She still hadn't made the last deposit to her business account.

Quickly she stuffed the folders into the case and snapped it shut. She'd swing by the bank before her meeting with Mitch, then stop by Mr. Maglioni's office to drop of the job. That settled she placed the briefcase in the chair, reached under the desk and retrieved her purse, but before heading out she again double checked to make sure she had everything. While she was in the midst of doing this she had an idea. On impulse, she reached for the phone, dialed and then stood waiting.

"Mr. Maglioni's office, Lisa Caldwell speaking."

"Hello, Lisa, this is Skye Sanders. How are you."

"Oh just fine Ms. Sanders. Would you like to speak to Mr. Maglioni?"

"No, this is more a social call. But first, I want to tell you that I will be dropping off a job for Mr. Maglioni this afternoon."

"That's no problem, Ms. Sanders. I'll let him know so that if he has anything else for you he'll be prepared."

"Thank you Lisa. Now, can I speak to Fran Russo."

"Sure, just one minute and I'll connect you."

In a moment she heard Fran on the line.

"Skye? Is that you. I'd just about given up on hearing from you again."

"I'm sorry, I've been frightfully busy, but I have to come down that way today and thought we could have a late lunch. Are you game."

"Sure, you name the time and place."

"What about Anthony's at say..." She paused trying to figure her schedule. "I guess we're looking at three, three thirty. Is that okay with you?"

"When you say late, you mean late. No, that will be fine. I can be there by three fifteen and get us a table."

"See you then."

By two thirty Skye was finally climbing in her car. Soon she was backing out of the garage and on her way down the street. Instead of going her normal route, she weaved through the development until she arrived at the intersection just before the entrance to the express way. "Damn," she said as the light turned red.

She sat there in anticipation, idly looking around and noticed the car waiting behind her. The man who sat behind the wheel looked as impatient as she felt, or was that an impatient expression? He seemed to be sneering at her as she watched him in the rear view mirror. All of a sudden she felt as though someone was sticking needles up the length of her spine. Before she had a chance to think about the sensation, the light changed. Much too quickly she stepped on the gas, turning left and then right onto 590N, the car behind doing the same.

She drove, keeping an eye on the rear view mirror as she dodged in and out of the traffic, trying to tell herself she was being silly. The car stayed behind her, matching each of her moves until she was pretty sure the man was following her. Not totally convinced or not wanting it to be true, Skye lowered her foot on the accelerator and watched the speedometer jump to sixty, then sixty-five. The car behind her did the same.

Anxiously she pressed the pedal down further and saw it pass seventy and then seventy-five as she drove recklessly down the left hand lane seeing the split in the highway just ahead of her. At the last minute she swung the wheel and prayed as she crossed into the next lane, turning the wheel sharply, and just making it onto the 490E junction.

Skye continued checking the rear view mirror, but couldn't find the car as she weaved recklessly in and out of the traffic flow. Finally she started to slow down until the speedometer again was reading fifty-five, all the time checking behind her.

She had lost him! Calmer now, she looked to her left and the adrenaline started pumping. He was driving right beside her!

Now she could see his features clearly as she looked through the side window. He was ugly. His features looked as though someone had pounded on his face more than once. He looked as though he was sneering at her with is meaty lips curled back, baring his teeth and his eyes mere slits on his face. He barely looked human. Snapping her head quickly around she forced herself to look away. What should she do now? she questioned herself frantically.

There were cars all around her on the three lane highway and she couldn't make a move. Frantically she stared out the front window, side glancing and praying. It felt like her heart would jump out of her mouth and she swallowed hard, concentrating on her breathing as she drove side by side down the highway with her pursuer. And that's what he was! He didn't make an attempt to cover the fact he was tailing her. Her only hope was to get into the far right hand lane and exit, but she knew he wasn't about to let that happen.

Her hands gripped the steering wheel tighter than necessary as she tried to figure out what to do. Finally she realized she only had one alternative. She was already in the proper lane to bear left, so why not stay there. It would take some quick maneuvering on his part to just get into her lane, let alone the next.

The decision help calm her nerves. She purposely avoided looking to her left, keeping to the speed limit as she drove with the flow of the traffic. She could see the split up ahead. Her pursuer could see it too. She could feel his eyes on her and she wondered if he would just swing over into the side of her car. But she couldn't think about that now, she had to keep pace with him no matter what.

She was there, not daring to look anywhere but straight ahead. She held her breath as she found her car going down the left lane and heading for downtown. Hesitantly she looked to her left then to see her pursuer's car captured in the traffic moving in the opposite direction. She breathed a sigh of relief. She had done it, she thought smugly. She had out maneuvered the bastard.

Skye released her firm grip on the wheel and felt the sweat on her palms as she twisted them around the steering wheel. Finally she saw her exit and moved over into the far right lane, slowing her speed as she did so. As she drove up the incline she saw the light was red and applied her brakes.

Her eyes opened wide, her jaw slackened as she realized she couldn't stop. Desperately she pumped at the brakes, but there was no reaction. At that moment before the impact, she knew she was going to crash into the car ahead of her, but there was no time to prepare.

Her head swiveled backwards on her neck, while her body pressed tightly against the seat of the car. As she smashed into the back of the car in front, her head flew forward until her face collided smartly into the steering wheel. She screamed, and then everything went black.

CHAPTER 36

She had fallen or been laid across the car seat. Blood had smeared the front of her white silk shirt which was the first thing she saw when she opened her eyes. Skye was having trouble focusing as she listened to the commotion outside. She heard someone yelling, "I was just sitting here at the light and she rammed right into me. I saw her coming, not braking or nothing. The next thing I knew I had a car ramming my backside." While she was still groggily listening, close to her ear another voice whispered persistently, "Miss, are you all right."

Then came the pain in a searing wave of fire that engulfed her brain. As if to cool it, she pressed her hands on the sides of her head, her face grimaced with anguish. It hurt so bad she wanted to cry. Skye squeezed her eyes shut and was consumed with the low roaring sound that filled her head. When she opened her eyes again, she still couldn't focus. There were several identical faces swimming in a circle above her. Dizzily she stared up.

"Are you all right," the stranger asked again.

She tried to shake her head, but it hurt to much. She realized someone was wiping her face with something cold, the hands gently rubbed her forehead, her cheeks and her lips. It felt so good, so soothing, so relaxing! The cloth moved over her eyes, tenderly it swept across her eyelids, then stopped.

Skye opened her eyes again, focusing much easier now.

"You fainted, Miss. Do you understand me?"

Summoning all her strength she managed to whisper weakly, "I think so."

"Would you like to try and sit up."

For the first time she recognized the blue uniform and knowing she was safe, it renewed her strength. Skye raised her head and looked appealingly into the officer's concerned expression, then tried again to speak only the words diminished and faded. As shocked and foggy as Skye's brain was, it struggled for lucidity. She pried her body up against the back of the car seat.

"Can you tell me what happened, Miss?"

She answered him softly, afraid to startle her head with the sound of her own voice. "I came up the exit ramp and tried to brake, but I couldn't." She paused, the effort taking it's toll. "Is anyone hurt?"

"No, everyone is fine."

"The car?" It was all she could manage.

"There doesn't seem to be that much damage to either vehicle. The man you ran into is angry, but unhurt. It's a good thing this ramp is steep or it would have been much worse.

Skye managed to slide her body up into a sitting position. Her head throbbed but she ignored it.

"How do you feel?"

"Much better. It's just my head hurts."

"I bet it does. I think we ought to take you to the hospital and have you looked at."

"That's good." It sounded more like 'goo' instead of good but the officer seemed to understand. Sit still for a moment, Miss. I'll be right back.

She wasn't going anywhere she thought as she tried moving her legs and then her arms. It seemed to be just her head that hurt.

"Miss?"

"Yes."

"There's no damage to the other driver or his car. His bumper took the full impact. He's upset, but asked me to tell you that he isn't going to report the incident to his insurance company."

"Isn't it required?" Skye asked hesitantly.

"No. I looked over your car and it also seems to be intact outside. Do you feel well enough to tell me what happened?"

"Yes. I was coming up the ramp and pressed on my brakes, but they didn't work. I couldn't stop. I guess I panicked then."

"Were you having any problems with your brakes before?"

"No." She hesitated wanting to tell him about her pursuer but decided against it. She had done enough damage for one day.

"I think you might have leaned forward once you found you didn't have any brakes. You might have tensed up causing you to fall forward. You obviously hit your head on the steering column." He paused, leaning down and looking closely at her. "Would you like me to call an ambulance?"

"No, I don't think that will be necessary. You're probably right. Outside of my head, I feel fine."

"Do you want to try and stand? I'll help you. We need to get you into my patrol car."

She smiled feebly. "I think I can manage that."

Skye reached over to the passenger side to retrieve her purse and briefcase.

"Here, let me help you with that," the officer said.

She waited while he situated the load then leaned heavily into the officer's body as he helped her out of the car and slowly walked her to his patrol car. and helped her in.

"Are you okay?"

"Yes, I'm fine." How many times was he going to ask her. Of course she wasn't fine. She was shook up and her head ached. All she wanted to do right now was take some Advil and lay down.

"I'm going to go move your car over to the side of the road. You wait here."

She rotated her body until she could look out the window. She watched as the officer climbed behind the wheel of her car and drove off the ramp and onto Monroe Avenue where another officer stood flagging the traffic to a halt.

Inside the car, the officer struggled. He pressed the brake pedal to the floor, but the car wouldn't stop. Turning the wheel roughly to the right he managed to get it facing in the right direction, then quickly reached down and pulled on the emergency brake. He climbed out, walked over to the other office and said something that had the other office following him over to the car.

The officer who had helped Skye, climbed back in the driver's seat, released the brake. At his signal the other man leaned into the front of the car while the officer turned the wheel to the right. Finally they had it up against the curb. The driver then pulled on the emergency brake, climbed out and locked the door.

She watched as the officer advanced. He climbed into the patrol car and turned his head toward the back seat.

"Miss, you were right. You have no brakes.?" I'm going to call in and have the automobile towed .

"You sit tight."

Skye was more than glad to oblige as she let her head lay back on the top of the seat. I'm going to take you to hospital now."

She felt the car moving and heard the siren wail as they went through the intersections until the patrol car was twisting up to the emergency entrance door. She allowed herself to be placed in a wheelchair and kept her eyes closed because it hurt to much to open them. She felt the chair being wheeled forward. Then she heard the voice of the officer as he explained the situation. After that the chair moved again until finally she felt hands lifting her up and placing her flat on her back. That's when she passed out.

When she came to, she opened her eyes to see Hank's face floating above her. Her first instinct was to move away, but her body ached all over.

"How do you feel?"

She recognized concern on his face and relaxed. "I'm okay."

Hank straightened, his face no longer in her line of vision. "They said I can take you home. They're going to give you something for the pain. Said you have a mild concussion and needed to get some sleep."

She tried to sit up.

"Do you need help?"

She did, but she didn't want to admit it as she forced herself into a sitting position, the movement making her head spin. The doctor entered the examination room and handed something to Hank. "Give her two of these when you get her home. If she has any of these symptoms", he added as he handed Hank a sheet of paper, "call me immediately and we'll take another look at her. I think she'll be just fine, a little sore, but just fine."

Hank thanked the doctor, watched him leave, then turned to Skye. "Well, you certainly don't look your best."

"Thanks," she retorted, then added as he extended his hand to help her from the table, "I'll manage." As she slid her feet to the floor, her eyes stared into the mirror across the room. The comical image made her stretch her sore cheeks, as she tried to smile. "I do look awful!"

Hank didn't say a word as he watched her climb into the wheelchair that had been wheeled into the room. He pushed her out the hospital door. She allowed him to help her climb up into his van before walking around and climbing into the driver's seat.

They drove in silence. When they arrived at the house, she didn't fend off his hand as Hank helped her to the door, but then did shake his hands away once they were inside.

"I can manage from here," she said.

Painfully she shuffled through the family room, pulling herself up the stairs until she stood in the kitchen. She took a deep breathe, then decisively continued until she made it to the bathroom. She entered and locked the door behind her.

The sight of her face stunned her. She could hardly bear to look at herself. It hadn't looked this bad when she saw her reflection in the hospital, but then it had been at a distance and this was up close. Tears rolled down her cheeks, burning as they flowed from her eyes. Her eyes were swollen, her cheeks puffy above lips that protruded hideously. She turned away. And then a terrible fury took over. It was his fault, somehow Hank had done this to her. Why did she think that, she wondered. Slowly she bent at the waist and turned on the shower. Holding on to the shower wall, she stepped in and gingerly cleansed her face and body.

She was a bundle of aches and pains now. She looked gratefully at the bottle of bellmira herbaflor, a eucalyptus herbal bath she had purchased on a whim, picked it up and poured a goodly amount into her wash cloth. Bravely she worked it into her body, feeling the soreness of her muscles with each move. It took much longer than usual but finally she rinsed herself off and stepped out of the tub. The effort of getting the bath towel off the rack was enough to make her want to skip the drying part, but she forced herself to try. She was finally done and feeling she had earned the privilege of falling into bed.

Seeing the blouse she had discarded lying on the floor she picked it up and rinsed it in cold water before opening the door and making her way into the bedroom. She seemed to be moving in slow motion as she dropped a nightie down over her head and shoulders until it covered her body, then she climbed into bed. A few minutes later Hank came in carrying a glass of water. He handed her two pills which she popped into her mouth and taking the glass from his hands, washed them down.

Finally she slid down in the bed and permitted Hank to pull the covers up to her chin. She watched as he went over and closed the blinds. Then she was alone, snuggling deep into the bed and thinking. There were so many secrets. So much going on behind each other's back. But that was as far as she got before she was engulfed in sleep.

***

"Hello, Brighton Police Station, Sergeant Andrews speaking."

"Hello, this is Hank Sanders."

"Yes, Mr. Sanders, how can we help you?"

"Well, my wife was in an accident this afternoon and I was told that her car was impounded... I mean, you guys have it."

"Hold on while I check. Ah, Mr. Sanders, what is your wife's name?"

"Skye Sanders."

"Just a moment."

Hank sat at the kitchen table with the phone to his ear. After making sure Skye was asleep he realized he had to know what happened to the car. Skye had told him the officer had the car towed and that only meant they had it. He had already called three stations with no success. He had to get the car before anyone had a chance to check it.

"Mr. Sanders? Are you still there?"

"Yes, I'm here."

"We do have you're wife's car."

"What seems to be the problem, officer," he said hesitantly.

"I don't know all the details, sir. Your wife's car was involved in an accident and the officer at the scene had it towed. That's all I can tell you."

"I see... Look, why don't I come and get the car and I'll take it in and have it repaired."

"Wait a minute, sir."

He could hear muffled voices.

"Sir?"

"Yeah, I'm here."

"It's not that simple, sir. Officer Bennington; that's the officer who was at the scene, had it brought here. There's something about the brakes, he wanted checked out."

"Look, she needs her car."

"Sure, I understand that."

Grabbing at straws, Hank ventured, "How bad was the damage to the car?"

"Very minor, Mr. Sanders. There wasn't much damage to either of the vehicles. Officer Bennington said that she was lucky that the ramp was on an incline. It helped to slow the vehicle down before the impact."

"Well, was the other guy hurt?"

"No, not a scratch on him."

"Then why are you wasting the taxpayers' money by checking my wife's car?"

"You never know, Mr. Sanders. The man was quite irate about the whole episode and may decide to sue. Or maybe we're dealing with a manufacturer flaw. After all Ms. Sanders car is quite new; too new to be experiencing brake problems. Like I said, it won't take long. We just need it for a couple of days."

Hank could see he wasn't getting anywhere and that perturbed him greatly. Minor damage, no one hurt.... It just didn't set well with him. But there seemed to be nothing he could do about it. For the first time he wondered how much of their personal life Skye might have shared.

"So when can I come get the car?"

His question was met with silence, then he heard the officer say, "Just a moment, Mr. Sanders."

Hank heard the phone being laid down, could hear the cop discussing the matter with someone, but not clear enough to ascertain what they were saying.

"Mr. Sanders, it looks like some time tomorrow afternoon we should be able to turn the car over to you. Is that okay?"

It wasn't, yet what else could he say, but, "Sure."

" Mr. Sanders, the Captain wanted to ask if your wife is okay?"

"Seems to be."

"Is she at the hospital?"

"No, I brought her home. The doctor gave me some medication to give her and she's been sleeping."

Muffled voices, as if someone had their hand over the mouthpiece. "Well, Mr. Sanders, we'll be in touch."

Hank hung up the phone.

He had the distinct impression they were not telling him everything. Something was definitely up and he was in a frenzy as he pondered his predicament. It was time to worry and that meant he had some figuring to do. This was certainly not part of his plan to have the car in the custody of the police. Police always thought in terms of a motive. They liked to classify and reduce things to basics; money, jealousy, revenge, passion, or whatever. He was going to be found out for sure and there was no excuse he could use in his own defense.

Of course they would have to prove he had done it, but even if they didn't know for sure, they would be watching him and he didn't like to have people nosing into his affairs. He thought he had allowed for error, but this conclusion hadn't entered his mind.

He addressed the possibility of the car being towed to a gas station, but not by the police. Even if there were only minor damages it didn't warrant alarm. Being towed to a gas station meant that once he gave permission, some grease monkey would fix the car and unknowingly throw away the evidence. That was his worse case synopsis then, but not now.

Worry was etched plainly on his face as he tried to determine what he should do. Everything he came up with was either dangerous or impossible, yet might be his only alternative. The issue that was as plain as black and white was the cops would find that the brakes were not faulty, but eaten away. That definitely was something to raise concern.

Hank couldn't sit still any longer. The fact of the matter was that his careful plan had gone badly awry. He blamed himself for not having known better and his attitude took on a glazed and sullen quality. Suddenly Hank rose from the table, turned, and walked to the window where he leaned over to stare into the backyard. He sought the latch of the window, started to open it then pulled his hand back as though it burned.

He turned back, his face full of shock looking over at the far wall. He took three steps and stood at the head of the steps, his hand still half-raised. He was going about it the wrong way! Chastising himself would not get him any where. He lowered his arm as he leaned against the wall, his mind a total blank. There is nothing I can do about it, thought Hank, any of it.

But there was something he could do!. He climbed into his van and headed for the Circle Bar. Halfway there he slowed, pulling over to the side of the road and made an unplanned turn into a side street. He needed money!

His mind worked quickly. He could get a cash advance on the American Express card. That was it. He'd get a cash advance. The van was already rolling and as he smiled eerily. Yeah, he'd do just that and make Skye pay it. He could just see her face when she opened that bill...

Now his thoughts were more serious as he went to make the withdrawal and then started toward the Circle Bar. Maybe with help he'd come up with some answers. If not he'll have the money to make a quick retreat, if need be.

***

Taylor sat at his desk looking over information he had received from Dan, he leaned back in his chair and let his mind relax. He wondered if Maglioni was experiencing the same success he was in gathering incriminating evidence to support his case. He doubted it. He, Taylor, had more time to devote and the manpower to help him. Maglioni, on the other hand, he thought, wasn't hungry enough and it took a real hunger to go through what he was to lay out a successful campaign.

Taylor smiled to himself, already feeling victorious. He didn't doubt he was about to prove himself a better attorney than Maglioni. No, the man didn't stand a chance against him.

While Taylor burned the midnight oil, Maglioni did too and his thoughts followed the same line. He was sure he had done all he could to help win the case, yet it was so important to him, he couldn't sleep. He had waited a long time for this opportunity and the chance of getting another was just about impossible. His life, his business was far from parallel to Taylor's and he knew this was it.

Maglioni got up from his desk and walked around the office trying to get the kinks out of his back and clear his mind. He didn't, couldn't allow himself to think about Taylor. He had to keep his mind on only the case. In that way he was sure to win. Slowly he walked over to the closet and took out his coat. He looked around the office before turning out the light and going home. He allowed himself to think about Taylor one last time, and he thought, the man was probably working overtime to set up his case. Well let him wear himself out. He on the otherhand would get the rest he needed. He had to keep sharp and that meant he had to sleep...

CHAPTER 37

Sam was in an icy, sarcastic mood as he sat at the bar with no one but Oscar to criticize and make miserable. He got like this when he thought about all those people who ignored him when he was trying to be friendly, who never smiled at him, who rushed past and seemed to look through him, and those who gave and took back. It was an attitude that craved revenge. But no one else was around.

Can't you get anything straight!" Sam snapped as Oscar sat a drink in front of him.

"I'm sorry Sam. I could barely hear you."

"So, why didn't you ask!"

"Didn't want to upset you," he replied meekly

"Well I am upset and you acting stupid doesn't help."

He had seen Sam in this type of temperament before and knew that it could be dangerous to his health. He had to stay out of his way! He kept looking around the barroom, wishing someone would materialize and take the pressure off. The last thing he wanted was to be the only person in the room with Sam Stillman and his sour mood. Oscar hurried to correct the error and placed a fresh drink on the bar in front of Sam.

Sam's sweat had left his face slimy and cold and that did nothing but add to his menacing appearance. He sat rigid for the moment, his throat tightening as he swore under his breath. The bitch had managed to lose him. He let out an audible sound of disgust.

Oscar who was pretending to be occupied with washing glasses, heard the spooky sound and rotated his face, his neck snapping painfully in the process. When he saw that Sam was not looking in his direction, he turned back around.

He continued to feed his wrath. Her face when she had turned to her right and seen him next to her, though! Now that did give him satisfaction, he had to admit that. Seeing her features distorted with terror had given him a sense of power, a sensation he managed to attain very infrequently these days. That, and knowing he was capable of making her worst nightmare come true were passions that fed the emptiness in his soul. Sure she got away, but not before he had scared the crap out of her!

A lascivious sneer crossed his face. She was a real looker all right, just the type to get a man's blood boiling and then throw him out. Just the type that he would like a chance to show who's boss and then snatch the life out of her. Oh, he wasn't stupid like his man Hank seemed to be. He knew her type, all sweet and innocent on the outside but inside was a different story. Her specimen could be shrewd, sly and meanly obdurate when they wanted to be. Beautiful women thought the whole world was put here for their pleasure and that anything existed more important than their own satisfaction was beyond comprehension. She was a pretentious, haughty bitch just like all the rest and he loathed them. Any man who had half a brain should be able to see that!

His meditation veered slightly until it was Hank who was on the chopping block. The pulse under his eye throbbed while red spots accentuated the sharp lines of his cheeks. His eyes were no more than black narrow pits spewing over with rage. Hank was nothing but a pussy whipped son of a bitch who grappled at his wife's feet. He hated men like him; especially when their stupidity affected his livelihood. He lifted his glass from the bar, tipped it to his lips and found it was empty.

"Hey Oscar, get me another." His tone was less ominous.

Nervously Oscar stopped what he was doing and fixed Sam's drink. Silently he placed the glass in Sam's outstretched hand, the sound of ice cubes as they knocked against each other rang in his ears as he moved to the far end of the bar. Sam emptied the glass, slammed it down on the counter and continued to deliberate.

Bitches were the cause of all the evil in the world. One way or another they forced a man's hand. Right now the bitch in his life was Paulette Locke. Every time he turned around she was there, waiting to shape and mold him. He growled silently. At first he had a little fun with it, making lustful advances until she'd find some excuse to leave, but after a while he got bored with the game. Now when she came with all her fancy ways trying to make him concentrate on how he spoke, articulating in a soft monotone, "Think before you speak! Try and use the right words! Watch those facial expressions!" all he wanted was to put his hands around her slender neck and squeeze the life out of her. It took all his willpower to hold himself back. Someone was paying her to be there and he had a good idea who that someone was, so he played along.

Finally the situation got on his last nerve and he pried it out of her. She was sent by Mr. Maglioni to groom him for his new life. Maglioni thought it would help his situation if he cleaned up his act! He was paying the man to defend him, not mold him into something he was not. Yet, the house, the car weren't too hard to take. He liked feeling equal to those who continued to look down on him. Yeah, he had gained from the situation and he knew there was more to it, but damn if he could figure it out. New clothes, nice furnishings--all of this added up to more than was on the surface, but that stupid dame swore she had told him all she knew. Maybe she was telling the truth, but then, maybe not.

What nerve, too! The idea of the rich, upper crust trying to pattern him into their own image served to increased his resentment. Well, they could try all they wanted to, but they'd never change him. Maglioni needed to stick to his job which was to get him off the hook for this murder rap. That was the extent of his obligation. The rest he could shove up his ass!

Sam was feeling the atavistic male lust to savage and to murder for all the injustices forced upon him and he yearned for satisfaction. His thoughts were interrupted when Hank exploded into the bar.

***

He stood at the doorway, adjusting his eyes to the dimmed lighting before finally making his way across the floor to stand beside Sam's stool. Without waiting for Sam to notice him, words rushed out of his mouth.

"Something's come up."

Sam turned slowly on his bar stool until he was staring into Hank's haggard face. "So, what do you want me to do about it." He replied sarcastically.

Hank ignored his tone. "Please Sam, I need your help. Can we sit down and talk?" He paused. "I'll buy you a drink!"

"Why, it has nothing to do with me. Remember, you threw me off the case!"

"Because I need your help."

Sam looked at him sharply. "What the hell." The words slid from his tongue as he lifted his body off the bar stool, tossing the words over his shoulder, he barked, "Oscar, bring us both our usual drinks over to the table. And you best get it right!"

Oscar's only rely was a nod of his head.

"Ah, Hubby at close proximity can't handle the little woman!"

Hank forced himself to back up. "Okay, let's switch gears for a moment. I'm sorry I had to cancel you're services, but I couldn't afford the cash. And yes I figured being back home I could handle it myself. I never thought I was better or smarter than you, it was a matter of finances." He stopped, waited a moment and then added, "Now that we have that out of the way, can we talk?"

Sam didn't like his tone of voice, but decided that would wait for now. "Are you paying," he said showing no concern.

"Yes," he said with despondency. Hank reached into his pocket and pulled out the money he had just gotten. He kept the wad low, under the table as he pulled off two bills and placed them on the table.

"Okay, what gives?"

"Well, the other night my wife infuriated me and I couldn't help but get back at her. I went into the garage and found some acid I had stashed away. I didn't even know what kind of acid it was. I had found it on some jobsite and taken it home. I can't remember why.

Anyway, I put the acid in her brake fluid and the next day when she went out, her brakes failed and she had an accident."

Sam stared in Hank's face waiting. When he didn't continue, he said, "So!"

"She had an accident and the cops impounded her car. They said because the brakes failed for no apparent reason, they were going to check it out."

"So they're just checking the car, that doesn't mean they'll find anything. Why are you so impressed with their level of competence. They ain't that smart my friend, no smarter than you, as a matter of fact!"

Hank caught on immediately. "Okay, okay so I should have run it by you and asked your opinion. I didn't because I knew it would cost me."

"Well, isn't that interesting. It's going to cost you anyway, but more than this," he said, fingering the bills that Hank had laid on the table.

"All right." Hank again reached into his pocket and peeled off two more bills. "Is that enough?"

Sam slowly placed his hands over the money and flipped each bill off the pile as if he were counting. "Yeah, this'll do just fine."

"The way I see it you have a fifty-fifty chance."

"Yeah, so what does that mean?" Hank questioned.

With impatience, Sam said, "They'll look at the damage to the brakes and depending on what type of acid you used, most likely the evidence will be gone. Maybe it will eat through the rubber parts, or even the metal. I don't know, but my guess is they won't figure it out."

"But what if they do?"

"Well, then you may be in deep shit my friend." Hank didn't hide his expression of worry and it was enough for Sam. "Stop worrying. By now anything made of rubber has disintegrated so the evidence will be gone. Or there may be some of the lining left to send for test. That's a fifty-fifty chance in my book."

Hank sat pondering the matter. Sam was obviously not offering any more alternatives. He picked up his drink as he leaned back in his chair. After a time, Hank looked over at Sam, saw his eyes narrowed, and his cheek twitching, but he wanted more than half a chance. "Why not steal the car back?"

He hated stupidity. Next to a conniving woman, ignorance was his second vice. Now it all transcended around him, the bitch out maneuvering him in the chase, the tension of the moment, the struggles in his life, it all came back to him. The man had asked for help then questioned it. He had all he could take.

Hank leaned back and after a moment again looked at Sam. He could feel the panic creep through his body as he stared into those blazing eyes. He had gone too far!

"Listen man, I'm not doubting what you said. I'm worried, is all. You can understand that. Here, have a cigarette and let me buy you another drink."

Sam was not to be appeased this time, but he never turned down a drink. A plan was already forming in his mind. He had noticed people coming in and now the bar was populated with bodies. Best to act like two drinking buddies sitting at a table, smoking, engaging in sporadic conversation. That's what he thought and that's what he did. At nine-thirty he loudly announced that it was time he left. He stood by the table and polished off the last of his drink, then headed out the door.

It was just after ten when Hank stumbled out of the Circle Bar and headed for his van. He wasn't exactly drunk, but he did reach his limit; if you could call it that.

He clambered up behind the wheel and while fumbling with the key, something nudged his right ear. Absently he batted it with his hand and felt the cold steel, barrel of a pistol. A chilly voice, said softly, "Start driving, my friend, and don't stop until I tell you to."

"What is this?" Hank said. "What do you want?"

"Do it!"

The pistol screwed into his earlobe painfully, and he hurriedly switched on the ignition and the headlights. He felt like vomiting, but Sam would like him showing weakness so he held it back. The pistol nudged him again.

"Come on! Move it! I haven't got all night."

Hank was fighting panic as he turned the key in the ignition again, heard that grinding sound of resistance, released the key and pressed down on the brake. He backed out of the parking lot, his wheels spinning on the gravel and turned the wheel sharply. The gun moved, but never left the side of his head.

Sam barked out the directions. It was some time before he paid attention to where he was going. By then they were driving down the lonely stretch of Erie Station Road, pulling into the stone driveway of an abandon barn when Sam told him to stop and get out of the van.

"Get ahead of me and walk toward the barn."

Hank did as he was told. He opened the barn door and entered, feeling the cool dampness of the interior, heightening the smell of old hay and lingering animal odors.

"Look, what is this?" Hank tried to sound firm. "What are you doing?"

"It's really quite simple," Sam said. "You have pissed me off and I am going to kill you."

Hank swiveled his head around in disbelief, but after one quick look at Sam's expression he knew it was no joke. He didn't want to die in this old smelly deserted barn. More to the point, he thought wildly, he just didn't want to die at all. His mind frantically searched for a way out.

"Come on Sam, stop kidding around. I've gotten the message. I apologize for being stupid. I want you to help me... I'm hiring you again..." Words, dozen of words flowed out his mouth as he stared at the pistol pointed directly at his face, possibly a foot away. He stared at the gun and suddenly there was an enormous flash, not like the normal flash you see when a gun is fired, but a white flash that exploded in front of his eyes. Then came the colors of red and orange, the heat flooding through his body and he knew he'd been shot.

Everything was slow motion and sound; like a dream sequence. The sound of the shot sending the bullet into his head, and the exploding of his eardrum. He fell back heavily into a pile of rotting hay and felt pain throbbing up his spine, colliding with the pain in his head. He rolled onto his side, blood spurted in an arc, splattering on the floor around him.

A great weariness came over him and he fought it. He didn't want to close his eyes, he didn't want to die. He tried to come up on his elbows to plead with Sam to help him, but Sam was gone. He was alone in this abandoned smelly barn in the middle of nowhere and on the verge of losing consciousness... That was his last thought as he his head dropped deeper into the hay.

CHAPTER 38

Dan Malone sat pensively in his office. It had been a long two weeks. He was exhausted but conscious of the fact he had all the answers. Now it was a matter of making all the pieces fit together. Soon he'd be able to spend time with his family again. Since the meeting with Taylor he hadn't been much of a husband or father to his kids, but that would change. He looked forward to putting it all behind him, so he could get back into the swing of his life.

It was Janet who had given him the lead he needed. Innocent and trusting she had supplied him with the information without knowing it. That evening as they sat drinking coffee while the kids went up to do their homework....

***

"Janet, what to you hear from your friend, Skye."

"Not much, honey. She's been up to her neck in work lately."

"What's got her so tied up?"

Janet shifted in her chair and leaned across the table. He knew that motion well. She had something interesting to say. He looked at her fondly, trying not to appear too anxious as she told him about her last conversation with Skye.

"Skye's gotten some very interesting clients lately, ones with money. She told me they had paid her a lot of money to do some simple work for them and she was worried about it." She paused as if reflecting. "Can you imagine being upset because someone paid her handsomely! Janet had an angelic expression on her face as she thought about her best friend. "That Skye, she's such a dear."

"No, I can't." Dan paused for a moment trying not to show too much interest. The last think he wanted was for Janet to start wondering about his questioning. He had to be casual about it. "Did she mention who these new clients were?"

"Some hot shots is all I know. If she mentioned any names, they meant nothing to me. Any way, whatever it was she was working on, it bothered her and then having them pay more than her normal fee made her worry all the more."

Janet displayed no concern as he continued to probe her for information.

"Did she mention anything else?" He tried to keep calm.

"No... Oh wait. Did I tell you she's getting a divorce?"

"I don't think you mentioned it." Here was something that just might shed some light.

"She is. She's finally going to divorce that husband of hers. I don't like him. He takes advantage of her good nature. I think she thought I'd be shocked when she told me, but I knew all along she wasn't happy. When I talked with her, he was in New York on some job, which was a blessing in disguise. You know he's been out of work for some time and not helping Skye with the bills. That's another reason I couldn't understand why she'd be upset, getting this windfall. She needed the money desperately."

Careful, Dan said to himself. Be very careful. He was on to something, but he had to try and wait for Janet to lead him to the punch line. Best now to be sympathetic.

"Skye is such a nice person. She's been an exceptional friend to you." Looking at his wife now he innocently added, "Has she gotten a lawyer?"

Janet looked puzzled for a moment and Dan wondered if she suspected something, but then her expression softened.

"A man named Mitch Cayman. She had called one of our divorced friends and asked about their lawyer, then ended up not using him. Skye told me it had come as a surprise when she called an old friend of hers; someone I've never met, and he gave her this man's name as the lawyer he had used."

"Why was she surprised."

"Well, she said that Mitch Cayman was one of the new clients who had overpaid her for a job she had done."

Bingo! He had what he needed. He wanted to end the conversation and get on the lead, but held himself back. "Is he expensive?"

"Maybe, but seeing as she knew something about him, she thought she'd fell comfortable talking to him. It must have the right choice because she ended up hiring him to handle her divorce."

"Well, that sounds like she's serious about the divorce. She's not wasting any time now."

"You bet she's serious. Why just the other day I called to see how she was doing and she mentioned she had contacted a real estate agent."

"She's selling the house?"

"Yes, but get this. Again its one of her rich clients. Here she had been worried about them and they're the ones who are coming to her aid. She said that a Paulette Locke stopped by one day and they got to talking. When she mentioned her situation, this woman offered to handle the sale of the house for her."

Dan was storing the names in his memory banks. His wife always surprised him. As clients they were nameless, but put them into a situation she could relate to and suddenly she remembered. There still may be more to learn, he thought, finding himself easily continuing the conversation.

"So she's planning on moving?"

"Yes, she says she doesn't want to stay in that house. Hank is fighting for all he's worth, too. She told me she was being followed and knew that Hank had something to do with it. He also had the house wired for sound. Can you imagine! It's like a melodrama to say the least.

"What, does he suspect there's another man in the picture? That's usually why someone goes to that extent."

"Who knows what he thinks. The only people who call are clients or her friends who Hank knows anyway." Janet let her eyes roll up to the ceiling. "Oh, it's such a mess, it bothers me to even think about it. I wouldn't trust that husband of hers no farther than I could throw him."

Janet was all talked out. He knew her well enough to sense that.

"Need any help cleaning up the kitchen?"

"No, you go ahead. I know you have work to do."

Janet stood and walked over to Dan, feeling the warmth of his arms as he hugged her tightly before lifting her chin and kissing her soundly on the lips. What a dolt Hank is, thought Janet with contempt. And to think he rules over Skye! It's outrageous. She returned Dan's kiss, selfishly thinking she was thankful to have such a wonderful, hardworking husband.

***

After that conversation with his wife, it had taken some time to follow the leads. He had managed to trace the fellow, Mitch and the woman Paulette to Angelo Maglioni, III and that had been his starting point. From there he had taken to tailing the two, then given up on Mitch and concentrated on Paulette who lead him to Sam Stillman. Tracing Stillman and asking some questions at a dive bar, he was able to connect him to the Angelino guy who had been murdered some time back. Now all he needed to do was organize the information he had gather and fill in the missing details.

In his office, Dan sat at the long table. Neatly, he laid out the rows of papers. He glanced at the clock on his desk. It was 6:30 p.m. He knew his wife's routine. She'd clean up the kitchen and then check on the kids to make sure they were doing their homework. That meant he had at least an hour before she'd come to check on him. He began trailing the leads in earnest.

His eyes went from sheet to sheet while his mind concentrated on finding the link between the pages. It was easy to surmise that

Paulette and Mitch had gathered information for the Stillman case and that they had probably been sent to Skye to have it typed up, which gave him the real connection between the three. Helping Skye with her divorce didn't fit into the puzzle.

The real enigma was that Stillman had hired Angelino to watch Skye. That he couldn't make hide nor hair of as he stared down at the names until he suddenly sensed danger. He could feel it coming upon him. His heart was pounding quickly in his chest as the details jelled. He tried to swallow the lump that had congealed in his throat, but his throat had constricted.

Something was hammering at his consciousness that was so overpowering he couldn't concentrate. "There is something I'm missing," he whispered.

Dan grabbed a blank sheet of paper, his mind working quicker than his hand as he wrote down disjoined facts.

Skye mentioned she was being tailed even after Angelino had been murdered.

Typing up the details received from Paulette and Mitch and most assuredly Maglioni. Getting a divorce...

To anyone looking over his shoulders, what Dan had written made no sense, but that wasn't the case where he was concerned. The missing details were swimming in his head. This time it was not a hunch. It was a certainty. "Damn," he said as he reached for the phone in the office, not aware that Janet stood in the doorway.

He was lucky. Taylor picked up the phone on the first ring. He could tell by his voice that he was extremely nervous. He had a right to be. The trial was only two days away and he had nothing. That is, until now. Dan delivered his message in a low, gruff voice.

"Taylor, I have to make this quick. I'm pretty sure that all the evidence we could possibly need is stored in a computer. I have reason to believe that someone else is interested in the data, too. They may be planning to make their move soon."

"Who has it?"

"A woman named Skye Sanders. She doesn't know what she has, but she's been doing work for Maglioni and his friends. Everything we need is probably in her system. That's not all, but I'll explain it later. Just leave it up to me and I'll get what you want."

"I'm running out of time."

"I'm well aware of that. Just sit tight and you'll have what you need, shortly."

"You're sure you've got it straight?"

"I think so." Dan's voice reeked with electrified urgency. Somewhere in the past hour, the fatigue had retreated; overwhelming numbness had anesthetized his anxiety. He could think clearly, almost abstractly.

"All right. Run it down for me." Taylor tried to keep calm. He had to be sure, had to know if Dan really had what he needed to win the case. This was no time to be irrational.

Dan recognized the symptoms in the other man. Taylor was coming to the end of his emotional tether, worrying if he'd have the information to win the case. Dan quickly filled him in on the details.

Janet moved back from the door to Dan's office. It's ridiculous, she thought, feeling suddenly confused. She leaned weakly against the wall in the foyer, her heart jumping spasmodically. She tried to calm herself, but her breath came in short spurts making her feel drunk and woozy. She had to get herself together and the only way possible was to stop thinking about what she had overheard.

"My god," she mouthed, her eyes wide with fright. She could hear Dan quickly shuffling papers in his office and she forced her feet to move into the foyer as though she was headed for the front room.

"Hi dear. Just let me clean up this mess and I'll join you in the living room."

Dan had materialized in the foyer and spoke to the back of his wife. There was a slight, barely noticeable change in her posture as she caught herself. She was to upset to speak, afraid he'd notice something in her voice. She was afraid to turn around too. So instead Janet nodded her head slowly and walked carefully across the foyer and into the living room.

Once safe from view, Janet turned around and was glad to see Dan hadn't followed her. Quickly she went over to the bar, opened the ice bucket. Picking up the ice pick she managed to break off a small chunk of ice and rubbed it gingerly on her face. She reached under the bar and grabbed a hand full of cocktail napkins which she used to gently pat her face dry.

Dan finished cleaning up his desk, haphazardly stuffing the papers into his briefcase. He stood for a moment looking around and when he was satisfied that he hadn't missed anything, he turned off the light and went to join his wife.

Janet, calmer now, stood in the center of the living room and glanced over when Dan entered. He looked cool and well-tailored in his cranberry and white striped shirt that still looked fresh from the iron. Even his slacks still held their crease and every brown hair was in place above his handsome face.

He walked over to her and ran a hand down the middle of her back. Before she could stop herself, she stepped forward, away from his touch, but Dan didn't seem to notice as he went to the bar and made them a drink.

Janet's eyes followed him, watching his usual foxlike grace as he moved across the carpet. "I love him so much", she said to herself.

"Honey, I forgot to tell you, I have to go out later this evening but I shouldn't be long. "Oh!" cried Janet, giving her husband an accusing look. "And why is that?"

"Business as usual, but let's not talk about that now. Did I tell you I saw Stanley and his wife the other day."

"Who?" asked Janet.

"Stanley, silly," he said fondly. "I invited them over for dinner this weekend." His back was to her so she wasn't able to see his face. If she could, she'd have known he knew something was bothering her. He continued to mix their drinks, then with one in each hand he turned around, expecting to see... he didn't know what, but not the sharp consternation that was on her face now. There was something like hatred in her flashing eyes. Dan quickly lowered his eyes trying first to convince himself he had been mistaken, but he was pretty sure that he hadn't imagine it.

"Sit down," he said, his fear increasing with confusion. He saw her clenched fists and the whiteness of her clenched lips. This was not his Janet, he thought, wondering what was bothering her and at the same time searching for a defense.

Janet only glared at him in a silence that seemed to charge the air. She had managed to convince herself earlier to stay calm and give him a chance to tell her something. Anything. But when Dan said he was going out she had seen red.

At that instant Dan knew that she had overheard his conversation. How much of it he wasn't sure. He had never lied to Janet. Yes there were times when he avoided answering, but never outright lied to her. To others, yes. But not to his wife. He slowly swiveled his body on the couch.

"What is it Janet? What's bothering you?"

"I heard you on the phone, I wish I hadn't, but I heard you."

Dan's cheek twitched and at first he said nothing. He thought about what he had said and frantically tried to console her. "I know you're upset, but it's nothing for you to worry about. I'm going to help your friend Skye. She doesn't know it, but she's in danger and I'm going to help her."

She didn't believe him. Try as she might she couldn't make herself believe what he said. "Tell me what's happening. Tell me now!"

"Sweetie, I wish I could, but you know I can't talk about a case. Besides I don't want to put you in danger, too."

Ignoring him, accusingly she said, "You tell me Dan. I said I heard your conversation on the phone just now so don't treat me like I'm stupid."

Dan frowned. "Okay, Janet, okay. Skye has been doing work for some people who are out to get my client. I wasn't sure at first, but I think she is in danger. Someone is going to try and get the evidence that she has accumulated innocently. I'm just going to warn her, is all."

"I don't believe you. If you hurt my friend..." She couldn't finish.

The thought of what was going through his wife's mind angered him. He felt a surge of hatred for Skye, her ignorance that had placed him in this situation that had his wife staring at him with hate in her eyes.

"You know I wouldn't do anything like that, Janet. Please listen to me. I am trying to help her." He was frustrated and scared now. "Tell me what I can say to make you believe me!"

She didn't let up. She continued to press him for some answers and as much as he wanted to relieve her fears, he knew he couldn't tell her the whole truth. It was to Dan, astonishingly curious that evening as he sat in their comfortable living room, his wife seated on the sofa at his side. This room had become their refuge. Where they met for their quiet time together. Tonight it was different. Tonight he would not see her smile or hear a word of conjugal kindness. At that instance he felt a part of him dying. There was a wiry strength he discovered in his wife, an obstinacy which would not yield, or, if yielding, remained obdurate and sullen. They argued through the night.

"For God sake, dear, it's nearly midnight. Give it up." Dan watched helplessly as Janet shook her head. Alarmed, he saw the firm set of her jaw and knew she still searched for some answers.

"No. I've got to know everything!

He knew it was useless to protest. Pulling up his body and moving closer to Janet he prepared his defense. His head was throbbing, and knowing what he still had to do tonight only made it worse. He was now quite sure she had heard the whole conversation and yet he felt there was still a chance.

"Darling, why don't you go on up to bed. It'll all look much clearer in the morning. I need to take care of something and then I'll be back. If you want to talk some more, I'll try and answer you're questions. Just try and get a few hours' sleep."

"Sleep?" Janet looked at him incredulously.

"Then rest," he almost snapped. "Go up to our room and lie down. I promise I'll not be long."

"Where are you going, Dan."

He swallowed hard before blatantly lying to her. "I need to take care of something right now, but it has nothing to do with this case. It's the one I was working on before, remember? I promised to drop off my report and I'm already late."

Janet looked at the clock. "It's awfully late to drop off files now. Why don't you do it in the morning."

He thought quickly. "Because I think we need that time to settle our differences. I'll just take the stuff over as I promised."

"You think that your client will be still waiting for you this late?"

"No, Janet, but I can put it inside the screen door and call him in the morning and let him know its there. That way I'll only need to make a phone call and can talk this through with you."

It sounded reasonable and besides she was too tired to talk any more. She needed time to think now, try and figure out what she should do.

"All right." Wearily, Janet walked out of the living room. She stopped in the kitchen to get a glass of water and was sorry she had. The minute she entered the room she remembered what she had been thinking just moments ago, remembered how lucky she felt to have a husband like Dan. But she didn't feel this way now. Silently she left the kitchen, went into the foyer, up the stairs, down the hallway past the children's rooms and the guest room to the master bedroom. Below she could here footsteps. Dan was walking around downstairs. Obviously she wasn't the only one who was upset.

She switched on the light and stood near the door, studying the room looking at the antique white furniture she loved so much. Dan had never cared for it. He had laughingly told her it looked barren and impersonal, like a motel room, but if it was what she wanted to go ahead. Before that they disagreed on the house. They'd bought it because she had wanted it so badly. She had said, "The house has real possibilities. Just wait and see. Give me six months with it." Now she felt the same way as he did.

Pulling off her shoes she wiggled her toes, stood up and took off her clothes and put on one of Dan's undershirts without thinking. She had a drawer full of sexy nighties but she didn't feel real sexy at the moment.

The room felt cool. She started to go back downstairs and turn off the air conditioning but instead she reached for the folded coverlet and drew it up over the spread. She touched the switch that turned off the overhead light.

The room was completely dark now. Outside the wind had picked up and she heard the sound of the branches of the dogwood trees as they slapped against the side of the house, then faintly the sound of the front door closing shut. Dan had left.

Janet dozed off into a light, uneasy sleep. She began to dream.

***

Her kids were calling out to her. "Help mommy, help!"

Janet jumped out of the bed, and ran into the hall, looking frantically from side to side. She was running through the darkness...running down the long hallway, passing the closed doors of her children's rooms as she followed their voices. It was that room, the one at the very end of the hall. Where had it come from, she wondered as she continued toward the closed door. She didn't remember a room being at the end of their hallway.

"Help us, please, mommy. Please!"

She moved quicker now, but realized she wasn't getting any closer to the door. It seemed to be moving away from her.

"Mommy's coming. Hold on. I'll save you!"

Suddenly she was at the door, pushing into the hard wood, trying to get in. The voices of her children rang out for her help and she turned sideways and bumped her side hard against the door again. It flew open at that instance throwing her through the entrance, her body falling hard on the floor, knocking her unconscious.

She felt herself coming back, forcing her eyes open, then shutting them against the bright light that filled the room. She called out, "Where are you children?" There was no answer. She called out again, and forcing her eyes to adjust she saw Skye lying on the floor, her body still...

***

After his wife had gone up to bed Dan spent his time pacing in the living room before finally turning and going into his office. He moved behind his large desk and stood there thinking about the scene he had just had with his wife. Forcing himself to stop thinking about he, he reached across the desk and turned on the lamp before digging into his pocket and pulling out his desk key. Slowly he leaned forward, the light illuminating the worry lines on his face. He seemed to be in a trance as he slid open the file drawer and removed his notes. He continued his far away gaze as he opened the upper drawer and removed three diskettes and placed them in his pocket. Standing up, he flexed his shoulders, vaguely aware that hours ago he'd been looking forward to going to bed, but not so now. With a quiet sigh he picked up his briefcase thinking that if Janet managed to get into his desk while he was gone, she would find nothing to further her idea that he was on his way to Skye's. He looked around the room as if assuring himself he had everything, then reached over and turned out the light.

As he stood in the foyer he thought about Janet. It was rare for them to disagree on anything, and arguing was something they never did. They were always happy with each other and trusted one another, yet tonight all of that had changed. One phone call had put them on opposite sides of the fence.

He found himself looking up the stair case, felt his feet guiding him toward the bottom step and with effort he forced himself still.

What could he say that would change things now. Nothing. He couldn't bare his soul, which was the only way to set things straight. And what if he were to tell her the truth? His hurt expression deepened, knowing that the distance between them would only widen.

"God," he said feeling the weight of the situation resting heavily on his shoulders, as he tried to think of a way to gain back the love and trust of his wife. "Oh, my god!" he whispered feeling the love of his life moving further from his reach. "What have I done! What can I do to make it all right!"

An enigmatic appearance now coated his handsome features as he placed a finger on his eyebrow. He loved her so much and the last thing he wanted was for her to form any doubts about him.

Again his expression changed. This time it showed his effort to gain the strength he needed to do what he had to do. As much as he wanted to run up those stairs and grabbed his wife to hold her close in his arms, he had to put it off for now. With the briefcase in hand, he grabbed his leather jacket off the coat tree and walked out the door.

***

Just as Dan walked out the door, Janet's eyes flew open. Frantically she looked around the darkened bedroom, a scream caught in her throat. She laid on her side, her body bathed in sweat and trembling. She felt claustrophobic, as if the ceiling had begun to descend upon her and shuddered convulsively. New beads of sweat popped out at her hairline before the realization hit her. She had been dreaming. It was all a dream.

As she slowly came to her senses her gaze went to the clock on the nightstand. It was after two in the morning. The house slept as she went downstairs.

It was peaceful in the house, very still and quiet as she moved slowly down the staircase, her hand sliding along the banister. But her mind wouldn't allow her to enjoy the serenity for long. It all came tumbling back to haunt her as she progressed slowly down the stairs.

"Oh, Dan, why did you let this happen," she said softly. In all their years of marriage they had managed to avoid arguing, but tonight made up for it.

No sooner had she spoken the words, visions of her nightmare swam menacingly in front of her and she had to grab hold of the banister to keep from falling. Not realizing what she was about to do, Janet moved firmly down the rest of the steps and hurried into the kitchen where she picked up the phone.

She could hear it ringing as she impatiently waited on the other end. Finally the line on the other end was picked up.

"Hello." A voice laden with sleep came to her anxious ears as her neighbor spoke into the receiver.

"Hi, Patricia, this is Janet. I'm so sorry to wake you at this ungodly hour, but I need to ask you a favor."

Patricia tried to shake herself awake, her eyes looking at the clock on her nightstand. "Hi, Janet." "Do you know what time it is?"

"Yes, I'm sorry, but I need some help." Afraid to give Patricia time to think, she added frantically, "Can you keep an eye on the kids for me. I need to go out."

Patricia was tired and didn't catch the urgency in Janet's voice. "At this hour!" She again looked at the clock. "It's almost three in the morning!"

"I know, but it's urgent. Please say you'll come over. I have to go somewhere."

Almost fully awake and lucid, Patricia registered the magnitude of stress in Janet's plea. "If it's that important, sure. Just give me some time to put on some clothes and let Fred know where I'm going. I'll be right over."

As soon as she placed the phone on the hook, Janet walked laboriously back upstairs. All her motions were lethargic and sluggish; her face pale and wan as she pulled on a pair of jeans and a short sleeve tee shirt before going into the bathroom. When she came out the hair about her face was damp, but combed into some semblance of order.

When Patricia knocked, Janet was standing in front of the door and opened it immediately.

"What's going on?" Patricia said upon seeing her friend's face. "You look like you've seen a ghost!"

"I'll explain later. I can't talk about it now. I need to get over to Skye's."

Janet grabbed her jacket off the coat tree and quickly slid her arms into the sleeves. She walked over to Patricia and hugged her.

"Thanks, Pat. I promise I'll explain everything later." Then she turned and opened the front door.

She stepped through into the blessedly cool October night. She walked over to her car and opened the door, pulling it shut as she put the key in the ignition, trying not to look over at the empty bay where Dan's car should be parked.

Within the car, the atmosphere was so tense and silent even the low rumble of the engine was a welcoming sound as she turned the key. She kept her eyes straight ahead as the car moved backwards until she was on the street, shifted gears and was on her way.

Janet dutifully, forced herself to drive conscientiously as she maneuvered through the dark familiar streets of her neighborhood, wishing she could cut the time in half. She lived twenty minutes from Skye.

The silence grew discomfiting as she drove down the street, turning onto the main road and proceeding toward her destination. Absently she reached into a case on the floor and pulled out a tape and engaged it in the deck without taking her eyes from the road. Soothing music filled the car's interior now, but its sensation was lost on her.

The light ahead turned red just as she approached and she forced her foot down on the brake. She sat very still, trying not to think about the situation, trying not to cry. She turned the dial on the radio and the music seemed to blast out around her, tears spilling uncontrollably from her eyes.

The light changed and she quickly started through the intersection, wiping her eyes with the back of her hand.

Luck was not with her as she found herself stopping at each light. As she approached the last one before the final turn, she had lost all patience and sped through not looking either way. She had to get there. She had to warn Skye. Finally she was just a block away.

Janet turned right off Calkins Road and was on Skye's street, prudently constraining herself to make the complete stop before crossing the intersection. This time she looked to her right, then left, her heart racing as she quickly turned her head left again.

There was a car parked, just a few feet away from the intersection. The car ignited her. Making her sense danger as she leaned her face close to her side window, squinting as she tried to see inside the dark car. No lights, no one inside, that she could make out.

Her car started rolling forward, but she put her foot on the brake abruptly and froze. Hadn't Skye mentioned something about someone watching the house? Yes, she had. Panic tightened her throat and tears spilled from her eyes as she pounded the steering wheel trying to made her mind work.

"What should I do? Why am I here?" She questioned herself as the tears blinded her vision.

"Stop it right now," she said in an authoritative voice. "You've come this far to warn Skye so don't blow it now."

It was as if her sub-conscious took over as she took her foot of the brake and found herself turning the wheel. Instead of going straight, Janet turned the car to the right.

Janet had been down this street before and knew it was a dead end road that was used by only the residents. It was a short street so there wouldn't be a lot of traffic. She passed by one, two, three houses and then pulled over to the side of the road and stopped the car. Quickly she turned off the headlights.

The engine purred softly as she adjusted her eyes to the darkness around her, using the back of her hand to dry the tears that filled her eyes. "You did good," she told herself as she began to feel her confidence rise. She had managed to overpower the panic that whelmed in the pit of her stomach, allowing her to ease the lump in her throat. She was okay now. Besides, she told herself, the car had been empty. It might belong to the people across the street from Skye. There was no reason to think otherwise. "Calm yourself, woman. Stop making a mountain out of a mole hill." A nervous laugh filled the car, taking away the silence and adding strength to her conviction.

Cautiously, Janet opened the car door and in one swift motion slide from its safety, pressed down the lock, and closed the car door so that the interior light was gone in a second. She stooped down moving around the car checking the other three doors to make sure they were all secured before making her next move.

She wanted to run to the corner house ahead, the house where Skye lived and pound on the door until her friend let her in. "But that would be foolish," she retorted rudely to herself. Visions of scenes from television came to her mind and she found herself acting out the antics of the characters that were part of the drama she had placed herself in.

She kept her body low, glad she had on dark clothing that would not announce her progress as she moved steadily along the side of the road until she was at the backyard of Skye's property line. Here she moved onto the grass and proceeded ever so slowly, looking around to see if anything had changed. No, she was all right. The houses were still darkened with only yard lights illuminating the area. Caught up in the drama of what she was doing, Janet giggled inside, lessening the tension as she wondered what anyone would think if they saw her. The giggle tickled her throat as she tried to keep the sound from being audible. A grown woman, stalking across the neighborhood, bent over and making her way in the wee hours of the night. Now there was something for the story books. Quickly she placed a hand over her mouth and forced the vision from her mind as she continued to move ahead.

In front of her now was the chain link fence that surrounded Skye's pool. Janet followed it's length until she was at the shrubbery that surrounded the patio. Cautiously she moved along the fencing, the back patio light shining on the top of her head, threatening to warn of her progress. She stooped even lower, making her way around the bushes until she was at the step up at the side. Here she paused for a moment, wanting to stretch up, her back aching now. But she didn't dare as she tried to decide on her next move. Should she knock on the sliding glass doors that allowed entry from the back of the house. No, she told herself. Skye wouldn't hear her unless she pounded loud enough for everyone else to hear her too. Then what? She continued until finally she had her game plan in line. She should make her way across the patio and go to the other end of the house.

Janet looked up and allowed her eyes to trail to her destination. That would put her under Skye's bedroom window on the upper level of the house.

That was all the strategy she could muster as she found her foot lifting up and maneuvering the step until she was on the patio. Still keeping low, she moved slowly across the space, bumping into the side of a chair, but moving so slowly, it didn't move or make a sound to cause a disturbance to her progress. Soon she was at the other end, stepping down and on the grass again.

Janet stayed as close to the house as she could until finally she was below Skye's bedroom window.

Janet straightened up and leaned up close to the side of the house. "Skye," she whispered. "Skye!" No response.

Not aware of what she was doing, Janet stooped down, groping in the darkness until her hand ran over the wood chips in the flower bed below the window. She filled her hand and then bringing it up above her head, brought her hand back and threw the wood chips at the window. She waited a few minutes and when there was no reaction, she reached down to gather another hand full and did it again. She continued to throw the chips until finally she heard movement above. Looking up she saw Skye's face outlined in the window.

Skye had been sound to sleep. At first she thought she had imagined the sound, but when it came again she forced herself awake. What was that sound. As she lay on her bed she was able to determine the sound was coming from the window and immediately alert she was filled with fright. Someone was out there.

Her first urge was to pull the covers over her head, but she forced her unwilling body to fall from the bed. Tense and scared now, edged up the wall below the window and carefully peaked through the side of the blinds. She could see nothing.

Janet below, saw the shade move. "Skye, it's me," she whispered. "It's Janet."

This time Skye heard the voice, the words taking a little more time to register. She moved to the center of the window, slid the window open and straightened her body trying to focus her eyes as she peered through the pane.

"Down here", came the voice again, forcing Skye to drop her eyes to the area below to window. "It's Janet."

Eyes peering down below the window, the moon cast an eerie glow on the figure below and suddenly she recognized her.

"Janet? Is that you."

"Yes. Skye, open up the sliding glass doors and let me in. We've got to talk."

Fully awake now Skye whispered back, "What are you doing here?"

"Please Skye. Open the damn sliding glass doors and let me in," Janet replied adamantly.

Skye moved back from the window. A chill went through her body as she reached over and grabbed her robe. Her mind questioned the presence of her friend standing below her bedroom window as she found herself hurrying down the hallway, forgetting to turn on lights until she was finally in the family room. She was fully aware that this wasn't a social visit.

While Skye hurried, Janet rushed back to the patio and breathed a sigh of relief when she heard the door sliding open. Quickly she stepped over the threshold and stood face to face with her friend. On impulse she reached out and hugged her and felt some of the tenseness of the situation leave her body. When she pulled back, she placed a finger on her lips.

"What is it Janet." Skye whispered with worry obvious in her voice.

"Come on, let's go downstairs. I need to talk to you."

***

While his wife sat downstairs inside the house talking to her friend, Dan drove around. He had seen the car at the intersection, only when he drove by it wasn't empty and he came to the same conclusion as his wife. Now he drove trying to figure out what to do.

Originally he had thought there was a good chance that he could break in through the front door, but he didn't dare chance it now. They were already here and he had to come up with an alternative plan. Normally he could come up with another tactic quickly, but with all that had happened, his mind wasn't as sharp as usual. He mustn't be hasty. He needed time to think.

So Dan continued to drive around, making sure he wasn't being observed and trying to figure out how he'd get into Skye's house without being caught. He should have contacted Walker, he thought. He was much too involved to think rationally. He should have had the sense to have Walker handle this for him. But, he told himself, he hadn't and it was too late now to think about that. He must figure out what he should do now and he was sure there wasn't much time left to reach that decision.

He tried to collect his thoughts. He had to get into Skye's house. That was his first objective and then he'd have to figure out his next move once that was accomplished. Absentmindedly he patted his pocket. He had the disks. He knew that once he was in it was a matter of getting into the office, bringing her system up and downloading the information he needed onto the disk. Then what? That was the question he next pondered.

He was in front of Wegmans supermarket now. He pulled into the parking lot, shut off the lights and tried to think. Carefully he went over the matter in his head trying to move the incident with his wife out of his head so he could think clearly. He had been on tougher assignments than this and managed success so why should he be incapable of finding a solution now. Even as he thought, he knew why and again he forced the thought to the back of his head.

He sat stone like trying to think the matter through until he came up with what he surmised as the only alternatives, then turning on the car lights, drove out of the parking lot and headed back toward Skye's house.

As he made another pass through the neighborhood he realized this time that whoever was in the car, was asleep, but he still didn't think it wise to chance going up to the front door. He turned down the side street and drove just far enough so he could see the back of the house.

Dan looked around the area noting the lights were out in the houses on the street. There were several outside lights on, but no street lights. That was good, he thought. Just enough light to guide him, but not enough to accentuate his progress.

Again he looked around, noticing there were several cars parked along the roadway, but nothing suspicious. He was confident this was as good as any a place to park and turned off the headlights.

Now Dan turned his attention to Skye's house. He'd have to try and get in through the sliding glass doors and if that failed, he'd have to hope that she hadn't locked the windows. With the matter resolved in his mind, Dan was able to concentrate clearly and decided that he'd have to delete the files after he had them copied onto the disk. That way if anyone else came snooping around, they'd find nothing.

He was ready. Dan reached over and placed his hand on the door handle, then paused, his mind working on its own now that he had managed to get it activated. What if he had to leave quickly, he thought. It would be wise to turn the car around, just in case he had to leave quickly Taking another look about, he again started the motor, not bothering to turn on the headlights as he drove further down the road until he came to the cal-de-sac. Carefully he drove the car around the circle until he was facing the way he had come. At the same spot as before, he moved the car over and turned off the engine.

Dan was so busy working on his plan that he didn't see his wife's car parked just a short distance behind him. He opened the glove compartment and took out a flashlight, turning it on with the beam facing toward the floor, to make sure that the batteries were still working. Satisfied, he then reached back into the glove compartment and pulled out his gun, checked to make sure it was loaded, while hoping he'd not have to use it. Finally he was ready.

***

Janet sat beside Skye in the rec room on the lower level of the house and told her everything, including that she was afraid that Dan had either already been there or was on his way.

"So what should we do?" Skye was now to frightened to think rationally. She could see how hard it had been for Janet to tell her, knew that warning her that her husband was involved had taken it's toll on her ability to provide an answer, but just the same wanting someone else to make the decisions .

"I don't know," Janet said wearily.

Skye's pulse was jumping now. "You're the one married to the detective. Come on Janet, think."

Janet focused her eyes on Skye who could see the hurt that was eating her up inside. That along with the horror of the situation of not knowing what to expect, let alone what to do was to great a burden. At that instance Skye knew she was on her own.

Well, they couldn't just sit here and wait for it to happen. They had to do something. Frantically she tried to think, tried to figure what to do. There was nothing they could do. Two frightened women, inexperienced and unarmed were no match for whatever was going to happen.

Skye's expression changed suddenly as she remembered the gun that Hank kept somewhere down here. She could get it and... Sure, right, she could do that and hope she had the stamina to pull the trigger. No, that wasn't the answer. Again her expression changed as she made a decision. She looked over at Janet. "We should call the police!"

Her answer came immediately. "No, Skye, please don't. Let's try and handle this ourselves, please." Janet was frantic now, trying to convince Skye not to call the police. Tears flowed from her eyes and her voice choked on each word.

"Okay, okay Janet, don't cry. We'll figure out something." She had no idea what, but she didn't want to upset her further.

Skye tried to think, but her brain wouldn't function. After a while she found her eyes looking ahead until they rested on the closed spare bedroom door. For the first time she thought about Hank. He must be in there. Where else could he be at this hour. She made a decision, thinking at the same time it may not be the smart thing to do, but she didn't have any other alternative.

"Janet, wait here. I'm going to get Hank."

She stared at her with frightened eyes. "Skye, what if Hank's in on this too. Do you think we should tell him!"

"What else can we do. You can't think of anything and neither can I. All I know is we can't handle this alone."

Janet knew that her friend was right. There was nothing else they could do, so she nodded her head. She watched as Skye walked across the rec room, heading toward the spare bedroom and for the first time was aware that they weren't sleeping together. She hadn't thought about it before.

Skye stood before the bedroom door and tapped lightly. When there was no sound, she turned the door handle and Janet watched as she disappeared through the doorway. In a matter of minutes Skye reappeared.

Janet stared across the room at her approaching form, wondering what was happening. Where was Hank and why wasn't he coming to their aid.

Skye was now beside her, reaching down and touching her shoulder, not concealing the terror that overwhelmed her now as she realized they were really alone. "He's not in there. He hasn't come home."

"So what now?"

"Janet, do you have someone watching the kids?"

"Yes, my neighbor, Pat is with them. What do we do now, Skye?" she whined.

"I don't know," Skye said in a soothing voice. "I guess we wait."

"But..."

"Janet," she added interrupting her friend, "All we can do is wait. Let's go upstairs. There's nothing else we can do unless you want me to call the police."

"No, please!"

"Okay, then. We go back upstairs and into my bedroom. Whatever happens we stay there until it's over or we change or minds and call for help. That's all we can do."

Shaking, Janet shook her head in agreement. She watched, wondering what Skye was up to as she made a second trip into the back bedroom. When she came out she walked into the bar area and Janet could hear her rummaging around. When she came out, she walked over to Janet.

"What were you looking for?"

"Hank keeps a gun down here somewhere, but I can't find it. Come on, let's go," she said resignedly.

As they moved toward the staircase, Skye asked, "Did you tell Pat were you were going?"

"Yes," Janet replied meekly.

"Did you tell her why?"

"No!"

"Come on, you had better call her."

Arms around each other, they moved slowly up the stairs, through the kitchen and into Skye's bedroom. Skye closed the door and locked it before turning toward Janet.

"Call Pat now."

Skye occupied herself by closing the blinds and climbing into the bed while Janet placed the call. When she hung up she said. "It's okay, Pat will stay with the kids as long as I need her too."

Janet put her feet up on the bed and leaned back against the head board. Skye did the same. Neither one said a word. Skye reached over until she felt Janet's hand and took hold of it. Then they waited.

Janet sat thinking about Dan, too scared to think about anything else. Her life had always evolved around Dan and life without him was unthinkable. They had to settle their differences, but how? She was tired, so very tired yet she couldn't sleep. She continued to sit there thinking until finally her eyes closed on their own and she knew nothing more.

Skye as exhausted as her friend, was unable to keep her eyes open much longer as she leaned against the headboard. She fought to stay awake until finally sleep overcame her.

***

Frank Jaffe woke up and glanced at his watch. He ran a hand across his eyes and tried to stretch. He hadn't spent a night in his own bed since he had taken on this assignment. He had done jobs for this lawyer before but they had proved much more interesting than this one. When he was given this assignment, Maglioni had told him that the woman was a friend of his and he wanted to make sure nothing happened to her. But now it was almost over. After he had reported in this afternoon stating that he hadn't seen or heard anything strange going on, he had been told he could call it off, but there was one more thing he wanted him to do. Tonight he was to get inside and as a safety precaution see if he could wipe the information out of the computer. He didn't know much about computers, but wasn't about to mention that. Instead he said it would be a cinch.

There had been no action all evening and he must have drifted off, he realized as he looked over at the dark houses up and down the street. "Time to make the move," he said to himself. Getting in would be no problem, figuring out how to turn on the damn machine and do the job was another ball game and at this moment he wished he had been curious enough about computers to at least have learned how to turn one on. Well, he thought, it was too late to worry about that now.

Frank Jaffe leaned back in his seat with a worried expression. There wasn't a lock he couldn't pick, a safe he couldn't figure out the combination to, and he was worried about turning on a computer? He'd figure it out. He was smart and quite capable of handling any obstacle that got in his way and he'd manage this one. He tried to believe that, but his expression didn't change. What if he couldn't? What then?

No time to think about that now, he thought as he silently opened the car door, the dome light illuminating the interior of the car for a brief second before he climbed out and shut the door. He patted his side to make sure his gun was tucked in his belt, then patted his chest pocket and felt the shape of his penlight. He was all set. He started across the intersection to the front door of Skye's house. He paused listening on the doorstep and took a last look around.

Jaffe reached out and tried the door handle, then reached into his pocket and pulled out a contraption, placing it into the lock. He worked silently on the front door to the family room, unaware of Dan doing the same at the back entrance to the room. At the same time they both heard the locks click. Frank pushed the front door in and stepped over the threshold just as Dan slid the sliding glass door silently on it's track, it's movement hidden behind the drapes. He stepped up over the frame and was in the room, his eyes trying to adjust to the darkness.

Instinct told him he was not alone and before he was able to make out the figure of the other person in the room, he was sweating profusely. Seconds passed as he tried to adjust his eyes, his hand already reaching for his gun. The surprise expression on both of their faces was hidden in darkness. He stood there for perhaps five seconds more, the gun pointed in front of him, both hands supporting it's weight and then he pulled the trigger.

Frank, just as aghast, managed to make the adjustment to the darkness of the room much sooner, but the shock delayed his action by seconds. Taking the same stance, his gun already drawn and ready, he aimed and fired. It was over in a matter of minutes. Their bullets passing each other as they met their marks.

There was no movement from the form that laid directly across from Dan Malone. His mind working quickly now, he took quick glances around the room as though expecting someone to pop up from behind a chair or emerge from the entrance doorway to the garage. His eyes skated across the two lamps at either end of the room and he thought they were the size of small people--they were small people to him as he laid dying on the rug. He instructed himself to get up, finally aware that he had fallen down on the floor.

That's when he felt the pain as it cut through his chest making him drop his head hard against the carpet. It was like a flashing bolt of steel cutting through his body, holding him in its grasp as he tried to over power it. He had to get up, take care of what he had to do and get out of here. But he couldn't move. He fought waves of blackness trying to take him into their grasp, his body paralyzed by the pain. For the first time he was scared. Raising his head up words seeped from his mouth. "Oh, man!" he said as his eyes saw the blood staining the front of his shirt.

***

The sound woke up Janet and Skye. As Janet bolted forward trying to get her bearings, she felt Skye grip her hand tighter, so tight that it hurt. Her mind tried to grasp what it was that had awaken her, while she looked around the unfamiliar darkened bedroom trying to figure out where she was. Finally it registered. She was with Skye in her bedroom. With frightened eyes, she glanced quickly into Skye's face, seeing the expression of panic and feeling it grow within her body.

She had heard a sound, a sound quite like the cannon that had been shot when she and Dan had taken the kids to Fort Niagara and they had staged a pretend battle. She remembered putting her hands over her daughter's ears while Dan had done the same with their son as he looked over at her laughing as she jumped from the shock of the explosion. But she wasn't at Fort Niagara now.

Janet tried to pull her hand from the vise grip of her friend's, the over powering panic spreading through her, using it to give her body strength.

Skye held her friend's hand in a death grip, her body frozen in time, not wanting to move from the safety of the bed. She felt the hand squeezing through her closed fist and he she fought determinedly trying to hang on until her fingers dug into the flesh of her own hand. Janet was free.

Skye jumped out of the bed and rushed around the foot trying to catch up with the momentum of her friend. She had to stop her. She didn't know why, but just that she had to.

"Did you hear it?" Janet's frightened voice spoke her concern.

"Yes!"

"What should we do? What was it?"

Skye stood beside her friend, barely listening. She walked over to the closet no longer in control of her actions.

"Skye, what should we do?"

The panic in Janet's voice registered, making her forget her fear for the moment. "Come on, we've got to find out what's going on."

Skye frantically looked around the room and saw the baseball bat next to the wall near the dresser. Quickly she walked toward it, snatched it up, making sure she was in front of Janet. Slowly she unlocked the door, listening for any sounds of danger.

She could hear nothing. She opened the door wider and reaching behind her, she felt Janet grab hold of her free hand. Giving it a slight squeeze of confidence, she pulled Janet with her into the darkened hallway.

Side by side they moved as one body. Skye was aware that it was getting light outside as they made their painful progress. Somehow the enormity of the situation lessened for her knowing it was almost morning. "Bad things happen in the dark," she recited silently. "Only in the dark".

They were at the doorway to the kitchen when Skye paused looking around before she allowed herself and her companion to step on the linoleum. The pressure of her gripe on Janet increased, restricting her from getting ahead of her as Skye sensed her urgency. Janet was probably remembering Dan. For the first time, Skye allowed herself to think about what they may find up ahead and again panic filled her body making her shake.

She could feel Janet leaning into her, trying to release her grib, trying to get ahead of her. "It'll be okay," she whispered over her shoulder, not believing it for one second.

Finally they reached the landing before the family room. Skye gripped the handle of the bat tighter while forcing herself to take the first step, then the next until she was standing on the landing before the doorway, Janet stumbling down beside her. Her eyes took it all in and before she could stop, an audible gasp escaped through her lips.

"What is it," came the frightened voice behind her. "Move out of my way, Skye," Janet said as she felt the pressure on her hand.

Skye couldn't move, couldn't make herself take the final step into the room. She was in the doorway now, unaware of releasing the grip she had on Janet as she clutched her robe closer to her body, then reached up to pat her hair. At the bottom of the stairs laid a man with blood soaking the front of his shirt. She could barely hear the moans coming from his mouth as his head moved from side to side. She head a scream, then realized it came from her. Then she yelled out in recognition, "It's Dan. He's been shot!"

Janet frantically hurled her body into Skye who was barely able to catch herself from falling forward as she stumbled down the step and into the room, dropping the bat and letting her hand press against the wall in time to break her fall.

Janet pushed forward, missing the step and falling to her knees beside the body lying on the floor. She screamed his name over and over again, her hands on either side of his face. "Dan, Dan, oh Dan!"

The tortured cries, the sight of the blood! Skye felt herself starting to sway, and leaned harder into the wall. "Oh, God," she wailed!" She prayed silently for the strength to endure while her brain digested the nightmarish scene. She fought the waves of darkness that tried to take her under. She couldn't faint. She must not faint.

Dan's body on the floor with the blood soaking through his shirt with Janet slumped over him and trying to raise his head. Her legs heavy now, Skye moved toward Janet wanting to comfort her, as she fought the nausea rising in the throat. As she stepped further into the room she saw the other body and was no longer able to fight the queasiness in the pit of her stomach. She sank back and fell down on the top step. She covered her mouth and eyes and leaned forward as her stomach lurched.

Skye kept her head down, afraid to look up. She wanted it to all go away. She had to be dreaming. This couldn't be happening. But it was. She could hear Janet sobbing and calling out her husband's name, frantically trying to rouse him. She had to open her eyes, she told herself and managed to obey.

Trying not to take in too much too fast, Skye refused to look down. Instead her eyes were drawn to the family portrait on the wall directly over the sofa. Suddenly there seemed to be a weird glow coming from the portrait. Skye felt herself draw back, tried to force her eyes to stay open while telling herself it had been her imagination. But it was more than she could muster to keep from screaming and her eyes closed tight.

She was certain she had seen it. Her eyes flew open while she forced herself to look at the portrait again.

Nothing! Whatever she thought she had seen, now had vanished. She was almost convinced when the light reappeared and she knew she wasn't imagining it.

It was too much for her to handle. Skye felt herself being pulled away from the trauma unfolding in the room. No longer in control, she felt her body rising from the step and moving toward the portrait. She felt the coolness of her hand moving across the glass as she fingered the picture, wondering what she was doing when her attention was drawn elsewhere.

There was a beam of light coming through the front window, lighting up her hand as she ran it across the picture. Cautiously, her stomach wanting to heave again, she moved around the body that laid directly in front of the door and glanced through the window that looked out on the front lawn. There were two police cars at the end of the driveway. She could just see the heads of the policeman kneeling down behind the cars.

Now she knew what had caused the glare on the portrait, as the officer again flashed the beam from his flashlight across the window. Skye jumped back away from the window, tripping over the body as she frantically tried to get to the other side of the door.

Sobs came from her mouth as tears streamed from her eyes. Skye reached up to wipe the tears away that blinded her vision. She wrapped her hand around the door knob, frantically trying to turn the handle which just slid around inside her hand. She was crying uncontrollably now, her body shaking as she wrapped both hands around the door handle and pulled toward her as she turned the knob, but she couldn't get it open.

Hysterically she looked down and sobbing louder she kicked out with her foot, trying to move the body further into the room as she continued to pull and turn until there was enough space for her to squeeze through. She felt the frame digging into her back as she pushed until she was finally outside. Immediately her body was bathed in the light that was fixed upon her.

Skye leaped backwards into the door frame, blinded by the probing light in front of her. She lifted her hand to shield her eyes from the brightness.

Not coming up from thier crouched pose, one officer yelled, "Hold it right there."

"Don't shoot," Skye screamed at that instance. I don't have a gun she wailed, sliding down the door frame, no longer to hold herself up. "In there. Please, you have to help us," she sobbed.

Slowly the officer who had yelled out at her, rose up. "Are you all right."

"No!"

"What's happened."

"Someone's been shot!"

She saw the officers coming toward her now, guns in their hands as the covered the short distance to the front step. She didn't wait. For the first time since entering the family room, she remembered Janet. Janet was in there alone with her husband. She had to help Janet. Somehow she managed to find the strength to stand on her own and turned pushing hard into the door until she was able to slip into the room. The officers followed, their guns out of their holsters.

Janet had his head in her lap now. She rocked back and forward moaning incoherently. One word was all that Skye could make out as she tried not to look anywhere but in Janet's face. "No! No!" she whimpered.

***

A face was floating somewhere above him as Dan forced himself back to the land of the living.

"It's all right, Dan. It's all right."

Skye's voice. It was Skye's face he was seeing.

"It's all over. We'll take you to the hospital and you'll be all right."

What was all right. Why was he here. He couldn't remember. He tried to shift his body, but the pain it brought forced him to wince and lie still. Why was Skye here. It didn't make sense. Suddenly his mind snapped at attention. Where was Janet? Where was his wife.

"Janet!" he cried out frantically, his voice feeble and unable to capture the urgency of his words. He was so weak. It was an effort to keep his eyes open... so much easier to let them close... He could feel himself sinking, wondering what had happened to him. He couldn't remember.

"I'm here, dear. I'm right here."

A hand in his, a hand he knew he had held many times before. He felt her lips on his cheeks, his forehead, his lips. He tasted the saltiness of her tears as she leaned over him.

"I'm sorry.... so sorry!"

The police were in the room now, leaning over the body at the door. "Does anyone know who this man is?"

Absently, with her eyes still captured on her friend's face, Skye shook her head. Janet demonstrated no change in her expression. It was as if she hadn't heard the question. No, Skye thought, it was as if she wasn't even part of the group gathered in the room. Her eyes, her body was involved with the figure lying in her lap as she rocked and sobbed above her husband's head.

The policeman pressed again, not catching the nod of Skye's head. "Do you know this man?"

"No!" The word came out as though it was an imposition for him to be asking her questions at a time when she could barely keep from fainting. That's what she wanted to do. Faint away and remove herself from the scene. She could hardly bare to look at the pain in Janet's face, but the alternative was much greater. So she continued to stare only at Janet. Continued to feel that the pain her friend was going through was her fault. She had caused this somehow. And what made it worse, she didn't know what she had done!

More animated now, the officer spoke again. "Madam?"

Skye forced herself to look away and watched as the officer came over to Janet and leaned down next to Dan. "This man is still alive. Call an ambulance!" He yelled over at the other officer before turning back to look down at Dan.

"Don't try to move," he said with authority. "You've been shot."

A puzzled expression squeezed through the pain as the words penetrated his brain. He'd been shot. Yes, he remembered now. He had been shot. The pain moved backwards and he could remember it all now. He had come to Skye's do get the information before anyone else had a chance to do the same. That explained why Skye was here, but his wife... Before he had a chance to finish his thought, the officer spoke again.

"I know it's hard, but can you tell me who shot you?"

Dan swallowed shakily. "No," he rasped, squeezing Janet's hand as her sobs grew louder.

"Why did he shoot you?"

It was getting harder to talk, much to hard. He had to reply, but it hurt so much to say words. Trying laboriously, he managed to respond. "Came through the door. Shot same time."

Witnessing the struggle for the man to reply, the officer turned his attention to Janet.

"This is your husband?"

Without taking her eyes from Dan's face she coaxingly acknowledged, "Yes. Is he going to be all right."

For the first time her head lifted, her gaze plastered on the officer's face, willing him to give her the answer she needed to hear.

The Officer looked down at the figure in her lap, staring at the crimson front of his shirt. He could see the hesitant lift and fall of his chest, the glassy stair of his eyes and he knew. He had seen it before and there was no doubt in his mind that the man could only last a short while longer. He lifted his head and looked fixedly at the woman who cradled the dying man's head, not saying a word.

"No, please, no." She cried harder now.

"I'm sorry madam," was all he could say.

Skye, witnessing the scene, crawled on the floor until she was directly beside Janet. She reached over, placing her arms around her shoulders, trying not to look at the figure in her lap as she cried with her friend, not knowing what to say.

"Don't leave me Dan. Please, don't leave me. Hang on darling."

"I can't anymore." The words came out in murmured intervals, spaced as if each word was it's own sentence. Janet leaned her ear down until it was over his mouth. " I'm so tired, so very tired."

Hysteria coated her response as Janet lamented, "No, don't leave me! Fight it Dan, please fight it?"

Wretched, searing tears fell from her eyes and splashed on his face as he looked up at his wife, trying vainly to smile. Her precious features were now etched in his mind and he wanted to tell her she was so beautiful and so dear to him, only he could no longer speak. Weakly he squeezed her hand, praying she could read his mind and capture all the words that were left unsaid.

His head laid heavily in her lap, his eyes glowed as they captured hers; his wife, his beloved.... His last thought as he slowly slipped away.

Terror clutched her tightly in its grasp. "Oh, no. No, I won't let you die!"

Janet's wail seemed to fill every inch of the room. Skye's hands flew up to cover her ears, and they rocked back and forth with the movement of her head. Her eyes were shut as if not seeing would block out the tremendous torture that had engulfed her.

The officers who had been intent on trying to identify the other body, spun in unison, to face the direction of the sound. There eyes stared at the scene before them. The woman on the floor had collapsed over her husband. Her hand clenched in a fist, she beat madly on the inclined body, screaming incoherently. On knees just behind her, the other woman's body weaved as she held her head between her hands.

No words passed between them as the officers covered the distance to the women. One officer was behind Skye, the other pushed Janet upward so that he could lean his head over Dan, then planted himself behind Janet.

Skye could feel the officer placing his hands under their shoulders, then pulling her up as he supported her. Skye fell back against him, unable to stand by herself.

She watched as Janet was lifted up, fighting and screaming incoherently as she was dragged away from the dead form of her husband. Skye lifted her arms to cover her ears.

"Come on, let's take them into another room."

Skye felt herself being almost carried up the stairs and into the kitchen. She could hear Janet sobbing and screaming out words at the other officer as she fought the pressure of his arms. She heard the officer soothingly and urgently pressuring her. "Please, madam, he's gone. It's for the best. Let me help you."

The officer was pushing her body down. She felt the chair arms, her body falling into the seat. She was in the kitchen now, her eyes looking around freely. This was better she told herself. Much better.

Hesitantly she allowed her gaze to fall on Janet. As if in a trance she watched as Janet was forced into the chair opposite her. The officer stood behind her, pressing down on her shoulders, keeping her in the seat. Her mind focused and she heard the words regretfully tumble out, "He's dead, isn't he?"

Janet frantically stared around the room until her eyes met Skye's. "No!" she kept repeating, her voice growing louder with each utterance.

"Get her some water," one of the officers said.

She was coming to her senses now. The officer who had helped her was already on his way to the sink. Skye found herself jumping out of the chair and immediately moving across the floor, pushing the officer out of the way as she reached in the cabinet to get a glass and carried to the refrigerator. "I'll get it," she said. She was alert and feeling stronger now as she stood waiting for the glass to fill. She carried it over to the table and placed in the other officer's outstretched hand.

She stood watching as the officer picked up Janet's hands, then placed the glass between, keeping his hand on the glass until he felt her taking control. Slowly the glass was lifted to Janet's lips and she drank.

There was a tap on her shoulder and Skye turned around. "Are you all right?"

"Yes," Skye replied firmly. "I can take care of her now."

"Are you sure."

"Yes. Do what you have to do. We'll... I'll be all right."

"Okay, we'll be in the next room if you need us."

Skye nodded her head and went over to stand next to Janet.

They were alone in the kitchen. The atmosphere was more toward normal now and Skye was in control. Aside from the whispered voices, the unidentifiable sounds coming from the room below it was almost as though nothing had happened. She could hear a clock ticking somewhere as she stood by Janet who now only stared straight ahead. Skye forced herself to ignore everything and concentrated on taking care of her friend.

Skye tried to soothe Janet who no longer seemed to be responding to anything around her. She sat in the chair looking straight ahead not a sound coming from her. She moved her chair next to Janet's and sat by her. Suddenly she heard a new voice below, her ears perked as she listened.

"My God! What's happened?" A pause. "Where's Skye."

"She's in the kitchen. Who are you?"

"I'm her neighbor from across the street. I'm the one who called you."

Voices were lowered and Skye could only catch snatches of the conversation. It appeared they were asking her neighbor if she knew either of the two men. There was no audible reply to their questions.

"Thanks. You can go now!"

When Selma stepped into the room, Skye looked gratefully into her face. Selma walked over and hugged her shoulders. "Sit still. I'll make some coffee."

Selma moved about the familiar kitchen talking as she began preparing the coffee.

"What happened, Skye?"

How much should she tell her was the first thought to enter her mind. It was all so complicated and she needed to talk to someone, only how much did she know?

"I don't know," she responded wearily. "Janet and I were sleeping and heard something and saw..." She couldn't finish the sentence.

"Do you know who the man by the door is?"

"No. I've never seen him before."

"Where's Hank?" Selma retorted not hiding the anger in her voice.

"I don't know that either. He hasn't been home."

Selma turned around and was about to say something, but seeing Janet's face changed her mind. "I think we'd better get her to lie down. Let's take her into the bedroom."

Mechanically, Skye got off the chair and with them on either side, they managed to get Janet to her feet and walk her back to the bedroom."

"Skye, stay with her and I'll go get Peter."

Selma left the room and hurried into the family room.

"Listen, Ms. Johnson, I need to ask you some questions first."

"Okay, make it quick, will you!"

"How well do you know these two women?"

"Skye I know very well. I've only met Janet a couple times when she was visiting Skye. Why do you ask?"

"Has there been anything strange going on here?"

"No."

"Think. Are you sure?"

"Well, no more than the usual. Skye is in the process of divorcing her husband, Hank. I wouldn't consider that strange."

"Can you tell me anything, anything at all. Something you might have noticed or heard around the neighborhood."

Selma concentrated. "Well, I did notice a strange car sitting at the intersection last night when I went to Wegmans."

He looked interested. "Tell me about it."

"Nothing to tell really. It had been sitting there several evenings. I mentioned it to my husband and he went out to take a look. He said there was a man sitting behind the wheel so he didn't get up close to the car."

"Did he know the man?"

"No. He could only see the side of his face. It was dark, probably around ten when he went out to have a look."

"Why didn't you call the police?"

"The people who live in the house where the car was parked have several automobiles. We thought, possibly they were moving it at the time. Later when I saw it again, I just forgot to mention it. It just didn't seem that important." She paused, then asked, "Can I go now?"

"Just one more question. You mentioned that you went to the store last night and saw the car?"

"Yes."

"Was there someone in it at that time."

"I'm not sure. Like I said, I wasn't too interested. Besides, I was more concerned with Skye."

"Why's that?"

"Well, it must have been around midnight when I left. I had procrastinated about going to the store all day to get cereal and milk for the morning and didn't get myself going until that late. Anyway, I noticed that all the lights were on in Skye's house. It bothered me since I only live across the street, I hear things. She and her husband argued a lot and more so after she asked him for a divorce. I wasn't being nosy, you see, but I wanted to make sure she was all right."

"So what did you do."

Hesitantly she replied. "I came across the intersection and parked the car to get out and check her garage. I saw that her car was in there, but not her husband's van. That meant she was there alone."

"So, do you know why she had the lights on?"

Sheepishly she replied. "Yes, I think so. Skye had told me a long time ago she was scared of the dark. It wasn't something she was proud of, but one time back when she and Hank were on better terms, they were over playing cards. Hank has high blood pressure and it was acting up so he asked Skye to get his medicine. Skye wanted me to come with her and when we were at the door she realized the only key she had on her was to the patio doors out back so she asked would I go around with her. That's the first time she mentioned her phobia."

It all made sense to the officer and he finally let her pass. Shortly she returned with her husband in tow. The officer noted he carried a black bag.

"Officers." he said politely, then taking in the scene added, "Are they both dead?"

"Yes," came the response.

Peter shook his head in sympathy. "I'll come back and give you a hand," he replied before following behind his wife.

"Are you okay, Skye?"

"Yes, I'm fine. Please take a look at her," she said pointing at Janet.

Peter examined Janet while his wife filled him in on what had happened. He sent Skye to get a glass of water while he got a sedative out of his bag. After Janet had taken them, he turned toward his wife. "Listen, I'm going to see if the officers need my help."

"Okay, I'm going to stay with Skye for a while."

He turned and left the room.

Janet was no longer crying as she stared through unseeing eyes. It was like it was happening to someone else and not her. She was aware of a hand smoothing her hair as her head laid on the pillow and then she drifted off, allowing the blackness to claim her.

Once they were certain Janet was asleep, Selma followed Skye into the kitchen. While Skye made a call to Janet's home, she poured coffee for them, then went to the head of the stairs.

"Would you gentlemen like a cup of coffee?" she said, careful not to look down at the floor.

"Yes. That would be nice, if its not too much trouble."

"How do you take it?"

"Both with two sugars and one cream."

Selma busied herself at the kitchen counter waiting for Skye to finish with her call. When she hung up the phone, she said. "Come and sit down, Skye. This will make you feel better."

They heard cars driving up followed by new voices in the front room. When Selma carried the coffee into the officers, they asked that she take them back to the kitchen and they'd be in later. Five, ten minutes passed as they drank their coffee, only hearing snatches of the conversations below. After a while Selma got up and poured the extra two cups of coffee down the drain. She removed the pot from the burner and replenished their cups then began a second pot. She then sat back down at the table.

They watched the sun come up through the kitchen window, the light making the whole situation less eerie. Skye got up a couple of times to go check on Janet, but found she was sleeping soundly. Silently they sat at the kitchen table, listening to the men in the front room.

The door continued to open and close, followed by more unfamiliar voices. It was almost seven when the officers joined them in the kitchen, carrying a Dunkin Donut box.

"Sorry, ladies. It took longer than we expected. I don't think we introduced ourselves with all the commotion. I'm Officer Sheldon and this is my partner, Officer Jefferson."

Selma and Skye nodded.

As if he had forgotten, Officer Sheldon said, "Oh, here, someone dropped these off for you."

Skye smiled weakly. "Thanks," she said as she took the box from his hand. "Please, sit down," she motioned, pointing to the two empty chairs. While they prepared to join them, Skye got out a plate and arranged the donuts on it before placing them in the middle of the table while Selma busied herself refilling their cups and carried them over to the officers.

"Skye, I'll get out the plates and napkins. You sit."

As she moved over to take her place, Selma crossed the floor again and got out plates and napkins. Finally she sat down beside Skye.

"I know this has been upsetting and that you're tired, but we need to ask some questions."

"It's okay. I understand."

"We need to speak to you both." He checked himself, then said, "I mean you and the decease man's wife."

"She's sleeping now. Selma's husband gave her a sedative. You'll have to wait to speak to her."

"Probably is best she rest. I could tell she was pretty shaken up."

Again the women nodded.

"Now, what can you tell me, Miss er..?"

"I'm Skye Sanders and this is my friend, Selma Johnson. The woman in the back room is Janet Malone and the dead... the man is Daniel Malone."

"Can you tell me why Ms. Malone was here with you?"

"She came here tonight to tell me about a conversation she overheard. Dan had spoken to someone on the phone about me and some clients of mine. From what she gathered, from Dan's part of the conversation, I had information that her husband's client wanted." Seeing the puzzled expressions on the officers faces, Skye quickly added, "Dan's a private investigator."

"What was this information?"

"Oh, I'm sorry. I run a computer business from my home. I've been trying to figure that one out and all I can come up with it's the transcripts that I typed up for several new clients..."

"I'm sorry to interrupt, but you're going to have to start from the beginning and tell me everything that comes to your mind."

Skye took in a deep breath as she looked around the table. Slowly she told them about getting the call from Angelo Maglioni. She explained that he needed her to type up a transcript. Later she was asked to prepare papers for three other individuals who she had to assume were sent to her by Mr. Maglioni."

"Why's that?" Officer Sheldon asked.

"Well, the papers I typed for them, dealt with the same case."

Officer Sheldon nodded. "Who were these individuals?"

"Two men and a woman."

"Do you remember their names?"

Skye watched the officers as they took down notes. "Paulette Locke and Mitch Cayman were two of them. But I don't remember the other man's name. It's in the computer." She added, "I could get it for you?"

"Later," Officer Sheldon said. "Do you happen to know who Mr Malone's client was?"

"No, I don't. I'm sorry."

"That's okay, Ms. Sanders. Is there anything else we should know."

She sat there thinking. "Well, I am getting a divorce, but I don't see how that has anything to do with this."

"It might. Has your husband said or done anything suspicious?"

She started to say, 'always', but instead said, "Well, he did have the house wired... I mean, I found he had wiretaps in the house. And, there was someone following me. I'm pretty sure he set that up too."

"Do you know why he did that?"

"I guess he thought that there must be someone else if I was going to divorce him. You have to know my husband to understand. He's the type of person who thinks the world belongs to him and he can do no wrong."

"I see," Officer Sheldon said with raised eyebrows.

"I don't think he had anything to do with this," Skye piped in quickly. "He's apt to do just about anything, but not this." Slowly she added, "I wish I could explain it in a clear, logical way, but I can't. Basically because Hank is not a logical man. He's a mishmash of emotions and fears and upbringing, and God knows what else."

Both officers were scribbling frantically in their notebooks. When they had finally caught up with her, they laid down their pens. This time she was addressed by his partner.

"You say you typed these transcripts into your computer."

"Yes, I did."

"Is the information still there?"

"Yes, I believe so."

"Where's your office?"

Skye got up and showed Officer Jefferson into the office. She watched as he walked behind the desk and stood before the system. Officer Sheldon followed. Excusing herself, Skye slipped in front of the other officer and sat before the computer, switching it on she worked the keyboard, and brought up a document on the display monitor. She gestured and Officer Jefferson leaned forward to look. It was the first transcript that she had typed for Mr. Maglioni. After a while, Jefferson reached around her and pressed the PgDn key several times, moving the document up to view the rest of it. They were engrossed, staring at the screen when Selma entered the office.

"Skye, if it's okay, I'm going to go home. If you need me just call. I'm not going into work today so I can come back anytime."

"Thanks Selma. Thanks for coming over and helping out. I really appreciate it."

"I know you do sweetie. You take it easy and try to relax, okay?"

"Sure, I'll do that."

As soon as Selma left the room, Officer Jefferson turned to Skye. "There's a lot of information in just this one report. Can you print them all out so we can take a copy with us."

"I can do that, sure. I guess I've already violated the privacy of my clients by letting you read the transcript, but I don't care. Right now all I want is to have someone get to the bottom of this."

Skye was about to print the first file just as the phone rang in the kitchen. She checked to make sure the printer was ready, initiated the print, then headed for the kitchen to answer the phone.

"Ms Sanders?" Officer Sheldon called out, "That might be for us. We gave the number to the station so they could get in touch with us."

"Okay", she said over her shoulder as she continued toward the extension. She picked up the receiver on the third ring.

"Hello."

"Hello, is Officer Sheldon there?"

"Yes he is. Just a moment please." She laid the phone on the counter and called out to the officer. "It's for you."

Officer Sheldon came into the kitchen, thanked her and put the phone to his ear. Skye went back in to finish printing the files.

"This is a nice set up you have here," said Jefferson. "Got a lot of clients?"

"More than I can handle lately."

Jefferson nonchalantly asked about her business and she tried to explain it while they waited for the printouts. Skye was standing by the printer when Sheldon rejoined them.

"Ms Sanders, could you sit down for a moment."

She looked at him with a surprised expression. "Why, what's happened?"

"Please, sit down. Jefferson, get her a glass of water."

"What is it? Is it my son? Tell me!" She didn't know why she said that. Suddenly each nerve was on end as she stared into Sheldon's concerned expression.

"No, it's not your son." He paused waiting until she was seated in her chair. "It's your husband."

Suddenly she remembered that Hank wasn't home. Now she looked inquiringly into Sheldon's face, waiting.

"Ms Sanders, that was the precinct. They found your husband's body out on Erie Station Road in an abandoned barn. He has been shot."

She couldn't speak for a moment as she stared into Sheldon's eyes, her mouth hanging open. Dead. Was he saying Hank was dead. It just couldn't be. More from shock then anything else, she burst into tears. She took the glass of water that Jefferson placed in her hands and drank in big gulps.

"I know this is a lot to handle all at once. Take your time and calm yourself. We'll finish printing the files while you rest in the kitchen."

"But..." She couldn't make her self say the words. "Is he..."

"Yes, he's dead. I'm sorry."

Trying to push the matter aside so she could thing, Skye managed, "Let me finish this."

"Don't worry, Jefferson here is a whiz with computers. He'll figure it out. You've already got it in the directory now so he can handle printing the rest. You just take it easy."

Skye managed a grateful smile no longer confident she could handle this and deal with the new information. With one last look at Officer Sheldon, she went back into the kitchen where she poured herself a fresh cup of coffee and sat at the table.

It didn't seem possible. Hank was dead? She didn't love him, but she never wanted him dead, she thought to herself. Bodies were falling all around her and she didn't have a clue what was going on. Sure she had her suspicions, but none of them lead to murder. The officer, Sheldon had said he was found in a deserted barn. A bar brawl she might have guessed, but what was he doing out on Erie Station Road.

She tried to picture the road that they lived just pass, before moving into the house. She saw fields on either side with a few houses, and yes, there was an old barn close to the end of the road where it butted up against East Henrietta Road. But what was he doing there?

"Feel any better." It was Officer Sheldon.

"Yes, it was just a shock. I told you we were in the process of getting a divorce, but as much as I wanted to get away from him, I never wanted him dead."

"Ms. Sanders, I need to take you down to identify the body."

"Oh, no, please."

"I'm sorry."

"But why? You already know it's him."

"It won't be that bad and I'll stay with you."

There was no way around it as she finally allowed herself to be helped from the chair.

"Give me a few minutes to get dressed and I'll be right with you."

"Take your time."

Skye walked across the kitchen and down the hallway. Silently she turned the handle of her bedroom door, trying not to disturb Janet who was still sleeping. Carefully she opened drawers and drew out pieces of clothing. She went to the closet and got out a jogging suit and a pair of shoes, then walking slowly across the room, she went through the door, closing it behind her.

In the bathroom she turned on the shower, then washed her face and brushed her teeth before getting undressed and climbing in.

The water felt good and helped to relieve some of the tension that had built through the long night. She was tired. So very tired she thought as she washed herself quickly and stepped out to dry and put on the clothes. A quick attempt at organizing her hair followed before she stepped out and returned to the kitchen.

Officer Sheldon rose from the chair as she entered the room. Without saying a word he walked her to the landing and felt the hesitation in her body as she stood there trying to gain the courage to enter the room.

"It's okay, Ms. Sanders. We've taken care of everything."

Skye managed to turn her body slightly and give the officer a grateful smile. Then feeling the light pressure of his hand as he pushed her forward, she made her way down the step and entered the family room.

The room looked as it usually did if you ignored the chalk marks that outlined the place where Dan had fallen and the body of the yet to be identified stranger. Skye looked around and noticed traces of white dust on the arms of the furniture and was afraid to look too closely, as she forced her eyes toward the front door and slowly progressed.

Feeling a slight pressure at her elbow, Skye moved aside so that Officer Sheldon could open the door. She watched as he stepped out on the front step, then slowly moved over to follow him.

They stood side by side, Officer Sheldon allowing her to adjust to the yellow tape that lined the sidewalk, curving gently toward the driveway. Taking a deep breath, Skye stepped down, Officer Sheldon supporting her as they made their way to his patrol car. Gently he helped her into the passenger car and she watched as he walked over to the driver's side, climbed in and turned to face her.

"Are you okay."

"Never better," she said shakily.

Officer Sheldon gave her a smile of encouragement, turned around and started the patrol car. Soon they were on their way up her street, turning at the intersection and heading toward the expressway that would take them downtown.

Officer Sheldon every now and then took sidelong glances over at his passenger, with a wondering expression on his face as though expecting her to say something. She was a strong woman. He could tell that now. All through the evening and into the morning he had watched her, expecting her to collapse, but she had managed to control herself and be there for her friend. He admired her strength. He appreciated her ability to help them so that they were able to take care of the police business. Now she sat quietly with all of it behind her, yet she hadn't asked him the question he expected. He wondered if maybe she was in shock and just doing a good job of hiding it.

He looked over in her direction again. No, she seemed okay. The further they drove, the more in control she appeared. He finally made up his mind to broach the subject. Obviously she wasn't about to ask.

"Ms. Sanders how come you haven't questioned if we thought you were involved with the murder of your husband?"

"I.. What is this? Are you saying the thought passed through your mind?"

Sheepishly, Officer Sheldon glanced over at Skye. "Seeing as you two were going through what appears to be a nasty divorce it was a logical conclusion."

"So, are you asking me now?"

"No. But only because of something your neighbor, Ms. Johnson said."

"What did she say?"

"She mentioned when we spoke to her that she had seen your car in the driveway the other night when she went to Wegmans. She only checked because she saw you had all the lights on and was worried something had happened to you. They think your husband was shot that night or early this morning and I know you were here this morning."

"Well, thank you Selma!" She looked at Sheldon. "No, I'm just kidding, I know you had to consider it."

"I'm relieved you feel that way, Ms Sanders, any time there are two people going through a divorce and one is murdered, the other automatically becomes the first suspect we check."

Skye changed the subject. "So what to I have to look forward to?"

"What?"

"I mean, what's involved with identifying the body." She couldn't bring herself to say, Hank's name.

"Oh, we'll go downstairs to the medical examiners office, and he'll ask you to make a positive identification of your husband." Sheldon replied, not wanting to go into any specific detail.

"How was he shot?"

"Are you sure you can handle it?"

"I think I ought to know. I have had enough surprises already."

"Well, I don't know all the particulars, but he was shot in the face, at close range."

Before she had a chance to ask any more, he changed the subject. "Did your husband have any enemies that you know of?"

"Everyone has enemies, but someone who would kill him? No, I don't think so. But..." She held it back.

"No, go ahead and tell me. It might be important."

"Well, Hank hung out in what I call, dives. He had a drinking problem, she said off-handedly.

"Serious," Officer Sheldon asked.

"I really can't say. I'm not much of a drinker myself. It takes only one glass of wine to do me in."

"How much did he drink?"

"Everyday. Sometimes he would have a drink in the morning. He'd pour his Jack Daniels into his coffee cup and drink it down.

She seemed far away as she continued to tell him about her husband. It was like she was somewhere else, just talking randomly as if nothing had happened.

"He was drunk a lot. He could handle a lot of liquor before it would effect him so I know he drank a lot. He'd add the liquor to his coffee, he'd say, because it would sober him up. I would keep tomato juice in the fridge for that purpose, but he preferred the laced coffee. Never understood that, but I guess it worked."

She was silent again. Officer Sheldon wanted more information about the places he went, but she obviously had forgotten his question.

"What can you tell me about the places he frequented," he asked again.

"They were real dives, most of them. The clientele was made up of people out of jobs, on drugs, or with an alcohol problem. When you said he had been shot, at first I figured it was in some bar." Again she paused as if concentrating on something. Finally she added, "That made more sense then some deserted barn in the middle of nowhere."

"Can you tell me the names of some of these places?"

"Well, there's the Circle Bar over on Jefferson Road. Then sometimes he would go to the Pussycat Lounge done on Main Street and the Half Dollar on Henrietta Road. That's just over the Jefferson Road intersection. That's all I can think of right now."

"That's good. We can start with them and maybe we'll get some leads. I've got a feeling that all of this is connected somehow, but the person that could have told us that was your friend, Janet's husband. I'm hoping she knows more than what she told you, otherwise we've got a lot of avenues to cover."

"Maybe," she responded slowly. "I have a feeling she doesn't really know any more than I do, but I thought I knew a lot of things..."

They were pulling into the hospital and Sheldon helped her out, holding her arm as they entered and took the elevator to the lower floor. He didn't release her arm as he moved in front of her to open the door, and then together they went inside.

Skye felt his light squeeze on her upper arm before he released her and walked over to a man in a long white jacket. The two whispered for a moment and the man in the white coat nodded his head. Then Sheldon was next to her, one arm around her waist, the other holding her elbow. The man in the white jacket disappeared.

She was shaking now, not knowing what to expect as she watched to figures wheel a sheet covered gurney in their direction. She could see the lump under the sheet and knew it was a body. She weaved slightly and leaned back against Officer Sheldon's arm.

They wheeled the gurney closer until it was only a few steps in front of Skye and Officer Sheldon. The form cloaked in a white sheet was still hidden.

She didn't want to do this. Didn't want the sheet to move down and expose the form below. Couldn't handle seeing what was hidden on the gurney. She tried to move away.

Skye felt the pressure as Sheldon moved her forward until she stood at the head of the gurney. The man who had moved to the other side, slowly lowered the sheet.

Skye looked away.

She heard the gentle probing voice of Officer Sheldon. "Please, Ms. Sanders. You have to do this."

Slowly she turned her gaze back to the gurney, lowering her head until she stared down into the face of Hank.

She was fascinated, her gaze transfixed on the hole where his nose should be. She thought to herself, someone did a good job of cleaning him up. Then it finally hit her and she gasped as she took in those eyes, the broad forehead, the beard covering his chin and high cheekbones. Her body leaned back harder against the officer and she felt the blackness coming over her. That's when she screamed.

Quickly the sheet was pulled up again and now it was only a lump under its covering.

"Is it him? Is that Hank Sanders?"

"Yes, it's him. Yes. Oh please, take me out of here!"

"Come on, we can go. It's all over. You did a good job. I'll take you home now."

This time they rode in silence. Skye had practically dragged Officer Sheldon out the door and into the hallway, hanging onto the hem of his coat. All the daydreams, all the nightmares could not compare with the horror of what she had just gone through. This evidenced her point. Reality was the supreme nightmare! She had to get out of here.

Now in the cold atmosphere of the linoleum floor, the whiteness of the walls seemed to sterile for comfort and she forced herself to find the strength to continue. She wanted to vomit, wanted to break down in tears, but she was afraid if she did, she'd remain here forever. So, tugging roughly at his coat, she forced Officer Sheldon to follow her to the elevator where she pushed the button and waited impatiently for the elevator.

The wait was short, but her mind now in overdrive, forced vision of the face she had been force to look at to float in front of her. Again she saw the crater in the middle of his face, the brown glassy eyes staring up at her before the man in the white jacket reached over and ran his gloved hand over Hank's forehead and down over the eyes. She heard the sympathetic tone of his voice as he said, "Sorry." Saw the lids of Hank's eyes when he removed his hands.

The lump in her throat rose to the top and she could not swallow. Her stomach lurched and she tried her best to control it. Blessedly it was over before she lost the power to move away and put the scene behind her.

The elevator arrived and Skye pushed into the small room, pulling the officer behind her. Only then did Officer Sheldon speak.

"Are you all right Skye?" he asked. Worry hung to his words as he looked hard into her face.

Skye managed to shake her head. It was all she could do.

The elevator seemed to take an eternity to reach the upper level. When the doors opened, they stepped across the threshold and their soled feet were planted on the carpeted floor. Skye looked around her, the soothing atmosphere of the hospital lessened the terror she had been forced to play a role in. She was finally all right.

"Come on, let's go", she said in a whiny voice. "I've got to get out of here."

"Maybe we should get you a glass of water first."

"No, I just want to go," she replied through clenched teeth.

Officer Sheldon didn't argue. Instead he walked her across the lobby and out the door. He helped her into the patrol car and soon they were pulling away from the nightmare and driving in the direction of home. With sidelong glances, he kept an eye on her, worried that she would break at any moment. But he had been right. This was a strong woman who was managing quite well, all considered.

When they pulled into the driveway in front of her house, Skye jumped out of the car and walked quickly up the sidewalk, not noticing the taped walkway . Officer Sheldon followed quickly behind her. At the threshold of the family room entrance, Skye hesitated for a moment before reaching out and letting herself in. Her eyes pointed straight ahead, she quickly made her way into the kitchen and plopped down into the first chair she came to.

"Ms. Sanders, let me get you some water," Officer Sheldon said, already heading toward the refrigerator without waiting for an answer. Hearing the sounds coming from the kitchen, Officer Jefferson entered the room and followed Sheldon as he carried the water to Skye.

Skye drank the water quickly while the officers stared at her. When she sat the glass down she said, "Thank you." She paused and then added, "Is there any more coffee?".

It was Jefferson who turned around and went to the coffee maker, getting cups and pouring a cup for each of them. He carried the first two cups over and placed one in front of Skye and the other in front of his partner who was now seated at the table. He then went back and carried a cup for himself.

They sat at the table drinking the coffee slowly. At ten o'clock Officer Jefferson got up from the table and disappeared into the office, then came back with the copies in his hand. At ten thirty, while he sat reading the transcripts and jotting stuff down in his notebook, Officer Sheldon made a call to the station, ordering four men to come out to the house. He sat back down to slowly explained his motive to Skye.

"Ms Sanders, are you feeling better now?"

"Yes, I'm fine."

Sheldon paused, looking closely at Skye to verify her statement, then sensing she was okay went on to tell her what he planned to do.

"I am going to have the house watched. There will be several officers here soon to set up surveillance equipment."

Skye gave him a wondering look, not sure what all this meant. Seeing her puzzlement he continued.

"We're doing this just in case someone tries to contact Hank or comes by to check on the other two men. Someone has to know why these men were here and the identity of the other man. Since this is the last place they were seen, it's obvious that whoever is behind this will try to make contact."

Grasping what he was saying, Skye asked, "What do you want me to do?"

"You will be instructed on that, but usually the procedure will be to place a wiretap on the phone and whenever the phone rings you should let it ring at least three times before you answer. That will give the men enough time to get on the phone. They will then need to have you hang on to the caller until they can trace the call."

"That's it?"

"Yes, basically. When the officers get here they'll go over this again with you. We'll be listening in on all your calls on both lines and maybe come up with something that will help us get to the bottom of this..."

"Four men to do that," Skye interrupted.

"No, two. The other two will be stationed outside. They will keep an eye on the place. We don't know what we're dealing with here and there may be more than one person involved. If you need to go anywhere, you must let one of the officers know."

Skye, sensing danger turned toward Officer Sheldon. "Am I in danger."

"Ms. Sanders we just can't take any chances now. You may be in danger, but I don't know for sure. That's the reason we are going to keep an eye on the house and hope we come up with something to explain what happened here."

Looking despondent now, Skye said, "I can't handle any more. Maybe it will be best if I left and went somewhere else."

"We need you. I'm sorry to have to say this, but it's the truth. Just hang in there a little longer. We'll be with you at all times. If you must go anywhere, one of the officers will tail you and keep a look out for anything suspicious."

"It all sounds so dramatic. I thought this was it. The men are dea..." She couldn't finish the words. Is all that necessary."

"Yes, it is. There were two homicides right in your own family room. We found your husband dead in some abandoned barn, and no matter how you chalk it up, it adds up to three homicides somehow tied to this house. I'd say there's enough reason right there! I'd be a fool not to put you under police protection."

"So, what do I do?" Her voice was filled with confusion as she repeated herself.

"Just follow our orders. It may help to clear this matter quickly if you try to think of anything else you should tell us, no matter how non-related it may seem. We'll keep you informed and maybe something will ring a bell with you."

The team arrived and Skye tried to stay out of their way as they went about setting up the equipment. At one point she looked out of the window with Officer Sheldon who pointed out two unmarked police cars and then introduced her to the officers who would be her bodyguards. At around noon she went to check on Janet.

***

Skye went into her bedroom and found Janet fully awake, staring up at the ceiling. The sound of someone coming into the room caught Janet off guard and she snapped her head in the direction of the door.

"It's okay, Janet."

"Is Dan..." she implored, not able to finish her thought.

Understanding what her friend was asking, Skye immediately responded, "Yes, everything has been taken care of.

Skye moved about the room getting out fresh clothes for Janet to put on. When Janet climbed out of the bed, they both looked at the spot on her jeans that screamed out a reminder of what they had been through. Quickly, Skye averted her eyes and said, "Janet, maybe you'll feel better if you take a shower and put these own. She held out the clothes, trying to keep her eyes from going to the blood stain on Janet's jeans.

"Yes, that would help," Janet said and without any further explanation she took the clothes from Skye and left the bedroom.

Skye sat on the bed. She heard the water running in the bathroom and she forced herself to concentrate on the sounds coming from that room. There were other sounds in the house, but she dare not let them enter her head. She had to be strong. She waited wondering and as hard as she tried, she couldn't help thinking about the drama of the night and where she had just been. It seemed so unreal, so foreign and yet she was part of it all. This was not happening to a character in a book or a movie. This was real.

When Janet returned, she looked much better. The white sweater that hung loosely on her own body, clung to Janet's full chest and tucked neatly into the waistline of the black jeans, emphasizing the slight flair of her hips. Trying to make light of the situation, Skye attempted a little humor.

"My sweater and jeans never had it so good."

"You picked them out," Janet responded lightly.

Taking on a more serious note, Skye added, "Are you ready?"

Hesitating slightly, Janet responded as she attempted a smile. "As ready as I'll ever be."

Together they left the bedroom and walked side by side down the hallway, holding each other's hand for support. When they entered the kitchen they were met by Officer Sheldon.

"Feeling better," he queried to no one in particular.

"Yes, we're fine," Skye returned. "Coffee, orange juice, water?" she questioned Janet as they made their way to the table.

"Coffee."

Skye went over to the counter and started preparing a fresh pot. She rinsed out the cups that had gathered in the sink and put them in the dishwasher before pulling out fresh ones to line up on the counter. She then turned around and leaning against the sink, watched as Officer Sheldon turned to face her friend.

"If you're up to it, I need to ask you some questions."

"Okay," was all Janet said as she sat stiffly in the chair.

"Can you tell me all that happened last evening. Everything you can remember, even it seems unimportant to you.

"Well, Dan and I had dinner with the kids, then spent the evening talking with them and watching television until it was time for bed. I took them up and Dan said he had to go into the officer for a while."

"Were's his office?" Officer Sheldon asked.

"He has an office in the house. He's a private investigator and his assignments are called into the house."

"Do you know what he was working on."

"Not really. We never discuss his work."

"Go on," Office Sheldon replied.

"Well, I finished getting the kids off to bed and came back downstairs to spend some time alone with my husband. It was our usual routine after the kids were down for the night we would go into the living room, have a drink and unwind and catch up on what the kids were doing... Just regular family things." Again she paused with a faraway stare.

"Please Ms Malone. I know this is hard but, I need to know."

"Sorry... Well, I came downstairs and was just outside his office door when I heard him talking to someone on the phone. Something about Skye... Her computer..."

"What did you do?"

"I don't know why, but I didn't want to let him know I had heard him so I went into the living room."

"How did you feel?"

"Mad. I was mad and afraid. Afraid because it concerned Skye." Her eyes traveled across the room to stare at her friend.

"Continue."

"Well, when Dan came into the living room I jumped all over him. You have to understand that all through our marriage we had managed to keep from arguing so this was unusual for us to be engaged in a headed discussion."

"Do you know who was on the line with him?"

"No. I tried to get him to tell me but he evaded the question. He also wouldn't tell me how Skye was involved. At least what he said seemed to be a lie. He never came right out and lied to me before," she said with tears forming in her eyes. "Never".

Trying to ignore her need for sympathy, Office Sheldon pumped Janet further.

"Did he admit he was lying to you or is this what you felt at the time?"

"No, he didn't say he was lying, but I know my husband. I know he was lying to me and that made me angrier. Skye is my best friend and I couldn't believe he would hurt her, but whatever it was he was about to do, concerned Skye."

"Do you think he came here to hurt your friend."

"No, that's not it! Janet replied adamantly. "That's not it at all. I think that he was coming here to get some information that Skye had in her computer. Information that had a bearing on the case he had taken on." Her eyes swept over to Skye again. "He wouldn't hurt Skye. No. He wouldn't do that."

"So then what?"

"Well, Dan kept telling me to go to bed. He said he was dropping off something for a client. When I countered him that it was too late. That the client would probably be in bed and why not wait until morning, he explained he wanted to take the file to the client and that it would save him some time the following day."

"Yes," Office Sheldon prompted.

"I could see he was adamant and nothing I could say would stop him so angrily I went on up to bed. I heard him leave and I must have fallen asleep because I woke up bathed in sweat. I had a nightmare."

"What?"

"A nightmare," she said again.

"What was it about?"

"I can't remember all of it, but I was in my house, walking down the hallway, hearing my daughter calling me. Then I saw Skye lying on the floor..."

Skye turned around to see that the coffee was ready. She poured three cups and carried them slowly over to the table, feeling the tension in the room as Janet tried to continue.

"Take your time, Ms. Malone."

Janet reached out and grabbed the cup from Skye. She took a drink of the warm liquid and then placed he cup on the table.

"Can you continue," the office implored.

"That's it. The nightmare frightened me so. I got up and put on some clothes and called my neighbor to come stay with the kids and I came over here."

"What time was that?"

"I don't know. It was very late. Maybe two in the morning.

"Why did you go to Skye's?"

"She was in danger. At the time I thought she was. I wanted to warn her and let her know."

"Anything else... Can you tell me any more?"

"No, that's all I can remember. I was here, told Skye what I had overheard and that Dan was coming to her house. We talked, went into the bedroom and then... Then...."

"It's okay, Ms. Malone. You've been a big help."

"Officer Sheldon tried to comfort her while he weaved what she had shared with the information Skye had given him.

"There's just one more thing. What is your address?"

"275 Hidden Valley Lane."

Officer Sheldon got up from the table and went into the family room. They could hear him talking to one of the officers. They sat there alone. Skye reached across the table and squeezed Janet's hand. Janet smiled wanly at her friend. Office Sheldon returned.

"Ms Malone, I have one of the officer's waiting to take you home. Janet turned toward Skye.

"You go on, now. You need to be with the children. I'll be all right."

Janet shook her head and got up from the table.

"Ms Malone. We've called in and asked for an officer to go over to your residence. He will be stationed outside just in case someone comes there looking for your husband. If you need anything he'll be right outside."

"That won't be necessary. We have a burglar system installed that rings at the Gates police station." Thinking she should explained further, she added, "We live in a quiet neighborhood. It is quite safe, but because of his business, Dan thought the alarm was necessary so he had it installed as a safety precaution." Fresh tears filled her eyes as she thought about her husband.

"I'm sure it is safe, but we just want to be sure. We've set up surveillance equipment here and need to do the same at your home. Two officers are on their way over there now. We cautioned them to wait until you get there so they don't upset your neighbor or the children."

Janet shook her head to let him know she understood. She walked over to Skye and leaned down to hug her. Quietly she whispered in her ear, "I'm sorry. So sorry."

Skye patted her hand and looked up into her face. "It's not your fault," she offered.

While Janet said goodbye to Skye, Officer Sheldon explained to his partner he would see what he could find over at the Malone resident and then drop back by. As soon as the other men were settled in, they would leave. That was fine with Jefferson.

It was after two when Sheldon arrived back at the Sanders home. He entered, checked with the surveillance team then went to find his partner. He found him in the office with Skye who was showing him her computer system.

"I hate to interrupt, but we best be going. Everything seems to be in order here."

"Did you find out anything more?"

"Yes, I did, but not at the Malone house. Whatever he was up to, he had it with him. They found Malone's automobile parked down the street and the car that belonged to the other man was parked just across the intersection. We now know his name. It's Frank Jaffe. Inside Mr. Malone's car was his brief case which had a lot of papers in it that mentioned most of the same names Ms. Sanders gave us. I've called in to have both automobiles impounded. As soon as they've had a chance to go over them thoroughly they'll give us a call at the station."

"Anything else..." The phone rang just as Jefferson started to speak.

"Skye looked imploringly at Officer Sheldon. She saw his signal to wait, the phone ringing eerily in the house that had suddenly become quiet. At his signal she picked up the phone.

"Hello?"

"Can I speak to Officer Sheldon," the strange voice asked.

"It's for you." Skye walked over, the phone cord stretching, and placed the receiver in Officer Sheldon's hand.

"Yes." There was silence as Officer Sheldon listened on the line. "Okay, thanks." He handed the phone back to Skye.

"They found a disk in Dan's pocket. Look's like he was coming here to get something out of the computer. My guess is that it's this," he added pointing to the printouts they had made from Skye's system. "They also found a disk in Jaffe's pocket. Obviously he was here for the same purpose."

"So what does this mean," Skye questioned.

"Seems that what we thought is exactly what went down. They were both sent here to get this information from your computer. The question is, why and who sent them."

"Do you have any idea."

"Yes, I do. But I need to be certain. Once I have a chance to go over the information and what you and Ms Malone have shared, I think it will make more sense."

"What about Hank's van," Skye inquired, the question popping into her head as they talked with each other.

"We already have that. I haven't heard anything back outside of it was taken in. I have a feeling we won't find anything there, but you never know."

"Is there anything else you want to ask, Ms. Sanders, before we go." It was Officer Jefferson.

"No, that's it. If I think of anything I can tell the officers and they'll get in touch with you?"

"Yes, that's how we will handle it. My advice to you would be to try and eat something and then get some rest, while you can. I don't think it's over yet, but we will handle everything." He saw the worried expression as it crossed her face. "Don't worry, we won't put you out of business, but I would rather my men question anyone who approaches the house. They've been told to say that there was an accident here and that they will take any packages they want to drop off. Any work that someone needs to pick up, I want you to give it to one of the officers to hand over to your customers. Or, we could tell them to come back later. Whichever way you prefer. By no means do we want you standing in any open doorways until we're sure it's safe."

"I don't understand. I know the faces of the people who you feel are part of this. Why can't I handle the others."

"Because someone could easily get a bomb inside," he said frankly. We know that it's the information we have now, that someone wants removed from your system and you can't be sure that there aren't others involved. In order to keep you safe you must follow our instructions. Stay away from windows and doors and don't assume you can trust anyone." He paused, then added. "Do you understand Ms. Sanders."

"Yes. I see," Skye said impressed by their thoroughness and again scared by the enormity of the situation.

"As for making any calls to clients that you know are due to stop by, don't call and cancel. We need to check out as many people as we can and would rather have everything running just as it should be. That is of course, with my men intervening for you."

Skye nodded in reply and then walked with Officer Sheldon and Jefferson as they prepared to leave.

CHAPTER 39

When Skye didn't showed up for her appointment, Mitch had his secretary, Stephanie phone her home. Stephanie reported she had gotten her answering service, so Mitch assumed she was just running late. At three he again asked Stephanie to call her home.

"Mr. Cayman, she's still not home."

"Thanks Stephanie. Will you keep trying?"

"Sure."

Stephanie called again at four and at five. She buzzed Mitch again.

"There's still no answer. Do you want me to keep trying?"

"No, Stephanie, thanks. You can go on home now. I'll see you in the morning."

"Okay, Mr. Cayman."

Mitch sat back in his chair, tired and wanting to go home, but he couldn't help thinking about Skye. It was not in her character to be late or not call to cancel. Even though he had known her a short time, he felt he knew her well. Not to show up at all had to mean something had happened. He had to find out. Mitch opened up the phone book and started calling the hospitals. When he checked with the Genesee Hospital he learned that a Skye Sanders had been brought in earlier that day. She had been in an accident.

"Is she all right?"

"Yes, sir she's find. She had a slight concussion, but we released her to her husband and he took her home."

So her husband was back. Mitch thanked the nurse and hung up the phone. He then dialed the Sander's resident. Hank answered.

"Mr. Sanders, I hate to bother you so late, but your wife had an appointment with me and when she didn't show up and I wasn't able to reach her at home, I called the hospitals and found out she had been in an accident. Is Ms. Sanders all right."

"Yeah, who is this?"

"My name is Mitch Cayman." He started to add he was her lawyer then thought better of it. "I'm a client of your wife's."

"Well, Mr. Cayman, she's sleeping right now. She had a mild concussion so they gave me some medication to give her and told me to make sure she went to bed. She's been sleeping ever since I brought her home."

"Well thank you Mr. Sanders. I was worried about her."

"Well I'm here with her so you needn't concern yourself."

"Will you tell her I called."

"Sure."

As he placed the phone in the cradle Mitch felt much better. He cleared his desk and picking up his briefcase, headed home.

***

Fran Russo was going through much the same thing. He had gone to the restaurant and waited for two hours before finally deciding she wasn't going to show up. At first he was upset, but then knowing Skye he figured it had to be some unexpected business that kept her from keeping their luncheon date. He sat at the table alone thinking about his morning. He had been busy gathering information for one of the lawyers and now it felt good to just sit. It was a stroke of luck he'd told the lawyer he was taking off early and would see him in the morning so he didn't need to rush. Of course them he figured he'd be playing catch up with his friend.

Fran finished his drink, paid the tab and headed home, thinking Skye would probably call him in the morning and explain.

The next day when she didn't call, at first he worried, but got so tied up with work, he didn't have time to think about it until he was getting ready to leave the office. He decided to call her home. He dialed the number and waited.

"Hello?"

It was a man on the line. He started to answer, then changed his mind and hung up the phone. He'd just wait until Skye called him.

***

He heard their footsteps as they came up the walk. Sam shrank against the wall and peered out cautiously. Two cops were approaching his front door! The cops looked around carefully, walked up and down the area, stared curiously at the front door, nodded to each other and continued up the drive.

He felt the cold sweat drip all over his body. His luck was running out. He could feel it. He walked briskly through the livingroom and into the garage. His car was there, ready to go. He'd filled it with gas at the station on the corner earlier this evening. Now he thought, he could climb in, raise the garage door and take off, only they'd follow him and eventually they'd catch him and it would be over anyway. Slowly he walked back into the livingroom and when the knock came, he unlocked the door and let them inside.

"Lean against the wall," one of the cops said, but he didn't move.

"I said lean!" The cop jammed his revolver into the small of his back, hooked a foot around Sam's ankle and pulled it back sharply. At the same time Sam felt the revolver shoved hard against him.

Sam grunted with surprise and said, "Watch out. I'll fall."

"That's the idea," the cop said. "And remember, this gun's loaded so don't try anything funny."

With Sam stretched out against the wall, the one cop frisked him, while the other pulled his hands roughly behind his back and handcuffed him. Then he was swung around.

"We can do this one of two ways. You can tell us where you keep your gun or we can tear the place apart and find it ourselves."

"Oh man, it's in the drawer of the table by the sofa. What's going on?" He tried to sound innocent.

"You're under arrest for the murder of Paul Angelino."

Sam watched as the other cop removed a plastic bag from his pocket and managing to slip the gun into it, lifted it up for his partner to see. He put it in his pocket. Then he was turned around again with an officer on either side of him, forcing him through his front door.

They walked to the patrol car and after the cop swung open the door he placed a hand on his head and lowered him into the back seat. The door closed behind him.

Sam watched as the cops opened the front car doors and climbed in. While one drove, the other called in on the radio to let them know they were bringing him in.

Sam looked out the window, knowing it was just a matter of time before they charged him with the other murders. Cops were like that. They'd find something on you and keep digging until they had every piece of your life fitted together. As he sat on the seat watching the scenery pass by he felt no remorse. As far as he was concerned what he'd done he had done for a good reason and the fact that he would spend the rest of his life in jail didn't seem to matter. At least now people knew he was not one to let anyone get away with anything. Not that bitch of a wife, her boyfriend, or the others who had tried to cross his path.

***

Sam's gun was sent directly to ballistics. The officers Pendleton and Fletcher who had arrested Sam took him directly to the interrogation room where they read him his rights and informed Sam they were holding him without bail. They asked if he wanted to call his lawyer. Sam told them, no, thinking to himself that no one could help him now. No one had ever really wanted to help him. That Maglioni fellow only said he would defend him because of the money. That he was quite sure of. No one ever cared about him. Not now, and definitely not in the past. And he thought further, he didn't care about any of them either.

Just as they were about to get started, there was a knock on the door and another officer entered.

"Here's the ballistic report you asked for."

Pendleton went over and grabbed the report. "Thanks," he said, impatiently waiting for the officer to leave. As soon as the door closed, he walked over to Fletcher and looking over Pendleton's shoulder, they read the report.

Pendleton let out a low whistle and looked at his partner. "Watch him. I think the Captain will want to see this immediately. What do you think?"

"Man," Fletcher whistled back. "This must be our lucky day."

"You may be right, partner. I'll be right back."

Pendleton hurried through the door and down the hallway, manuevering through the room ahead until he was at the captain's door. He tapped his knuckles lightly against the frosted glass.

"Yeah, who is?" came the rebuttal.

"Officer Pendleton, turned the door handle and walked in. "Think you should see this. It was just delivered to me."

Pendleton remained standing, watching his captain read the ballistic's report. He didn't say a word or take a seat. He waited patiently to hear his orders while he watched for Captain Andrews impression.

Captain Andrew finished looking over the report and looked up at Pendleton. "Look's like Stillman's been a busy man."

"I'll say," Pendleton said Trying to act nonchalant.

"Did you read him his rights?"

"Yes."

"Did he ask for a lawyer to be present during questioning?"

"No. He waived his rights to a lawyer."

Captain Andrew picked up the phone. Pendleton waited, watching as he dialed.

"Sheldon, get Jefferson and come into my office. Do you see Pierce and O'Malley?"

"Yes, Captain."

"Tell them to come, too."

Jefferson looked up. "What's up?"

"I don't know, he didn't say. Come on, he wants us in his office right away."

As they walked through the aisles they stopped at Pierce's desk. "Hey, you and O'Malley, come with us."

"Where we going?"

"Captain wants to see us in his office."

"All of us?"

"That's what he said."

They walked single file through the maze of desks until they were outside Captain Andrews office. They could hear him talking to someone. They opened the door.

"Shut it and get in here," he roared.

Captain Andrews always roared. It was in his nature to do that, especially when he had something interesting to say. He was an over weight, soon to retire, old geezer who had little patience these days. He stood behind his desk, his snow white hair in it's usual state of disarray, his fingers tucked in his belt loop and perspiration spots growing in his armpits.

O'Malley pulled the door shut behind him and walked in to lean against the plate glass window, next to his partner. Pendleton sat in one of the side chairs and Sheldon occupied the other. Jefferson stood leaning on the top of his partner's seat.

"I've got something you all should see." Andrews waved the report in front of him and then handed the paper to Sheldon.

Sheldon read it while Jefferson looked over his shoulder. When he finished, Sheldon let out a low whistle and passed it to Pierce, who studied it with O'Malley. Not a word was said until Pierce handed it back to the Captain.

"Well, gentlemen, what do you make of it."

"Looks like we just got lucky!"

"Not so fast, there. Nothing's that easy, O'Malley."

"I just meant..."

"I know what you meant," he glared. The captain paused making sure he had their attention. Four sets of eyes were on him, eagerly waiting for instructions. "Pendleton, fill them in."

"We read Stillman his rights and asked if he would like an attorney present during questioning. He said, no. We were just starting the interrogation when we got the ballistics report. As soon as I read it, I showed it to my partner and hightailed it down to the captain's office. That's about it. Fletcher's waiting with Stillman."

"Okay. Now we're all at the same spot. How do you want to handle it?"

Pendleton piped up. "Since my partner's in there, why don't we take it from here. You men can stand behind the glass and if you give me a few details I'll see if I can get some answers."

"But...", Jefferson piped up.

"No buts, men. Fletcher and Pendleton have been working on the Paul Angelino death for some time. They were the ones who bought Stillman in and they should handle it from here."

Captain Andrew's glared into the faces in the room. He couldn't help thinking that this was quite a note to end his twenty some odd years of service. This was not your run of the mill happening in Rochester and he would receive the credit for doing a job well done. That thought made him smile. Coming back now and seeing the expectant faces, he turned to Pendleton again.

"Tell them the rest of it," he gloated.

"Well, as you know, me and my partner were assigned to the Paul Angelino case. The one.."

"Yeah, yeah," Captain Andrew's pushed. "They know that."

Pendleton looked sheepishly at the captain and then continued. "Anyway, we got a lead that lead us to Sam Stillman. We checked it out and had enough information to warrant an arrest. We found that the car Paul Angelino was driving belonged to a man named Sam Stillman and checking through the records we learned he owned a gun that matched the caliber of the one used to kill Angelino. We followed Stillman, learned where he lived and the places he frequented. With some cajoling we got the bartender at the Circle Bar to fill in the missing details. That's it in a nutshell.

Sheldon spoke first. "We're concerned with the killing of Hank Sanders in a deserted barn up on Erie Station Road. The coroner puts the time at late last night, or early this morning. He was shot once, at close range, dead in the face." He waited to let this information sink in. "Think maybe our man Stillman had something to do with that?"

"Depends," Pendleton said.

"Depends on what?"

"What type of gun was used in the case."

"The ballistics report we showed to the captain matches the one that you found at the Stillman's residence. He also was known to frequent the Circle Bar. That's what his wife told us."

"I talked with the captain," Pendleton said as he looked at Captain Andrew's for permission. Not getting a yes or a no, he continued. "I know very little about your case, but from the information the captain gave me, along with the fact that the bartender mentioned Mr. Sanders talking with Stillman, I would say there is a good chance he's involved in both cases."

"You done?" It was O'Malley.

"Yes. Unless... Need any more details Sheldon?"

Sheldon who had been writing down what Pendleton shared, stopped writing. "No, that'll do."

"Then, let me fill you in on another coincidence. Me and my partner are on the Palma case. George Palma was stabbed in the back, several times with a butcher knife that we think belonged to him. Apparently he was sleeping when the killer gained access through a basement window, got the knife and went into the bedroom and stabbed him."

"What makes you think it was Stillman," Pendleton asked.

Pierce answered for his partner. "Because asshole, his damn fingerprints were taken off the knife." Obviously he wasn't too concern with covering his trail, or figured maybe it would be overlooked. He threw it in the kitchen sink, for God sake. Maybe he thought he'd get lucky and some idiot would figure he'd slaughtered a pig or something!" The room broke out in laughter.

"Don't get nasty with me. I'm saving you some legwork if I can get a confession out of him," Pendleton snapped not seeing the humor.

Clearing his throat, Captain Andrew's said, "Well, we don't have all day. If we can cut this short, let's do it!"

Single file they left his office. Pendleton entered the interrogation room while the Captain and his entourage went pass the entrance and down to the next door. They lined up behind the one way mirror to watch. At the Captain's signal, quiet ascended the room. The speakers were turned on.

Samuel Stillman sat at a table, facing the one way mirror, glaring as though he was seeing them standing on the other side. His hands were in cuffs and his ankles were chained, yet Sheldon thought, he was glad he was not on the other side. The questioning began.

"Do you understand that by waiving your rights to have a lawyer present, everything you say can be used against you in a court of law."

"Yeah," he sneered.

"Did you give Paul Angelino a car?"

"Yeah, I lent him my old one?"

"Then why did you turn around and kill him?"

"Who says I killed him?"

"This report," Pendleton flipped it on the desk. "In here it says that your gun was used in the killing of Mr. Angelino. It also says that your finger prints were all over the car."

What did it matter, he thought. He had gotten his revenge. "Yeah, I killed him."

"Why? Did you fight over the car?"

"Naw. The man tried to lie to me so I killed him."

His voice was cold, as though stating a fact of life. Pendleton didn't like being in the same room with him. He cleared his throat, then continued.

"Do you know a man named, Hank Sanders?"

Stillman raised an eyebrow, which was the only sign of any surprise. "Yeah."

"Did you shoot Hank Sanders in an abandoned barn out on Erie Station Road."

"Yeah."

"What did this man do that made you want to kill him?"

"He took away my job?"

Pendleton looked at his partner and shrugged his shoulders. He turned back to Stillman. "What do you mean, he took your job?"

"He asked me to keep an eye on his wife and take care of things for him."

"Yeah, so, then?"

"I did as he asked, hired someone to help me and then he pulled me off the case."

"I don't see..."

"I bet you don't see," he sneered. "I had to pay my man, only I didn't have the money anymore."

"Who was this man?"

"Angelino, you dumb shit!"

Pendleton heard his partner snicker behind him, assumed the others behind the mirror were getting a kick out of it, too.

"Listen, smart ass, just answer the questions."

No response.

"What about the name, George Palma? Ring a bell?"

"Yeah. Another lying bastard!"

"What did he lie about?"

"His name, for one. But I found out though. He thought I was stupid, but he don't anymore."

"Did you stab him three times in the back with his own butcher knife."

"Thought it was more!" That was all Stillman said.

CHAPTER 40

Sheldon moved the papers around on his desk until he found his pad. "Let's see, we have Hank Sanders, George Palma, Paul Angelino... Our concern was Hank Sanders and why Malone and Jaffe held a shoot out in the Sander's living room. But I'm afraid we're now dealing with two additional murders that are going to somehow tie into our case. We already know the connection between Sanders and Angelino. It's not a direct connection, but it figures in."

Jefferson walked around to sit at his desk. "We know that Palma was one of Ms. Sanders clients. He's the one she couldn't remember."

Sheldon picked it up again. "So, we know that this George fellow was connected to our man, Maglioni. I suggest we pay Maglioni a visit in the morning."

"Right," Sheldon responded. "And Ms Sanders gave us a list of places where her husband frequented. I say we check out the places now and see if anyone can tell us something we don't know."

They grabbed their coats and left the station. As they walked to their car they decided to start at the farthest point, the Circle Bar. They'd swing by the Half Dollar and then back toward town, stop at the Pussycat Lounge and call it a day. They climbed into their unit and headed out. A half hour later they parked and climbed out their car.

Inside the lights were dim and it took a while for their eyes to adjust. They saw two patrons sitting at the bar who had been engrossed in a discussion, but now stared at them as they stood at the door. Besides the two, the only other person was the bartender. Slowly Sheldon started walking and Jefferson followed. They sat down o the bar stools and waited for the bartender to come over.

"What can I get you." Oscar tried to appear calm, but already he was shaking. This was the second set of cops who had come into the bar. He didn't know what was going on, but he knew it had to do with Stillman. He smelled the overpowering sent of trouble.

"Just some advice," Sheldon said. "First off, what's your name?"

"My name's Oscar," he said, his voice rising as he pronounced his name.

"Oscar, do you know a man by the name of Samuel Stillman."

Oscar drew back at the mention of Sam. His reaction was not missed by Sheldon or Jefferson who watched him closely.

"Yeah, I know him. So what!" Oscar spoke offensively, telling himself to be careful. Ratting on a man like Stillman was nothing to take lightly.

"Well, Stillman is sitting in jail right now, charged with murder."

"So what does that have to do with me?" Carefully he tried to hide the relief of knowing Sam couldn't get at him. At least for the time being.

"Nothing so far. We need to ask you some questions. We know that a man Hank Sanders comes here frequently. Do you know that name."

He started to deny any knowledge of the name, but thought better of it. "Sure I do."

"Did you know that Sanders is dead?"

Again Oscar's reaction gave them their answer. His expression was one of genuine surprise. Before he had a chance to ask, the officer continued.

"Did Hank ever talk with Stillman?"

There was no need to try and cover up, Oscar thought. Stillman was already in jail so he didn't have to worry what he'd do if he said anything. He was scared of the man. They had enough evidence now to put him away so he couldn't get revenge for a long time. Besides, he needed to get it off his chest. Once he started, it was hard to shut him up.

Oscar told the cops his suspicions that Stillman had murdered his wife and that the man came in here always bragging about how he got even with her and her boyfriend.

"He used it to get business. He'd joke about it and watch the reactions then get some poor soul suckered in who was having troubles at home. He'd act all sympathetic and convince the guy to let him handle it for him. I've seen him do it over and over again and it made me sick to my stomach."

Jefferson asked, "What about Paul Angelino. Know anything about him?"

"Only that he was a friend of Stillman's, if you can call anyone his friend. He's some kind of private eye. Sam used him when he thought his wife was whoring around."

"Did you ever see Hank Sanders talking with Angelino?"

"No, never."

"Oscar was it?" Oscar nodded. "Oscar you've been a big help." Sheldon looked around the bar. "Is it always this empty?"

"Naw. It's usually filled to the rafters," he laughed nervously. "The people who come here pop in and out all day. But when it gets late, that's when it gets busy around here."

"Oscar, we can trust you not to mention our little conversation to anyone. Can't we?"

Again Oscar nodded, then watched as the cops got up, turned and walked out the door. In the parking lot Jefferson talked as they walked over to their unit. "So Stillman reeled Hank in with his story, or something like that happened. My guess is Sanders didn't know Stillman before the time he hired him, and I'll bet Sanders didn't know the Angelino guy at all."

"Yeah, that's how I see it to. It looks like the end of the trail on these two. I guess we picked the right bar to start with. I can't see any need to check out the other two."

"Me either. Let's go with what we got for now and if we need more, we can check off the other two, later."

"So what now?" Jefferson asked.

"Back to the station, and then home," Sheldon replied allowing himself to give in to the fatigue.

CHAPTER 41

Ginny was sitting reading in the living room when Sheldon got to the house. She looked up as he entered the room.

"Hi honey, you look exhausted."

"I feel exhausted," he said as he unbuttoned his shirt then lowered himself on the sofa and took off his shoes.

"Can I get you anything?"

"Yeah, a couple aspirins would be nice!"

"Oh honey, she said. She pulled him nearer to her and forced his head back on the sofa, commencing to massage his temples."

"Oh, you always know the right medicine."

Her hands felt good as they kneaded his forehead. He felt the tension leaving his body and the headache disappeared.

"Come on, let's get you into bed."

"You're right again." Sheldon got up on his feet and went up the stairs with Ginny behind him. He stopped at the bathroom door. "I'll be in shortly?" He kissed her and watched as she walked away.

Sheldon undressed carefully, brushed his teeth for two whole minutes, then took a hot shower. He felt a little better as he entered their bedroom and climbed in beside his wife, his thoughts on something other than sleep.

Ginny was small and her skin soft and fragrant when he put his arms around her. She kissed his ear as he pulled her closer. The next thing he knew, it was morning.

***

When Sheldon arrived at his desk, Jefferson was already on the phone.

"It's ringing," he said.

"Hello, Mr. Maglioni's office, Lisa Caldwell speaking."

"Hello Ms Caldwell, this is Officer Jefferson. Can you put me through to Mr. Maglioni."

"Just one moment, please."

"This is Mr. Maglioni. What can I do for you Officer Jefferson?"

"Well, if you have some time on your calendar, me and my partner would like to pay you a visit."

"Can I ask what this is about?"

"Sure, you can ask, but we'd rather tell you to your face."

Angelo frowned. "Sure, officer. When do you want to stop by."

"Now, if it's all right with you."

He glanced at his calendar. "Now is fine. Just tell my secretary when you arrive that I'm expecting you and she'll show you right in."

"Thanks. We appreciate it." Jefferson hung up the phone.

"We're in. Finish your coffee and let's get rolling."

***

When they entered the reception area, Jefferson let out a low whistle as he looked around. At the same time he was wondering why would a lawyer who was this successful, bother with the case of a man like Stillman. He could tell by the expression on Sheldon's face that he was thinking the same thing. They walked up to the secretary.

"I'm Officer Sheldon and this is my partner, Officer Jefferson. Mr. Maglioni is expecting us."

They waited in front of her desk, listened in as she pressed the intercom button and announced, "I have Officer Sheldon and Officer Jefferson here in the reception area."

"Show them in Lisa."

Lisa stood. "Gentlemen, will you follow me."

She lead them down a short hallway to a massive oak door. She turned the gold knob then stepping to one side, allowed them to enter the room, closing the door behind them.

Mr. Maglioni came from behind his desk and offered his hand, first to Sheldon and then Jefferson. "Can I get you anything, gentlemen? Coffee, tea, a soda..."

"No, we're fine for now." It was Sheldon who spoke.

"Well, then gentlemen, please have a seat."

Angelo waited until they were both seated then he sat down. "Now, what can I do for you, gentlemen?"

"For starters, are you aware that your client, Samuel Stillman, has been taken into custody."

"Yes, I am." He offered no explanation.

"How did you find out."

"A little birdie told me." Mr Maglioni looked into the faces of the officer. "Listen, does it matter how I found out? I know that Mr. Stillman was picked up for suspicion of murdering a man called Paul Angelino."

"Not for suspicion, Mr. Maglioni, sir, he has confessed to murdering Mr. Angelino. We have a ballistics report on his gun, which we brought with us. Would you like to see it?"

"Sure, if you don't mind." The report was handed to him. Not waiting until he finished, Jefferson asked, "Do you know a Hank Sanders, or a George Palma!"

Both names rang a bell, but it was the last that really shocked him. He had been trying to reach George for several days with no luck.

"What's happened to Mr. Palma?"

They could tell they had taken him by surprise.

"Sure I do, but I don't remembering seeing anything about George... Mr. Palma. What's happened to him?"

"He was knifed in his bedroom."

"Is he dead?"

"Yes."

"Before we go any further, gentlemen, may I ask a question."

"Sure, what is it?"

"Why didn't I read anything about Mr. Sanders or Mr. Palma. Nothing was in the media, unless I missed it. I do remember seeing something about Paul Angelino being murdered."

"Well, Mr. Sander's body wasn't found until this morning. He had been killed in an abandoned barn up on Erie Station Road in Henrietta. The coroner determined he died the previous night, or early yesterday morning. As for Mr. Palma, a friend of his tried to reach him by phone and when he didn't answer she stopped by. She had a key, so let herself in and found him in the bedroom. She immediately called us.."

"I see," Maglioni said.

"We know that George Palma was working for you. We're not sure what his assignment was, but figured you would tell us that."

"I'll be glad to. I hired George to gather information on Sam Stillman. He's... I mean, he was a good detective. I've used his services on lots of cases and he always managed to get the information I required."

"Do you know why Stillman might have killed him?"

"That's a good question Officer Sheldon. Let me think for a minute."

Jefferson and Sheldon watched Maglioni carefully why he pondered the matter. He seemed to be an honest man and they were pretty sure he wasn't hiding anything.

"It is my guess, and I mean just that, if Mr. Stillman is the one who killed George Palma it must be that he found out he was following him. That's just an assumption on my part, gentlemen."

"We understand, but at least it gives us something to go on."

"Is there anything else?"

It was Jefferson who spoke up. "Are Paulette Locke and Mitch Cayman two others hired by you? From the information we have, these two people were also involved on the Stillman case."

"Yes, that's correct." There was a frown on his face, but he answered thoroughly. "Paulette is a real estate agent and I hired her to handled two property deals for me. Mitch is a lawyer who was willing to help me out on the case. They are both good friends of mine and I can vouch for their character."

"That won't be necessary." Sheldon added, "We also know that you had these people, including yourself and George Palma, hire a Skye Sanders to type the information.

"That's correct." He looked puzzled. "Can you tell me where you got that information."

"Yes, but first let me explain something. Early this morning Skye Sanders house was broken into. A neighbor called after she had heard what she thought was gun shots. When we arrived there was one man, a Frank Jaffe, dead at the front door and another man who was just barely alive, lying on the floor across from him. The wife of the other man was there staying with Ms. Sanders. Her name is Janet Malone and her husband, who died shortly after we arrived, was Daniel Malone."

"Excuse, what..." He seemed shocked.

"Ms. Malone had come over to warn Ms. Sanders about a telephone call. She had overheard her husband making a call to someone about information her friend, Ms. Sanders had stored in her computer.

"Oh my god! Is Ms. Sanders all right."

"Yes, she's holding up quite well. She's quite a lady."

"Do you know what happened."

"Mr. Malone tried to tell us that. The best we could make out was that he had entered through one door at the same time Jaffe came through the front. They both shot, fatally wounding each other and died in Ms. Sanders family room."

"So why? Do you know why the men were there?"

"That's what I'm getting at. From what Mrs. Malone told Ms. Sanders and later us, she had a suspicion her husband was going to get that information out of Ms. Sanders computer. I have to figure that the other man, Jaffe was on the same errand. What I can't figure out is who sent him." He paused fingering his chin. "Anyway, we told Skye she had to think about her own safety and show us what she had stored in her system. There was no other choice, but to concede.

I have printouts of the information that she pulled up and it led us to you."

"Well, I hardly blame her for that! I can imagine how scared she was finding two men dead in her house. No, I don't hold it against her for giving you the information you wanted. Not at all."

"I'm glad to hear that. She was really worried about invasion of privacy by supplying us with this information, but I told her anyone would understand, under the circumstances."

"These men, you mentioned, do you know how they fit into the picture."

"I guess we can't answer that right now. We thought maybe you knew."

"No, I don't recognize the names," Maglioni responded innocently. He paused. "Now wait, I may have something for you. The prosecutor on the Samuel Stillman case is a man named William Taylor. It may be that he found out, somehow, that I was using Ms. Sanders to type up the transcripts. If he knew he might have hired at least one of the men to get the information for him. It's another guess, but the best I can come up with. As for the other man, who knows?"

Sheldon thought about what he had said. "You might just have something there. It makes sense. At least it's worth checking out. Is this Taylor the same man who is the District Attorney?"

"One and the same."

He couldn't hold back asking the next question. Sheldon turned to Jefferson who nodded, then faced Maglioni. "Tell me something Mr. Maglioni, its been puzzling me to no end. Why would a successful lawyer like yourself and the District Attorney want to be involved with the Stillman case? I can't figure that out for the life of me!"

Angelo figured he might as well tell them the whole story now instead of waiting until they found it out for themselves. It was a matter of public record anyway. Slowly he told the officers about the case held so long ago and his dealings with Taylor. He admitted that when he saw Taylor's name he had seen red, remembering that time so long ago. He decided to take the case. He just couldn't pass up an opportunity to face Taylor again. He imagined that Taylor decided to handle the case on his own and not turn it over to one of his men, for the same reason.

"Well, Mr. Maglioni, sir, this has been enlightening. I can't say that I approve of your choice in clients, but it has been interesting, to say the least."

Angelo stood up and the officers followed suit. They shook hands. "Officer Sheldon, Officer Jefferson. As Mr. Stillman's attorney, I expect that you will be in touch?"

"Yes, well, that's another matter."

"What do you mean?"

"Stillman doesn't want a lawyer."

"Well," Maglioni said looking directly into Sheldon's eyes. "He has a right to an attorney and it's my guess he'll change his mind and want me to defend him. I can't say that I want to, but if he asks, I will comply."

"Well then, yes, you'll be hearing from us," Sheldon said, "And thanks for seeing us on such short notice."

Mr. Maglioni walked them to the door and showed them out.

***

Back at the station Sheldon and Jefferson informed the Captain of their meeting with Maglioni.

"Captain, Maglioni suggested we might check with William Taylor."

"You mean the District Attorney, Taylor?"

"The same."

"Explain."

"It's possible Taylor sent one of the men to the Sanders residence..."

"Why would the District Attorney do that!"

"For a personal reason that deals with the lawyer Maglioni." Slowly Sheldon filled him in on what they had learned. He's named the prosecuting attorney on the first Stillman case. You must have read about Stillman killing..."

"Yes, I read the papers... So let me see if I get this right. Maglioni thinks that our District Attorney was trying to get a lead on how he'd play the case?"

"That's how I see it," Sheldon said.

"Jefferson. You feel the same?"

"I'm with my partner. Right now we have two dead men and no witnesses. The only thing that ties them together is they were after something in the Sanders house. That's all we got."

"Okay, go ask some questions and get back to me?"

"Will do, Captain."

CHAPTER 42

"I'll call Taylor's office," Sheldon said to his partner. But before he could pick up the phone, it rang.

"Hello, Officer Sheldon speaking."

"Hey, Sheldon, this is Manigan."

"Yeah Manigan, what's up? Everything okay over there?"

"Outside of reporters swarming all over the place, we're doing okay..."

"That's to be expected. I would prefer that Ms. Sanders not speak to them. Understand?"

"Yes, we've been keeping them away from the house. I'm calling because Ms. Sanders received some news that I thought she should tell you about, right away."

"What is it?"

"Hold on. I'll get her on the line." A few seconds and Manigan said. "Okay, Sheldon, she's on!"

"Ms. Sanders?"

"Yes, Officer Sheldon I think I have something that will help you?"

"Go ahead, I'm listening." Sheldon pulled a pad in front of him.

"A while ago I received a call from Adam Snyder."

"I'm sorry, who's Adam Snyder?"

"Oh, he's a client and a good friend. We've known each other since I started the business; about five years."

"What's his line of business, Ms. Sanders?"

"He's a lawyer." She paused. "I did tell you that he was the one who took care of the wiretaps for me?"

"No, but continue."

Skye's train of thought was forgotten, then it came to her. "Yes, well, Adam was checking to make sure I was all right."

"What did you tell him?"

"I know I wasn't suppose to say anything, but he is a friend, so I ignored your men and told him about the murders. Just about the two in the family room, is all?" she said to defend herself.

"It's all right Ms. Sanders, just tell me everything."

"Okay, after Adam got over the initial shock, he asked me to look out the window and see if there was a car watching the house. Of course I didn't need to check, so I mentioned that the one man who was killed was named Frank Jaffe..."

Sheldon could feel himself getting excited, it must have showed because his partner now stood beside him with question marks in his eyes. He couldn't wait and interrupting Skye Sheldon said, "What did he say?"

"He said, so that's why he hadn't been able to contact him. He was talking about Jaffe. Adam told me that Jaffe had been working for him. He had Jaffe keeping an eye on me since the day we talked at the restaurant. He was worried, especially after he had done some checking on the names I'd given him."

"I don't follow all of that, " Sheldon said, " but, let me ask you this. Did he give any reason why Jaffe had broken into the house?"

"Yes, I was coming to that. He said that he decided to take Jaffe off the case, after Jaffe's last report. As a safety precaution he told Jaffe to delete the files in the system so if anyone did snoop around they would think it was a bum lead." Skye sighed, "What a mess, huh? Your men thought I should let you know about this immediately."

"Thank you, Ms. Sanders. If I were there, I'd hug you."

"It helps that much?"

"Yes, that much. Listen, we have one more lead that should complete the picture, thanks to your friend Adam. We'll check it out and get back to you."

"Okay," Skye said.

"Manigan? You there?"

"Yes, I'm here Sheldon."

"Okay, fill me in on the rest of what's happened."

"That was the highlight," Manigan said, then gave his report. Sheldon learned that four people had stopped by with work. He gave him the names, told him they checked out okay. Paulette Locke came to pick up a job and talked with Ms. Sanders about selling the house.

Sheldon listened as he listed the calls coming into the office and verified they had all the names in their report.

"That's about it," Manigan added. "Besides that, Ms. Sanders received a call from her mother, her son and her sister Mary on the home line."

"Keep your eyes and ears open. Looks like we're about to wrap it up." Sheldon raised his eyes and looked at his partner when he said the last part.

"You've got it," Manigan said and then hung up the phone.

"What? What did you find out?" It was Jefferson.

"Well, we're down to one. It seems that a friend of Ms Sanders, an Adam Snyder had hired this Jaffe guy to protect her. He called her today and when she told him about the murders, he disclosed that Jaffe was his man. So now that leaves us with finding out Malone's connection."

"Well partner, I'd say we've put in quite a day's work. Are you ready for a drink."

"You bet I am. A stiff one and then a good night's sleep. We should have this all cleared up tomorrow."

Jefferson added, "Why don't we wait until tomorrow to fill in the captain and finalize the report."

"I'm with you partner."

They tried to organize their desks, turned off the desk lights and went into the locker room to change into their civilian clothes before going to the bar around the corner from the station. After one quick drink they climbed into their own cars and departed company.

CHAPTER 43

At nine o'clock the next morning, Officer Sheldon placed a call to the District Attorney's office. By ten thirty he and Officer Jefferson were seated in Taylor's office.

"Mr. Taylor there's been a series of murders and we're hoping you can shed some light on an individual named, Daniel Malone."

"What's happened to Dan," Taylor asked as he leaned over his grey metal desk. "Is he all right?"

"Do you know Mr. Malone, Mr. Taylor?"

"Yes, he does work for me. He's a private investigator."

"Did you hire him recently to check into the Samuel Stillman case?"

Taylor looked from one officer to the next, suspiciously. "Obviously you know the answer to that question or you wouldn't be here now."

"Will you answer the question Mr. Taylor. Did you hire Mr. Malone recently."

"Yes, I did. Now will you answer my question. Is he all right."

"No, I'd say he was far from all right. Mr. Malone is dead."

Taylor's jaw dropped down, his eyes widen to their limit as he stared dumbfounded at the two officers. "What... What happened?"

"Mr Malone was killed yesterday, sometime around two in the morning."

"Who killed him? What happened?"

"He was breaking in through the back door of the Sanders residence and when he entered, he was face to face with a man named Frank Jaffe who had just broken in through the front door of the same resident. They surprised each other and fired. Jaffe died instantly, but Malone was still alive when his wife and Ms Sanders found him laying on the floor."

"What did he say. Did he tell you anything."

"No, if you mean did he mention your name. He was very weak by the time we got there and barely able to tell us more then what had happened. It was information we got from another source that lead us to you."

They watched as Taylor tried to recover, then Jefferson spoke. "Mr. Taylor, we already know about the Samuel Stillman case and the part you're playing. We've talked with Mr. Maglioni and he thought it might be beneficial to talk with you."

For some reason the idea of Maglioni sending the cops to him did not bother him. Not in the least. He was so shook up over the death of his friend.

"What would you like to know?" Taylor invited.

"Do you know what Mr. Malone was doing at the Sanders house?"

"Yes. I didn't know all of it. He called me earlier that evening and told me he knew where he could get information that would help me on the Stillman case. The name, Sanders was never mentioned."

"I see," Sheldon said not responding to his last statement, his mind caught up on something else. "So you were the one on the other end of the call that Ms. Malone overheard."

"What, I don't follow."

"It's not important."

"Anything else?"

"Just to summarize, would it be correct to say that you hired Dan Malone to do investigative work on the Stillman murder case. That in performing this assignment, Mr. Malone found out that Ms. Sanders had typed information for the defendant, Mr. Maglioni and that he called you the evening before his death to advise you of his findings."

Taylor shook his head in agreement.

"Mr. District Attorney, you have been most helpful. We'll make sure you get all the details of our investigation."

"I'm sorry, is there more?"

"Yes, Mr. Stillman is currently in custody for the murder of Mr. Paul Angelino and two other people."

"What two other people. I thought you said that Dan was killed by this Jaffe fellow."

"Yes, that's correct. Stillman confessed to the murders of a Mr. George Palma and Ms. Sander's husband."

He asked the same question as Maglioni. "I didn't see anything in the paper about these men being murdered. What are you telling me?"

Jefferson provided him with the same details he had given Maglioni and told him they would send him a copy of their final report on the investigation.

"Do you have any further questions, Mr. District Attorney?"

"No, not at the moment."

"Here," Jefferson said as he handed him his card, "if you need to get in touch with us, just call that number."

***

Back at the station, Sheldon went directly into the captain's office while Jefferson went to start the paperwork. When Sheldon joined him, Jefferson was just getting started. Both men were two finger typist and they poked at keys, stopped and looked over their notes, then continued. They began at five. At six thirty, Sheldon went for food and they ate at their desk. At eight they were still at it when the captain stopped by their desk.

"How's it coming."

"Not much longer Captain. We should have the report on your desk when you get in."

"Okay, men, I'll see you in the morning."

At nine they had the whole picture in front of them. Sheldon placed his hands on his neck, massaging the sore muscles, wishing he were home with his wife. He looked over at Jefferson who was standing, stretching his body and walking around to get the circulation going.

"I've finished the report on Malone and Jaffe," Sheldon said.

"The Sander's one is done, too," Jefferson replied as he stopped for a minute, then walked some more.

"So we need to summarize it all now." Sheldon was up now. They talked their way through the full realm of what they had uncovered, then Sheldon sat at the typewriter with Jefferson standing behind them. They began.

The clock ticked somewhere off in the distant, but neither man heard as they struggled to put their findings down on paper. When the coffee pot was empty, Jefferson got them more from the machine in the hallway until they finally reached the end. It was then, shortly after midnight.

They passed the report between each other, reading it over and commenting on the details. When they were satisfied it was all down correctly and in good order, they laid the paper aside.

"Well, ready partner," Jefferson said. "Let's drop this off in Andrew's office and get some rest.

***

The murders were solved, yet as tired as he was, when Sheldon got home he could not sleep. He sat downstairs in his recliner and picked up the book that Genny had been reading to get his mind off the case. An hour later he was drowsy, climbed up the stairs and barely got his clothes off before tumbling in the bed.

"Want some breakfast," Genny questioned as he entered the kitchen the next morning.

"No, just coffee."

"What time did you get in?"

"Late. Some time after midnight. I was exhausted, but once I got in I was too stressed out to sleep so I read some of your book."

"Did you like it?" He could hear the laughter in her voice.

"Let's put it this way. It had me dozing in less than an hour!"

The tingling of her laughter filled the kitchen. "Me, too. Why am I reading it?"

Sheldon got serious. "Probably because you're bored waiting for me all the time. I promise you it's going to get better. We finished the case last night so I should be keeping decent hours again."

Genny didn't say a word, just turned and gave him a grateful look. He sat and drank his coffee while making the final call to the Sander's resident. The phone rang the prearranged three times and then Skye's voice came over the phone.

"Hello."

"Hello, Ms. Sanders, it's me again."

"Oh, hello Officer Sheldon." He could hear the relief in her voice. "Want to speak to the officers?"

"Yes, but you too. Can you put Manigan on the phone with us."

Sheldon waited feeling the relief of making his last phone call on this case. Until caught up in this dilemma he thought he had heard and seen it all. Obviously that wasn't true. He heard Ms. Sanders voice.

"Manigan?"

"I'm here."

"Are you saying it's safe now?" It was Ms. Sanders who spoke.

"Yes. Dan was working for District Attorney, William T. Taylor. From what he told us Dan was going to download the information onto disk and give it to Taylor to use in building his case against a man named Samuel Stillman..."

Skye listened as Officer Sheldon told her everything. It still made no sense to her. Still she was having a hard time believing this was happening for real and it was not a dream. When Sheldon told her that Sam Stillman had killed Hank, Skye felt nothing. She was beyond feeling now as he continued until she knew all that he had to share.

"So what now," Skye questioned knowing Sheldon had completed his report.

"You still there, Manigan," Sheldon asked.

"Yes, I'm here, Sheldon."

"That's about it," he added. "Ms. Sanders, how are you holding up?"

"Oh, I'm okay. I slept like a baby last night and was able to get a lot of work done. As much as I like the company, I'll be glad when it's over."

"Well, that should be soon." Hearing a different voice, Sheldon interrupted their conversation. "Who's on the line?"

"It's me, Seco."

"What is it?"

"Nothing special. The media is camping out on the lawn now. Thought you should know that. Also, there were nine calls on the private line, most of them from her girlfriends who had heard about the accident and wanted to console her. And, the woman from across the street called and came over to visit with Skye. She had two customers drop off jobs, all clean, and three office calls that were for new jobs. Yes, and five customers called to check on jobs they had dropped off earlier. That's about it."

"Very good, officer, but we've got our man in custody and all the loose ends tied up."

Sheepishly, Officer Seco, added. "I didn't know that."

"I know. That's what Manigan was just told."

"So what do you want us to do now," Seco inquired.

Seco being new to the force tried to merit having Manigan as a partner. He tried very hard to be helpful and thorough. Sheldon knew this and respected the man who was barely old enough to warrant the title. Having a good partner was what kept officers alive.

"Well, I guess we clear out of there tomorrow. When you get to the station, be sure and drop off your logs with me. I'd like to look them over before turning them into the captain. And when you finish it, I'd also like a copy of your written report."

"Anything else."

"No, I guess that's all for now. I'll see you at the station tomorrow."

"What time should we plan on leaving here."

"Don't rush it. Take your time and gather up all the equipment. Just play it by ear and when you get here, you get here."

"That soon?" It was Skye.

"They can stay longer if you want them to, Ms. Sanders."

"No, that's not what I meant at all. I'm okay with that, it's just that I thought it would be longer."

"I think that should do it."

"What about the press?" She asked shyly not wanting to sound like a baby.

"It's whatever you decide. Talk to them or not. I think the stories should be out by the time my men leave so they will have calmed down. If not, don't hesitate to call the station and we'll get them off your back."

"Thanks. Thank you for..."

"Doing my job, Ms. Sanders," Sheldon finished for her.

CHAPTER 44

Every channel carried the story of the murders. Skye got so she couldn't watch the news anymore. The newspapers were no differ. It became headline news, written in minute detail with all the gory facts highlighted for the world to see and read. There were pictures of the dead men, including Hank and some of herself and Janet plastered in amongst those of the others who played a role in the drama.

The media had missed nothing. They carried a separate store on herself and Hank's impending divorce. How they got the news she didn't know or care. She was thankful it was over.

The picture of Paulette was stunning. She had been caught coming out of her house, dressed in black and white. Her hair was tucked up under a wide brim felt hat with wisps falling to her shoulders. She looked totally in control of the situation as she stood there smiling sweetly into the camera.

Skye tried to avoid most of it, but had to read the story on Hank. Tears came to her eyes and her heart went out to him.

***

On September 20, the body of Hank Sanders was found in a deserted barn on Erie Station Road in Henrietta. Mr. Sanders had been seen earlier that evening at the Circle Bar on West Henrietta Road. In questioning it was learned that Mr. Sanders spent the evening talking with a man named Samuel Stillman. The bartender stated that they had been engrossed in conversation for over three hours that evening.

At some time around nine, Mr. Stillman left the establishment and Mr. Sanders followed shortly thereafter. An eye witness who asks to be kept anonymous, had been at the Circle Bar that evening stated that he saw Mr. Sanders climb into his van and start the engine.

He hadn't been paying particular attention until he heard a grinding sound, the type of sound you hear when the engine is on and the key is turned again. That's when he looked closer at the van and saw a figure leaning up against the back of Mr. Sander's seat. It wasn't until Mr. Sander's peeled out of the parking lot, did he notice that there was a gun pointed at Mr. Sanders. He recognize the man as Samuel Stillman.

When asked why he withheld the information, the informer said he didn't want to get involved. When asked why he changed his mind, he said because it had bothered him and he wanted to come clean. His information only helped to seal the case that had already been solved by the police.

Mr. Hank Sanders was shot once in the head, the bullet entering his brain. It is assumed he died instantly. Mr. Sanders was in the process of a divorce.

Samuel Stillman has confessed to the murder of Mr. Hank Sanders. He also has confessed to the shooting of two other men; Mr. George Palma and Mr. Paul Angelino. Mr. Stillman is being held without bail at the county jail.

***

"Oh my god," Skye screamed, her hands covering her mouth. It all coming to light now. He had died in a deserted bar. He had died all alone. No one deserved to die that way. As she looked down, a sentence seemed to move from the page as if it was three dimensional,

"It is assumed he died instantly". She tried to block the words from her mind. It was too horrible to think about.

Skye's family arranged the service at the Presbyterian church, and friends stopped by afterwards to consoled Skye. The tears keep flooding from her eyes and they were all for Hank. She couldn't help feeling sorry for him. All she had wanted was to give them both a chance to start a new life, one that was happy and one that was built on love. Only Hank would never get that chance now. She was a widow. Strange word she thought. She would have been a divorcee, but now that had changed.

She looked down at her black dress, the black stockings and black heeled pumps that blended well with her mood. She was glad when the service was over. She welcomed the chance to be alone.

Her mother insisted on coming home with her after the service and at first Skye said, no. Finally she gave in and her mother stayed the night. The following evening her sisters had them over for dinner. Again she wanted to refuse, but was glad she didn't. The conversation was comforting and later they all watched a movie together. No one mentioned what had happened and no one asked about her feelings.

Scott was there too. He took three days off to be at her side. He suffered the most, though he insisted he was okay and tried to be there for her. When they were alone together they talked about it, Skye filling him in on all that had happened.

He loved his father and she was glad that he did. Hank had always been great with him, taking the time to go to his games, yelling and cheering and losing his voice as he screamed the team to victory. Those were the times that had kept her from severing the ties. It was the wonderful relationship that Hank had shared with

Scott that she never wanted to ruin. And now, after what they had gone through, she had to admit she was glad she had waited to ask Hank for a divorce.

Skye looked over at Scott, seeing Hank's features on a face that she so dearly loved. Scott would miss him, miss him terribly and that made her happy, not sad. Hank had earned the right to be loved by his son. He had been a different man when the two of them were together. He hadn't known how to be a father in all aspects, but he had come close in their relationship. Hank had shared a deep and loving friendship with Scott.

***

Scott returned to his studies and her mom went home. After all the activity Skye was glad for the solitude. She kept to herself for the next few days, not answering the office line when it rang. She wasn't ready to face that just yet. There was still something she had to do.

Gathering up the courage, Skye was ready to talk with Janet. At first she had been too busy, she thought, but later realized she was avoiding the issue. She hadn't talked with her friend since that morning when she had left with the police escort. She hadn't even told her about them finding Hank. She told herself it was because of Janet's own lost. Now she wished she had, as she sat wondering how Janet had taken the news.

She had started to call Janet after the arrangements had been made for the funeral, but someone had mentioned to her that Dan's funeral was the same day. As she sat there thinking about it now, she couldn't even remember who had told her. Still she should have called, she told herself.

Skye sighed softly as she dialed Janet's number.

Janet's hesitant voice came over the phone and Skye forgot her own problems. "Janet, this is Skye."

"Skye? Oh, Skye, I thought you hated me."

"No, what gave you that idea?"

"You know."

"Well take that silly notion out of your head." Feeling totally in control now, Skye inquired. "Janet, we should talk. Can I come over."

"Oh, yes, Skye. I'll fix us some lunch and we can talk. I can't wait to see you."

It had been easy. She had put it off, only to find it wasn't going to be as hard as she had convinced herself. Sure the memories were there, but she realized that Janet needed her and Skye worked best in that situation.

Janet's tears came from the heart. The days following Dan's death had been very hard on her and it was visible on her face. She told her friend she slept all the time, heavily sedated so that dreams wouldn't interfere with her rest. Knowing that made Skye feel even worse.

"So what will you do now, Janet," she inquired.

"Well, Dan planned well for our future. The kids will continue at their private schools. Dan had taken out insurance that will pay off the mortgage on the house and left me quite comfortable from what our lawyer has told me."

"How do you really feel Janet."

"Oh, I was hurt at first, then angry at Dan for what he did. But now, I just don't feel anymore." She paused then quickly added, "I still love him. I can't help that."

"You should love him. He loved you. He loved and cared for you and the kids when he was alive and planned well so that he can take care of you now. He deserves your love."

"Thanks Skye, I appreciate that. And you, what about you?"

"Well, it'll be different, but you know I was going to divorce Hank. I guess I'm thankful it's over and a little scared about the future."

"If you need anything, money or a listening ear, I'm going to always be here." Janet managed a smile. "That's what friends are for, right?"

"Right," Skye responded, returning her smile.

"Oh Skye, I miss him so much. I wake up each morning in that bed wishing he were there with me. There is so much I need to tell him. I didn't even get a chance to say goodbye."

"I know, Janet, but you were with him, don't forget that. He knew you loved him and he loved you back. That's what you need to remember, and not the end."

"I'm trying," she said tearfully, "I'm really trying."

"I know you are. Just remember that you still have friends who care a lot about you and need to see that smile of yours again."

Janet's eyes were glistening as she hugged Skye. She whispered in her ear. "I'll come back, just give me some time."

***

In a way she was lucky, Skye thought. Sure she had to work, but she enjoyed it immensely. She'd have to give up the house, but she never wanted it anyway. Her life would go on much as it had before, but Janet's would have a hole in it that would never seal itself shut.

***

With the trial set, the media had another heyday. All the incidents were again in the news. Samuel Stillman would face a total of four trials: the first on the murder charge of his wife, Evangeline Winters-Stillman, and her lover, Peter Stiles, the second for the murder of Paul Angelino, the third for the murder of George Palma, and fourth for the murder of Hank Sanders.

The murders had received such coverage, they were slated to be held in the large court room of City Hall.

Skye had been there, seated with her son on one side and Janet on the other. There was plenty of room for the media that came in droves to see Samuel Stillman face all the murder charges.

Before court began, Samuel Stillman was brought into the court room flanked by two deputies, his hands cuffed and a long chain coming off of them and hooked to the chains encasing each ankle. He was restrained throughout the proceedings.

The pretrial motions to use Stillman's taped confessions were damaging to the defense, and the judge ruled in favor of playing them for the jury. To Skye this meant nothing, but for Angelo Maglioni,

III it meant he would enter the courtroom with one more strike against him as he faced the prosecuting attorney, William T. Taylor.

It took ten days to select the jury. Following the selection the case began with the opening statements of the defense and the prosecuting attorney. At first neither one noticed the change. Taylor had a lot of time to think before the trial date was set and it did him good. As the days progressed he realized that he no longer felt vindictive toward Maglioni, that he wanted to enter that courtroom and let justice prevail. Of course some would say that was easy since Stillman had signed his own death warrant, but that had nothing to do with his decision. It might well have been because he had carried it around for so long, this hatred for Maglioni, that it died a natural death, only he didn't think that was the reason either.

Daniel Malone had been one of the few people he could call, friend, and now Dan was dead because of his lack of respect for the law. That was what he credited his change in attitude. If he had acted judiciously maybe Dan would still be alive. The fact that he played a role in the murder, plagued him viciously. Night after night he found he could not sleep and he spent those hours reading through his law books and it finally sank in. He was a servant of the people. People like Dan looked up to him as someone they could trust. Being a lawyer meant he served as a prosecutor or defendant in a court action, acting as an agent for another. Well from now on he determined, he would earn that title.

He began investigating the facts and the evidence for the first trial. He prepared and filed his pleading in court. At the trial he introduced substantiated evidence, interrogated witnesses and only argued questions of law and fact as they pertained to the case and his client. He played it strictly by the books.

For Angelo it was much easier to let go because he never lost his respect for the law. His vice was seeing the lack of respect that Taylor represented, and when he realized Taylor had come to his senses he felt much better.

Maglioni went into that courtroom and play his part like he always had. It wasn't a matter of winning, it was a matter of protecting the rights of his client and that's what he did.

At first Angelo thought he imagined it, but during the jury selection, Taylor seemed more relaxed, more professional than he remembered. Now as he listened to his opening statement he knew this was not the same man he remembered.

A parade of police witnesses took the stand first. They supplied the details and pictures of the crime scenes, the ballistic findings that proved that the gun owned by Samuel Stillman was the murder weapon and presented the gun as evidence.

Doctors were called to the stand to state the cause of death. The testimonies that followed told not only were the bullet entered the victims, but how the wound caused their demise.

Other witnesses were called to the stand to fill in the details that gave reason for the crimes or placed the suspect somewhere near the scene and they were matched by those who provided extenuating circumstances that might have forced the suspect to commit the murders.

The trial ran for almost three weels. The jury presented their verdicts of guilty for each count of murder after three days of deliberation, and sentencing was set for two months later. Samuel Stillman received four life sentences, without the possibility of parole.

CHAPTER 45

Paulette handled everything with ease and style. She was there, showing the house and pointing out all its wonderful features. When it was time for the household sale, Paulette was there to help again. Then came the day when she took Skye to see the house she had told her about.

It sat in the middle of an oversized lot that had been professionally landscaped so that it looked like a park with trees, bushes and rock flower beds. The house had natural wood siding and it looked as though it had grown in that spot. The driveway was two car widths wide and two long allowing ample parking for her clients. There was a brick walkway that lead to the front door and another on the far side of the driveway that lead to the office area. Skye felt like she was looking at a picture.

Inside it was breathtaking. The ceilings were high with windows running from the baseboards on up. The center of the house was open to the roof with a spiral staircase going up the center. The whole left side of the upstairs was the master bedroom suite which included the bedroom, a dressing room, walk-in closets and a huge master bathroom with the vocal point being the Jacuzzi that sat in front of a floor to ceiling window. There was also a shower and a makeup area. On the right side of the staircase were two additional bedrooms, separated by a bathroom.

The first floor rooms were spacious. There was a formal dining room, a living room with a stone fireplace, a very modern kitchen with built-in appliances and a separate eating area, and a den with built-in bookcases on two walls.

A door off the kitchen led down to the finished basement. Here there was a workout room, laundry room and the office which had a door entrance from the outside.

It was so much more than she could ever have imagined and Skye fell in love with it. Paulette went to battle. She made phone calls to the owners, their Realtor and back around again until she had the price as low as it would go, then she called Skye.

"Paulette, you can represent me any day. You should have been a lawyer!"

"I told you, didn't I?"

"Told me what?"

"That I use to be a lawyer?"

"No, I don't remember you mentioning that."

"Well I use to do matrimonial work. I quit because it wore me down. Too many tears, too much rage and suffering. It was too high a price to pay. But it taught me to see people, including myself, far more clearly than I ever did before. That's how I met Angelo."

"But isn't this hectic."

"No, I call this fun. Helping people fine houses and get rid of the one they don't want is very rewarding work and I just love it!"

***

Everything played in tune. The closing date for the house was at ten o'clock in the morning, and at one in the afternoon she closed on the new one. The previous owners had moved out two days before and informed Skye she could start moving her things in whenever she wanted. She knew Paulette had something to do with that.

When the day arrived, when the moving van pulled up at the door, all that was left was the furniture she had set aside. All the boxes and crates had been carried over by friends and family. Everything was stacked neatly in each room.

At ten o'clock exactly the transfer began and by ten thirty she signed over the deed to the house to its new owners and wished them well. It was as she was leaving that she finally realized she had been worried. She knew Paulette said that they would go through with it, but her own hesitancy of buying a house that had been a murder scene kept her from believing it would happen. Paulette had been honest with the perspective buyers who were moving here from out of state. Paulette swore she had. She had taken them through the house, made sure they were aware of all that the house had to offer and just aware of the attractive price. She had told them in her own way about the incident that had taken place in the house, adding whatever she needed to cement the deal. She admitted they were shocked, but they did want the house.

Now Skye breathed freely. She had been more than willing to lower the asking price when Paulette made the suggestion, and told her to go even lower if necessary. After all the money she had made from Mr. Maglioni and his friends, she could afford to be generous. She just didn't want to end up with the house still in her possession. And now it was over and she had gotten a fair price for the property.

Before the next closing, Skye scooted out to what would soon be her new house to find Janet waiting in the driveway.

"What are you doing here?" she said gleefully as she got out of her car.

"Waiting for you!"

"Well you're lucky, Missy. I'm not suppose to be here."

"Paulette said you'd come, so I came on over?"

Skye remembered she had mentioned to Paulette that the telephone people were installing the phone and the cable people were scheduled to show.

"So what else did Paulette say?"

"That you could use some help. Since you would both be tied up in closings she thought it was nice of me to volunteer to help out."

"I swear I don't know how she does it," Skye replied shaking her head. "She's always full of surprises! By any chance did she give you a...." There was no need to finish as she saw the key dangling in front of Janet's smiling face.

"Come on Skye. I fixed us some coffee. You are to relax until it's time for the final closing."

***

The second closing went slower than the first. The owners were late getting there and then their attorney called to say he was running late. If it hadn't been for Paulette's and Janet's foresight, Skye wouldn't have been sitting calmly chatting with Paulette. Once everyone was present, the closing concluded quickly. Skye accepted the keys, responded to the congratulations and walked beside Paulette as they made their way to the parking lot.

"Now Skye, what I want you to do is go to your car and say something wonderful to start out your new life."

"What? What are you talking about."

"You want this to be a start of a wonderful new life, don't you?"

"Well, yes."

"Then say something that will start it out right and I'll see you later."

Skye looked with astonishment as Paulette walked by her, climbed in her car and took off down the road. After a while she shrugged her shoulders and walked over to her car, climbed in behind the steering wheel and sat. Paulette had steered her right all along, so why not give it a try.

Taking a quick look around, Skye allowed herself to smile as she said, "There is nothing I can't do and I won't ever look back."

www.ingramcontent.com/pod-product-compliance
Lightning Source LLC
Chambersburg PA
CBHW030823310726
48980CB00006B/612/J

* 9 7 8 1 9 2 8 6 1 3 6 8 8 *